Twisted Truth

AMY CRONIN

POOLBEG
CRIMSON

Published 2023 by Crimson
an imprint of Poolbeg Press Ltd.
123 Grange Hill, Baldoyle,
Dublin 13, Ireland
Email: poolbeg@poolbeg.com

A catalogue record for this book is available from the British Library.

ISBN 978178199-710-9

www.poolbeg.com

About the Author

Amy Cronin is a writer from Cork. She began writing stories at a young age and was rarely seen without a book in her hand. Her debut novel *Blinding Lies* was released in December 2020 and *Twisted Truth* continues the story.

You can follow Amy online @AmyCroninAuthor (Twitter) and @amycroninbooks (Facebook).

Acknowledgements

Thank you to Paula Campbell, David Prendergast and all the team at Poolbeg for the opportunity, for your encouragement and support.

To Gaye Shortland, thank you for your enthusiasm for this story and for your expert guidance.

To my sisters Laura, Stacey and Shauna, and to Ber, Linda, Trish and Suzanne, thank you being so supportive and excited about my books! There will be bubbles this time!

To my beta readers – you are invaluable and so appreciated. Will, I look forward to plotting with you *in person* soon!

I am lucky enough to have friends who are generous with the knowledge and expertise of their chosen professions. Sandra, thank you for answering so many random questions. (There will be more for book 3 – *sorry!*) And to Katrina for your generous and invaluable insight. You've both helped this book come alive.

The artwork that Tom Gallagher admires in Chapter 1 is by Cork artist Rick McGroarty. View his stunning collection at www.rickmcgroarty.com. Thank you, Rick, for allowing me to (fictionally) hang one of your pieces in Tom's office!

Thanks to the Terrific Two (as they like to be called), for character-name ideas and understanding when I had to write. Kevin – thanks for the mugs of coffee, for turning my laptop and the kitchen table into an ergonomically sound workspace, and for listening and nodding encouragingly throughout the plotting process.

Finally, thank you, readers! I hope you enjoy following Anna's story in this second instalment of the *Blinding Lies* trilogy.

Dedication

To Valerie who passed on her love of books,
and to Kevin who always weaves a great story.

Prologue

It was dark.

But not so dark Seán couldn't feel the stirrings of excitement at the possibilities of a new day. Usually, he hated the month of January, with its bleak mornings and the early creep of night in the darkening afternoons. Today, as he pulled back the bedroom curtains and watched the first rays of the weak morning sun puncture the horizon, he felt his spirits lift. Winter would soon be over.

His shift in the Cork University Hospital was due to start soon and he was already late – breakfast would have to wait until he reached the staff canteen. He packed his lunch, the remains of a roast beef dinner his sister had provided filling his sandwich, relish oozing over the crusts. From the bedroom he grabbed his training gear and stuffed his lunch, wallet and phone into the small bag.

On Thursday nights he played five-a-side soccer with a bunch of local men in their fifties. They had grown up together and still met up once a week. Seán was looking forward to it. He knew he needed the exercise and could do with losing

1

some weight but, mostly, he looked forward to the company. Since his dad had passed away last year, the dark winter nights had proved to be long and lonely. Heaving his gear bag onto his shoulder, he left the house, buoyed by the thought of the camaraderie with his friends later.

Heavy rain had lashed the house overnight, but the morning was dry and cold. Dodging puddles on his uneven driveway, he hurried to the car. Clonakilty was over forty minutes' drive from the city, even longer with heavy morning traffic. His dad had nagged him over the last few years to get a job closer to home, to spend less time on the road. There were so many accidents these days, he had argued, and Seán was "spending a fortune on fuel". But he liked his job and, truthfully, didn't mind the commute. The drive home always helped him to unwind after a busy shift. And besides, he knew all the back roads to make up time. He decided to stick to those back roads now – it was his usual route, and even if they were a little waterlogged and muddy from the downpour, he'd take his chances.

Dawn broke and the tentative rays of sunlight he had seen earlier now peaked strong on the horizon. The roads were deserted and in the growing light he picked up speed. Despite having the heating on full, his breath fogged the air in front of him and he shivered a little.

Up ahead, he saw something that caused him to abandon the building speed and press hard on the brakes. He winced as the wheels skidded on the wet road. The car came to a stop a few feet in front of a jeep that was pulled into the verge at a haphazard angle. Perhaps there had been an accident, he wondered, throwing off his seatbelt. Cheeks stinging in the cold air as he climbed out of the car, he jogged forward, and peered in the windows. The jeep appeared to be empty. He exhaled in relief – whoever had been inside had obviously made it safely out. Perhaps it had been abandoned by a driver conscious he'd had one too many pints last night, he thought with a chuckle. Turning back to his car, he felt a flicker of anxiety – he needed to get back on his journey.

But something caught his eye. From behind the jeep, on the ground, a pair of legs were stretched out, shoes pointing in opposite directions. The sound of heaving and grunting reached him then, as though someone was exerting himself, struggling. His heartbeat quickened and he strode to the back of the jeep, ready to help. On the ground a woman lay still, her eyes closed, her mouth slack. A man knelt beside her, his hands knitted together on her chest.

With pounding adrenaline, Seán knelt down.

"I'm a nurse, let me help!"

Without a word the man sprang to his feet. Seán noted that his baseball hat was pulled low, and what he could see of his face was pale and scarred, skin sagging around his chin. The man kept his head down, not making eye contact. He must be in shock, the poor man, Seán thought, inching a little closer to the woman, ready to start compressions.

"Have you phoned for an ambulance yet?"

When he heard no reply he looked up at the man. He was looking off to the side, a little distance away. There, resting on the muddy verge of the road, was a tripod, and on top of it a video camera. Its red light flashed on and off, on and off. Seán's brow furrowed in confusion. Were they being filmed? What was going on?

A tiny sound, a giggle, escaped from the woman on the ground. His eyes flew to her. She was no longer still. She opened her eyes and stared at him, her face growing red as she fought visibly to stay composed.

Confusion turned to fear.

His hands had been poised over the woman's chest, ready to begin compressions – they began to tremble uncontrollably now as laughter erupted from her. In the quiet of the empty road, it had a shrill, manic sound that enveloped him and fear gripped his hammering heart. He stood up, willing his shaking legs to hold steady.

"What's all this?" he asked, raising his eyes to the woman's companion.

The woman squealed in delighted laughter on the hard, cold ground as the man stared at Seán. There was something wrong with his eyes and mouth … but Seán's attention quickly went to his hands, which were wrapped around something black. It was pointed at Seán's face.

A gun.

The crack of the gunshot broke the tranquillity of the early winter morning. Resting birds took flight from nearby tree branches. Rolling on the ground, the woman's laughter reached a deafening pitch. The only other sound was the thud as Seán fell.

1

The office at the back of Tom Gallagher's house was warm, despite the chill outside. As dawn broke he was sitting behind a large desk, which was empty save for a stack of pens, some enlarged photographs, and the mug of coffee his housekeeper Jessica had brought him. He had opened the window just enough to hear the morning birdsong without losing the cosy heat of the room. Sipping his coffee, he rested his head against the leather seat and listened, eyes closed. It was a moment of peace before the madness of the day began.

When he opened them again his eyes rested on a large watercolour painting of the Fastnet Rock. Blue waves swelled and ravaged against the rock, but the lighthouse stood tall and strong. Tom often felt like that lighthouse, a beacon of strength amid the crashing waves around him. Lately, that had never felt so true. He marvelled at the brushstrokes, at the skill of the artist, and momentarily felt peace roll over and around him. He savoured it for a long time, before finally turning his attention to the photographs on the desk, his calm evaporating quickly.

They were images from CCTV that had recently come into his possession, taken in an alleyway in Cork city. He had spent days studying them obsessively and knew every grainy detail. They showed two women crouched on the ground outside the bathroom window of the Mad Hatter nightclub in the city centre. A competitor's club, where the manager had agreed to turn the security cameras off for the night – this was an image from the street cameras. A second photograph focused on one of the women as she faced a thickset man who was blocking the exit from the alley. Even with the poor quality of the image her eyes looked wild, her teeth bared like a cornered animal.

Kate Crowley.

Tom's fists clenched on the desk as he looked at her. Her hair was cropped and dark but shortly before that image was taken it had been long and wild, with fiery auburn curls. She had cut it short and died it a darker shade, to hide from him and the law after what she had done.

After she had killed his son David.

He knew that after that photograph was taken, Kate had attacked the man standing in front of her – *his* man. She had kicked out and the hardman he had sent to find her had crumpled to the ground like a rag doll. Kate had then run into the night and kept running. She remained out of his reach but never far from his mind.

Her green eyes invaded his thoughts, despite all he did to be free of her. At night, when sleep eventually came, it brought no relief. Kate's eyes became David's. In his restless nights he dreamt of his youngest son lying on a cold slab in the city morgue. His skin was waxen and icy to touch, the sheen of death glistening on his face. A hole in the side of his neck told the story of his death – the bullet

6

wound that had caused him to bleed out and die, alone, on Kate's living-room floor. The nightmare was always the same: David would turn his head to look at his father, open his eyes and speak words Tom could never hear. And, always, his eyes were the same bright green as Kate Crowley's.

He awoke from such torture every night, clutching his chest to calm his pounding heart, to find himself alone in his bed. His wife Mae had taken to sleeping wherever she passed out. Usually the sofa or an armchair, sometimes the floor. He was used to sleeping alone now and had grown weary of his wife's breakdown, of the stench of liquor and vomit that infused the air around her. He let Jessica clean her up in the mornings when she arrived at the house. But he knew it was his fault – he had promised Mae he would bring Kate to her. It seemed to him the only thing that would appease his wife would be to bring her the woman who had killed her son, to do with as she pleased. So far, he had failed to keep his promise. Kate evaded him still while his wife drank herself and her memories into nothing. She was diluting herself, the person she was once. Watching her spiral into a shell of a human being added to Tom's fears and anxieties, amplifying those that had consumed him since David's death. He drowned out the nagging worry about Mae's drinking with his determination to get justice for David. And for John, their older son, who had been tortured and beaten because of Kate's actions. He was home, alive, recovering … but the wounds of the past few months felt fresh and deep.

Too much time had passed while Tom was steeped in grief. Burying a son should be enough for any man to deal with, but he'd had to watch Mae slip away from him too. John's rehabilitation had become a project and given him a reason to get out of bed. Now he was focused on finding the woman who had delivered his family to the gates of hell. He should have acted sooner – precious time had slipped away and Kate had disappeared. But he was a patient man, with assets at his disposal. It wouldn't take long … and now he had these photographs. Now he had a lead.

"Tom?"

Ely Murray stepped inside the office. His bulk filled the doorway. Tall and broad, with a scar that ran from his ear to his lip, he was an imposing figure. He had earned that scar working in the Gallagher business and wore it proudly. His dark eyes observed the man he had called "boss" for over thirty years. He had always admired Tom Gallagher … but lately he seemed troubled, a man who was less interested in the world around him. A man lost to an inner chaos. Ely had bad news to impart – again – and he dreaded the boss's response. Frustration had begun to penetrate his thoughts where his employer was concerned. He had never felt this before – he suspected it might be time to move on.

"News from Dublin airport. Alan Ainsley has finally surfaced. He was spotted in the departures lounge with a female. Our man didn't get a photograph of her but we presume it's his wife. They flew to London."

Tom picked up a pen and tapped it on the tabletop, side to side. Ely knew the signs of the man's agitation – a vein pulsing in his neck, the whites of his eyes more bloodshot than usual. His dark hair was gelled off his face – even in turmoil he was well-dressed, with a pressed shirt and aftershave, groomed and presentable – but it accentuated the deep lines on his forehead and around his eyes. Though tall, and physically an imposing figure, the boss was ageing. Recent events had taken their toll on Tom Gallagher and his family, and on his enterprise.

The weeks after David's death had brought too much heat on the family in Ely's opinion. The Gallaghers ran a number of successful businesses in the city – nightclubs and bars – which in turn facilitated the more lucrative end of the business: drugs and hiding stolen goods. They had built an empire by staying hidden from the gardaí but David's actions, and his death, had caused so much scrutiny of the family that the business would be lucky to survive. Associates still distanced themselves, preferring to use other avenues that were not under enquiry. David had made too many mistakes.

And now he was dead.

"Tom?" Ely prompted.

His boss's eyes refocused and he looked at him as though seeing him for the first time. He appeared tired, defeated, and Ely's annoyance increased. He wished the man would snap out this malaise and get back to the real world.

"I want to send some men to London, try to determine Ainsley's next move," Ely said. "He's been in hiding for weeks now. We should take our chance."

The mention of the Englishman's name again awoke something in Tom. Ainsley had been a useful middleman, but he had helped David to broker a deal behind his father's back with a German gang, and it had cost David everything. Tom had a list of people that needed to be dealt with, and Ainsley was right at the top. His eyes bored intensely into the man in front of him while he thought things through. Ely had been his go-to after David was shot and his older son John had gone missing. He had proved himself both capable and calm under pressure over the last two months. He was a valuable asset.

"No. Don't send anyone to London. It's a waste of resources. Ainsley could have flown to practically any other airport from there. Keep a man watching his house and at our usual spot at Cork airport – he'll be back. He has a daughter in Trinity College and his mother-in-law is in a nursing home in Waterford. I want to know as soon as he lands back in the country."

Ely nodded appraisingly, pleased to see there was a spark in his boss yet. Perhaps it was too early to write him off.

"The shipment due in on Saturday night –"

"Forget all that!" Tom waved his hand to indicate that he should sit down and slid one of the CCTV photographs across the desk. "Take a look at this. At *her*." He jabbed with his finger, his voice a hiss between clenched teeth.

Forget the shipment? The shipment, and others like it, were how Tom Gallagher made money. How Ely got paid. Suppressing an irritated sigh, he leaned forward and studied the image. Instantly his breath caught in his throat. Here she was, crouched beside Kate Crowley, the girl who had knocked him unconscious in the ladies' bathroom in the Mad Hatter nightclub. He had barely seen her face at the time, but he would never forget it.

Ely and some of his men had gone there to bring Kate Crowley in, to answer for what she had done to David. She had been trying to buy a passport to leave the country. But when he had been about to grab her in the bathroom, *this* girl in the image had shown up. Kate's friend perhaps – he didn't know. What he *did* know was that she had some karate or other self-defence skills because she had knocked him out cold. That had never happened before. He was glad Tom had arranged for the CCTV inside the club to be turned off for the night – he would not like to have to explain how a girl half his size had bested him. He studied her face, her wide brown eyes, her short blonde hair.

"She helped Kate Crowley that night – if you remember, they jumped from a window at the back of the club into this alleyway."

Ely did remember. He wouldn't forget this girl easily.

"See what our Garda source knows about her. I want to know *everything*: who she is, what she is to the Crowley bitch, and why she was there that night."

"Where did you get this?"

"An old friend – don't worry about that." Tom's eyes darkened in annoyance at the interruption.

"You think she can lead you to Crowley?"

Tom leaned back in his chair, gazing again at the watercolour on the wall.

"This girl is our only lead. Kate has disappeared. My solicitor is pressing the gardaí but they've nothing, no clue where she is, except they suppose she made her way to France to link up with her sister and the two kids. David deserves justice. Let's just see what she knows."

The anger that burned in his eyes thrilled Ely. He had his own reasons to want to find the girl in the alley. He would enjoy interrogating her. She wouldn't get the better of him twice. And if it brought answers that resulted in the boss focusing on more important things again, like keeping his business operational, even better.

"*Find her!*"

***

John Gallagher was standing at the door, out of sight but within earshot.

11

So, his father was still caught up in finding the woman who had killed David. And he was entrusting the task to Ely Murray, not his own son …

John remembered Kate – she was aunt to his two nieces, practically family. Her sister Natalie had been David's partner for years. Compared to her sister, Kate was stuck-up and opinionated and not afraid of him. That had been intriguing. Amusing, even. As far as he could figure, she had shot his brother in self-defence, and he had to admit David had given her good reason. Many people thought David Gallagher had got what was coming to him, and long overdue. In a way, he missed his brother – things were different without him. But David's actions had changed everything. If he were still alive, John would remind him of his family duties, and to keep his head down and stay off the Garda-radar.

He could clearly remember the day David died last November – but the days after were blurred to a medley of pain and torture. David had called him, screaming about being robbed of goods he was holding for a German gang, the Meiers. He hadn't mentioned he was also missing a memory key the Meiers were to buy from him – he had kept the rest of the family out of *that* business deal, for reasons John could still not forgive.

He could tell his brother was in such a rage he would no longer be able to see reason – when David lost his temper, he usually ended up attracting attention. He had warned him to stay put, to calm down. Staying calm in a dangerous situation allowed a man to stay in control. Allowed him to come out on top. But, of course, David didn't listen …

Be prepared for anything was John's motto – the men he usually dealt with in this business were unpredictable.

Staying ahead in this game meant never being taken by surprise. A lesson he thought he had mastered until his car was almost driven into the water at the docks, and he was ambushed by the very men David was afraid of. The Meiers. A group of criminals from Germany that his father had forged a business alliance with through Alan Ainsley. Ainsley had brokered many deals for the Gallaghers over the years, and the Meiers had been repeat customers. Business was lucrative, and so beneficial that Alan Ainsley was like family.

Until he helped David to strike a deal that destroyed everything. David had acquired classified security details for a political conference that took place in the city last year. Through the middleman, he arranged to sell it to the Meiers, leaving his father and brother out in the cold.

What was his brother thinking? Had David successfully sold the data on to the Meiers, it would have seriously compromised the safety of several leading politicians in Europe and made him a very rich man in the process. But his gamble had led to his death.

On the day David was shot, the Meiers had been so desperate to locate the memory key that they had taken John to a remote farmhouse and tortured him for days to pressure his father into finding it. To think that Kate had it all along, as well as thousands of euro of David's money, fuelled a pit of rage inside Tom Gallagher night after night. John felt the anger radiate from his father every day. The man spoke of nothing else. When the whole world was there for the taking, Tom chose to focus on one stupid girl. John could understand – she owed the family.

He had tried to forget his days of torture – the Meiers were dead, beaten to death and their throats slit by his father and his men in the hallway of this house. The walls

13

were freshly painted and the floor tiles replaced, but he imagined the stench of death and decay hanging in the air, and he liked it. It reminded him that *he* had won and *they* had lost. All that was left of their flesh and bones were particles of ash, scattered on the winter wind. Whereas John had only started making his mark on the world.

He rubbed at the stump of flesh where his finger had been. When they had finished breaking his bones the Meiers had hacked it off and mailed it to his mother. The stump was not yet fully healed, and his doctor had advised keeping it covered to protect from infection, but John like to push and pull the lumpy, mottled flesh. The nerve-endings were dead, the remaining flesh causing him no pain. The memories did, but John kept himself busy to bury them deep into the bowels of his consciousness. Listening to his father's plans to find Kate Crowley stirred an excitement in him. He wanted in on this, and not as Murray's number two either.

His parents were treating him as if he were a precious figurine made of glass – their one remaining son, tortured and barely alive when he was rescued. But his bones were healing and his scars would fade. He was ready to return to the fore, to the business that would be his. The men needed to see him, to see that he hadn't changed, that his force hadn't been diluted. He had been happy to indulge his mother's desire to keep him close and out of trouble – he had other businesses he was interested in, other ways to pass the time. But he was growing restless. He would have to convince his father to cut him loose again.

Sometimes he thought he understood his brother's need to strike out on his own. Every man needed to make his own mark. Unlike his brother, when he chose to go it alone, *he* wouldn't be making any mistakes.

14

2

Victus, as always, was busy at lunchtime. The coffee shop near the Lee Street Garda station was Anna's favourite, its aromas and sounds a warm, familiar hug. When Vivian had suggested lunch, there was nowhere in the city that was a tempting alternative. A wave of scents reached her as she pushed open the door – roasting coffee beans and the sweet smell of pastries. The barista Louisa smiled in greeting and nodded towards a table at the back where Vivian was waiting, her head bent over a laptop, a steaming mug beside her.

"The usual?"

"Thanks, Louisa! And a chicken panini too, please."

Anna grinned as she weaved between the tables to where her friend was sitting. Vivian had spent much of the previous year in New Zealand. After finding her birth mother a few years previously, last spring she had decided to travel to Auckland to finally meet her in person. So much had happened while she was away that she and Anna had been meeting to catch up as often as possible, and still there was so much to share.

15

Anna sat down opposite her, smiling, waiting for her to look up from her laptop.

"Hello!"

Vivian raised her head, her blue eyes bright with excitement. Anna knew that look – she called it her 'Lois Lane' expression.

"Anna! Hi!"

"You're working on something," she said. "You've got that look on your face again!"

Vivian grinned and closed her laptop. She bent and slid it into its case on the ground. Her brown hair was tied in a neat bun at the nape of her neck, her trouser suit a smart navy. She had secured her job as a reporter for the city's busiest newspaper almost as soon as she'd returned to Cork, and Anna marvelled at how professional and grown-up she looked. She was conscious that in her black trousers and green woolly jumper she looked like her casual younger sister. As clerical support in the nearby Lee Street Garda station, she never met the public, and didn't have to dress as smartly as Vivian did for the office. Collating statistical reports for the Department of Justice depended on her degree in mathematics and post-grad in statistics more than her fashion sense, thankfully. Vivian, on the other hand, was front and centre to the public, and rarely was a hair out of place.

"There's a big story breaking and yours truly is assigned to it!"

She paused as a server brought Anna's lunch and coffee to the table.

Sipping the milky froth of her latte, Anna waited for her friend to continue.

"There's been a shooting in Clonakilty early this

morning. On one of the back roads towards the bypass. A man shot dead."

Anna's hand froze, her coffee suspended in mid-air. She had been immersed in the files on her desk all morning and this latest crime hadn't filtered through the news channels at work yet. She felt her breath catch in her throat. It was January, a new year full of fresh starts and potential, but already there had been a shooting. It seemed to her that since November she had been immersed in shootings and serious crime, at work and in her personal life.

Lowering her coffee, she gave in to a chill that shook her body from head to toe.

"Are you OK? You've gone pale! Is it one of your migraines again?"

"No, it's not that. I'm fine." Anna had battled migraines for the last ten years. The headaches had grown steadily worse in the last few months. "It's just, not too long ago my colleague told me there'd been a shooting, and we both know how that ended."

Vivian nodded, sombre now. "Still no word from Kate?" she asked, her voice low and her eyes wide.

Anna shook her head sadly. "No, and I don't think there will be. She's long gone."

"I still can't believe she killed him!" Vivian didn't dare mention David Gallagher's name – Cork was a fairly big city, but small where it counted.

"Me neither. But she did. Whether it was self-defence or not."

Anna had initially assumed their old friend had shot David Gallagher to save herself but, as time went on, she was less sure. While searching for information online, she had discovered that after their paths had diverged and they lost touch, Kate had become a kickboxing champion in college. It had thrown the self-defence theory into doubt. Anna had many lingering questions that she feared she would never know the answers to. She still wondered why she had let herself get drawn so quickly and completely into the case. As soon as she was assigned to the file last November, she had thought of nothing else. She believed Kate hadn't meant to kill David, but she had certainly used Anna's friendship to her own advantage in the end. Whether Kate was guilty or innocent, she knew she would never hear from her again.

"Lee Street will be working on this morning's shooting." Vivian gulped her coffee and pushed the last of a sandwich into her mouth, chewing quickly.

She did everything as if she were in a hurry, and Anna realised that today she probably was.

"The local station in Clonakilty doesn't have the resources right now. My boss mentioned DS Ryan taking the lead."

"Well, if DS Ryan is taking charge, the investigation is in good hands then." Anna wanted to change the subject from the shooting – no doubt the report on it, in all its gruesome details, would make its way to her desk before too long. "How are things at home?"

Vivian's face darkened and she sighed. Her adopted brother Gareth had been difficult since she had returned from New Zealand. They had never been close, but lately his attitude towards her had changed from ambivalence to anger. He was livid with Vivian now, accusing her of turning her back on their parents in favour of her birth mother. Her parents assured her they didn't feel that way but Anna knew the strain in her relationship with her brother really hurt her friend.

Vivian groaned. "Not great. Gareth seems less angry, but that's only because he's not actually speaking to me. I feel bad for him – when he reached out to his birth mother she didn't want to know. I suppose he feels a sort of double rejection from her. I wish he could focus on how lucky he is with Mum and Dad. He's going to flip out when I tell him the latest news." She took a deep breath, rubbing her temples with both hands. "Brenda is buying me an apartment, here in the city. She's insisting. And she's planning to visit in the summer."

Anna watched her friend frown and reached across the table, rubbing her arm.

"That's great! You don't seem happy though – you should be thrilled!"

"I am … it's just, Gareth is being so difficult …"

"Please don't let him spoil this for you. You've nothing to feel guilty about."

Vivian couldn't help but grin. "Oh Anna, I can't wait for you to meet her! Brenda's warm and funny, and so creative. I really like her!"

Anna smiled fondly at her friend. Since they were teenagers, Vivian had wondered about her birth mother. There had been endless conversations imagining who she might be, whether she looked like Vivian, if she'd had more children. Anna was delighted her friend finally had some answers.

"I'm thrilled for you. I know how much this means to you! And don't worry about Gareth – I suppose it's natural that he's envious that you have a bond with your birth mother. I'm sure he'll come around."

Vivian nodded, grateful for the support. "I just feel a bit guilty. Mum and Dad have given me so much, and here I am, so excited about Brenda. Plus, I'm not long back and I'm planning to move out … it's a lot!"

"Your parents know you love them! And your brother knows you love him too."

Vivian swirled the last of her coffee around in her mug and nodded. Then, with a start, she checked a slim gold watch on her wrist, another gift from Brenda.

"Oh, I have to go! I'm hitching a lift down to Clonakilty with the photographer from the newspaper. I want to see if there's any developments at the crime-scene and speak to the locals, get their reaction and find out more about the victim. But, quickly, speaking of brothers … have you spoken to yours yet?"

Anna pushed her hands through her short blonde bob and sighed.

"No. And I'm not sure how to. I gave him the photographs and newspaper articles about Mum days ago and I've heard nothing back from him. I've tried to give him time, and obviously we need to talk … it's just, I'm not sure where to begin!" She smiled sadly as she remembered William Ryan's words of advice, offered not so long ago: *I find the start to be the best place to begin.*

3

Detective Sergeant William Ryan crouched on the ground, his dark woollen overcoat trailing on the wet concrete. The victim, a man in his late fifties, was undeniably dead. All that remained of one of his eyes was a dark gash, where blood and bodily fluids had oozed and now resembled black lava grown still and crusting. The Tech Bureau team were satisfied it was a gunshot. There was no exit wound – the bullet would be still lodged inside his head.

The road was a back road, not often used, but known to the locals. It was thronged with people now. The Garda Technical Bureau's team of forensic experts were in the process of scrutinizing every inch of the terrain, and a couple of bystanders were assembled by the white-and-blue crime-scene tape, keen to watch the scene unfold. The grassy verges of the road were a muddied blend of green and brown, owing to the torrential rain the night before. A man he suspected of being a journalist crept around the edge of the tape, observing everything with hawk-like curiosity. It wouldn't take long for more of his ilk to descend, like crows to feast on a carcass,

William thought sourly. At least the victim would soon be afforded some dignity inside the crime-scene tent, which was in the process of being erected. The state pathologist was due shortly.

He noticed his supervisor, Chief Superintendent Frank Doherty, step under the tape, flashing his ID in irritation at an approaching garda. The bulk of the man was intimidating, his scowl even more so. William met his eyes, and they shared a mutual half-nod. Immediately Frank demanded answers of the people with the misfortune to be standing nearest him.

William, observing the shoulders of the forensic garda tense at the diatribe of demands carrying over the cold morning air, grinned and muttered "Good luck!"

He turned to the young man who was bent over, hands on his knees, breathing deeply.

"You OK there?"

Colin Forde was local to the area but stationed in Lee Street in the city after recently being allocated to detective duties. He had already expelled his breakfast onto the grass and, judging by the way he was heaving, William suspected there was more to come. He wasn't wrong. Once the man had finished, he passed him some tissues and turned his back to let him compose himself. This was his first murder scene. He was considerably shorter than William, his smattering of freckles and wide blue eyes making him look a lot younger than he really was. William had heard good things about this young man; this case was about to put that to the test.

"I wonder what this is?" Colin moved slightly to his left, still bent low to the grass. "Eh … Sergeant Ryan, have a look at this."

William stepped gingerly to the spot, careful to avoid the little pool of vomit. "What do you see?"

"Marks, here. Three holes in the mud. And the grass is all trampled down around it – the mud is all scuffed. It looks flatter that the rest of the verge here."

William bent low to look at the markings, moving the blades of grass aside with a plastic-gloved finger. Colin was right. Three holes in the mud, making a triangular shape.

"Yes ... someone definitely concentrated on this small area. I wonder what those marks are from ..."

He straightened up. This could be nothing and might not even be connected to the crime scene, but it could be something. He raised his arm and signalled for the forensic photographer, who was still concentrating on the body.

"Over here, please! Photograph these marks in the grass. Pay particular attention to the mud for footprints or anything useful."

He moved towards the victim's car, leaving Colin to finish cleaning himself up. The car had been examined already, yielding nothing of interest, except for the fact that the motive for the shooting wasn't theft – the victim's wallet and phone were still inside a bag on the passenger seat. A card inside the wallet identified the victim as Seán Doyle, a nurse in the emergency department of CUH – Cork University Hospital. There was a packed lunch and a sports kit. William had sent two gardaí to the hospital and the near-retired local garda to the next of kin. He had made a positive ID at the scene, and it was better to have the news broken to family by a familiar face. The cause of death was obvious. All that was left to do was find the person responsible and enough evidence to secure a conviction. Along the way he hoped to establish a motive, although in William's experience there didn't always need to be one.

Colin ran a hand over his short, red hair and smoothed

down his jacket, keen to make sure everything was looking as it should. He watched the tall, thin detective from the Lee Street station pull off his shoe-covers and lever himself up with ease to stand on the bonnet of the victim's car. He had heard William Ryan was a little eccentric, but effective, and wondered what he was up to. He looked forward to working with the man – there was much he could learn from him – but this was the last thing he had expected to face this morning. Squaring his shoulders he breathed deeply, hoping to quell his embarrassment at emptying the contents of his stomach in the middle of the crime scene. He watched as the senior detective moved in a full circle on the bonnet of the car, taking in all that was around them.

"You're a local man, Colin. What's over there?" William pointed across the field that ran parallel to the road. "That large green shed?"

"That's Conways' land – that's their farm shed, I suppose."

William hopped down quickly. Peeling off the plastic gloves, he pulled his own black leather gloves from his pocket and pushed his fingers into them. The air around him had an icy chill.

"The shed's fairly close. If they have security cameras, we'll need to take a look. Might tell us something." He spoke quickly, his eyes roaming around the crime scene. "Those tyre markings in the ditch tell us the other vehicle was bigger than the victim's, probably a jeep or Land Rover, but it'll be difficult to get anything definitive, I think – it's a bit of a mud-bath. Other than that, the killer left nothing behind for us to go on. Nothing obvious anyway, but maybe the tech team will get lucky. And let's hope Conway has cameras and that they are switched on. Now!" He patted the Detective Garda's back. "Feeling better?"

"Eh ... no, not really."

"Good. Time for lunch!"

Colin Forde enjoyed the sound of his new job title: Detective Garda. His mother said it had a ring to it. So far, this was the least enjoyable day of his career. He was certain he would never get the images he had seen this morning out of his head.

He would much rather have had just a cup of tea, but William Ryan had insisted he eat something. The steaming bowl of mushroom soup in front of him might not have been a wise choice. An aroma of garlic mixed with cream rose steadily from the bowl and he fought the mounting nausea that threatened in waves.

"Have you ever seen a dead body before, Colin?"

William was tucking into a heaped plate of carvery. He pushed a forkful of roast turkey slathered in dripping gravy past his lips as he spoke. Colin had to look away and cupped a hand around his mouth.

"Once," he answered through his fingers. "I saw my grandmother at her wake in the sitting room. But nothing like ... nothing like earlier."

"Ah yes." William swallowed and took a mouthful of water, swilling it around his teeth. Colin squirmed in his seat. "I don't blame you for feeling queasy! Terrible thing to see. An eye blown into the back of a man's skull ... awful!"

A memory pulled at William's consciousness, of his former Chief Superintendent dead and bleeding out, slumped over a computer screen. The events of last year were still being investigated, still darting into his mind at random times of the day and night. He pushed the images away and concentrated on his food.

Colin decided it was rude to just sit there and took a cautious mouthful of soup – it tasted good. And salty. DS Ryan was right – it would settle his stomach. If he concentrated on not thinking about the victim on the ground this morning, he might be able to eat it.

They were sitting in the bar of a hotel on the main street in Clonakilty. It was almost full, bodies snaking to and from the carvery counter – they had been lucky to get a table. Their corner of the bar was warm and both had shrugged off their heavy coats due to the heat from a blazing fire nearby.

"Is it always this busy at lunchtime?" William enquired.

"Most days. They do a good lunch trade here."

A young waitress arrived at their table. Tucking a strand of hair behind her ear, she blushed slightly. "Hiya, Colin. I heard you got a promotion. Shame we won't see you around as much. Can I get you anything else? Anything at all?"

William raised his eyebrows – these two obviously knew each other well. He realised Colin still couldn't muster a smile and was struggling to speak – he could almost *see* nausea inching up the man's throat.

"Tea for two, please, Jan!" he answered, reading her name from the tag on her blouse. He adopted a casual tone. "Busy here today. Is the hotel full this time of year?"

The young girl snorted with laughter. "Full? Are you kidding? It's January – we only really stay open for the lunch trade. Who in their right mind would go on holidays in January?"

"So, no hotel guests then?"

"Just a few businessmen – they come here every month for a few nights. And an American couple on honeymoon – imagine coming to Clonakilty on your honeymoon in

January! I'd head to the sun myself." She laughed again and stole a glance at Colin.

He was giving her all his attention now and, despite his sickly pallor his eyes were bright and bored into the girl's. William smiled – Colin could sense a lead. He was impressed.

"Oh really? Honeymooners?" Colin attempted a warm smile. He cleared his throat before continuing. "Are they still in the hotel?"

The girl glowed under his attention and sat down on a stool beside their table, her eyes locked on his face.

"No, they checked out this morning. They've had such rotten luck."

"Rotten luck?"

"Poor things were robbed on their way here! In the airport, the woman said. Their hand luggage lifted right off the trolley! It had their passports and wallets in it. All their credit cards, their ID, everything, gone! They were lucky they had some cash stashed in another bag – the woman was quite dramatic about that actually, praising God out loud in reception. People were staring!" She giggled, remembering.

"And what about her husband?"

"Oh, he never spoke at all. One of those silent types, I guess."

Colin met William's eyes across the table. He felt his nausea abating.

"Jan, I'm going to need you to tell me everything you can about that American couple."

4

"Yes, this is much better!"

The woman lay in the middle of the king-size bed and spread her arms and legs wide, moving them up and down, making a snow-angel on the crisp white sheets. She was still speaking in an irritatingly exaggerated American accent, and he wished she would shut up.

The man sat at a small desk near the window, studying booklets and other tourist paraphernalia supplied by the hotel. He had turned his back to her, to discourage her from making the sound she never tired of making. Eventually she stopped speaking and picked up the TV remote, flicking between channels. That didn't bother him so much. Finally, she was still, no longer messing up the bedsheets. He hated untidiness.

His thoughts darted to the mess made this morning, to the blood and flesh that had spurted into the air. Their target had been so shocked it was difficult not to laugh, remembering the look of confusion on his face. The process had been simple. To check into a quiet hotel in a quiet town, to survey the back roads, the nooks and crannies of the place, and find their spot. If this town hadn't worked out, he would have moved on to the next. He had read about using a roadside ambush to achieve their objective in the true-crime books he favoured, and it had been so easy in Clonakilty, with plenty of back roads to choose from.

The town wasn't *that* quiet though, and to avoid being seen it was soon obvious their film would have to be made either early in the morning or late at night. Owing to the need for natural light, the morning was the most obvious choice. Even though the sun was barely up that early, it was enough. He had spent the previous three mornings driving slowly around the countryside in their stolen jeep, through the back roads, his baseball cap pulled low. The licence plates were fake, the jeep stolen in Dublin and driven south – he didn't expect to come to anyone's attention. And he needed to research the area – to discover things, for example, like the fact the school bus travelled mostly on the main road but made six stops on two wider back roads. On the road he had eventually chosen, the lone driver had travelled past him each morning at almost the exact same time. He had made up his mind, and it was taking a risk to assume the driver would always be alone, but it had paid off. In his experience, life was a series of risks and rewards. If he continued to take calculated risks, the rewards would be great.

The woman had chosen alter egos for them. Codenames – Bonnie and Clyde. He didn't like it – it was juvenile. She could be childish like that. But he had no real desire to argue with her, so he let it go. It excited her, this fantasy she was creating. And they stayed anonymous. The quality of the film had disappointed him though – the angle afforded by the tripod was almost useless. The camera needed to move, to be fluid … he would have to make sure they created a better film next time.

He shifted in the leather chair at the desk and looked out the window, across the South Mall. The hotel was luxurious and extremely restful, the style old-fashioned as it dated from the 19th century. He had been in Cork before, as a child, and remembered the sounds and smells, especially the English Market. The smell of the fish and the sight of their gutted bodies had enthralled him. He felt restless now, his leg bouncing on the thick carpet. After the exhilaration of this morning his body felt tightly coiled, his breath coming in sharp bursts. He knew that pounding the city streets would help but he was fearful of being outdoors where street cameras could track their movements.

She called him paranoid, reminded him they were *incognito*. She was loving this, the accents, the wigs. And maybe she was right. But everywhere they went he felt eyes watching him, probing his skull. Still, it might be better than staying inside a small hotel room with her. She was talking again – she rarely stopped. Listening to the whine of her voice he wondered how long he could remain inside here.

She moved across the carpeted floor and perched on his knee, drumming her fingers on his shoulder. Immediately he sighed in annoyance. She was too thin – he was always telling her that. Her bones pressed uncomfortably into his thigh and he pushed her off. Unfazed, she gazed out the window at the tree-lined street.

"There's a homeless man over there." She pointed to the left side of the street. "Two of them actually. What do you think? Should we go and say hello?" She giggled, unable to pull her eyes away from them.

He yanked her arm roughly until she was back by his side, then jabbed a finger at the leaflet spread out on the table in front of him.

"Here. Tomorrow. You'll need to book us an appointment."

"'*The Rebel Event Centre*'," she read from the page. "Open for private tours throughout the winter." She stared at the smiling photograph of '*Marian Selway, Marketing Manager*'.

"Won't there be cameras? CCTV?"

"Maybe. But aren't you the one who keeps saying that the cameras don't matter? That we're in disguise?" He pointed at the leaflet again. "It'll make a better film. We need to up our game."

Moving towards the end of the bed, he smoothed out the wrinkles she had made on the sheets. He lifted their suitcases onto the bed. Unzipping them, he unloaded the contents in neat piles: clothes, her bag of wigs, shoes, toiletries and finally, a mask in a soft velvet pouch. It was made of mixed materials, mostly rubber. It was the closest thing he could find to a death mask of his father's face. He touched it gently, reverently. The eyes and lips were sealed shut, the skin pale cream, almost white. The rubber over the eyes was thin enough to allow him to see through, as though behind a veil. It was enough. Tiny holes at the nose allowed the wearer to breathe. It wasn't comfortable, but it wasn't worn for comfort. It was worn for disguise – and terror. His intentions were clear: he would avoid identification by wearing this and she could do whatever she liked.

"Book us in." He gestured to the hotel phone on the bedside locker.

The woman clasped her hands together in excitement. "Will we be American again? Or how about English this time?"

"I really don't care." He headed for the bathroom, keen to scrub off the flecks of flesh and blood he imagined crawling on his skin, lingering despite two earlier showers. He locked the door.

With a delighted squeal she picked up the phone.

5

"Anna!"

Anna laughed as she was bowled over by the ball of excitement that was her niece. They fell together onto the rug on the hallway floor. Chloe wrapped her small arms around her aunt and hugged her tight.

"Hey, little one, give your aunty some room to breathe!" Alex laughed, pulling Chloe up and offering his sister a hand. He was considerably taller than her at six foot, but they both had their mother's light-blonde hair and their father's brown eyes.

Anna twirled her niece's blonde ponytail playfully. "Wow, you're strong for a five-year-old!"

They walked into the kitchen, where Alex carried on the task of cutting a chicken pie into portions. Anna inhaled deeply, the smell of cooking and the familiarity of her brother's house as soothing as a physical embrace.

"How was your day?"

"Good. I met Vivian for lunch."

"I was allowed help with the salad," Chloe said, beaming.

"I gave you four tomatoes!"

"Wow! How did you know they're my favourite?" Anna laughed as she carried her plate to the table, Chloe leading the way. Her niece insisted on carrying her own as usual, but she did consent to her dad cutting her pie into smaller chunks.

"Where's Sam this evening?"

Alex busied himself with handing out napkins as he answered, not meeting Anna's eye.

"She's working late. Now, let's tuck in!"

Anna did – it was hours since her panini in Victus, and she was hungry. She ignored the obvious question that followed Alex's statement – his wife was working late *again*?

Every Thursday evening Anna taught 'Taekwon-Do Tykes' in her local community-centre hall, assisting her own instructor Jason. She loved teaching even more than her own training. She had achieved her black belt and was keen to progress. The enthusiasm and innocence of the youngsters was always a welcome salve after her busy job in the Lee Street station. After teaching, Anna always had dinner with her brother and his family. Alex lived near her own home, in Kinsale. They were close – he was the only family she had.

For months now his wife Samantha had been working late at a stockbroker's in the city. Anna knew it had been causing tension between them – Samantha had a new supervisor, and she described him as "demanding". Alex worked from home as an accountant, running his firm from the house. It was a set-up that worked for them, but Anna hated to think of her brother and his wife arguing.

"But for the fireplace, the place looks almost as good as new!" she commented, looking through to the sitting room.

Less than two weeks ago, and not long after Chloe's fifth birthday party, a chimney fire had caused considerable damage. No-one had been injured and the fire had been contained quickly, but the room was completely destroyed. The fireplace had to be ripped out, a gaping hole still marking where the hearth had once been. The windows were still bare of curtains, but the furniture and carpet had been replaced and the smell of fresh paint had begun to overpower the odour of soot and charred material.

"Thanks. We are still dealing with the insurance company, of course!"

She smiled at him, conveying her sympathy, familiar with the story of her brother's struggle to claim on his house insurance. She knew they had used their savings to redecorate and rebuild so far.

"It's early days yet – it will probably be sorted out soon," she said.

"I really hope so."

"Aunty Anna, I got a new schoolbag!"

"That's great – will you show me after dinner? I thought school doesn't start until September?"

"Try telling Chloe that! She can't wait!"

The rest of the meal passed in relaxed conversation. Anna looked forward to Thursday nights with her brother's family – she had grown increasingly weary of living alone, of an empty house every day after work and a quick salad or frozen pizza for dinner, eaten in front of the TV. She missed feeling part of a unit – the smell other people infused in the air as they moved and breathed, the scent of a family. In contrast, her house felt sterile.

She hadn't always felt this way – up until recently she had loved living in her childhood home. Now she realised she was spending as much time as possible *away* from the house lately. As richly imprinted as it was with memories of her parents, it was also tainted by the recent break-in by Dean Harris, the man who had intended to seriously harm her. She had hoped to live in the only home she had ever known for the rest of her life – now she wasn't so sure.

She tucked her niece into bed and, after reading the three books Chloe had lined up, made her way back downstairs to Alex. He was putting freshly brewed coffee on the low table in the sitting room as she walked in. The room was cold.

"Gosh, you'd miss the heat from the fire!"

"I know! Hopefully, it won't be too long before the new stove is installed." He threw a blanket to his sister. "Here, use this."

"It's nice to look out and see the stars," Anna murmured, sipping her coffee, her gaze on the night sky outside.

Alex laughed. "Try telling Sam that! She said she feels exposed without curtains and blinds. The new ones will be ready next week."

Silence stretched between them. Normally, it was an easy silence, comfortable. Tonight, there were things to be discussed, and neither felt too keen to start.

"Have you spoken to Myles? How is he doing?"

A broad smile spread across her face. She supposed Myles was her boyfriend now, although nothing had been officially confirmed. She wondered if people still did that – make their boyfriend/girlfriend status official – it was so long since she had dated anyone.

Alex laughed at the look on her face.

"What?"

"You look besotted at the mere mention of his name!"

"Don't tease!" She threw a cushion at him, and he laughed as he held his coffee cup high to avoid a collision.

"If you must know, I spoke to him yesterday, and he's staying with me for the weekend." She lowered her eyes, hating the blush that stained her cheeks. Her brother's eyebrows shot up, disappearing under his dark-blond hair.

"None of my business," he said, but he was grinning.

She knew he was happy for her.

"How's his leg and shoulder?"

"Healing, thankfully."

Anna shuddered, her normal physical response to remembering the events of that night. She hated to think about when Myles had been shot. Had it really only been the end of November?

She had first met Myles Henderson at work, at what was the beginning of one of the most difficult few months of her life. Through her job analysing and collating criminal cases across the county, she had uncovered a link between files that led to identifying the man responsible for a series of sexual assaults which had remained unsolved. She had approached Frank Doherty, then the Detective Superintendent, about it, only to be publicly humiliated in the open-plan office. His response had not been entirely unexpected – the man was a known bully and gruff to deal with on his best day. She remembered the sympathy that had radiated from Myles across the room – it was their first meeting. He had been introduced to her as a detective from Dublin, drafted in for the upcoming political conference in the city. He had asked her out, and they had grown close.

Myles had been in a meeting with the former Chief Superintendent the night Kate had called to Anna's house and confessed to shooting David Gallagher and stealing from him. When Kate produced the memory stick, and Anna realised the contents seriously compromised security for the conference, she had brought it to that meeting. She had hoped Myles' computer skills could help – but her decision had almost got him killed.

He had told Anna he worked for the Special Detective Unit in Dublin. Later, when his injuries were healing and he was no longer stationed in Cork, he admitted that had not been completely true. He confessed that he had been undercover, searching for the culprit of a security breach within the Lee Street station. Anna understood the deception and, even though she knew she might never know the truth about his job, she missed him. He had made her laugh in a way she hadn't in years. He helped her feel less *alone*.

He had also tried to help with the mystery that hung over her and her brother – the mystery of their parents' disappearance. Using his computer skills and the access he had, he had looked over their missing-persons case. What he discovered was now what Anna wanted to discuss with her brother. Talking about Myles offered the natural lead into the topic of conversation that had hung over them both over the last few days. Trepidation settled in the pit of her stomach but she tried to ignore it, setting her mug onto the coffee table.

"We need to talk about what he gave me, Alex. To be honest, I thought you might have called me days ago … can I see the file again?"

Alex sighed and rolled his neck from side to side, cracking the joints. He had known this would come up. He had stalled as long as he could, but his sister was hungry for answers. He didn't have any, and he didn't know how to go about finding them. Or even if he wanted to find them. This wasn't something a private investigator could look into. It seemed bigger than that. And he worried that if they did go digging any more into the past, they would both end up regretting it.

Resting his own mug on the coffee table he walked wearily to his work-from-home office at the back of the house, returning with a cardboard folder. Anna had given him the newspaper articles days before, shortly after her meeting with Myles. He wasn't sure yet how he felt about the guy meddling in their family affairs – he barely knew them yet had taken a liberty and opened up a Pandora's box.

He passed the newspaper articles over without a word. He had studied the contents closely, committing every word and image they contained to memory, poring over them long into the night when his insomnia prevented sleep. A tiny part of him had wanted to destroy them, to forget they ever existed. But he knew his sister would never forgive him. He also knew she was right. The file contained images of their mother that cast what they knew of their parents into doubt.

Anna's lips moved as she silently read the headline on the first page.

Moscow Orchestral Reserve Wow at the Royal Albert Hall.

He watched her finger trace over the photograph of a group of musicians standing outside the Royal Albert Hall, stopping on the face of a woman of average height and build, with the same soft features and large oval-shaped eyes as Anna. The woman's hair was bundled into a fur hat. Her coat was thick and knee-length, with four large black buttons – it was the coat he remembered as his mother's. Bright fire-engine red, it had been in the attic of Anna's house since after his mother and father had disappeared.

In 2008, just over ten years ago, their parents had vanished following a car accident. No sign of them, no bodies, no overnight bags or personal items in the car, nothing. Alex had been twenty-five and Anna just sixteen. He still marvelled at how their world had fallen apart and then been rebuilt. It was as if he was remembering events from a different life. The Garda investigation had been huge but ultimately unsuccessful. The prevailing theory was that there had to have been a third party involved – where were their bodies, their belongings? Foul play was suspected but nothing was ever discovered that could lead to a conclusive answer.

To Anna, it was a mystery she was tired of enduring. Last year, as the ten-year anniversary of their disappearance approached, she had consulted a private investigator and had begged Alex to help her in trying to discover what had happened. He struggled to understand why she thought a private investigator could do what the gardaí had not, but he had agreed to support her. She had confided in Myles. And then *he* had taken it upon himself to do some digging.

Alex was still reeling from what Myles had uncovered. According to him, their mother, Helen Clarke, was born Yelena Vasilieva in 1956 in the Russian town of Omsk. Her father was a businessman. She played cello with the Moscow Orchestral Reserve and, while staying in London, on the night of the 4th of September 1978, she disappeared.

The woman in the two newspaper clippings Myles had given to Anna definitely *looked* like their mother. But he had never heard mention of Russia while growing up. Their mother had claimed to be only a fan of orchestral music, and not proficient in the instrument she kept in the attic and never played. But she had listened to Bach's cello pieces so often, a wistful look on her face, that Alex didn't feel shocked at the image of her standing beside a cello outside the concert hall … rather he felt that a jigsaw piece was slotting into place.

He had to admit there were things that kept him up at night. The fact that neither of his parents had any siblings or living parents. The fact that before they moved to Ireland and Anna was born, the little family had moved from town to town in England, never settling, never making friends. And the mysterious appearance of Bob, a man claiming to be his father's friend. Alex had never heard him mentioned before he turned up. He arrived at the house in the days after their parents disappeared and told Alex of a trust fund his father had set up. He gave him details of how to access the money and left a business card. They had never heard from him again. Alex had called the number on that card a few times after the shock had worn off and he had questions for Bob, but the call was never answered.

"It's *her*. I've been up to the attic and compared the photograph to the coat. It's *her*, Alex!"

"Yes, I think you're right."

"She loved it – she said it was her favourite winter coat." Anna had a wistful look in her eyes. "It was winter when they crashed, but she didn't have it with her …"

"It was at the dry cleaner's – she was annoyed she couldn't wear it to Dublin." He smiled, remembering.

"So, what do we do about this?"

He paused, weighing his words, fighting to keep his tone patient and even. The excitement in her voice filled him with a dread he could not ignore.

"I'm not sure there's anything we *can* do. So Mum was Russian. So what? For whatever reason, Mum met Dad and

41

fell in love and then decided to leave her old life behind. We should accept that."

Shock stilled Anna for a moment, and when she spoke she was aware her voice had risen significantly. "*Are you serious?*" She thought of Chloe asleep upstairs and continued in a lower tone. "Our mother was Russian, and a man turned up with half a million euro in a trust fund after our parents crashed their car and disappeared, and you're OK with that? It sounds to me like … like maybe she was a spy or something …"

"Don't be ridiculous, Anna!"

"How can you say that? Mum concealed the fact she was Russian from us! And the money Bob gave you! There's nothing normal about this, Alex! To think she could have been a Soviet spy is hardly outside the realm of possibility! Maybe she defected and had to keep it a secret!"

He rose quickly and turned his back to her, tracing the stonework on the half-built fireplace with one finger. Staring at his back, Anna felt anger rush through her – he had spoken harshly, as if incredulous at her wild suggestion. Yet she knew the thought had crossed his mind too – it must have!

"Alex, we never knew who she really was. The detectives investigating their disappearance didn't either. They didn't know her real name. Why did she keep her past hidden? *How* could a person hide this?"

He turned around again. His face was blotchy with pent-up emotion, and it caught her off-guard.

"This isn't a movie, Anna! This is our life! Mum could barely use her mobile phone – there's no way she was a spy or whatever cliché you're thinking of!"

"Look … I understand you don't want to accept this possibility. Neither do I – it's incredible. But you're not

42

making sense. All the signs are there! Aren't you intrigued to know who she really was?" She pushed on, seeing the pain on his face, but she felt past caring. How could he contemplate not finding out the whole truth?

"I *know* who she really was! She was our mum! Our parents were Helen and Michael Clarke, end of story! After the last few months, after everything that happened to you, I just want a bit of normality. Mum and Dad are *dead*, Anna. There's no other explanation. I wish you'd accept that!"

"But what if they're not? What if –"

He covered the distance to her quickly and knelt down, gripping her arms.

"They're gone, Anna. I wish you'd let it rest!"

His voice broke and she felt guilt hover around the edge of her anger.

"Clearly Mum had a life prior to meeting Dad, and she never told us about it," he said. "So what? Parents are people too, with lives of their own. Obviously, it's nothing we needed to hear!"

She shook her arms free from his grip.

"*But they lied to us!* The cello she never played? She said she was just a fan of the music. She was obviously talented enough to play in an orchestra! And she said she had no living family members."

"That might be true!"

"She never said she was Russian!"

"What does it matter? *Anna – they are not coming back!*" He emphasised each syllable, every word a little dart that stung her, each one more painful than the last.

She blinked quickly, tears threatening to fall, and jumped up. Grabbing her coat, she left without saying goodbye, closing the front door softly behind her.

From the middle of the sitting room, Alex watched her go. They hadn't argued in ten years. He had always made sure of it, always anxious to keep their relationship smooth and even-keeled. She was his responsibility, and he took that seriously. He was sorry he had upset her, but he wanted this to end. He *needed* it to. The mystery surrounding what happened the night of the car accident had endured for too long. Adrenaline fired inside him, fuelling the insomnia that had ruled his life for ten years. Sitting down again, his head in his hands, he wondered would this nightmare ever end.

When Anna stepped inside her front door and dropped her keys into the bowl on the hall table, she froze. A little less than two months ago she had done that very same thing and realised someone had been in her house, had moved things around on the hall table and left the cold air in through the still-open patio door. And a few nights after that, he had waited for her upstairs, creaking the floorboards as he hid. With a shake of her head, she switched on the lights and moved through the house.

Dean Harris was in custody – he couldn't harm her.

In the kitchen she poured herself a glass of wine and moved through the arch into her living room, her coat still on. The house was cold. She put her mother's favourite record on: Bach's Cello Suite No. 1 in G Major. Settling on the sofa and staring into the emptiness of the unlit stove, she let the music wash over her, strengthening her resolve. She would find the answers that had been so elusive for too long. She was tired of the constant ache the not-knowing caused her – the sudden onslaught of memories that derailed her day, the restless nights. The images and ideas that swirled in her head as she pounded the punchbag in the gym with

Jason. The underlying and never-ending fear that, one day, one of the files she picked up at work would detail the remains of two adults, lying rotting and overlooked.

Her brother had been only twenty-five, not yet a qualified accountant, when suddenly he was responsible for his teenage sister while dealing with the knowledge that not only had their parents suffered a serious car accident, but they were also missing. Traces of their blood had been positively identified in the car, but there was never any sign of them afterwards. Alex had liaised with the detectives at the time, and Anna knew he believed their parents were dead. They had often spoken late into the night, voicing their hopes and theories, in this living room. Anna thought he had shielded her from the worst of the possible scenarios over the years, but it was clear their parents were not coming back.

Now Alex seemed to have moved on – he was married, with a daughter and a busy accountancy practice. He had agreed to support her last November when she had broached the subject of hiring a private investigator to examine all the evidence they had of the accident and Garda investigation. But that had come to nothing. Once he had studied the newspaper article Myles had provided, instead of it igniting his curiosity as Anna's had been, his resolve to move on had hardened.

When the record ended, she rinsed out her wine glass and made her way to bed. More and more she hated the stillness of the house, the silence that followed her from room to room. As she drifted into sleep she remembered that Myles would arrive tomorrow evening and thoughts of him with his curious brown eyes and wild dark curls soothed her. Then another thought nudged into her romantic reverie: Myles had found out this much – perhaps he could uncover more? And maybe, if he were prompted, he could search for more information on their father, Michael Clarke. Perhaps understanding who *he* was would shed light on why their mother had hidden her own past.

6

London, 1978

"Patrick Michael Clarke, if you don't get down these stairs, so help me God!"

He descended in a thundering run, the sound reverberating around the small kitchen. She hadn't had to shout very loud – the terraced house was so small. The kitchen door was propped open by a chair leg, as always, and he rushed in, straightening his tie. Bending to almost half his height, he kissed her cheek.

"Sorry, Nan!"

"Let me look at you."

She cupped his face in her hands and he smiled patiently. His shoulder-length curls were smoothed into place, his brown eyes bright and amused. The navy suit he wore was second-hand, or maybe third – she had borrowed it from a neighbour. The shirt was new though – bright white and crisply ironed, it set off the red tie. That had been her husband's – now their only grandchild was pushing it into place. Swallowing a lump in her throat, she released his face and he straightened up, grabbing a half-slice of toast from the table. She had poured a cup of tea, with two sugars as he liked it, and he drank half of it in one gulp.

"Put these on," she said softly, sliding a white cardboard box from a chair where it was concealed under the tablecloth.

He stopped chewing and stared as she opened the lid, pulling out a pair of plain Oxford shoes, the black leather gleaming.

"You can't be … I mean, how did you ever afford … Nan, we really can't …"

She grinned broadly. "Oh, shush your bothering, you need to look the part. Come on! Put them on!"

He did as he was told, kicking off his scuffed brown shoes and sliding the cap-toe Oxfords into place.

"I can't believe it!"

"I'm not having my only grandson start his first job as a professional bookkeeper in tatty old brogues."

"But where did you get the money?"

"That's for me to worry about and you to put right out of your head. Now go on – you can't be late on your first day!"

He smiled at her and, wiping crumbs from his mouth, looked around the small kitchen as though he had forgotten something. Suddenly he grabbed her into a bear hug, swooping her up.

"Thank you, Nana," he whispered, his voice thick with emotion.

"Will you go away out of that!" She swatted his hand and smoothed her skirt, but her eyes glistened when she met his. "I'm very proud of you. They would be too." Both their eyes moved to a photograph on the wall, where a young couple gazed at each other, arms linked, their faces full of love and promise.

After a pause, she thrust a small paper bag into his hand and began to gently push at his back.

"There's your lunch. Now off with you!"

At the front door he shrugged on his coat and pulled a flat cap from his pocket, securing it into place as he pulled open the latch.

"*Stop!*" she called, startling him. "What on earth is that on your head?"

"You know what it is!"

"Take it off this minute! Lord help me! Here you are in a smart suit off to a respectable job with your father's old cap on your head. Michael would turn in his grave."

"I *always* wear his hat!"

"Not today you don't! Today you make a first impression, and you won't get that chance again. You want to be taken seriously!"

He didn't argue with her. With a smile he pulled his father's cap off his head and hung it on the coat hook. Just today he would leave it at home.

She watched him go, sauntering the way he usually did, pride in his step. Tears welled in her eyes again and almost spilled over, but she knew better than to let the neighbours see her cry. The cobbled lane was full of children playing quick games before they returned to school after the weekend break. One little boy stopped amid a game of bulldog to watch Michael walk by. Turning, he strode to the open front door.

"Where's Michael going, Nana Clarke?"

"He's going to work, Jerome."

"Dressed in a suit? He never wears a suit to the factory."

"Nothing much slips past you, does it! He's got a *new* job, a *better* job."

49

"That's good. My daddy says us Irish won't amount to much. Not in London."

Nana Clarke reached out and ruffled his hair.

"You tell your daddy Michael has got himself a job as a bookkeeper for Mr Lewis, the textiles trader at the port."

"How did he manage to get that then?"

Her patience had run out. "*Ugh!* He got the job because he studied hard and passed all his exams in night school! Now off you go or you'll be late for school." She slammed the door.

Walking back to the kitchen she shook her head, to push Jerome and his father's ignorance out of her mind. She opened the sitting-room door and sighed – it was wall-to-wall with piles of clothes waiting to be ironed, extra money to be earned. She had time to make a quick start before she left for work at the greengrocer's. Switching on the radio, she smiled. The station was playing Brendan Shine and her grandson was off to his first proper job, one with prospects. It was a good day.

Michael walked the cobbled narrow street outside his house to the bus stop, dodging running children and a football that just missed his head. Terraced houses lined his walk, rows on either side. He could walk this route in his sleep – his feet knew every loose cobble and every neighbour was as familiar to him as his grandmother. For twenty-two years Warburg Street had been his playground and his home. Zipping up his coat against the breeze, he turned the collar up, hunching into it. Smiling as he passed the kerb where he had fallen and split his head many years ago, and the corner where he had first kissed Meg Collins, he picked up his pace a little. His whole life was here, in this street.

Adrenaline pulsed inside him with the sure certainty that everything was about to change.

He had been to the port of London only once before, when he had been interviewed for the job, and it didn't take long to get his bearings when he alighted from the bus. He signed in at the security hut and greeted the man there, who engaged him in conversation for so long he was beginning to worry he'd be late for his first day. He backed out of the little hut, nodding and smiling. The man was clearly bored and lonely, and he didn't want to be rude, but he had to jog to the warehouse door.

He had been inside the warehouse already for the interview and remembered the layout of the business. The stock was stored in wooden boxes on the main floor, and there were two high-ceilinged offices up a flight of metal stairs at the back. The last time he was here he had discreetly admired the fine fabrics, the colours and quality cuts of the cloth that were lined up on shelves waiting to be checked-in and packaged to go back out. His own suit was borrowed, but Mr Lewis was paying a good wage, and Michael knew he'd soon be decked out in fine clothes. His first priority was to pay his grandmother back. The list of things she had provided lately far exceeded the expected cost of raising an orphaned grandson – his night-school tuition and the Oxford shoes, for a start.

He pulled off his old coat before he stepped inside – she had warned him – his suit looked smart but his overcoat certainly did not, so he was to remove it before he stepped inside the building. During their interview Mr Lewis had confessed to being clueless when it came to his business accounts, and he wanted to keep things straight, as he put it. He had warned Michael that he had a tough task ahead sorting the dockets and ledgers, half-heartedly filed, and stuffed into a cupboard. Michael had assured him he could handle it. Resting his hand on the warehouse door now, he paused and took a deep breath. He hoped he was right.

A man approached him as he stepped inside. He was about Michael's age, his shirtsleeves rolled up, a cigarette resting behind his ear and another hanging from his lips.

"Alright, mate?"

Michael rubbed the back of his neck. "Eh … my name is Michael Clarke. I'm here to start work. I'm the bookkeeper."

The man smiled and extended his hand. "Robert Evans. You can call me Bob."

His handshake was firm and Michael was able to meet his eyes – rarely was anyone his own height. "Come on up, Michael."

Michael noted the cockney accent mixed with the lilt of an Irish brogue, and the muscular curve of his shoulders under his shirt.

They ascended the metal stairs quickly, Michael jogging to keep up with the other man.

"Lewis is upstairs." Bob glanced back at Michael. "We all call him 'Lewis' though his name is James. You can call him 'Mr Lewis' until he tells you otherwise." A smile and wink softened his words. He had a knack of balancing his cigarette on his lower lip as he spoke, as though it was moulded to it.

"Of course. Understood."

Bob grinned as he pulled open another door at the top of the stairs. He clapped Michael on the shoulder as he ushered him inside. "Alright then!"

The office was bigger than he remembered, even with

three rectangular desks squeezed into it. The linoleum floor was sticky under his new shoes and he was conscious of the leather creaking as he stepped inside. One wall was taken up with a large window that allowed a view of the warehouse floor below.

A much older man was sitting at one of the desks, a telephone receiver pressed to his ear, and he held one finger up to indicate he would be with them shortly. Mr Lewis, looking as dapper as Michael remembered from the job interview. Michael noted his slicked-back grey hair, and finely cut suit. He looked like a movie star about to walk on set.

Bob led Michael to the desk at the back of the office.

"Set yourself up here."

It reminded Michael of the table he had used in school – if he spread his arms wide they would extend well beyond it. The desk was empty, the surface pit-marked with scratches.

"And here," Bob said, with a hint of humour in his voice, "is the filing cabinet with all the accounts." He pulled open the door of a tall, floor-to-ceiling cupboard, and grinned as stacks of white paper fell from the overcrowded shelves onto the floor in front of them.

"*Sweet Jesus!*" the exclamation escaped Michael before he could stop it.

Bob laughed heartily. "He said you were warned!"

"But there must be *years* of accounts here! Don't you have a filing cabinet? How does anyone keep track of things?"

"We don't – that's why I hired *you!*"

Michael turned around to face his boss, who had finished the call and was standing behind him. He held out his hand.

"Good morning, Mr Lewis."

"Good to see you again, Michael." He returned the handshake with less vigour than Bob had and gestured to the mess of papers. He had spoken on the phone just now with a distinctly posh English accent, but now that faded significantly into more cockney tones. "I told you I want to get the business accounts straightened. I don't need any nasty surprises if the Inland Revenue decide to visit! As I said before, I'm trusting you to get it in order and set up a system we can run going forward. Got it?"

Michael felt slightly queasy. He guessed there were thousands of sheets of paper on the floor and much more stacked in the cupboard. He had promised at the interview he could handle the accounts but now he felt panic prickling through his veins.

"Mr Lewis, this might take some time. As I told you in my interview, this is my first job after night school, and as I'm seeing all this now," he gestured to the overflowing cupboard, "I'm not sure I'm the right man to –"

"Now that's a load of old cobblers!" Mr Lewis smiled and patted him on the shoulder. "You came top of your class and were highly recommended by your tutor. I trust you'll be honest and diligent. Bob here will give you some money from petty cash to buy whatever you need – notebooks, proper ledger books and so on. Take one of the cars from outside to bring the stuff back with you – you did say you can drive, didn't you?"

Michael nodded.

"And take as long as it takes to do the job – any revenue man that might come calling will be satisfied as long as it's being done."

His eyes roamed over Michael's suit and rested on his

coat, slung over one arm. "There's a rail of suits and coats at the back – excess stock from some of the shops I supply – they send us samples from time to time. Find a few suits that fit, and a coat too."

Michael opened his mouth to protest but his boss silenced him with a raised hand.

"You work for me now, so you represent my business. Every time you walk in and out of that door downstairs you show off my goods and services. You're a smart lad but you have to look the part. In this life, a man has to walk the walk, as the saying goes. Got it?" His tone, suddenly, invited no discussion.

Without waiting for a reply, he returned to his desk and gathered up his own coat and scarf.

"Bob here will take you for a pint after work and fill you in on who's who and what's what. Now!" He patted his pockets. "I have to see a man about a horse – I'm off." And he was gone, a whirlwind of expensive cologne and tweed wools.

Bob laughed softly and Michael met his eye.

"He does that. You'll get used to it. Just do as he asks and keep your head down." Glancing at his wristwatch, his eyes bulged slightly. "I have to see about a shipment. The petty cash box is here." He pulled a silver metal box from his desk drawer and set it on top. "I'll see you here later and we'll go for that beer. If you need anything or if there's any problems, you'll find Boxer and Roy downstairs, probably skiving!" Grinning, he pulled on his coat and left, his boots clattering down the stairs, a cloud of cigarette smoke trailing in his wake.

Michael was suddenly alone. Moving to the window he observed Bob move quickly through the warehouse floor and out the front door. Two men moved between crates, one smoking, the other talking animatedly. His mate laughed and they continued working. Boxer and Roy, he assumed. He turned again to the pile of papers. Bending to pick one up, he examined it, his heart sinking. It contained three dates, various different amounts, and one company name ... the bare bones of a ledger entry. There was no indication if this was money paid or owed. He groaned and dropped the page back onto the ground.

Later, as he and Bob reached the pub nearby, he was feeling even less enthusiastic. Bob called a greeting to the barman and ordered two pints of lager. They settled on a high table with stools near the back.

"So, what do you think? Will you stick around?" As Michael exhaled and took a long swallow of beer, Bob laughed. "It's not so bad. Lewis isn't looking for anything fancy, just enough of a system to get the accounts in order. He's had some trouble with the police poking around and wants everything shipshape as the saying goes!"

"The police? I thought he was concerned about the Inland Revenue?"

"Oh, it's nothing serious! Just some nosy detective being jumpy about documentation. Lewis wants everything in order, that's all. Just straighten out what you can and set up some type of easy accounting system and you'll be fine."

"OK, I'll do my best. It's just – I don't really have the experience – I'm fresh out of night school. I'm sure Mr Lewis could find someone better suited."

"Lewis likes you. Just give it a few weeks."

"He certainly seems generous." Michael ran a hand over the thick new coat on the stool beside him.

"Yeah, pays well too." Bob dipped his head. "He expects loyalty. His business is no-one else's business if you know what I mean. The industry he's in – it's competitive. Best to keep the business cards close to your chest." He lit a new cigarette from the stub of the one resting on his lip and exhaled towards the ceiling.

Michael had noticed that Bob smoked quickly, one after the other, the next cigarette always waiting behind one ear. He studied the other man over the rim of his glass. He guessed there wasn't much between them in age. Bob was his own height but broader, with a more athletic physique.

"Is it just three men employed in the business?"

"And now you." Bob signalled to the barman for two more pints. "Many of the textile mills have closed recently. Sign of the times! The sad truth of it is that it's cheaper to import some goods, for now at any rate. Lewis imports textiles, a mixture of leathers, wools, other fabrics. He brings in the most cracking leather from Turkey, seriously high-quality stuff! Most of his customers are based here in London, some further south, and one customer in Scotland. I look after security and keep the other two boys in line." He grinned. "I do a bit of everything, me, whatever Lewis needs. I'm like that saying, 'A Jack of all trades'. Boxer and Roy do all the grunt work. They're tough lads, but hard workers. Not too bright if you know what I'm saying."

"Boxer?"

Bob laughed. "I can't even remember if it's his surname or a nickname. It suits him though! He has a shiner or a split lip most Monday mornings. Tends to have heavy weekends, does our Boxer."

Fresh beers were placed in front of them and he raised his glass, observing Michael for a moment. "There's no need to be nervous – you just need to sort out the accounts and keep things straight. It'll be fine." He brought his pint to his lips, downing almost half of it, managing to keep his cigarette in situ.

Michael nursed his pint, letting all he had absorbed today sink in.

"Have you worked for Mr Lewis long?"

"About four years now. I live with my brother and his missus but I'll be getting my own place soon. Lewis pays well, as I said. He's a self-made man, you know. Took over the business from his father, who came here when he was a child. He takes a lot of pride in the fact that his family worked their way up and that *he* built the business up even further. He provides some of the textiles used by one of the tailors for the Royal Family, you know!"

Michael noted the pride and loyalty in the other man's voice, and he was impressed too. It was hard not to be.

"Listen, me and the other boys play a bit of footie on Saturday afternoons if you'd like to join us?"

Michael shook his head. "Thanks, but I train in Taekwon-Do – I'm going for my black belt right now actually. I train in a working-men's club near me."

"Tae-*what*?"

Michael laughed – he was used to this. "It's a martial art. Sort of like what the movie star Bruce Lee does. Have you seen any of his movies? *Enter the Dragon? Fist of Fury?*"

Bob raised his eyebrows, looking impressed. "Sure I have. Bit unusual for an Irishman. I thought you lads were into the Gaelic footie and that. Still, fair enough."

"Aren't you Irish?"

"I was born here." Bob carried on talking, the beer loosening his tongue. "Both my parents are from Clare. I've never been, but I hope to change that someday. What's your story?"

"The whole family are from Kerry and moved over here long before I was born. I was raised by my grandmother … I owe her everything really."

"What happened to your parents? If you don't mind me asking."

"My dad worked at the docks and he was killed in an accident when I was a baby. My mother got sick and died shortly after – a broken heart, my nan says." He smiled, noting the pity in the other man's eyes.

"Nice lady, your nan?"

"The best!"

Bob raised his glass in a toast and Michael met the glass with his own, smiling.

"To you! And your nan! And Bruce Lee!"

Laughing heartily, they clinked glasses.

Later, Michael confided his fears to his grandmother.

"I don't think I'm qualified enough for what Mr Lewis wants. He needs a whole filing system created. There's no proper accounting in the business whatsoever, it's just slips of paper! He did it all himself over the years. Times have changed and he needs it done properly now. But you'd imagine he'd want someone with years of experience behind him, not some kid fresh out of school!"

Nana Clarke nodded, staring into the crackling fire.

"Look … he pays well, and is generous, but my guess is he chose a fresh lad like you because he'd have to pay an experienced bookkeeper a lot more. And he obviously thinks you're trustworthy and smart."

Michael smiled at her, then turned his gaze to the fire,

watching the flames dance and twist around each other.

She leaned towards him and grabbed his hand from the armrest.

"I'm proud of you! Lord rest him, my Michael would be proud of you too. It kills me he never got to see you grown up … his son. And Mary too, God rest her …" She sniffed, but quickly pulled herself together, as she always did. "Remember, all you can do is your best!"

He squeezed her hand. It wouldn't be an easy task, sorting through the mountain of papers. Yet the business was medium-sized, the turnover appeared modest … maybe he could handle it. He had studied hard for a job like this for over two years, and she was right – he had to believe in himself. His Taekwon-Do training was teaching him confidence and perseverance, and he knew the task of coming up with a decent filing system was a test of sorts. And an opportunity to put all his training and studying into practice. He should feel excited.

So why did he feel on edge?

7

Cork, 2019

Mae Gallagher was sitting alone in a wide armchair in the reading room of their mansion overlooking the heart of Cork city. The architect had called it a 'reading room', and the interior designer had filled the walls with heavy oak shelves that were laden with books, from literary classics to contemporary fiction and everything in between. Mae wasn't sure if her sons had ever picked out a book and settled down to read. She and her husband certainly hadn't. Like many things in this house, she realised, it was a ruse. A pretence, to show the world the Gallaghers were normal. Normal and in control of their world.

Tom had built a successful business by appearing calm, measured, a trustworthy man of impeccable self-control. He rarely lost his temper, publicly. He enjoyed expensive whiskey and the finer things in life. He had showered her with every material pleasure money could buy and did his best to shield her from the world he had created around them. His word was his bond. Yet for all those attributes he was a very dangerous man. She had closed her eyes and ears to that reality a long time ago.

Almost two months ago he had promised her he would find and deliver Kate Crowley, to answer for her crimes. At the time, she had lived for the moment she would have the girl within reach. Kate Crowley had shot her youngest son and set in motion events that had cost her almost everything. Kate's sister Natalie had left too, taking her two young daughters ... Mae's grandchildren. One of Tom's Garda contacts had told him they flew to France after David died. She had lost so much that day. She felt the pain of her loss in every joint, every muscle of her body. It hurt just to open her eyes in the morning. Thinking of her son brought waves of nausea that were best kept down with alcohol. The numbing elixir was keeping her alive.

Pouring brandy into the crystal glass, her hand shook only a little. There had been whiskey in it before and she swilled the remains of it into the brandy. She could no longer taste what she drank, craving only the feeling of emptiness it offered.

Her eyes strayed to a collection of photographs on one of the bookshelves and she rose to her feet, wobbling and spilling liquid onto the flowered chair upholstery. That would have bothered her before ... before everything changed. She gripped the photo frame – her boys, David and John, arm in arm, buckets and spades on the ground at their feet. She didn't recognise the door they were standing in front of for a moment, and then, as she sat back down with the framed photo in her hand, it came flooding back.

The boys were probably ten and six years old, posing at the front door of their first home. It had been in a housing estate in Blackrock, close to the city, and quite a prestigious area in Mae's opinion. Far better than where she had grown up. Tom was building the business then, with one club in the city, and making more contacts and deals every day. She was surprised to find her eyes fill with tears – for the past few weeks she had been too numb to feel much. But the memories of her little boys filled her with so much sadness. She looked at their faces, their dark hair and shining eyes. She could barely look at David's face … it was too much. Her eyes rested on John. He was smiling. He had always been a smiling child. It was a smile that hid so much … she gulped at her drink, remembering.

She had loved living in the housing estate – she couldn't remember the name of it now, but they had been happy there. Initially. The houses were set in a semicircle around a large green area, and there were a lot of children of the boys' age to play with. She had worked hard to better herself – practising speaking with a different accent, styling her hair the same as the other women in the estate – and was delighted to be included in their coffee mornings and walks after the school drop-off. It was easy to forget where she was from – she cut off contact with what remained of her family, focusing on her future, on her *new* family. They were everything to her. Tom was busy and loving his newfound success. He was planning to take over a bookies and had made a new business contact he referred to as 'The Englishman'. Things were looking up. Everything was perfect.

Except it wasn't.

Mae supposed there were warning signs, but hindsight offers so much clarity. It began with David complaining that the other children wouldn't play with him. When she probed, she found out it was because David was John's brother. This worried her – what did the children have against John? He was a child too, only twelve when they left the estate, so he was even younger when all this started. She tried to find out as much as she could but the other parents clammed up. No-one was keen to criticise another's child. It bothered her to have her son excluded and, if she was honest, she worried that exclusion might spill over to affect *her*. She liked things as they were. Tom told her not to worry – John was boisterous and tough by nature. He was probably being heavy-handed and things would settle down.

It was one of the few times her husband had been completely wrong.

The escalation of the situation started with the next-door neighbour's cat. It was found, in a bush at the back of the green area, with its stomach slit open, its intestines spilled out onto the grass. Naturally, everyone was horrified, and blamed a gang of teenagers from a nearby estate. For a week or two, nobody spoke of anything else. Until the next animal turned up tortured and decapitated on its owner's doorstep. Horror in the estate grew. But no-one felt it as much as Mae, when she found a long, thin-bladed knife with dried blood and animal fur stuck to it, under John's bed. Or when she saw John's smile when she quizzed him about it.

He denied harming the animals. But he couldn't stop smiling, a grin that spread across his face whenever the subject was raised. He thought it was funny – he was enjoying himself. Mae knew then that John had what her grandmother called "bad blood" running in his veins. Perhaps there had been other signs – if so, she had ignored them. She tried to hide her shock from her son, not wanting him to think badly of himself. Perhaps that too had been a mistake. The horror continued, despite her and Tom's efforts. Now she realised they hadn't gone far enough to help their son.

They moved to a new house and moved again when the pattern was repeated – neighbourhood children were afraid of John, and he made no friends. During his teenage years he sought no friendships, not even with his brother, happy to just exist alongside him. As he grew into a man, he made no lasting relationships, and women never stuck around for long. Where he seemed happiest was working with his father. He thrived in the business, his unnerving smile always in place. He still lived at home – unusual, perhaps, for a man in his thirties – but he was close to his father, and it suited him. Mae knew that if anyone could be ruthless enough to turn Tom's enterprise into something even more memorable, it was John. She had worked hard to push the knowledge of who he was, *what* he was, far into the back of her mind. She forgot about the animals and the children in the estate. John was happy, the business was thriving, her family was just as Tom had always promised her.

But then John was tortured by the Meiers in the sequence of events that she held Kate Crowley accountable for. John, once the torturer, was now the victim. Now he was home, rescued by his father's cunning, the Meiers gone from their lives – how, Mae didn't want to know, so she didn't ask. John frightened her now, the look in his eyes, the stiff set of his shoulders. She knew her son – he was aching from the inside to hurt someone. To put right the wrong that had been done to him, even though the Meiers were dead. John was a caged animal, needing to wreak a havoc so great that the whole world would know his hurt. So she kept him close to her, begging Tom to shield him from the business, to let him recover and take more time. Daily she drowned the truth, poisoned it in liquor – the truth that in reality, it wasn't John she was shielding from the underworld her husband had immersed them in. It was the world she was shielding from him.

She roused herself, draining the last of the brandy, and decided to go to bed. It was weeks since she had woken up beside her husband. Sometimes he cried out in his sleep, loud enough that she could hear him from her armchair. She knew Tom suffered. He had done terrible things to bring John home. And he would do it all again to avenge David's death. She loved her husband – tonight she would hold him while his nightmares ravaged him.

Gripping the banister, she hoisted herself up the stairs, step after step. The ground swayed and she swallowed hot, searing vomit. On reaching the landing, she noticed a light shining under John's bedroom door. Feeling a pang of sadness, she stopped outside it. It was so long since they had connected in any way. She couldn't remember the last proper conversation she had had with her son. His bruises were almost healed, his ribs too, yet the distance between them had yet to mend.

Swaying on her feet, she pushed open the bedroom door.

He was sitting at his computer, the monitor illuminating the room. He hadn't heard his door open, and when she called to him softly his head whipped around. He sprang from his seat, his eyes wide and wild. She recoiled at the look of unbridled anger on his face. Pushing her roughly from the room he slammed the door, muttering *"Fucking drunk!"* as he turned the key.

Sobbing, she stumbled to her bedroom. Tom lay in bed, sheets tangled around his legs, moaning softly. Climbing in beside him, she wrapped her arms around his back. The peace that sleep required wouldn't come, and she remained wide awake. Every time she closed her eyes, she remembered John's face and the wild look in his eyes and realised the horror she had worked so hard to quash all those years ago had risen again.

She felt afraid.

8

Friday dawned bright and crisp, a hint of spring in the air. After her workout and training session with Jason, Anna drove to work with the windows down. Fresh wind and birdsong accompanied her from the coastal town of Kinsale into the city centre, the din of traffic eventually intruding to remind her that Cork city was the throbbing heart of the county. She closed the car windows and switched on the radio.

The shooting in Clonakilty dominated the news headlines. Gardaí were appealing for witnesses, although the report had said the victim was shot on a quiet back road in the early hours of the morning. Anna doubted there would be anything of value from the public appeal. Still, she felt certain that, with William Ryan at the helm, progress would be made.

The tables in Victus were mostly unoccupied, customers choosing takeaway rather than sitting inside. She joined the queue, browsing her mobile phone as she waited. A message from Myles made her smile.

Train leaves at 3pm. No need for my surfboard for obvious reasons! I'm begging you, no seafood on the menu for the weekend. Did I mention I miss you?

"You look happy!" Louisa grinned at Anna as she reached the counter. "The usual this morning?"

She nodded, feeling a little silly. Myles made her happier than she could remember in a long time, even though they had known each other less than a few months. When Anna had first encountered him, she had been struck by his bright smile and large brown eyes. His unruly black hair was a mass of curls that he sometimes wore in a bun. He was a surfing fanatic, an IT genius, and his role in the Department of Justice was strictly confidential. She had been drawn to him from their first conversation in Victus. Sometimes, at night when she struggled to sleep, she thought about how close she had come to losing him before she ever really got to know him. Once Kate had given her the memory key, her decision to bring it to Myles had almost got him killed. He had been shot in the upper arm and thigh and still relied on a walking stick – he had a pronounced limp when he tried to do without. His arm remained stiff – no amount of physiotherapy could compensate for the healing nature of time, and so his surfing days were on hold for now.

In the open-plan ground floor of the Lee Street Garda station, Anna deposited a cappuccino and croissant at her colleague Lauren's unoccupied desk before turning on her own computer. An orange sticky note grabbed her attention – placed conspicuously on her screen, the writing in heavy black ink.

See me, FD

Frank Doherty, the Chief Superintendent of the Lee Street Garda station, promoted after the violent death of his superior the previous year. She sighed and swirled her coffee in the cardboard cup, watching the brown liquid blend with the white foamy milk, wondering what he wanted.

Her relationship with him was better this year than it had been in the previous three years she had worked here. She had little dealings with him generally but, when their paths *did* cross, he adopted a gentler tone with her than the other clerical staff. Still, she felt uneasy around the man. He barked orders more than anything else, his demeanour of dissatisfaction with his staff a constant, despite the events of recent months.

Her desk was cluttered with stacks of folders and memos, a collage of sticky notes littering the walls of her cubicle. One bulky folder had a note stuck to the front, in handwriting she recognised as William Ryan's. It was the file on the shooting in Clonakilty. She had been expecting it, and her heart fluttered in anticipation. She'd heard the scene was horrific and didn't relish opening the section of the file with the crime-scene photos. She could put off starting on it for a while yet – Frank Doherty was waiting.

Securing the lid back on her coffee cup she set it beside her keyboard, before making her way to his office on the third floor. The door was open, and he was sitting at his desk, twisted around in his chair, rummaging in a desk drawer. She knocked gently.

"Chief Superintendent Doherty?"

He straightened up in his seat and glared in her direction. She suspected a glare was just the natural resting expression of his face. His white shirtsleeves were rolled up, the dome of his bald head glistening in the overhead fluorescent lights. Even sitting down the man was huge, so big he was the same height as Anna while she was standing before him. His shirt buttons were straining against his stomach and he often chewed on blood-pressure tablets. Based on the red colour of his face, she would wager he needed a higher dose.

"Ah! Nancy Drew herself! Sit down." It was an order, not an invitation, and Anna complied.

The first time he had called her Nancy Drew had been to mock her – she had found a common link between unsolved sexual assaults in the county and, as DS William Ryan had been on sick leave, had brought her concerns to his supervisor, Doherty. The man had accused her of thinking she was the famed fictional sleuth instead of clerical support and urged her to go back to her desk and leave solving crimes to the detectives, "like a good girl". Later, after Anna had been attacked, he had referred to her as Nancy Drew in what could be called an affectionate tone.

"What can I do for you, Chief Superintendent?"

He looked at her quizzically. "What?"

"You left a note on my desk to see you," she prompted, fighting to keep her voice upbeat.

His eyes cleared and his expression darkened.

She wiped her sweating palms on her trousers as her sense of foreboding increased.

"I thought you should know. This case with Dean Harris …" He trailed off, watching her carefully.

She felt the hairs on her arms stand to attention under his gaze, her heart rate spiralling.

"What about it?"

Memories of the night he had entered her home were etched in her subconscious, jabbing into her dreams and waking thoughts without warning. She remembered the surge of adrenaline as she hid behind her living-room door, hearing the creak of the staircase and watching his shadow as he moved towards her. The self-defence skills her father had trained her and Alex in when they were young, as well as her black belt in Taekwon-Do, had saved her then. She had fractured Dean Harris's jaw defending herself, before fleeing to her neighbour's house while he lay unconscious on the floor. As far as she was aware, he was still in a prison cell while the Director of Public Prosecutions prepared a case against him.

"Whoever carried out the sexual assaults in question left DNA at each scene, and up until Harris's arrest, we had no match for that." He adjusted his shirtsleeves as he spoke. "When he broke into your house he was arrested, and naturally then a DNA sample was taken. We assumed it would be a match to the unresolved cases, but it appears there's been a problem."

Blood rushed to Anna's face and her heart felt like it would explode out of her chest. Dean Harris had been carrying a bag with him that night, a "rape-kit" as one of the arresting gardaí had called it – tape, condoms, latex gloves … he was prepared. He had been at the scene of each of the sexual assaults, installing security alarms after a robbery, with ample opportunity to spot a potential victim. All the evidence was there … surely he was going to prison for a long time?

"I don't want you to worry unduly. Forensic Science Ireland are due in soon to explain what's going on, and the man is still behind bars." He cleared his throat. "However, it appears there was an error somewhere along the line with processing his DNA. So we have what's known as a 'technicality' of sorts that could see him out on bail while it gets sorted."

Anna met the Chief Super's eyes and found anger there.

"Out? On the streets?" Her voice was merely a whimper and she cleared her throat.

He nodded and pursed his lips. "Unfortunately, yes. His solicitor is pushing for temporary release while all this is being cleared up. I imagine he'll get it too – I've seen it happen before."

"Does DS Ryan know?" He had been involved in the case, arresting Dean Harris in hospital the morning after the attack.

The Chief Superintendent pulled a handkerchief from his pocket, wiping sweat from his brow and the back of his neck.

"He's due in shortly." His eyes travelled to the wall clock.

"I ... I don't know what to think."

"I wouldn't worry. It'll get straightened out, one way or another. In the meantime, keep this to yourself and keep your wits about you."

She nodded, unable to form sentences around the jumble of thoughts in her head. An awkward silence filled the office. Anna assumed there was no more to be said on the matter. She half rose from her seat before changing her mind.

"Have you had any update on ... the events of last year? Any sign of Kate Crowley?" she asked quickly, before she lost her nerve, wincing at his dark expression. She figured she would ask the question now that she had the man's time. He usually didn't stop to chat with the staff on the office level. At the mention of the case his forehead creased, a red blush colouring his neck.

"No! She remains missing, even now after weeks of searching."

"And no new information on who the buyer was for the memory key?" She knew she was pushing him now. It was with some relief she turned on hearing a noise at the office door as William Ryan rapped his knuckles in greeting.

"Update on the Clonakilty shooting in ten minutes." His light-blue eyes rested on Anna and he smiled warmly. "Anna! How are things? I left a file on your desk this morning."

She nodded her head slightly and rose from the chair.

"That's fine, I'll make it a priority."

He smiled. "Are you OK?"

"I've been better."

She left them to it.

Lauren's eyes bulged behind her glasses when Anna filled her in on the conversation with Frank Doherty. She was last to arrive in the office today, even though her apartment was only a short walk away. Gulping her coffee, she put her hand on Anna's arm.

"Christ! Imagine him back out on the streets!"

"You'll have to keep it to yourself for a while, but I'm sure the whole building will know before too long."

"Of course, no problem." Watching her friend digest the news, Lauren tried to inject more positivity into her voice. "This will all get straightened out, I'm sure of it."

"I hope so!"

"Give it time – these things always get sorted!"

Lauren's conviction was comforting. Anna exhaled all the pent-up air she had been holding and felt her heartrate slow down and her shoulders relax.

Lauren pulled a magazine from her bag, grinning – her

wedding was only weeks away, and her productivity at work was seriously suffering. The finer details of her wedding were far more interesting.

"Let's change the subject ... what do you think of this headpiece for the bridesmaids?"

Anna picked up her latte again, relieved it was still warm, and leaned in closer. Glad as she was to discuss a more light-hearted topic, she struggled to be tactful as she looked at the headpiece. She was almost lost for words.

"It's a bit ... *um* ... big?"

"Yeah, maybe you're right." Lauren finished the last of her croissant and turned the page to a feature on wedding dresses.

"What about this dress?"

"I thought you picked out yours last year?"

"Not for me ... for you! What time are you collecting Myles today?" With a grin she ducked to avoid Anna's swatting hand.

Anna turned her chair to face her workload again and, despite the grim conversation with Frank Doherty, couldn't help smiling. Myles was staying for the weekend, and Lauren was singing at her desk, a song about Anna and Myles going to a Chapel of Love. She could always count on her friend to lift her spirits.

With a deep breath, she opened the first file of the day. The crime scene images from Clonakilty stared back at her – they were as horrific as she had been warned.

She dedicated her morning to compiling all the evidence into a report, typing up job-book entries and detailing things to be followed up. Though her mind was occupied with the task, Dean Harris crept into her thoughts here and there, breaking her concentration.

So ... he was in jail right now but there was a problem with the DNA ...

She tried to reassure herself. He had been arrested after breaking into her home, with a bag of items suggesting sexual assault was his intent ... he would surely spend time in jail for that alone. And Anna reminded herself that she had bested him once and could do it again ... if the need arose.

Couldn't she?

9

"Fill us in, DS Ryan, and be quick about it," said Frank Doherty. "The day is long but my time is short! The press conference is at midday. Give me something to work with!"

At the front of the conference room William faced the gathered detectives and gardaí. He was aware of a slight tremor in his hands as he held the file containing his notes. The news Frank Doherty had imparted earlier had spiked an anger in him that had yet to dissipate. A representative from the main forensics body in the country had scheduled a meeting next week – he knew it would take a Trojan effort not to pin the man to his office wall if they had messed up the investigation into Dean Harris's crimes. Frank Doherty didn't care to conceal his resulting anger as William did. He stayed to the side and let the detective take the lead on this one, huffing and muttering, his red face glistening with sweat. The bulk of the man remained on the edge of William's line of sight.

For now, William tried to focus on the case at hand. Two enlarged photographs of Seán Doyle were taped onto the noticeboard at the front of the incident room. One in life and one in death. His sister had provided the image of the victim at his nephew's wedding – smiling, jovial, cheeks ruddy from a few pints. The Garda Technical Bureau had provided the death photo: waxen skin, a dark hole where his left eye had been. The assembled women and men were sitting quietly, waiting. There would be no smart comments, no fidgeting. This would command all their attention.

"The victim is Seán Doyle, an A&E nurse in the CUH, aged fifty-six at the time of death. The state pathologist has given preliminary findings, but obviously tests are ongoing. The scene is still being examined. The cause of death appears for now to be a single gunshot wound to the head."

"What's the scene-of-crime take on this?"

"The scene is almost pristine. There are no bullet casings at the scene and the pathologist is expected to find the bullet inside the victim's skull. We await information."

"A revolver then? The shell casings remain in the cylinder."

"Or the guy could have picked up the casings?"

William held up his hands. "We'll have clarity on that soon. There was one tyre mark in the grass verge, and nothing else that's of any use. Castings of the tyre mark were impossible – the surface was like a mud-bath after the downpour the night before. But we have photographs and they are being examined, so let's hope that brings results. No traffic cameras or on-street CCTV in that rural area, but footage from a wider area is being examined."

William pointed to a third enlarged photograph on the wall.

"These marks were observed at the scene. Three holes in the ground making a triangular shape and the grass around them is flattened down – again, no possible footprints of use."

He turned to the room. "Your input here is welcome."

Silence greeted him. The assembled gardaí looked to each other for inspiration. William nodded at Colin Forde, who leaned over a computer at the desk at the front of the room and selected a video from his email account. After a few seconds he turned off the lights, pointing at the white screen at the front of the room.

"Detective Garda Forde is about to press play on a video of security footage of the incident, albeit of poor quality. A nearby farm belonging to Jim Conway has CCTV cameras mounted on a large shed used to house machinery. It offers little to go on unfortunately"

The video opened. The image showed the back road where Seán Doyle had been shot. But the angle of the footage was higher than was truly useful. The road appeared deserted until a large beige-coloured vehicle pulled into the grassy verge of the road and stopped on the left-hand side. Only the roof was visible and the collective force in the room leaned forward in their seats as if to see more.

Frank Doherty stopped sucking his blood pressure tablet and watched, his eyes riveted.

"Is this it? This is useless. The ditches are blocking everything!"

"Agreed," William muttered, "but it's all we've got."

Faint movement, slivers of glinting light, pierced the stillness of the footage.

"We think that is the front passenger door and driver door opening," William said. "So, we are looking for two perpetrators."

"Presumably they exited the vehicle to flag down a passing driver," Frank said.

"Yes. But the footage is inconclusive. By the position of

the body on the road in relation to the partial tyre print, it's clear the victim was shot behind the vehicle. The ditches are too high to offer more conclusive information."

William tapped his pen against the surface of his desk and nodded to Colin, who switched off the recording and turned the lights back on.

"As I said, this is all we've got. This is the only activity on the road in the time frame and the location where this vehicle stopped matches where the body was found." He exhaled in frustration.

"That's it?" Frank Doherty's eyes bulged and he rammed his hands angrily into his pockets. *"There's nothing here! I'll be eaten alive at the press conference!"*

"I appreciate that but there's very little to go on. *Yet.* There are no missing or reported stolen vehicles matching the height and colour in the area, and the search has been extended nationwide. I'm waiting on a report back. I know it's early days in the investigation but I'm confident the deceased had no enemies – he lived a quiet life. We've spoken to his family and friends and to the local gardaí. He was a popular local man and a good neighbour. Detectives are at the CUH to speak to his manager and colleagues, to find out if there are any grudges against him from a patient or work colleague, but given what we know about him, it's unlikely he was targeted for any personal reason. This may have been a random crime where our killers waited for the victim to arrive. There must have been a ruse to get the victim to pull over and leave his car. He was travelling from the opposite side, heading to the main Cork Road."

"If it was a random attack, presumably the killers must have waited for a driver travelling alone," a garda said.

"Is it a road Mr Doyle travelled every day?" asked another.

William smiled. His colleagues were invested already, every angle being teased out.

"Yes, it was his route to work five days a week. And one of the quietest roads in the area, according to locals. So it's likely the killers assessed the roads, looking for a pattern, a lone driver. We've begun the process of speaking to residents in the locality, to see if anyone saw a strange vehicle driving around the roads in the days prior to the attack – particularly in the early morning." He pointed again to the photograph. "The deceased's sister, Mrs Sheila Barrett, was quizzed as to why her brother might stop for an unfamiliar vehicle on his way to work. She said he was a good sort of guy, always keen to help others. And he was a medical professional – a nurse."

A young garda from the back of the room raised her hand. "Is it possible the killers knew this – that he was a nurse and would be more likely to stop than the average person if there appeared to be an emergency?"

"Garda ...?" William smiled – he liked intelligent questions. He hated that he couldn't yet remember the names of all the staff in the station.

"Detective Garda Grace Thompson."

"Well, that's a good point. It is possible."

"However, that still wouldn't prove they had a personal motive to kill him," she said. "Just that they knew he was a likely target who would probably stop."

"Correct." William was impressed. She was astute, this young woman. He guessed she was in her late twenties, like Colin. She was tall and thin, her long legs tucked under the seat, her shirt sleeves pushed up, black hair pulled back off her face in a low ponytail. She looked as eager to solve this as he felt, her grey eyes watching him intently.

"Anything else?" Doherty's jaw was grinding now. "Any suspects at all?"

William gestured to Colin Forde, motioning for him to continue the update.

Clearing his throat, Colin addressed the room.

"An American couple booked into the local hotel on Sunday afternoon, so that's four days prior to the shooting." He looked down at his notebook on the table. "A Mr and Mrs Parker-Barrow. They claimed to be on honeymoon. A member of staff, Jan O'Neill, told us about them and remarked how unusual a destination Clonakilty is in winter for a honeymoon. We agree – it's odd."

A ripple of chatter ran through the room.

"Why on earth would anyone honeymoon in Ireland in January? All the way from America?"

"Maybe they like the cold and rain?"

William held up his hand for silence.

Colin continued. "Miss O'Neill informed us this couple claimed to have had their bags stolen and were therefore unable to give their passports on check-in or pay using a credit card. They paid in cash, the woman loudly praising God she had stashed some euros in her pocket before everything was taken. She was described as 'dramatic'. Miss O'Neill presumed they had reported the theft at the airport. We checked – they never did."

A collective intake of air whistled through the room.

"*Jesus Christ!*" Frank Doherty blustered, his eyes bulging. "What are you doing to find them?"

"Statements from the staff have been taken, but unfortunately there's no security footage available from inside the hotel," Colin responded. "A sketch is being worked up of the couple. So far we are looking for a tall, dark-haired male who never spoke throughout interactions with staff, and an exuberant and chatty blonde woman, about a foot shorter than her companion. CCTV of the streets surrounding the hotel and forensics in the room are being examined."

He finished and sat down, looking relieved.

"Frank, what are your thoughts?" William asked.

"Any other sighting of them in Clonakilty? Any restaurants that might have CCTV?"

William exhaled his frustration. "We're working on it. There's dozens of cameras and hours of footage. According to the hotel staff the couple didn't socialise in the hotel. They kept a low profile. The hotel doesn't have a car park so they must have parked any vehicle they used in the surrounding streets or public car parks. CCTV is being examined, as Colin said."

Doherty thought on it a while longer, eyes now boring into the opposite wall.

"I don't know if we have enough to consider them suspects. Certainly, in the press conference later, I'll ask them to get in touch to help with our enquiries. At least it's something – it might distract from the absolute lack of progress otherwise!"

Grace Thompson spoke again from the back of the room – "Did you say their name on check-in was Parker-Barrow?"

Colin nodded and she felt the eyes of the room on her. "It's just ... they had no ID to verify that?"

"None," William confirmed. "What are you thinking?"

"Well, just that it's a fake name."

"I think that's pretty obvious!" Doherty muttered through gritted teeth, glaring in her direction.

Grace shook her head slightly, as though to dismiss the man.

"I mean, those are the surnames of Bonnie and Clyde.

Bonnie Parker and Clyde Barrow. You know, the infamous criminal couple in America?"

This silenced the assembled men and women. Doherty, in particular, looked perplexed. He turned to William.

"Did you realise this? What do you think this means?"

Rubbing his hands together slowly in front of him, William could only shake his head. "No, I didn't. Honestly, I don't know what it means. Maybe it was just a fanciful thing, or maybe they're fans of the duo."

"Or maybe they're lunatics," someone muttered from the back of the room, and there was an assembled murmur of agreement.

Grace raised a finger again. "Bonnie and Clyde went on a two-year crime spree and were notorious bank robbers. We should check if there are any other unsolved robberies or murders with a similar M.O."

"Good idea," Frank nodded, "but I'll be keeping this away from the media for now. Until we know what it means."

"The woman was described as chatty," Grace continued. "Did she give any clues as to where they were going when they checked out?"

"No, unfortunately. Details in the job book will be completed on a rolling basis and the latest update will be sent to you shortly. This is a priority case. Communication will be sent to all stations in the city and county. And, folks, keep this image in mind …" He pointed at the triangular markings in the grass. "It might be nothing, but if it was made by the killers it's one of the few things they left behind."

The gardaí and detectives left the room quietly – the photographs of the deceased had been disturbing, the case intriguing. Random, seemingly motive-less shootings were uncommon in Cork, especially in the countryside. There was usually a grudge that could be explained by the locals and traced back to the killer. This seemed to be a completely indiscriminate murder, where the killers had lain in wait for their victim. That was unsettling for even the most seasoned of staff.

William motioned for Colin Forde and Grace Thompson to stay behind, busying himself with pinning a map to the noticeboard while the others filed out of the room. When it was just the three of them, he turned and smiled.

"Quick thinking on the Parker-Barrow angle, Grace, although God knows what it means. I need good detectives on this. I'd like you both to work exclusively on this case. Colin, bring Grace up to speed on all the details and then follow up with the technical team, see what's what. Find out where we are on whether residents in Clonakilty reported any suspicious vehicles driving through the area. And I like the idea of looking for similar crimes. Let's hope this is an isolated one, but better to know if it's part of a pattern."

Both nodded, Grace slightly more enthusiastically, William thought. He noticed Colin kept his eyes firmly away from the photographs of the victim. He felt for the man, but there was nothing he could do to shield him from the images – they were an essential part of solving the crime. Colin had an inquisitive mind and a sharp eye for detail and William was determined to use his skillset.

"If this was a completely random shooting then it could happen again," William said. "They didn't rob the victim … maybe they did it for kicks?"

"Who knows? Our most pressing requirement is to *find* this couple," Grace muttered, staring at the images on the noticeboard.

William exhaled heavily. "Agreed. But they could be literally anywhere."

10

Two streets away, the couple walked through the lobby of their hotel on the South Mall and onto the main street. Marian Selway was booked out for tours until Saturday, so they would just have to wait. The man's mood had plummeted on hearing that news, but there was nothing that could be done. He toyed with the idea of choosing another lead in their film, but time was already against them. And this felt *right*. He had mulled it all over while she prattled on endlessly over breakfast. They had time, and the Rebel Event Centre was a spectacular setting. It was perfect.

He hadn't spoken in two hours. He avoided looking at the woman, but couldn't avoid hearing her ...

She talked non-stop, bouncing beside him as they walked. She had convinced him to go outside to get some air – and a change of scenery was a relief if he was honest with himself. The hotel room had become claustrophobic. The buzz from their little roadside set-up had faded and he was restless.

The woman had a large fur hat on today, fake of course, and a matching coat. She looked ridiculous. At breakfast she had affected a Russian accent with the waitress in the hotel dining room, and the man had to remind her they had been Irish on check-in. She had spun her overly dramatic story about being robbed of their bags again – it worked again – but he was growing irritated by her antics. Daily her wigs and her accents changed, and he had trouble keeping up. Sometimes she was many different personalities in one day, and his head would spin so that he had to squeeze the flesh of her arms to make her be quiet. In bed, too, she spoke in different accents, but he was better able to drown her out then.

At the end of the South Mall a cluster of men were drinking from bottles wrapped in paper bags. They were sitting on low wooden benches and chatting amongst themselves, oblivious to the world moving around them. The woman stopped her bouncing walk and stared at them. Her head was cocked to the side and she appeared to be in a trance. The man tugged her arm, uncomfortable – they must not draw attention to themselves. But she would not be moved. With her feet planted into the ground she continued to stare, and when she had the attention of a few of the group she began to laugh. Loud shrieks that cut through the chilly morning air. The men stared back, some mouths open in shock at the display in front of them, others too lost to the liquor to register any surprise.

The man pulled hard on her arm.

"Move! Now!"

She fell into step beside him again, linking arms once more.

"Let's get some coffee. And flowers. I assume there's a florist in this city!" She spoke as if the parade of her mania had never happened.

He kept his head low and walked fast. Rage was mounting inside him, pulsing and pulling at his fists. He wanted to claw the stupid smile from her face with his fingers. She was drawing attention to them – there would be CCTV of the streets, and they couldn't afford to be noticed. He walked so fast she had trouble keeping up.

"The flowers?" she prodded, yanking his arm. "Take me to the market you talked about, the English one. I want to see it. We can get croissants and coffees and bunches of roses and pretend we are shopping on the Avenue Montaigne in Paris." Her pronunciation had slipped into something he assumed was an attempt at a French accent.

He turned to face her, his fists balled and ready. She smiled at him, in the charming way she could when she knew she was on the edge of danger. He sighed and moved off again.

Behind him her laughter echoed in the city street.

11

At lunchtime, Anna joined Vivian outside a new block of apartments near Blackrock Castle. They couldn't yet go inside – the building contractor was working on the snag-list and not quite finished. The two friends stood opposite the entrance, excitement radiating from Vivian to the point that Anna couldn't help but laugh.

"I've never seen you so happy!"

"Well, I've never had anything of my own before, not even a car! I just can't believe Brenda is buying me an *apartment*." Her eyes shone as she took in her surroundings. "I mean, the view – it's just stunning! This is going to be *my* view every morning! Sometimes when I wake up I wonder did I dream it, that I'll have my very own place!"

"Well, it's not a dream, it's real!" Anna laughed and squeezed her arm.

The apartment block held just twenty-four new homes, set in a crescent shape around a large communal green area. Half grey-brick and half white-pebble dash, the buildings blended aesthetically into the surrounding landscape, with Blackrock

Castle and the river behind it a visually stunning backdrop.

"Your parents must be thrilled for you!"

"They are." Vivian smiled. "Gareth hasn't said a word about it though."

"Still not speaking to you?"

Vivian shook her head sadly.

"Well … time heals things. He'll get over it, I'm sure. Don't let his resentment spoil this for you."

Vivian pulled her into a hug. "Thank you! I really mean it."

Not for the first time, Anna's happiness at having her best friend back in her life was a physical rush. It really had felt like such a long time apart while she was in New Zealand.

They walked the short distance to the courtyard coffee shop in the castle and ordered lunch. It was bright and dry, a beautiful crisp day that the cold couldn't diminish. Wrapped in their coats and scarves, with a nearby patio heater on full, they almost felt cosy. When their soups and coffees arrived, they tucked in, their casual chat turning inevitably to the shooting in Clonakilty the day before. Vivian had attended the press conference earlier at the Lee Street Garda station, and her report had been on the lunchtime news update online.

"Your Chief Superintendent is a gruff man, isn't he? Not exactly media-friendly. It doesn't seem like there's much to go on. From what I gather, the shooting appears to be completely random."

Anna tasted her soup and nodded. She knew more about the case now than Vivian did, having typed up the job book for DS Ryan earlier. She wondered if she should confide in her about the problems with Dean Harris's conviction but decided against it for now.

"It's awful, that poor man!" she said instead.

Vivian shook her head, her ponytail waving. "Let's talk

about something else. How are things with Alex?"

Anna sighed, feeling the weight of the fight with her brother rest heavily on her shoulders.

"We had an argument about our parents – he doesn't see why we should dig into their past. He wants to let things as they are! Can you imagine it – carrying on as if you haven't just been told your mother was a Russian cellist, who disappeared from her family as a young woman? I mean, that's mind-blowing, and he wants to ignore it!" Her voice broke as tears filled her eyes, and she looked away, at the observatory tower behind them. She had replayed their conversation over and over in her mind and was still incredulous at her brother's reaction. Neither had contacted the other since she left his house abruptly – she felt nauseous every time she thought of it.

"You two haven't argued in years! I'm sure things will sort themselves out."

"I feel the complete opposite to Alex … I *need* answers! I just don't know where to start."

"What will you do?"

"I've thought about asking DS Ryan. He's really nice, and I know he'll help if he can, but the shooting has taken up all his time and … I don't want to bother him, I suppose. And, besides, if there was something he could access in the files about my mum, Myles would have done it already."

Vivian sighed theatrically and grinned. "Honestly, have I taught you nothing? *Everything* is accessible online, Anna – the internet is a fountain of knowledge. You have your mother's real name. If I were you I'd search for newspaper articles with that and see where the trail leads you."

Anna nodded slowly, feeling her earlier sadness nudged out by a growing motivation. Her friend was right. She remembered how she had found enough information online to realise Kate Crowley was more than capable of defending herself without shooting David Gallagher. The images she had seen and the information she had found had turned her certainty that Kate was innocent into doubt. She wondered what she would discover online about her mother – in fact, she had already started by keying in her name, looking through a handful of newspaper reports on the night she disappeared from London. But Anna had not gone any further, and she thought she understood why – without her brother's support in this she felt vulnerable. Though she longed for the truth, she was nervous about finding it alone.

"It's so nice here." Vivian looked around her and nodded at the road beyond the courtyard. "And a bus stops here, heading into town. It's perfect." She glanced at her friend who had a faraway look in her eyes. "So what are your weekend plans?"

Vivian's question brought Anna back into the moment.

"Myles is coming to stay, remember?" A wide grin spread across her face, and she marvelled that even thinking about him could lift her mood so much.

Vivian gasped, her eyes growing wide. "Of course! I can't believe I forgot! I hope I get to meet him."

Anna grimaced. "Maybe next time. It's his first time staying in Kinsale with me, so I think we'll keep it low key." Time spent with Myles, in person and not just in conversation over the phone, felt precious and she wanted to make the most of it.

Vivian wiggled her eyebrows and laughed – Anna couldn't help but join in.

* * *

At six o'clock, she was waiting nervously at the arrival gate at Cork's Kent station. She wondered why the butterflies danced and fluttered in her stomach – she *knew* Myles, even if it was weeks since they'd met in person. Every day she looked forward to his morning text and his evening phone call. She wanted to talk to him all day long. Everything that happened, even the tiniest minute thing, became an instant *"I must tell Myles later"* moment. She chided herself at how ridiculous it was, yet it felt right. He made her happy.

There was so much she didn't know about him yet – his precise job within the Garda for one thing. She hoped they would have that conversation this weekend. But she was happy that she knew the important things about him: his love of surfing and his hatred of seafood, despite his Greek mama's insistence. How he made her laugh, how he made her feel … how he had saved her life less than two months ago, even though it made his own injuries so much worse.

She ran her hands through her blonde bob – she had cut her long hair recently and was still unaccustomed to the feel of it brushing against her neck – and filled her lungs with a deep breath, letting it out slowly. She had cancelled her customary Saturday morning Taekwon-Do training session with Jason, a thing she had only done once since her training resumed after her parents' disappearance. She had stocked the fridge, no seafood of course, and was so nervous about having him stay for the weekend she was almost giddy.

As the passengers departed the train and began to filter through the gates, she was standing on tiptoe to better see through the crowd …

Suddenly, there he was. Tall and thin, in drainpipe jeans under a short, padded coat, Myles walked towards her with the limp she had very nearly forgotten about, his walking stick glancing the tiled floor. His dark mass of curls was as wild and unruly as she remembered, his smile the same bright white against sallow skin. A grin lit up his face, brown eyes twinkling behind his glasses as he reached her and pulled her into a hug.

"Hello, you!"

Words caught in her throat – she was overcome with emotion. The trials of the last few days – the argument with Alex, the never-ending thoughts about her mother's past, the news that Dean Harris might soon be released – she felt it all evaporate as she buried her face in his chest, breathing him in. He felt solid and warm, and she felt her tension unfurl as they embraced. Finally, she looked up at him, her own brown eyes shining brightly.

"Hello you too!"

On only their second date she had told him everything about her parents' disappearance. It felt natural and easy to open up to him. Seeing him now, in the flesh, after weeks of phone calls, she found herself forgetting about everything except the fact that he was finally here. Perhaps, just for the weekend, she could stop worrying and wondering about where her parents were, and who they had been.

12

London, 1978

Nana Clarke played "Night Fever" by the Bee Gees so often at home, Michael found himself humming it throughout the day at work. If it irritated Bob, he never said, but he did suggest they get a radio in the office, laughing at Michael's sheepish expression.

It was three weeks before he made any impression on the stacks of papers. He had sorted them into piles on the floor: debtors, creditors, orders pending and completed. The linoleum floor was grimy, and the pages were often marked with dirty shoeprints, cigarette burns and what he hoped were coffee stains. He had bought a filing cabinet and enough notebooks and ledgers to require a new set of shelves for the small office. Mr Lewis said nothing about his expenditure, which must have exceeded what he meant when he said to take money from the petty cash. He was rarely in the office, but he was at his desk when the filing cabinet arrived and Michael roped Bob into helping him carry it up the metal staircase.

Mr Lewis watched them quietly, twirling a pen across

the fingers of one hand, his expression unreadable.

Bob winked at Michael when he saw his nervous glances at the boss.

"Don't worry about him – if he's quiet he's happy. It's when he makes noise you have to worry!"

Slowly, Michael began to form a system. There were a number of main suppliers of cloths and fabrics, namely one in the Netherlands and another in Turkey, and a handful of smaller suppliers, who were rarely used. The warehouse was busy, with orders coming in regularly and prepared to be shipped out again by Boxer and Roy. Lewis seemed to be the only one who prepared the customs paperwork, and Bob oversaw the rest of the operation, consulting a clipboard, shouting instructions at the other two men, ensuring things went out on time. They seemed to have an easy relationship and an efficient system. Michael often found himself alone in the office and it suited him – the work of sorting the papers into a system was tedious, requiring all his concentration to just decipher handwriting in some instances.

Any time he felt weary of the work, he remembered his grandmother's eyes when he presented his first paycheque – the tears that shone there told him she could stop the extra work she had taken on and begin to repay her debts. He knew she must have borrowed money to pay for night school, even though she told him not to worry about it. Knowing the cost of the course, he estimated that within a year she would have repaid all the money she had borrowed. For now, he was happy she could relax more in the evenings. His long-term goal was to support her retirement – he owed her that.

Mr Lewis seemed happy to trust Michael to get on with his work. Occasionally he asked questions, and one morning Michael realised his workstation had been rearranged overnight, the piles of documents moved and no longer in order. He didn't mind – if it was his company, he might want to check up on the new guy too. And he was happy there. He was well paid, Bob was fun to be around, and felt he was getting through the workload, his earlier trepidation at his lack of experience evaporating every day.

There were a few inconsistencies that niggled him though. The orders from the company in Turkey were rarely itemised, mostly just listed as 'stock' and there was no paper trail to disclose how the orders were paid for. No cheque stubs, no bank documents – nothing. He would need more detailed records than that kept in future. If the accounts were to be independently audited, no bookkeeper could be seen to accept that! A couple of times a year orders were shipped to a company that supplied clothing to stores in Scotland and Northern Ireland, but order dockets were either missing or so illegibly written that it was impossible to determine what the docket contained. It seemed to Michael that Mr Lewis was owed a lot of money by that company – he could find no evidence of payment in the last six months. These were inconsistencies, possible problems. He knew the Inland Revenue could audit the books at any time – Mr Lewis would have to keep his accounts in order, and that responsibility was his now. He just hoped Bob and his boss would agree to keeping detailed records. And to type out the orders that came in.

In June, Nana Clarke's musical obsession had changed to John Travolta and Oliva Newton-John's "You're the One That I Want". He was glad of the radio at work – at least while he was there he could listen to something else.

His Taekwon-Do training increased to five nights a week. The Grand Master of his school was due to visit London at the beginning of July. He would expect demonstrations and would award black belts to the worthy few. Michael fully intended to be among them. Bob had grown accustomed to the gear bag slung over his shoulder every morning, and the sight of him running out the warehouse door at six p.m. sharp each evening, calling a quick goodbye. Boxer was jovial, calling out impressions of Bruce Lee as Michael hurried past him. Roy never commented, keeping his back turned and his manner as aloof as it had been since Michael joined the company. He had given up trying to form any type of working relationship with the man.

On the last Friday in June, Michael had stood up and stretched, ready to leave, just as Mr Lewis arrived at the office. His arrival was heralded by loud thumping up the stairs. Bob and Michael looked at each other and their friendly banter ceased.

Lewis was a walking advertisement for the luxury fabrics he imported – in a three-piece-suit of soft grey wool, a pale blue shirt and matching tie and handkerchief – but his face was darkest night. He pulled off his cap and dropped it onto his desk, his bushy eyebrows furrowed low, his mouth set. He appeared not to have noticed his employees until Michael walked past his desk and said, "Goodnight, Mr Lewis."

His head snapped up and he appraised the young man critically, his eyes finally resting on the gear bag.

"What's that you've got there?"

"This?" Michael held up the bag. "It's my training gear."

"Training? For what?" He stepped closer.

Michael was taller than average height but suddenly he felt dwarfed by the man. His boss had his hands in his pockets, his elbows jutting out, his physical space wide. He eyed him suspiciously and Michael felt unnerved by the sudden chill in the air, the change in the man he was growing to like.

"It's Taekwon-Do. I'm training for my black belt."

Lewis's eyes bulged and colour began to flood his face.

Bob rose and moved to his side quickly.

"It's a martial art, Lewis. Like the movie star Bruce Lee."

Michael looked at Bob quizzically, feeling the unexpected tension from them both – in the older man's intense stare and in Bob's tight smile. Suddenly he felt sweat begin to dampen his shirt between his shoulder blades.

"Show me. Open the bag." Lewis gestured to the gear bag with one hand, his other still inside the pocket of his suit trousers. The icy drip of his voice permeated the air, and the office suddenly felt claustrophobic.

"No problem," Michael murmured, moving back to his desk and dropping the bag on top. He pulled out his white top, pants and his belt, his towel and shower gel, his bottle of water. Lewis stepped to his side and stuck his hand inside the bag, moving it left and right. He found it empty.

Michael looked questioningly at Bob and the man gave a tiny, almost imperceptible shake of his head.

Lewis smiled, revealing rows of gleaming, false teeth, too big for his mouth. Michael had never noticed that before.

"Never mind me, young Michael, I'm growing paranoid in my old age."

Michael felt the man's hand clap roughly on his back.

"You're doing a great job with the accounts – don't think

I haven't noticed. I know I can trust you." He kept one hand clamped on Michael's shoulder and looked him in the eye as he spoke. "I want you to collect someone and bring her to my house. Drop her at the door, eh? Bob will give you the address. Her English isn't great. Just make sure she's at my house within the hour."

"*Um* ... now?" He was confused at the man's sudden change in demeanour.

Lewis had turned his back and now ignored him.

"Bob, we need to discuss tomorrow's shipment." He moved across the room again to the door. His eyes met Michael's. "I expect her at my house in an hour." His tone left no room for failure or negotiation, and he crossed the hall to the meeting room where he sometimes met with other businessmen.

Michael appealed to Bob – his arms spread wide, his eyes pleading. "I can't! I need to train!"

Bob tore a piece of paper from a notebook on his desk – he had been bent over it, writing. He pressed it into Michael's hands. "Just do this. It's simple. Take one of the cars outside, OK? One night off your training won't hurt!" Then he too was gone, into the meeting room behind the boss, closing the door firmly.

Alone in the office, Michael looked at the scribbled instructions in his hand. Under his boss's address was written **Banks Hotel, Room 47, Yelena Vasilieva.**

He narrowed his eyes, considering the brief but tense encounter. The boss had called himself paranoid – did he suspect Michael of stealing fabric in his gear bag? There was very little money in the petty-cash box ... was that it? The last few minutes had been a complete shift in personality, a side to Lewis Michael had never experienced before. And who

100

was this girl? He knew the boss was married, with teenage daughters. So, who was Yelena Vasilieva? Irritated though he was to miss training, he was also very, very intrigued.

The London streets whizzed by in a blur of lights. He did his best to concentrate on the road but found his mind was on his Taekwon-Do demonstration. Mentally he ran through each move in formation. He was ready, and excited at the prospect of finally achieving black-belt level. He would have preferred another training session first, but it was not to be.

Luckily, he was familiar with the location of the Banks Hotel, having passed it on the bus many times on his way to night school. He was surprised to find parking easily outside, and quickly made his way into the lobby. It was so luxuriously decorated he stopped and stared for a moment – it was like nothing he had ever seen before. Four crystal chandeliers dominated the space, casting twinkling lights on the marble pillars. A mirror the length of the long reception desk reflected the area, the guests moving at a leisurely pace, basking in the extravagant setting. Cream-leather couches, where drinks were served and air-kisses swapped, filled one corner. He became aware he was standing still, with his mouth hanging open, and he laughed to himself as he moved further into the lobby. He would bring Nana Clarke here for tea as soon as he could arrange it, he decided, glad Mr Lewis had insisted he look the part for his job. Without the expensive suit, he would have felt hugely out of place here.

He spotted an elevator opposite the reception desk and made his way there, hoping he was affecting the air of a man who knew where he was going. Being an Irishman in London city had its drawbacks these days, and he had learned that if he appeared confident and sure of his right to be there, he could blend in unnoticed.

Finding room forty-seven was easy and she was waiting, pulling open the door as soon as he knocked.

She wore a blue-and-green minidress, her hair hidden under a stylish hat. Her eyes were the palest blue he had ever seen.

"You are not Bob!"

Her accent was one he had never heard before.

He felt stunned, momentarily, then quickly grinned. "That's true. I'm Michael."

"I was told Bob would come for me."

"He was needed elsewhere. I'm to take you to Mr Lewis's house."

Her oval eyes bulged slightly in what looked like alarm but she masked it well, nodding as she pulled the door closed behind her. They eyed each other for a moment, neither moving. Clearing his throat, Michael motioned to the hallway in front of him and she led the way to the elevator. He noticed she was carrying a small bag and a red coat over her arm.

"Did you see two men, in dark suits, probably reading newspapers, in the lobby?" she asked as soon as they were inside the elevator.

"No." He remembered how he had been dazzled by the marble and the crystal chandeliers – he wouldn't have noticed anyone reading a newspaper. "Should I have?"

"It is not a problem. They know I am to visit Mr Lewis." Her voice was soft and slightly shaking. She was nervous – his intrigue grew. He almost reached out to pat her arm reassuringly, and felt mortified – they had just met – why did he feel this urge to protect her? He was being ridiculous!

"I've a car parked outside."

"How long will the journey take? I forget."

"Traffic is light – I would think about thirty minutes."

"Will you be staying with me? At the house?"

Momentarily he thought she sounded as though she wanted him to stay. He remembered Mr Lewis had said her English wasn't great – as far as he could make out, it was perfect, if just a little difficult to decipher under her thick accent. To Michael, she seemed afraid.

"No, I'm to leave you at the door." There was apology in his voice but there was nothing he could do. "I'm sure Mr Lewis will drop you back or call a taxi."

If this perturbed her she didn't show it. He opened the passenger door of the car and she slid inside. Hopping into his own seat, he manoeuvred into traffic again and silence descended on them for a few minutes. Twilight was settling over the streets, but the city lights were dazzling.

"Have you been to Mr Lewis's house many times?" he asked then.

"Just once before." She kept her gaze on the passing streets. After a brief silence, she spoke again. "I have not seen you before. You are new in the business?" She turned her head slightly. The fading evening light glanced on her cheekbones.

She looked younger than himself, he thought, maybe by a few years. Which would mean she was in her early twenties. He wondered why Mr Lewis wanted to see her, what their relationship was.

"Yes, I started a few months ago."

"You like it?"

"It's OK. It pays well."

She turned away to look at the passing buildings again.

"I live with my grandmother, and we need a good wage." He mustn't start rambling. "Where are you from? I wasn't told anything about you."

She kept her face turned away from him. "The Soviet Union." It was barely a whisper.

He decided to press on with his questions, to fill the void of silence if nothing else. His discomfort about this whole thing was increasing.

"How do you know Mr Lewis? Are you ... *um* ... his girlfriend?" As soon as he said the words he regretted them.

Her head snapped around and she looked at him in disgust.

"Do not be so stupid!"

He blushed and was glad she turned her face away, staring at the road again.

They drove the next twenty minutes in silence. He felt her tension bounce across the space between them – the tight set of her shoulders was such that her body barely moved with the gentle sway of the car. He cursed his stupid question, wondering how to return to conversation. He doubted she'd be interested in his upcoming Taekwon-Do demonstration ... he wondered if he should tell her more about his grandmother ... or perhaps a geography lesson of the roads they drove through?

In the end, her red coat was the catalyst to break the silence.

"I like your coat. It looks heavy – very warm for an evening in the English summer though."

She continued to look out the window, turned away from him, but she did reply.

"My sister has the same. A gift from our grandparents. I always wear it."

After a few more minutes she turned to face him.

"He is a business acquaintance of my father's."

Michael realised she was answering his earlier question, about how she knew Mr Lewis. He nodded and offered a smile.

The icy layer around her was beginning to thaw and she looked at him now as she spoke. "What do you do for Mr Lewis?"

Relief that she was speaking again flooded through him. "I'm a bookkeeper."

"You keep books?"

He laughed softly. "No, I keep accounts. You know, debtors and creditors, that sort of thing." Her face showed only confusion, so he elaborated. "To put it bluntly, I look after the money."

Her stare was so intense he began to squirm.

"Ah. The money. It is always money. Tell me, Michael, are you as bad as the others?"

He looked at her blankly and she smiled.

Sitting forward, she pointed to a turn in the road up ahead. "Turn here," she said and unbuckled her seatbelt as he followed her directions and turned into a wide driveway. They had arrived at Lewis's house and she knew it … she had been here once before, as she had said.

She hopped from the car the moment he stopped.

"Goodbye, Michael." She ran lightly up the steps and didn't look back.

He watched the door open, narrowing his eyes to see better as she stepped inside, head bowed. He couldn't make out who had opened the door, and it was quickly shut again. Sitting in the car, the engine idling, he took in the front of the house. Its private driveway off the road marked out Lewis's wealth. It looked old, its brickwork faded, mature ivy growing thick on the front walls. He assumed it was a family house, probably where Lewis himself had grown up.

With a heavy sigh, he turned the car and left her behind.

It was only when he was halfway back into town that Michael realised he hadn't taken the turn off to drop the car back at the warehouse. But he was near the Banks Hotel. He drove faster than he should, eager to find a parking space. The first available was a few streets away and he swung the car into it. Then he walked quickly back to the hotel. He wasn't sure what he was doing, or why, but he kept walking, his head bowed under his father's flat cap.

Across the street from the hotel was a bar he had noticed earlier. He found a seat near the window and ordered a beer. It lasted him two whole hours. The head had gone flat and it tasted sour by the time she returned. Ignoring ill-tempered stares from the barman, he watched her step from a taxi, her red coat distinctive under the lights from the hotel entrance. She pulled her bag and a small black suitcase from the back seat of the taxi and walked quickly through the hotel's revolving doors, disappearing into the lobby.

Michael stayed in his seat, swirling the last drop of beer in circles, thinking. Who was she? What was in the bag? It was light, she had lifted it easily. She had said her father was a business associate of Mr Lewis but he knew there was no business in the Soviet Union on the company's books. He wondered if her meeting with Lewis had had anything to do with the man's changed mood. And he was curious as to how Bob knew her exact room number at the hotel ... Yelena was beautiful, yes, but that didn't quite explain why he felt so drawn to her. Was it her vulnerability? Certainly, the fact that she seemed nervous about visiting Lewis's house had intrigued him.

He had so many questions.

13

Cork, 2019

"Don't you think you've had enough, my love?"

Tom gently prised the glass of whiskey from his wife's hand. Sitting still, she offered no protest as he took it, her glazed eyes staring into the distance. When he touched her skin, she slowly turned to look at him. Her face was puffy and lined, red spider-web veins tracked across her cheeks. She rested one hand on the arm of the chair, and as she raised the other to touch his face, it shook violently.

"This can't go on, Mae," he said softly. "You're drinking yourself to death."

The only other sound in the room was the clicking mantel clock. It amplified each passing second as she gathered the strength to speak. He had to lean closer to hear the rasp of her voice.

"You promised me. You said you'd find her."

With a sinking feeling, he knew who she was referring to. Kate Crowley. He understood her obsession, he felt it himself – the woman had killed their son and robbed from him. From them all. She had a debt to repay, a life for a life, in his opinion.

"I'm doing everything I can, my love. I've found her friend, the woman who helped her when she was hiding from us. After she ... after she killed David. This friend can help us. And I have people working on tracing her from Paris. I'll have information on her exact whereabouts soon. I promise you it won't be long! She'll pay for David's death, and we'll take back the girls too. Wouldn't you like that, Mae? Our granddaughters here in this house?"

She smiled, a faint twitch of the muscles of her mouth, but it was enough for him. She didn't protest when he suggested bed. When he lifted her from the seat, he stifled a sob at how light she was. She had lost so much weight. When had she last eaten a meal? He would ask their housekeeper Jessica – in fact, he would task her with keeping a closer eye on his wife. The idea of a rehabilitation facility popped into his mind from time to time, but he knew his wife would never forgive him, would consider it an indignity not to resolve their own problems privately. *He* would have to be the one to help her.

After he had settled her into bed, Tom stormed downstairs. Room by room he purged the house of alcohol, bottles clinking in the bin bag he carried. He stuffed the bag into the outside bin, punching it down and slamming the lid. His knuckles hurt and anger still vibrated through him. With clenched fists he gazed at the stars, the cold air prickling his bare arms and neck. Their bright lights pierced the dark sky, pinpoints scattered in patterns he knew were constellations but meant nothing to him. Lighting a cigarette from the packet in his pocket, he sucked on it and watched the exhaled vapour fade into the sky. There was something soothing in the way it twisted in the breeze and evaporated.

Somewhere, Kate Crowley could be watching the very same sky as him. She could be gazing at the night stars with her sister and nieces, his granddaughters, never knowing all the ways he was plotting his revenge. Killing her was the only way to repair the damage she had done, and to heal his wife. And, if he was honest, to heal himself.

The chill of the night made him shiver, and he welcomed the discomfort of it – he felt alive. Rousing himself, he walked to the front of the property, approaching the two security men stationed at his electric gates from behind, slowly and quietly. Inside the small wooden security hut, one man flicked through a magazine with disinterest, the other stared into the nothingness of the road in front of the house. They didn't realise he was watching them, assessing them. The men were new – replacements after the regular guys were killed by the Meiers last year, their throats cut and bodies dumped in the hallway of the house as a warning.

In Tom's mind it had all started with Kate – she stole the memory key that brought the Meiers to Cork in search of it, that caused them to torture John until Tom was forced to act. Dealings with the Meiers had come to a pleasing end: they were history now. But still, David was dead, and John … John appeared unchanged by what he had suffered and by the death of his brother. *Unaffected.* The thought troubled Tom and he angrily flicked away his cigarette.

Kate Crowley would be found, and dealt with, and he would repair his family if it killed him.

Ely Murray pressed harder, grinding the leather sole of his boot into the soft flesh of the kid's neck. The guy writhing on the ground couldn't be more than seventeen: skinny, with a shaved head and a ratty moustache, one eyebrow pierced, and the word *"Nan"* tattooed on his wrist. He twisted and turned, thin hands pushing uselessly at the boot, his terrified eyes bulging around the red veins bursting inside them. Ely was tired of asking questions that yielded no answers. His impatience pulsated from him to the walls around the small garage workshop.

"Where did you get the gear from?" He released the pressure on the kid's neck a fraction – he wanted him to talk.

Gasping, desperately drawing for precious air – "He'll kill me!"

"No, *I'll* kill you!"

"Please! If I tell you anything I'm dead!" The kid on the ground began to cry, curling into a foetal position on the concrete floor.

Ely turned to his men, four of them positioned around the room, with an almost helpless expression.

"What the fuck am I to do here? This kid here is selling coke he didn't get from me. From any of us! Selling on *our* streets, without even so much as a by-your-leave." He kicked the kid in the stomach.

Moaning and coughing filled the room.

Ely's rage had been replaced by confusion – who was supplying drugs on the Cork streets without Gallagher's say-so? Who was the kid so terrified of that he would rather be beaten to a pulp than talk? This was the type of fear Tom Gallagher used to instil, or rather John Gallagher when he had involved himself in his father's business. These days John amused himself in his room with his porn or video games, Ely didn't care what. But he *did* care that the business he had been a member of for thirty years was beginning to crumble around him, and none of the Gallaghers seemed in any fit state to do anything about it.

His mobile rang in his pocket and he yanked it out, turning away from the kid, who was sobbing now. Ely recognised the number – a garda. His source.

"What?"

"I have the information you looked for – about the girl?"

"Go on."

"A word of warning – she's one of us."

"She's on the force?"

"Clerical staff. I wouldn't touch her."

"For fuck sake, that's hardly –"

"She's capable too. I really wouldn't go there with this girl. Whatever Gallagher needs, she won't have it."

"I'll decide that!"

"One other thing. The gardaí have never been able to touch Tom Gallagher but, with what David was involved in last year, the detectives are working through mounds of information from a personal laptop and phone. They know what David was up to, and all about Alan Ainsley as well. The spotlight is going to shine on Gallagher's business soon, and there'll be nothing he can do to escape this time. I thought you'd appreciate the warning."

"Give me a minute."

Ely took the phone from his ear and rubbed his hand through his hair. He wondered what Tom would make of this information. The pursuit of Kate Crowley was his driving force now. Ely's respect for the man was being whittled away by his dogged hunt for a woman that was long gone.

The teenager on the ground, crawling now to a corner of the garage, was proof that Tom had been too quiet of late. Men were invading his city, and nothing was being done to stop it. Ely knew Tom was shielding John, trying to appease his wife by keeping him off the streets. That needed to change, fast! Now, the girl he wanted was Garda staff and his source was right – she was best left untouched. But perhaps if Tom Gallagher exorcised this particular demon he could get back to business …

"You still there?" He returned to his source.

"Yeah."

"The girl. Give me her details. And anything else you've got."

He ended the call, knowing her details would light up his phone screen shortly. The garda was too far down the hole he had dug for himself to ever wriggle out and would do what he was told. Pocketing his phone, he returned his attention to the teenage drug dealer who was about to squeal like his life depended on it.

14

The woman had expected Marian Selway to be younger – she certainly looked a lot older in the flesh than in her brochure photo. But she took care of her appearance. Her smile in greeting was dazzling white, her make-up subtle, every short hair in place. She constantly touched a string of pearls around her neck with one hand, a nervous tic perhaps. In a cream trouser suit and high black heels, she looked every inch the marketing executive. Her eyes were curious, but not yet suspicious.

Suspicion would come, but by then it would be too late.

The couple in front of Marian looked … unusual. She remembered the woman's name from the brief glance she had given the slip of paper the receptionist had left on her desk – *Miss Hyde* – but she couldn't remember the man's, and he didn't offer it.

"Welcome to the Rebel Event Centre, Miss Hyde and …?" She left the sentence open, waiting for an introduction, but he didn't turn to look at her.

"Oh, call me Jacquelyn!" The woman shook her hand delicately, her eyes roaming the vast entrance hall of the event centre.

The man beside her kept his head to the side, gazing out the window, with one hand gripped around the handle of a carrier bag. He didn't speak, but his companion seemed unable to stop. Marian moved further into the building and they followed, Jacquelyn Hyde's voice echoing loudly in the spacious atrium as she followed. They were event organisers from a company in London, she said. Over to scout out possible locations for a celebrity wedding. Their clients wanted complete confidentiality, and to have their ceremony in the bride's birthplace. Cost was not a consideration. Marian thought it unusual they hadn't given her more notice – normally such people were very organised, lining up tours well in advance. This seemed a bit spur-of-the-moment, but she decided to go with it – if she secured a celebrity wedding the Rebel Event Centre would be placed securely on the VIP map. The receptionist had taken the scantest of details about the booking, as usual, and as she didn't work weekends had left the rest to Marian. This was the last thing she wanted to spend her Saturday doing and hoped it wouldn't take too long.

The couple intrigued her though – the woman wore a fur coat, fake in Marian's opinion, and lots of badly applied make-up: bright-red lipstick and heavily kohled eyes. Her exuberance more than made up for her companion's quietness. He wore a dark coat and trousers, with a baseball hat pulled low, and looked like the woman's minder, not her colleague. What she *could* see of his face was extremely pale. The skin around his jaw and neck sagged grotesquely, as though scarred and puckered. His very presence unnerved her.

115

Marian had a strange sensation that the hall was closing in around her as the woman's posh English accent billowed in the space, bouncing off the white tiles and chrome finishes.

"It's chilly in here!" The woman clutched her fur coat around her neck theatrically, brushing aside her long red hair.

"Yes," Marian smiled. She was feeling more uncertain with each passing second. Her eyes lingered on the woman's hair for a moment too long – there was no way such a vibrant gloss was real. She smiled quickly, pulling her gaze from the woman's garishly painted red mouth.

"Without the crowd the centre is built for, it can get cold, especially in winter. Most of the external walls are of thick glass, which makes the building quite hot in the summer but a little cold in the winter, I'm afraid!"

"How many bodies does the centre hold?"

"Bodies?" Marian paused, then laughed uneasily. "We can cater for groups of up to one thousand. We've some big musical acts lined up for the summer and tickets are sold out already!" She had begun her sales pitch and briefly felt more relaxed with the familiar spiel. But her eyes flicked to the man continuously, nervously.

The woman calling herself Jacquelyn Hyde ran her tongue along her thick coat of red lipstick. Marian suddenly felt like a small, weak animal cautiously eyeing a larger predator on the food chain.

"One thousand! Well, that's just perfect – our client has a guest list of seven hundred. But today it's just three?"

Marian's fingers flitted to the string of pearls again. "Yes, just us today. Let's begin the tour." She turned away and walked briskly to the middle of the atrium, her heels clicking on the cream tiles. She glanced nervously at the man's lowered face, then down to the carrier bag in his hand – he really didn't look very professional – but she was resolved to get this tour over with quickly. Pausing in the middle of the large open atrium at a marble sculpture depicting two men holding sticks in the air, she returned to her dependable marketing pitch.

"This statue was commissioned specially as homage to Cork's great hurling achievements. The sticks you see there are called hurleys and you can see one of the players is holding a ball – that's called a sliotar. The sculpture really draws the eye, wouldn't you agree? It would be quite a feature in any wedding photos!"

The woman nodded enthusiastically and pulled a small handheld video recorder from her bag.

"You don't mind? It would help my client to get a feel for the place," she said sweetly, her eyes large and innocent, fake eyelashes fluttering.

Marian *did* mind but she didn't object. She nodded, her eyes finding the man again, her nervousness spiralling. He didn't look at the sculpture but continued to stand with his head lowered, his demeanour one of complete disinterest.

Marian squared her shoulders and smiled brightly, the effort of it concealed.

They followed Marian to the foot of the staircase on the left of the atrium, the glass wall showing little traffic on the road beyond the car park. As they ascended, Marian talked non-stop. She turned around occasionally to speak directly to the couple, but only the woman engaged in the conversation, her video camera held aloft in her arm. The man's head stayed low, only the top of his baseball cap visible to her. At the top of the stairs, she strode forward, on carpet this time, the sound of her heels muffled by the soft wool.

"Here is our hospitality suite. We have a long bar as you can see here, with capacity to serve food to eighty patrons in one sitting. The restrooms are along the side there," her arms gestured to guide their view, "and our wedding venue is through to the left. Would you like to …"

Her voice trailed off and she stared in jaw-dropping, undisguised horror. The man had taken his baseball cap off and raised his head. His face looked … melted and then reshaped, muscles sagging, flesh clumsily piled around bones. There were no eyes – in the space where the eyes should have been, there were deep indents the same colour as skin, as though the eyelids had been sealed closed. The lips were pale and barely distinguishable from the rest of his face – they looked sewn together by invisible thread, pressed and distorted into a grotesque shape, like rotting flesh held in place. As she stared in muted shock, a dark stain spread from the crotch of Marian's cream trousers down her leg.

The sound of laughter startled her and she spun to face the woman, who had moved to stand behind her, camera raised to eye-level. The woman was laughing so hard she had trouble keeping her hand steady, so gripped the camera now with both hands. Tears of laughter rolled down her cheeks, and she let them fall – they made her eyes a chilling, watery blue stare. Black mascara lines halved her face and her wide, red mouth hung open. She looked like a monster.

Something glinted in the light of Marian's peripheral vision – a knife. The longest blade she had ever seen. The man stepped towards her, and Marian's screams were lost in the manic laughter of the woman who just managed to keep the camera steady.

Later, he drew his own blood by scouring his skin to the point it tore off. He let Marian Selway's blood and flesh mingle with his own and wash away in the hotel-room shower, scrubbing his body to a state beyond raw, to a state of pain so intense it brought relief. The heat of the water was almost as unbearable as the feeling of her speckles of flesh. He had washed the death mask already, his father's face. Finally, he felt clean.

The woman was sitting in front of her laptop at the desk in their hotel bedroom. Every so often she erupted into giggles, but when she heard the flow of water end she did her best to suppress them. She suspected it bothered him.

He stepped onto the carpeted floor of the bedroom and she smiled radiantly. His bare skin looked so red and raw it repulsed her slightly. But his eyes were sated, calmer than they had been in days. When she spoke, he noted she wasn't yet done with the English accent.

"Shall we go for dinner?" she asked brightly.

15

"Where's John?"

Tom Gallagher raised his head at the sound of Ely Murray's voice. His man, Marco, shifted his bulk in the seat and stood up, stepping slightly in front of his boss. The message was silent yet loud and clear, and Ely raised his palms to Marco in appeasement. He had no desire to start a fight.

Tom was standing at the bar of his club, the Oracle. It would open in an hour and he was doing his customary walk-through. He was a man who liked his staff to know his face. Now, he eyed a new barmaid as she polished glasses at the other end of the bar.

"What do you want, Murray?"

"We have a problem."

Tom dragged his eyes away from the girl and focused on the man in front of him. Ely was ageing, balding, the scar that ran from his ear to his lip sagging a little. No sign of a paunch though – he was keeping himself in shape.

Tom drew himself up to full height and squared his shoulders.

"I pay you to deal with problems. Is there something you can't handle?"

Ely's eyes narrowed. "I usually have John to ... assist. Is he still 'resting' or is he planning to get back in the game?"

"Is there something you want to say, Murray?"

The venom in his voice gave Ely pause – he needed to proceed with this carefully. He changed tack.

"I caught a young fella selling on *your* streets. Only we didn't supply him. So, you're not getting a look-in. He won't say a single word. We're holding him, giving him a chance to change his mind. But he's too *scared* to talk. This has never happened before, Tom! The guy's too scared of his supplier to talk to us! We need John back on the streets! Word has got out that he's stepped back, and fellas are getting cocky now that John Gallagher isn't around to keep them on the straight and narrow!"

Tom stepped behind the long wooden bar and poured two shots from a bottle of Jameson whiskey. He slid Ely's across the bar, and the man downed it one gulp. Tom savoured his, swirling the liquid around the glass, holding it to the light briefly before taking a sip. His lips pursed around the heat of the whiskey as he considered his words.

"John is chomping at the bit, but in truth he needs more time. Losing David has had a terrible effect on Mae and, well, John suffered terribly." He pointed a finger at Ely, anger charging his voice. "You were there when John's finger was delivered in a cardboard box! They hacked it off! You know what it did to Mae, seeing that! And the night we saved John ..." Tom's voice trailed off, his eyes darting to Marco. "When Marco pulled John from the boot of the Meier's jeep he was barely alive! Beaten like a dog, mutilated ..." His hand clenched around the glass and he clamped his lips shut to quell the tremor in his voice. A deep breath steadied him. "All because of that bitch Kate Crowley!"

Ely shook his head. *Back to this again!*

"What have you got on that girl? The one who helped her," Tom demanded, his eyes blazing.

"Did you not hear what I just told you! Another dealer is supplying the streets! In *your* city! And you still want to go after –"

"Just tell me what you found out!" Tom's teeth were clenched around his words in a warning Ely knew better than to ignore.

The barmaid had set down the glass and now moved away from the end of the counter to safer territory. Ely sighed, resigned, and rested his hands on the bar.

"She's Garda staff. We might need to reconsider this – it could bring too much heat. Also, my man inside told me there's trouble coming your way – the investigation into David's death and his dealings with the stolen data have given the gardaí more information on your business than they've had in years. I'm told they're looking into your affairs and are doing everything they can to bring a case against you."

"Looking into my affairs?" Tom repeated, veins bulging in his reddening neck. "When they can't even find the woman that shot my son!" He downed the remains of his whiskey but gripped the glass a while longer, deep in thought. "Finish the kid. Make it public – leave him on the street to send a message to whoever supplied him. And I want that message heard loud and clear! But I also want that girl, Murray! Garda staff or not, she involved herself in David's death and tried to help *her*, and I want to know why! You got that? If she knows where Crowley is then we'll make her talk."

He left Ely standing in the bar, Marco hot on his heels like a faithful guard dog.

As they pulled into traffic, Marco glanced back from the driver's seat.

"You really think this girl is the key to finding Kate Crowley?"

Tom shrugged, keeping his eyes on the streets in front of him.

"Perhaps it's time John got more involved ... just saying."

The heat of Tom's glare was so intense Marco imagined it could burn a hole in the back of his head. He decided to keep his counsel to himself and concentrate on the road.

Once the car had pulled away from the kerb Ely strode purposefully through the bar and into the office. He had keys both to the door and the safe, and enough confidence in his stride to evoke no questions – he was *supposed* to be in the boss's office while he was out. Once inside, he locked the door and unlocked the safe. He counted the contents: two hundred thousand euro in bound stacks of notes, mostly small bills. He exhaled deeply. So much money... so much potential for more. Yet someone was muscling in, threatening to destroy all they had achieved. He couldn't shake the idea that the Gallagher business was sinking, and he refused to be dragged down with it.

One thing he could do to stem the disintegration was to facilitate revenge for David's death. And that meant finding the girl and bringing her to Tom. He resolved to do just that, Garda staff or not – he could placate the boss and at the same time quench the flame of embarrassment the memory of her ignited in him.

He left the office, careful to leave everything just as it had been.

John was sitting alone in his room. He knew his father was at the club. He should be there too, but his father insisted he take his time in getting back out there. John had eventually agreed, even though the need to be in the thick of things was itching like a scab waiting to be scratched. The men that worked for the Gallagher business respected him – at least they did before the attack by the Meiers, and he was sure nothing had changed. But they needed to see his face. Front and centre, handling things. This had formed the basis of his argument with his father.

"Let me be involved!"

"There's no need to rush back. Ely has everything under control."

"At least let me handle the girl. I can find her and sort that."

"No, son. Give yourself time. You promised your mother – she couldn't take it if anything happened to you too."

The argument had raged, over and over, and in the end it was his mother's cold hand over his that stayed his rising temper.

In a way, he understood. David was dead … their tight circle had been breached and one of them was dead. In the days after the attack by the Meiers he had felt vulnerable and, for the first time in his life, weak. It was uncomfortable to realise how easily the gang had ambushed him. He barely remembered the details of the torture, just his fear when the door to the room they had kept him in opened and he heard the heavy footfall towards the chair they had tied him to.

But he was *made* for this life. He had served his apprenticeship on the streets and was ready to go back. His body was healing and his mind was clear. Only his parents tethered him. He decided to indulge them a little while more. After all, there were businesses to explore other than the empire his father had built up.

His bedroom was as dark as night, and he had no idea what time it was, or when he had last eaten. None of that mattered. He drummed his fingers on the small table and clicked into his emails, reading with a growing interest. His new business venture was advancing – it was unchartered territory for him, and he doubted his father would be interested. But it was profitable, and it made him feel alive. Mostly, it drove the memories of those days tied to a chair in a cold farmhouse out of his head for a while. Certainly, it was a useful pastime until his mother relented and eased the pressure to stay in safer territory.

He felt sweat on his palms and he wiped them on his jeans, then pushed the stump of flesh on his finger over and over. He felt a stirring inside him, a growing excitement, and he unzipped his fly …

His eyes darted to his bedroom door. A noise – a creak on the floorboards outside.

His mother.

The time had come to leave this stifling house. Big as the property was, he needed privacy.

16

Myles took over the space in Anna's small house with such ease it was as if he was moulded into it. His clothes slotted into the wardrobe as though they had always been there. The space between the sofa and the coffee table in her living room was the perfect size for him to stretch out his leg. He already had a favourite mug in the kitchen and didn't try to reorganise her 'junk drawer' when searching for the backdoor key. It was as though he'd lived there forever.

She had never invited a boyfriend to stay before and had been apprehensive about bringing him so firmly into her space – since Alex had married Samantha and moved out six years ago, she had lived alone. She had thought she liked it that way, but the sense of independence she had once enjoyed had morphed into a crushing loneliness. Solitude was sapping her soul.

Yet she had still worried about bringing Myles here. Perhaps being alone for so long had made her set in her ways? Last year she had realised how routine and ordered her life was – cutting off her long hair had been a drastic step to make a change. She had wondered if this weekend was a change too far.

Quickly she realised she needn't have worried. Myles accepted her invitation to make himself at home and blended into her life seamlessly. And she laughed more than she had in ages. He was funny, in his commentary on things, his observations on life and his place in it. She enjoyed talking to him about every topic that came up. He listened to her opinions, and on most things they shared the same outlook. The rise and fall of their conversation filled the house and chased away the silence, and she loved every second of it.

On Friday night they had dinner in Kinsale, followed by a slow walk around the winding streets in the bracing wind. Electricity fizzed in her when he held her hand. Every time he kissed her, she felt her love for him rush through her. The power of the emotion took her by surprise – she knew they were moving fast but it felt right. For the first time in what felt like a very long time, she thought of nothing but the moment at hand.

On Saturday morning she woke before sunrise, her body clock accustomed to rising early. Usually, she and Jason trained for over an hour. But this morning, she didn't want to leave Myles' side.

She lay beside him, watching him sleep in the half-light of the rising sun, steadying her breath. She had dreamed of that night again ... the nightmare tormented her, disturbing sleep, her heart pounding in panic upon waking. Seeing him beside her she felt instantly calmer. He lay on his side, bare-chested, arms crossed in front of him, his long dark eyelashes resting on his sallow skin and his curls fanned out on the pillow. With a shaking hand she traced a scar on the flesh of his upper arm – still pink, it was fading, and would be a silvery starflower shape before long. The bullet wound – the first gunshot. Anna knew his walking stick was somewhere near the bedroom door. He planned to discard it as soon as his physiotherapist allowed. Her heart tightened as she watched him sleep. Just as she had found him, he had almost been taken away.

Rain poured heavily all day, a continuous downpour that lashed the windows. The accompanying wind whipped and screamed around the house. Anna usually found days like this depressing and claustrophobic – hours lined up one after the other with only boredom to fill them. But with Myles here, it was entirely different. She felt peace settle over her as the day wore on. They cooked while listening to music and made easy conversation as they ate.

In the afternoon Anna lit the stove and they settled on the sofa, books in their laps, Myles' leg propped up on the coffee table. As evening wore on and darkness settled, he prepared a pizza in the kitchen while she selected a movie. Watching him lay food onto plates at the kitchen table she marvelled at how happy she felt. Happy and at peace. She realised she hadn't felt the throbbing pulse of a migraine in the time he'd been here. Somehow he managed to cast light all around her, chasing away the shadows. She felt safe.

As he chatted from the kitchen she rose to draw the curtains, not noticing the car parked at the kerb across from the house, nor the man sitting watching her, the scar from his ear to his lip marring his face.

* * *

128

On Sunday morning Alex texted at dawn, Anna's mobile phone vibrating on the bedside locker. She snatched it up. Myles was breathing deeply, lost in slumber. Her heart skipped a beat as she read the message – she had almost succeeded in pushing her brother and their disagreement from her mind since Myles' arrival Friday night.

Anna, I'm sorry we argued. Can I call this evening after Myles leaves? Obviously, we need to talk.

Tears filled her eyes and she quickly typed a reply, relief flooding her.

I'm sorry too, I shouldn't have left like that! I'm dropping Myles to the train station later and will be home by 6. Call any time after.

His reply came quickly but made her frown.

Sam is working today. I'll call as soon as she's home.

Working, on a Sunday? This was a first. For months Samantha had been working overtime in the evenings, but never at the weekend. Anna felt uneasy about it, yet knew it wasn't really any of her business. She replied with a 'thumbs-up' emoji and snuggled closer to Myles.

After lunch she drove them to Garrettstown beach. The last time Myles had been here he had surfed the swell of the waves, not perturbed by the bracing November cold. Now that was out of the question. It was dry but still windy, and they were wrapped in heavy scarves and winter coats, sitting on a low wall. As he watched the waves surge and roll she studied his face, finding his expression impossible to read.

"Do you miss it? Surfing, I mean. Are you sorry we came here?"

He shook his head. "Seeing the water again makes me

more determined! The next time I stay I'm bringing my surfboard." He kissed her ear and she rested her head against his shoulder. "That's assuming I'll be invited again?"

"How could you even ask! You're the perfect house guest. You don't snore and you make a great pizza! What more could a woman want? And the next time you stay, I must show you my mother's cello ..."

She had decided not to mention her parents during Myles' visit – she didn't want him to think she was hinting for his help. He had already shed so much light, yet it had cast her parents into darkness. Still, she felt that she had held something back from him by not showing him their photographs or playing her mother's favourite music.

"That'd be nice," he said slowly. "I saw their photos on the wall in the hall ... you look very like your mother. You and Alex have your dad's brown eyes though."

Anna turned to look out to sea, into the foaming waves.

"I'm sorry I can't help any further, Anna." His voice was soft. "There's really nothing more I can do. Not on any official files anyway, because it seems as though Yelena Vasilieva no longer exists. After she disappeared from London there's no trace of her. Online of course is another angle and we could –"

She kissed him to silence him – they had been through this. She had already assured him she knew he had done what he could, and she had no desire to get him into trouble at work.

Over the weekend he had explained that he worked in the Crime and Security Branch in Phoenix Park, in Garda headquarters in Dublin. Not long after they first met, he had told her that his skills in I.T., namely hacking, had brought him to Garda attention, and he was *encouraged* to join the force, as he put it. She knew his job involved intelligence analysis, and that he had been undercover when he was in Cork. He kept the exact details of his job private, and after serious deliberation on issues of trust, she had decided to accept that. One day he would fill her in properly and, until then, she cared about the man, not about his position in the force.

When he had brought the newspaper articles about her mother to her, she'd had so many questions but quickly realised he couldn't answer them. Not because he needed to protect his job – but because he didn't have the information. Even with his talent and position, he could only access certain files. Others were sealed, and that was not an area where he was prepared to flex his computer skills to access what she needed. She remained infuriatingly in the dark, but there was nothing more he could do.

He had explained that he had first accessed the Garda report concerning Michael and Helen Clarke's car accident. Next, he had read the file from the Missing Persons Bureau. He told Anna all had been as it should, just as he had expected: a thorough investigation, but no survivors found. No bodies, either. He had remembered Anna telling him her parents were English and moved to Ireland shortly before she was born. So, he attempted to dig a little further. This involved calling in a favour from an old college friend who now worked for the Met Police in London. He in turn put Myles in touch with a contact, who then stopped the search in its tracks.

The implication of this was something Myles had decided not to discuss with Anna. A sealed file, classified information … he wasn't told the specifics, but it further burdened the mystery. All he had was a name, and an online search led to newspaper articles that detailed the case of a missing cellist, giving some background information on her family. Anna's reaction to the article's photographs had confirmed he had found the right person, but the full truth remained unknown. She had told him of her argument with her brother, of his desire to let the past lie where it was ... Myles couldn't help but feel it would be safer for Anna if she felt the same.

17

Saying goodbye to Myles at the train station hurt Anna more than she had expected it to. To distract herself on the drive home, she began to plan how she would search for her mother's family online, if there were any still alive. Myles had offered to help, but she wanted to do this herself. She had already scratched the surface of the search, but held off probing deeper until now, hoping it would be something she and Alex would do together. She was relieved he was planning to call but she didn't hold out any hope that it would be to search for more information on Yelena Vasilieva. More likely it would be to clear the air. And perhaps convince her to let it go.

So, she decided, she would begin the search herself.

Myles' revelation that her mother was a promising cellist who disappeared from the orchestra in London in 1978 was the sliver of information that she focused on now. There were many newspaper articles covering it. The disappearance of a woman always drew media attention, especially one from a foreign country. She still considered it a possibility that her mother could have been a spy, despite what her brother said – after all, she had consciously decided not to return home to what was then the Soviet Union, at a time when defections were more frequent. She felt sure the internet would be a "fountain of information", as Vivian had put it, yet perhaps only from the perspective of the UK press. She wondered if Soviet newspaper articles from that time were available online. Even if her search yielded nothing of value it would pass the time until Alex arrived.

The streets in her housing estate were almost empty, most cars parked in their driveways. The rain had started again in earnest, and she imagined families clustered around TV sets, squeezing the last of the weekend in with their loved ones before careers and school took them apart again the following day. Letting herself into her house, Anna swallowed a lump in her throat, her response at the vast emptiness of her small home. Myles had quieted the deafening roar of the silence that stalked the space.

By ten o'clock she had begun to hope Alex wouldn't call over. Her eyes stung and her back ached but the hours of searching had yielded the name of a woman she felt certain was her aunt, her mother's sister. She didn't want to share the news with him just yet, didn't know how he would feel about it, and she didn't want him to stifle her growing excitement. Desire to keep searching flared in her and, despite wanting to repair the damage from their argument, she dared to hope he wouldn't show up.

But he did arrive. Anna shivered in the cold draft as she ushered him in – at the sight of the dark-grey Audi parked at the kerb opposite, a thought flickered and died. Alex's brow was lined with deep creases as he muttered a greeting. He shrugged off his coat and accepted her offer of coffee, despite the late hour. He lowered himself onto the sofa, the worn brown leather creaking slightly. She had lit the stove and the glow of the flames warmed the room.

He always felt instantly at ease in the house that was once his childhood home, and as the minutes passed he relaxed, his mood brightening. His sister had kept the structure of the house the same after he moved out, but had redecorated, and he loved the new feel of the house. Her bookcases were still in place, one on either side of the fireplace, every shelf bursting with books. Anna's taste was eclectic – she read everything from Jane Austin to J.R.R. Tolkien. Books on mathematics and statistics were wedged among the literary classics, her chosen educational path merged seamlessly with her recreational reading. Their father's record player still had pride of place on the deepest shelf, his record collection alongside it. Anna had found a lot of her furniture in flea markets and second-hand stores, and they blended together in a mismatched cosy way. He admired her style. She kept a collage of family photos in the hallway by the front door, the family of four posing at the beach and around a Christmas tree, always smiling. He thought of his parents every time he stepped inside the house.

"So," Anna began, hating that her heartrate was spiking nervously, "again, I'm sorry about the other night."

Alex smiled and it was tinged with sadness. "Yeah, me too." The argument between them needed no more discussion. He sipped the coffee she had given him before perching the mug on the small table between them.

"Sorry I'm so late. Sam was working until half an hour ago." He ran his hands over his short blond hair, his eyes downcast. "She's doing so much overtime and seems kind of distant. If I wasn't such a trusting kind of guy, I'd think she was having an affair!" He laughed a little, but it was forced, weak.

"Don't say that!" Anna felt alarm curling inside her – Samantha had never given her brother cause to doubt their relationship. But she had never stayed so late at work before either. For weeks.

He shrugged helplessly.

She noticed he had brought a carrier bag with him, and she eyed it with interest, keen to distract from the air of despair around him. Motioning to the bag, she smiled. "Did you come bearing gifts?"

"More of a peace offering!"

He pulled a bronze trophy from the bag. About twelve inches tall, it depicted a man in martial art clothing, cast in mid-kick. Anna's breath caught in her throat.

"Remember this? Dad won it when you were about ten." He passed the trophy to her, looking away from the tears in her eyes.

"Oh my God!" She held it aloft, turning it in the light. "I *do* remember this! Dad was thrilled with himself!"

"Remember we went out for chicken wings after? And Mum was a little tipsy by the time we got home!"

They laughed softly together. The memory was a happy one but mingled with sadness.

Anna went to hand it back but Alex shook his head.

"You keep it for a while."

Resting it beside her father's record player on the bookshelf, she felt emotion bubbling inside her. She returned to the armchair, blinking tears away quickly, folding her legs beneath her.

"I also found this." He pulled a business card from his pocket and passed it across to her in the armchair. She read it with interest.

"Who's Robert Evans?" On the small cream business card was the man's name, a phone number, and a PO Box number in London. Her eyes grew wide with the realisation of who had given Alex this card. "Dad's friend Bob gave you this! Right after they disappeared!"

The man had been a stranger to them but spoke of their parents as if he was an old friend. He had sympathised with them, asking if there was anything he could do. He had also told them of a trust fund their father had set up a long time ago, of which he was trustee. He had facilitated the transfer of money and disappeared from their lives again.

"Have you tried the number again?" She spoke in a rush, her excitement uncontained. Anna knew Alex had tried the number over and over years ago, but the call had never been answered. Life took over, and eventually trying to contact Bob Evans stopped being a priority.

"I tried it again today. It's disconnected."

Her shoulders slumping, Anna stared into the orange glow of the stove. An idea crackled for attention.

"Could we find out anything from the post office box?"

But Alex merely frowned. "I've no idea how to go about checking if it's still in his name. I mean, it's ten years ago. Privacy laws are different now to what they were – I doubt we can just phone up and start asking questions."

"I guess you're right. I really don't remember much about him." Suddenly sitting up, she was excited. "The trust fund! There must have been a paper trail at the time!"

Even as she said the words Anna knew it was pointless to think anything new could be learned now. If there was anything to find out, her brother would have done it ten years ago.

He ran a hand over his face, pulling at the skin of his cheeks, his stubble rasping beneath his fingers. Exhaustion was etched in the lines around his eyes and in the pallor of his skin.

"I've been over every document I still have in the house – there's nothing."

Anna remembered the feeling of utter shock at learning her father had amassed a trust fund of five-hundred thousand euro. They hadn't lived as if that much money was tucked away. She knew her father had an accountancy firm in the city, but they had lived a normal life.

"You know, I still don't buy it," Alex said. "Bob Evans turning up like that was weird and suspicious at the time, and it still is."

Alex remembered the feeling of unease the man had evoked, but he had spoken about Michael Clarke with enough knowledge and familiarity that Alex believed him, telling stories about their time in London, about Michael's love of martial arts and proficiency in bookkeeping. Then, when the trust fund money came through, everything seemed legit. Alex had had an accountancy degree to finish and a teenage sister to look after … Bob had faded from his mind.

"Do you think Myles could have a look at the card, see what turns up? He found the newspaper articles about Mum." He shrugged. "It's just an idea."

Anna nodded enthusiastically, the relief that her brother was on board with the search for information chasing away her earlier tiredness. He'd had a complete attitude change since last Thursday night. "Myles said he'd help in any way he could! I'll send a photo of it to him now. Fingers crossed he finds *something*."

As she tapped on her mobile phone, they fell into silence again, each lost in their own thoughts, the only sound the spit and crackle of the logs in the stove.

Anna picked up her mug and drank slowly as the memories of that time flashed in her mind. She found the heat from the mug grounded her, preventing her memories from flooding her emotions.

"Five-hundred thousand euro though! I never had a clue Dad had that kind of money."

"To be honest, now that time has passed and I've thought about it, I don't think he really did. Dad was careful with money – the mortgage was paid on this house, but other than that they didn't have much in the way of assets."

Anna didn't remember any of this. She had been sixteen, grieving, lost in the mystery surrounding her parents' disappearance. The finer details of their day-to-day lives and cleaning up the mess the two adults left behind, had been left to her brother. While she had cried in her room or stayed in this living room by the telephone, waiting for news, he had dealt with every aspect of the disappearance. At twenty-six, she was just one year older now than her brother had been when he'd had so much despair and responsibility thrust upon him. She wondered how she might cope in the same situation.

"A few months after the accident I met the other employees of Dad's practice. There was one other accountant and a receptionist. The accountant was happy to take over. I examined the books as best I could – he gave me everything he had. The business was ticking over and not making a loss but was by no means making a fortune. He paid a fair price to take over the business and I was happy to let him do it – one less thing to worry about, to be honest. But there was very little money in the business bank account." He leaned forward, looking at her intently. "To be perfectly honest, Anna, it doesn't add up, literally!"

"So where did the money come from? And why would Robert Evans lie about it?"

He could only shrug.

"You and Mum and Dad moved here when I was a baby," Anna said.

"Just before you were born."

"And you don't remember anyone else significant from your time living in England?"

"A couple of kids here and there, from school and that, but no-one stands out. As I've told you, Mum and Dad kept to themselves."

He resumed drinking his coffee, sitting back into the sofa cushions. Chatting with his sister in front of the blazing stove was comforting, familiar. Despite the topic at hand.

"And you still don't want to consider that Mum being a spy is an option we should take seriously?"

The look he gave her left Anna in no doubt about how he felt about that line of thought.

She stared at the business card again. "Can I keep this?"

"Sure. But I've already searched for the man on Google, LinkedIn and in social media. There are plenty of Roberts Evans but none of them look like the same man. From my memory of him anyway."

They finished their coffees in silence. Anna hoped Alex's interest in Robert Evans was a sign that his steadfast desire to leave the past to history was morphing into a quest for answers.

"Why do you think Mum never played the cello?" Anna asked then. "If she was talented enough to play with an orchestra and travel around the world, how could she just leave the instrument in the attic all those years?"

Records of orchestral music had been played so often in their home, they had once joked it was the soundtrack of their childhood. Now that Anna knew the reason her mother loved it so much, the memories of her closing her eyes in apparent tranquillity at the sound of the cello seemed tainted.

"She loved the sound of the cello but maybe to play it brought back memories she wanted to forget?" Alex suggested. "If she chose to leave everything behind and start a new life ... I guess that makes sense ... Dad bought her that cello when I was little." He smiled to himself, lost in a memory. "Actually, I do remember her playing it once or twice, but then she asked Dad to put it in the attic. Look, about Mum being a spy ..." He reached for her hand and squeezed it. "I just can't get my head around that, OK? But if you want to search for answers again, I'll help you. I haven't slept an unbroken night's sleep in over ten years. I've come to a point where I *need* answers now. As much as you do, if I'm honest with myself. If only to close my eyes and sleep peacefully. If we have any chance of putting this to rest, I want to take it."

Anna gripped his hand between hers. She wasn't able to speak, choked with relief at his words.

"My opposition the other night was ... fear, I guess," he said. "The more I think about this the less I think we'll like the ending." He sighed deeply. "I'm scared you – *we* – won't be able to cope with what we discover. But not knowing is terrible too. Maybe Myles can help us further –

he seems a handy man to know. But I said this to you last year when you wanted to hire a private investigator – we must accept whatever we find out and try to move on."

"I understand how you feel! And I agree that not knowing is probably worse than the truth, even if that truth is awful!"

"Did Myles mention if the Garda file on their disappearance detailed the name Yelena Vasilieva?"

She shook her head quickly. "It wasn't in their file – it was only when Myles looked back at their English records that he found it, but that's as far as he got. Just a name, and that was only through a contact of his. The files were sealed. He looked the name up online and found the newspaper articles."

Alex exhaled slowly, his brow furrowed deeply. "So, Mum's name was changed in England and that fact was never discovered by the Irish authorities. Sealed files ... I don't like the sound of that."

"And yet you still think my spy theory is crazy!"

"Yes, well, maybe what you said about her defecting could have some truth to it. I'll contact the liaison in the Missing Persons Bureau. It's new information if nothing else. I have his details in the box of paperwork in the attic. Is there anything up there belonging to Mum and Dad?" His eyes strayed to the ceiling, to the attic of their childhood home.

She shook her head. "Just boxes of clothes and school things."

Pushing his hands onto his knees, he stood up to go. It was midnight.

As Anna saw him out, she noticed the tired slump of his shoulders.

"I hope to meet Myles properly someday. Did you enjoy the weekend?"

She couldn't hide her smile. "Talk to Sam," she urged. "I'm sure everything is OK and you're worrying needlessly."

He hugged her quickly and turned to go.

When he was gone she yawned, feeling completely exhausted. Even though she was desperate to keep searching, she knew she needed to rest, and decided to continue the next day. As she walked wearily up the stairs, she checked her mobile for messages. There was one from Jason, asking if their morning training session could be postponed until the evening. She quickly texted back her agreement, relieved to be able to sleep a little longer in the morning. She needed to talk to him about her parents – he had been her father's closest friend. She had never asked him if her father had ever confided in him about their lives in England. She doubted she would find answers. Surely, at some point in the last ten years, he would have told them if he knew anything that could help.

The other message on her mobile was from Myles. He had arrived home safely and missed her already. He promised to search for information on Robert Evans as soon as he could.

Smiling, she made her way to bed, wondering what he might discover, if anything – for now, it was just another piece in the puzzle. Without knowing exactly what information he had access to, it was hard to know what to expect. But she *did* know he had access beyond anything she ever hoped to have at work and was gifted with computers.

Excitement hovered around the edges of her apprehension – she felt closer to the truth now than at any other time in the last ten years. She lay staring at the ceiling for a long time, her thoughts rolling over each other. Sleep refused to come. Was this the torture her brother had endured since their parents disappeared?

Eventually, she popped in her earphones, and as the opening chords of *Bach* began, she drifted into sleep.

18

Alex stood in the bedroom doorway, watching his wife sleep. Earlier, she had returned from work so late she was exhausted. She had kissed him lightly on the cheek and mounted the stairs wearily to bed before he made his way to Anna's. She had her back turned to him now and was lost in slumber, her shoulder rising and falling softly with each deep breath. She had always been able to sleep, no matter what life had thrown at them. She was lucky that way. He was a natural insomniac – at least, for the last ten years he had been. He was predisposed to tossing and turning whenever something played on his mind, before eventually giving up on sleep altogether. Usually, by the time the sun was rising, he eventually found clarity of thought. Lately, even that was escaping him.

He was sitting at the kitchen table nursing another mug of coffee when he heard Chloe stir. With a jolt of shock, he registered the rising sun outside and realised he had been up all night. Deciding to let Samantha sleep, he got their daughter up, dressed and fed, before dropping her at playgroup. He enjoyed the one-on-one time with his little girl. She was full of boundless energy and questions, excited that Daddy was dropping her off today. When they arrived, he had to spend time admiring her artwork on the wall and see how tall she had grown on the giraffe growth-chart before she reluctantly let him go. Her innocence made him smile, and for a fleeting moment he forgot the conversation of the night before with Anna, and the pressing situation with his wife.

When he returned home, Samantha had already left for work and the house was empty.

"Well?"

"Well, what?"

A deep intake of breath while Tom Gallagher steadied his swelling fury.

"It's Monday morning. Where is she?"

"She's at work, I imagine."

"You had all *fucking* weekend! I want her here, in this house!"

"She had company this weekend, day and night. A detective from Dublin stayed until Sunday evening, and then another man called to the house late on Sunday night." Ely sourly remembered thinking he would surely freeze to death sitting in the car. "I'll make my move when she finishes work this evening."

"Well, you'd better! I want this wrapped up! Do I need to assign this to someone else?"

"Leave it to me."

19

London, 1978

When Michael arrived at the warehouse it seemed busier than usual. Boxer called out a quick greeting and continued moving large packages and crates with the forklift. His own greeting was lost in the noise so Michael raised his hand instead. He waved to Roy and the man nodded – it was progress.

Bob was in the office already, poring over documents, his eyebrows knitted. He barely looked up as Michael walked in and shook off his jacket.

"How's it going this morning?"

"Good."

The reply was blunt and Michael remained quiet for the rest of the morning, letting the man get on with his work. He could ask his questions about the Soviet girl another time.

Hours later Bob raised his head and finally broke the silence.

"You got on alright the other night? With the girl at the hotel, what's her name …?"

"Yelena. Yeah, good. Who is she?" He tried to sound casual.

Bob gathered the paperwork in front of him into a neat stack and pushed it into the desk drawer beside him. "You remember her name, eh?" His tone was teasing. "Don't get too attached – the boss has his eye on her!"

"I thought he's married?"

"That's never stopped him before! Come on, let's get some grub, it's clocking-off time. I'll throw in a few cheeky ales!"

They went to a pub near the port, a place that was fast becoming their regular. Over steak-and-kidney pies and the pints Bob had promised, Michael attempted to steer the conversation back around to the girl who had intrigued him so much. He couldn't yet understand what it was about their encounter that he couldn't forget. She was beautiful, yes, but he knew it was more than that. She had seemed both afraid and resigned to her fear. Her tense body language, the words she spoke … and the suitcase she had collected from Mr Lewis. He couldn't shake off the feeling she was in trouble.

He dabbed a napkin at his mouth as he spoke. "So, the girl, Yelena. She said her father is an acquaintance of Lewis's. I didn't know we imported stuff from the Soviet Union. Is that even possible?"

Bob paused mid-sip of his ale, the glass left hanging in mid-air, his cigarette balanced on his lip as always. "I told you, Lewis has many different contacts in this business. The only thing you need to worry about are the accounts. Why so interested?"

Michael shrugged. "She seemed a bit … vulnerable, that's all."

"Probably tired or something. She performed in a concert the day before. Lewis and some of his cronies had tickets. It's proper highbrow stuff."

"What do you mean 'she performed'?"

"Violin or cello or something. She's part of a big orchestra that tours the UK every now and then."

Michael raised his eyebrows, surprised. "Will she be back?"

Bob grinned and elbowed him in the side. "Jeez, you really fell hard! Don't worry, I won't tell Lewis!" He laughed as he pulled the cigarette from behind his ear and lit it from the other.

Michael decided to drop the subject. He hadn't mentioned the bag she had brought back with her to the hotel from Mr Lewis's house. His interest in her was starting to sound crazy, even to himself. He resolved to try to forget Yelena Vasilieva.

Back in the office he could see the meeting room was occupied. Mr Lewis's loud voice boomed across the hall – there was a burst of laughter and then more serious tones. Bob gathered up some papers and headed downstairs to the warehouse. Michael intended to get stuck into his own paperwork again. It was slow and tedious, but he drew some comfort from the fact the pile of documents was reducing in size. The air in the office felt dead, oppressive and after lunch he felt sluggish. There were no windows to open and allow fresh air to liven up the room. He crossed to the door and opened it, propping it open with a small wastebin.

After a short time, he heard the meeting-room door open across the hall. Mr Lewis stepped out, followed by two men. They went down the metal staircase and into the warehouse. Curiosity piqued Michael's interest and he stepped to the large glass window that overlooked the warehouse below. The men wore jeans and leather jackets, looking the opposite of Mr Lewis's professional attire. He wondered who they were. They inspected several boxes and spoke to Bob for a brief moment, before making their way outside. He noted the men pull their caps down low as they walked to a car parked a short distance from the large door.

As he watched, Mr Lewis turned and met his eyes. Michael raised a hand in greeting, feeling only slightly perturbed at being caught watching the interaction – he often left his desk to stand at the window, to rest his eyes from the paperwork as much as to stretch his legs. Mr Lewis eyed him without expression, his hands hanging by his sides. Roy stopped what he had been doing and followed his boss's gaze, he too staring at Michael with what he could only describe as hostility.

Feeling his heart racing a little, Michael turned back to his desk. Back to sorting through piles of paperwork, the job he was being paid to do, resolving to keep his questions and his curiosity in check in future.

20

Cork, 2019

Frank Doherty had opted to leave the Monday-morning press conference to William Ryan.

The detective felt as though the collar of his shirt was suctioned to his neck and ran a finger along the space in between. He looked around at the assembled bodies, members of the press, a scattering of gardaí and Anna Clarke from the clerical staff downstairs. She handed out briefing documents, a single sheet of paper with the scantest details of the case he could get away with releasing, then took a chair at the side of the room.

William remembered Colin Forde vomiting onto the grass a few days before at the sight of the victim on the ground in Clonakilty. That crime scene was a mere rehearsal for what had transpired at the Rebel Event Centre. Colin had managed to hold it together there on Saturday evening, though had stopped short of looking under the white sheet covering the victim. Grace Thompson had had no issue with the grim sights in front of them, staying professionally curious and alert. He had been impressed with her reaction and had high hopes for his team.

After Marian Selway's body had been found on Saturday evening, the hours had seemed long, and yet William felt the breathless rush of a man scrambling for time. Watching the security footage from inside the Rebel Event Centre had left everyone in the viewing room speechless – he couldn't remember when last that had happened. Marian Selway had suffered a death so violent, the thick cream carpet of the Centre was a deep crimson where her body had fallen, blood-spatter on the glass walls and marble pillars illustrating the goriest crime scene they had ever witnessed.

When he closed his eyes the images replayed in vivid colour, and he welcomed them. The woman's face, the man's knife ... they had *filmed* it! The details of the murder were fuel, and the fire they had ignited was burning inside him. He would find these people and he would stop them! There was no other alternative that he could accept. So with every passing second he was a man on fire from the inside – interviewing the victim's family and friends, requesting CCTV around the Rebel Event Centre, pressing Doherty to assign a profiler. Every minute of his consciousness burned with the need to catch the people responsible, but he was gripped by a reality that wound itself around him and crushed the air from his lungs – he had almost nothing to go on.

His team had hardly slept. In the few snatched hours away from the case, their phones had been rarely still, vibrating as William communicated each thought and idea. They relished it – anyone who had viewed the footage of Marian Selway's death would not find peace until the killers were stopped. Now he intended to pull the media along in helping to catch the duo on the CCTV, but he knew he could only show them select still-images from the footage.

As Anna watched him, her brown eyes narrowed in concern. A sheet of sweat coated the detective's face and he pulled at his collar repeatedly. The man at the top of the room was flustered. She had never seen him this way, and she knew it wasn't the image he would want to project to the assembled press. They locked eyes, and she mouthed "Are you OK?" He gave a brief nod, but she thought her expression of concern had hit home as he squared his shoulders, visibly pulling himself together.

She could understand his reaction to the crime-scene photographs – she had worked on the file earlier and typed up notes for the press. Even though she had forced her eyes away from the images after a brief second, they stayed in her mind. She looked forward to her training session with Jason later, to physically propel the pictures from her brain and punch away her fear and frustration.

She recognised Vivian's neat bun and smart suit jacket. She was sitting in the front row, her mobile phone on her lap, recording, and her pen poised over an open notebook. She was staring at the detective in anticipation, hungry for information. Unease at her friend's obvious excitement fluttered in Anna's stomach, and she pressed her back into the wall for support.

"Ladies and gentlemen, thank you for your time, we'll now get started."

Silence fell over the group.

"The victim, Marian Selway, was found dead by her husband on Saturday evening at her place of work, the Rebel Event Centre. She had failed to return home after a scheduled private tour and wasn't answering her mobile, so he checked her workplace. The state pathologist is finalising the report, but we can say with certainty the victim suffered a violent assault that led to her death."

"Do you have a lead on the suspect?"

It was Vivian who had asked.

"Suspects, plural. A couple, claiming to be from an event management company in London booked a private tour of the Rebel Event Centre for Saturday afternoon. In her capacity as marketing manager, Mrs Selway was conducting the tour."

"Can you give us names?" Vivian again.

A brief hesitation as an internal debate flashed across his face. "Only one name was given, and we believe it to be fake. The booking was made for a Jacquelyn Hyde from London. No event-management company name was given."

"*Jacquelyn* Hyde? As in *Jekyll and Hyde*?" Vivian's voice rose several octaves. "Is that a joke?"

"We are looking into it."

"The suspects in the killing of Seán Doyle checked into a hotel using the obvious fake names of Mr and Mrs Parker-Barrow," she said. "That's clearly a reference to Bonnie and Clyde."

William bristled, feeling the blood drain from his face. This information hadn't been given to the press yet. The journalist sitting in the front row – her name tag said *Vivian Keating* – had somehow got herself an exclusive. His teeth clamped around the flesh inside his cheek as she continued.

"And now a reference to another famous killer. Both Bonnie and Clyde and Dr Jekyll, once he changed into his alter-ego, terrorised people. This pattern must concern you, detective." Her voice was shrill and rang loudly through the room.

William felt all eyes on him, like pinpricks piercing his skin, waiting for his response. He exhaled heavily, the weight of the case pulling his shoulders forward. He made an obvious effort to stand straighter and wiped a hand over his face.

"Obviously, this *is* the American couple you are looking for in relation to the killing of Seán Doyle on Thursday morning in Clonakilty, isn't it?" Vivian pressed him. "Only they're not American, are they? The gardaí have no idea of their actual nationality."

He was taken aback by the statement, by the quick way she had joined the lines in the two killings. He didn't want to answer any more of her questions – he knew where it would lead. To panic, hysteria. He knew he had to tread carefully.

"Obviously we are concerned. Yes, we believe it could be the same couple. And yes, we believe they are concealing their identities in every way possible. The suspects are using disguises, fake nationalities and unusual names. We urge the public, particularly those working in front-of-house positions, to be vigilant for any suspicious names used in bookings."

"So, we are looking for two serial killers here?"

Anna gasped and stared at the side of Vivian's face as her questions landed and had the desired effect. Murmurs resonated from the assembled press, their mumbled horror reverberating around the room.

"No," William answered firmly, his eyes stern. "It's too early to speculate on that. Besides, killers tend not to be defined as *serial* until there are three or more victims –"

"But some researchers say it can be as low as two victims. At the very least, we have a couple that have killed two people in violent circumstances. Isn't it fair to say the people of Cork should be scared, detective?"

Anna knew the blush that coloured William Ryan's face was more from anger than anything else. The press conference had completely run away from him. She looked at her friend in alarm, her eyes aiming a *'What are you doing!'* glare that Vivian couldn't see. She was lost in the scent of a front-page headline.

William held up his hands to silence the growing commotion and try to regain control of the small crowd.

"Let me reassure you, and the people of Cork – we are doing everything we can to bring the killers to justice. There is no gain to be had in panicking."

The screen behind him blinked to life. The images portrayed there of two adults, a man and a woman, were next to useless in identifying the suspects. The man's face was mostly hidden by a baseball hat pulled low – in one shot he had removed his hat, but his face was so distorted it was impossible to discern any identifiable features. The woman's hair was obviously a wig – bright red, it matched her lipstick. Her eyebrows appeared to be painted on, her skin an artificial shade of white. Her face resembled that of a blow-up doll.

"If Ms Keating here has finished with her speculation about serial killers, we can get on to the real business of sharing all the information we have."

William's tone was brittle and stern, but Vivian merely smiled in return.

Anna felt stunned. Her friend really was dogged in her search for an angle. Wasn't a brutal murder enough?

"These pictures show our suspects. The images are taken from CCTV inside the Rebel Event Centre. As you can see, the images are designed to mislead investigators as to the identity of the suspects. The woman is evidently wearing a wig and her make-up is used, in our opinion, to exaggerate her features and add further confusion as to her appearance. We can only surmise the man was wearing some type of mask to distort his face. CCTV shows he kept his head lowered throughout the tour of the building. If Mrs Selway felt threatened by the couple it wasn't obvious. They travelled to the Rebel Event Centre by taxi – we have traced them to a taxi rank in the city centre and further work is being done to establish from where they entered those premises. The driver has given his statement – the couple presented as English and paid in cash. The man was described as quiet by the taxi driver, the woman as chatty. They did not book a return journey. We continue to examine on-street CCTV."

William pulled at his shirt collar, his eyes moving around the room before resting on Vivian. "Your job here is to alert the public and to publish the images and details as they are presented to you. Speculation about serial killers is unhelpful and likely to incite panic. Public panic is something I would hate to have to hold you accountable for, Ms Keating."

Anna lowered her head to suppress a smile at his cold stare and stern tone. Vivian was seething – even from the side of the room, Anna could see it in the tense jerk of her shoulders as she half-rose from her seat in protest.

"Now, thank you all for your attention. You have been given an A4 sheet with all the details we have to date. We will not be taking further questions at this time."

Vivian's protest was lost in the sea of bodies and the wave of noise as the room burst into life, the assembled reporters shouting questions that went ignored. After a few minutes of being ushered out by a garda they began to make their way to the exit, keen to gulp fresher air and coffee, meet deadlines and file reports.

Anna had no doubt that Vivian's protest centred around censorship of the press – she had heard the speech many times. She loved how passionate her friend was about journalism. Just occasionally, Anna was reminded that her passion sometimes had an edge to it that made her feel uncomfortable.

"Can you *believe* him!" Vivian muttered as she reached her.

Anna kept her eyes low and moved aside to let her friend pass. She was far too disciplined to ever talk to a member of the press about the details of her work but being seen to be overly friendly with a reporter wouldn't be a good thing.

"I'll call you later," she muttered.

Vivian took the hint, joining the throng of people leaving the room.

Anna moved to the front of the conference room, collecting discarded papers as she went. When she reached William Ryan, some of the members of his team were there with him, discussing the potential fallout from the press conference.

"I can understand now why the Chief Super stayed out of this press conference!" Grace Thompson muttered. "Frank Doherty can blame you when the shit hits the fan!"

William groaned and leaned his weight against a table behind him, his body sagging.

"It's inevitable really. Two random, violent killings without any real leads. The suspects pretending to be foreign and using ludicrously fake names. It's very worrying. People need answers!"

"So you're satisfied it's them. The same people?"

William nodded. "There's no doubt about it. She wears wigs and speaks with different accents. She was a blonde American in Clonakilty, an English redhead in the city. He is quiet, giving nothing away. What do you think covered his face? The skin around his neck looked like scar tissue. We said a mask just now, but I've never seen a mask like it."

None of the detectives had any idea to offer.

Anna hovered at the edge of their little group, unsure why she had stayed behind, just keen to offer support in some way.

"Look into cases where masks were worn, at home and abroad. The internet is a minefield and perhaps these people are copying something they saw online. Even in a film. The research on this case is going to be tough but we need to get inside their heads. I've requested a profiler to help. By choosing the alias Mr and Mrs Parker-Barrow, the killers opened the door to their psyche. Bonnie and Clyde were legends, in a way – the public were obsessed with them. It could be the killers are trying to stir up media interest using their names. Or just some sick fantasy they're playing out. And Jacquelyn Hyde … it's subtle enough to be missed at the time of first hearing it but laughs in the face of investigators when working backwards and trying to piece things together."

"Exactly!" Grace said. "They didn't check into the hotel in Clonakilty using the names Bonnie and Clyde. That was too obvious. And who'd wonder about the name Parker-Barrow unless they really knew their crime history?"

"Did anything come back on unsolved murders with a similar M.O. or robberies by a male and female couple?"

"No, nothing."

"Is there a reason you didn't tell the press the woman filmed the killing?" Colin Forde was standing a little to the side, his back to the images on the screen.

William opened his shirt top-button and loosened the knot in his tie.

"I don't know … perhaps it adds nothing only to show how perverse the killers are. Certainly, it would give the press an angle, but it'd serve to … sensationalise these people more. We don't need anything more disturbing in the public mix for now."

"It'll probably leak anyway. By the sound of things, the press have got hold of more information than we wanted to release just yet," Grace added glumly.

William sighed. In his experience, the more sensational the details of a crime, the faster they were leaked.

William noticed Anna, standing a little to the side of the group. Her hands were full of white pages, collected from the assembled plastic chairs – the contents had been emailed already to the journalists, and so most of them were discarded and left behind. She was paler than usual, her brown eyes wide and staring into the distance.

"Anna? What is it?"

She cleared her throat, a little embarrassed. "Do you think they only filmed this killing? Or did they film the other one too? The shooting in Clonakilty."

William shook his head. "I've no idea."

"I mean, why would they *film* it at all? And why record one but not the other?"

Colin moved quickly to the desk and computer, his fingers flying across the keyboard. In seconds, images from the shooting of Seán Doyle appeared on the screen. At the image of the three holes pushed into the muddy grass on the verge of the road, he turned to face the expectant faces. He was slightly breathless.

"Last year, when the Chief Superintendent was killed, the press came to the funeral. Do you remember, they were only allowed outside the church, and some of them assembled their cameras and gear on the grass? They were waiting so long … their video cameras were mounted on tripods."

"I remember that!" Grace said, excitement in her voice. "An elderly man approached me outside the church, asking to make a complaint. I guess he saw the uniform and wanted to vent to someone. He was the caretaker of the church grounds and he was really unhappy about the holes the camera crew were making in the grass!" She stepped up to the screen, her eyes roaming between the three holes. She traced lines between them with one finger. "Anna's right. Why film one murder and not the other? I bet these three marks are from a tripod!"

Anna's voice was a disgusted whisper as she stated the obvious. "So they filmed the murder in Clonakilty too."

"Using a tripod because, for some reason, the woman was unable to hold the camera that time."

The sides of William's face began to tingle – tiny pinpoints of pressure. The sensation trickled along his neck and into his chest, a mounting adrenaline. This detail had added to the utter horror that was etched onto the faces of his colleagues in the room.

"Now why do you suppose they would want to do that?" he said.

Later, at the Rebel Event Centre, William stood on the first floor near the dark bloodstain on the cream carpet. The building was empty, the forensic evidence already collected. With his eyes closed, he stayed still, breathing in the odours of the room, and letting the muted sounds wash over him. He stepped to his left and turned to face the stairs, then turned around again, his arm raised as though holding a camcorder. Trance-like, he was an unusual sight.

Grace watched him from across the wide space, leaning against a cream marble pillar. It was far enough away from where Marian Selway had died to have avoided any blood-spatter. She watched him move slowly, absorbing the scene with his eyes closed. Colin stood with his back to them, staring out into the view of the city. He had witnessed enough Saturday night and Sunday to fill his nightmares for years.

William opened his eyes and blinked in the glare of the winter sun. Glass walls to his left amplified the light bouncing off the chrome finishes.

"They spared no expense on this place," Grace said, moving towards him.

He didn't respond. Crouching down he touched the drying blood on the carpet with a gloved finger. It would soon be a stain so cavernous it would need cutting out. He imagined the whole carpet would be ripped up and replaced, the walls repainted. If the place ever opened up again. After such a grisly crime, and the coverage in today's press, he couldn't imagine anyone ever booking in for dinner or a concert in future. But maybe he was wrong, he thought – some people enjoyed the macabre element of mystery.

"Tell me about the victim again."

Grace pulled a small notebook from her pocket and flipped to the current page, although she didn't really need the notes to remember the details. The anguish of the victim's husband was still fresh in her memory. She and Colin had been unlucky enough to have to speak with him shortly after he found his wife murdered and had interviewed him twice since Saturday night.

"Marian Selway, aged fifty-nine, lived with her husband Graeme, no children. He runs a boarding kennel and she

162

helped out. It seems they lived a quiet life. Before the role as marketing manager here she worked for a hotel chain. This job was taken to reduce her workload, to spend more time at home." She snapped the notebook closed. "Graeme Selway is from Essex originally but moved here as a child. Marian is from Cork. She had many friends, was involved in an animal-welfare charity. Certainly, she had no enemies her husband is aware of."

"It wasn't personal," William said.

"The same as Seán Doyle. What do you think?"

He straightened up and pulled off his gloves. He was still lost in his thoughts, his eyes unfocused.

"Bonnie and Clyde and Jekyll and Hyde ... who *are* these people?" he murmured. "Jacquelyn Hyde ... say it fast enough and it rolls off the tongue. Almost like someone's idea of a little joke."

"The receptionist who took the booking by telephone is a part-time student and it seems she didn't find the name unusual. If the victim did, she didn't mention it to anyone."

William met Grace's eyes with a deep sigh of frustration. "I'm getting absolutely nothing here!" He looked around the room one more time.

"We'll have the forensic report soon enough." Colin turned from the glass wall and the view over the city, to face the room.

William shook his head. "I don't mean DNA and such like. Last year, when the Chief Superintendent was killed, it was different. I had a sense of what had happened – I could picture where she lay dead, where Myles Henderson lay wounded on the ground. I could *feel* the terror Anna Clarke had felt hiding in the storage closet. But now ... aside from where the victim fell, I've got nothing!"

"You had a victim statement then – Anna Clarke's. Now all we have is CCTV. And that's not exactly helpful."

"It's more than that. There is always a residual feeling left at a crime scene, and sometimes you can tap into it. Fear, panic, anger. Here … there's nothing. Marian Selway was taken so completely by surprise that she died before she had much chance to feel anything."

"A small mercy."

"And the killers … there's nothing. No motive. No rage. He was calm … he killed her without any hesitation. Just a calculated execution captured on their personal camera."

"I've thought about that. Why not use a phone to film things? Mobile-phone cameras are great these days."

Colin stepped towards them. "Only if they had the latest model and camcorders would still be superior, capture better imagery and so on. But who would want to do that?"

William rested his hands on his hips and shook his head, exasperation in his voice.

"The woman's appearance … the wig, the make-up and fur coat … it's all so distracting. It's very clever really. Her appearance was so vulgar it completely side-tracked Marian Selway from the danger they posed. And the man … he kept his head down and his face hidden. Compared to the woman, he was nothing. She was a pantomime and he was a shadow. They might as well be ghosts."

21

The moon sliced into darkness with blunt precision, chunks of light casting long shadows across the ground. Puddles hissed softly as new rain fell, misting and swirling in the wind. John Gallagher waited in the hulk of darkness behind a stack of pallets, his collar turned up and his eyes alight with anticipation. He had ached to be here, had longed for this part of his old life. Life *before.* Now, as adrenaline spiralled inside him, his body almost vibrated with pleasure. He had missed this.

The dockyard appeared empty, but men moved among the crates and boxes, shadowy figures that darted from the darkness before being sucked into it again. Voices were low and eyes accustomed to the half-light. A man appeared to his left – shorter but stockily built, hours lifting weights etched in his shoulders and arms.

"What's the problem?" John spoke to the darkness in front of him, never turning to the man, never making eye contact. His ribs were still healing, and movement hurt some days more than others. Today was one of those days, so he stayed still.

"It's good to see you out here again, John." The man's voice was cordial.

"What's the problem?" He dipped his head in the direction of the pallets and crates in front of them. He had no time for chit-chat – he had asked his question twice now, and the man should know better than to expect it to be asked a third time.

He cleared his throat softly. "Ninety pallets were expected but we can count only fifty."

The slight tremble in his voice pleased John. He felt alive. This is how things should be.

"So … either you've forgotten how to count, or we've been robbed. Which is it?" He pushed his hands deeper into his coat pockets and kept his eyes focused on the men in front of him, moving quietly between crates, counting, searching. Irritation and excitement pulsated into the air around him, in the stiff tilt of his neck, in the way he sucked air between his teeth.

"The shipment docked earlier than expected. High winds tonight. The pallets were unloaded by the time we got here. The crew are long gone." The man cleared his throat louder this time to hide the quiver in his voice.

"So, we've been robbed. Is that what you're telling me?"

John turned his head to look at the man and noticed him take a small step back and swallow hard. He *lived* for the fear in the man's eyes.

"We … we … it looks that way, yes."

John pursed his lips and stared out into the inky-black sea. Almost half the containers had been taken before his men arrived to make their usual collection … he turned back to the man beside him, whose clipboard was shaking slightly now in his hand.

"No-one's ever dared to rob us before. Someone is muscling in. But they can't do that unless they have information, wouldn't you say? So, someone is talking to people they shouldn't be. What do you think of that, Ken?"

He spoke so quietly, so calmly, Ken wanted to turn and run. It was dangerous to be near John Gallagher when he was calm and angry – it was a deadly combination he had witnessed before, and he often had to look away before John was done. He had always felt safe in the protective circle of being *in* with the Gallaghers. Being on the outside was a very dangerous thing.

"Where's Ely Murray?" John demanded. "He normally oversees the deliveries."

"He's in Kinsale, as far as I know. Chasing some girl for your … for the boss."

John tilted his head to one side with a low groan. The muscles stretched and creaked – too much time spent sitting at a computer. "Call him. Get him here. This takes priority."

Ken moved away into the shadows to make the call. Immediately his breathing steadied. He was somewhat unnerved to see John was recovered from his torture by the Germans. He had been among the crew of men assembled to drive the Meier's vehicle with their dead bodies inside to a back road far from the city and set it alight. He remembered the boss the following morning, calmly inspecting the new tiles and paint job in the hall of his house – the place where he had beaten the leader of the gang to death with cold determination. *His own home.* The thrill of it all, the rescue of John and killing of his torturers, had moved the Gallaghers into a new class in the underworld. Was someone really attempting a hostile takeover? As he dialled Ely's number he was glad to be out of John's way and felt a stab of pity for whoever dared to cross the Gallaghers this time around. It was suicide.

Ely had some fleeting hope he could grab Anna after work, before realising she was parked in the staff carpark. Forcibly grabbing a garda clerical officer from the Lee Street station carpark would not be his wisest decision. So instead, he had followed her, staying two cars back until she left the city and passed the airport, where traffic thinned and there was no-one between them. He kept enough distance not to draw attention to himself but close enough to notice if she turned left or right. She didn't. It was a straight run into Kinsale.

Anna pulled into a hotel carpark, taking a gear bag from the car as she exited. Ely waited fifteen minutes before following her inside. The hotel gym was easy to find, its glass wall offering a direct view of the sweaty, red-faced occupants. She was among them, with a man about twenty years older. They were in a corner beyond the treadmills and bikes. He held a punchbag while she pounded into it with so much force that the man had trouble keeping his feet steady. Ely was rooted to the ground at the sight – the slight girl of medium height, blonde hair in a ponytail, landing precise blows into the red punchbag. He was reminded of the night in the Mad Hatter, when she had quickly palmed away his attempt to grab her, before landing a sucker-punch to his kidney and a fast kick to his knee that saw him slammed head-first into the sink. For the first time in his life, he had been knocked unconscious, and by a slip of a girl too! Remembering that night, Ely's teeth bored so hard onto his bottom lip he tasted the metallic sting of blood.

He watched her through the glass, finding a place for himself among the shadows. She and her partner stopped briefly, to drink water and to chat. Their topic of conversation drew a frown from her, and he thought he saw her eyes glint with tears. The man put a hand on her shoulder and Ely considered inching closer to try to hear, or at least attempt to lip-read their conversation. He was intrigued. But before long they put their water bottles away and returned to their training session and he returned to wait in his car.

Ninety minutes after she had arrived at the hotel she emerged again, waving goodbye to her training partner. Ely eased the Audi out of the car park, staying two cars behind her. He imagined she was headed home at this late hour, and he was right. By the time he parked at the kerb two houses down from hers and across the road, her car was in the driveway and her living room lights were on.

He watched and waited. She drew the living-room curtains after a few minutes, yet her bedroom curtains remained open, the light off. She was still downstairs. Ely craned his neck to look around him – the housing estate seemed to be quiet, curtains closed against the night, most houses set in darkness. Would he prefer to surprise her lounging on the sofa, tired after her training session, or asleep in bed? He knew which was the safer option, for him, but watching her pound into the punchbag had fired him up. He was in the mood for a challenge. Grabbing his scarf from the passenger seat he wound it around his face and pulled his woollen hat low, before climbing out of the car and crossing the street in a quick jog.

Her driveway was short and the car parked there provided cover from view. Within seconds he was standing at her front door. A nearby streetlight offered some illumination and he examined it – the door was an old model, with the traditional high latch, not the modern door handles most new builds had. He tested it against his shoulder – the wood was heavy. This would not be his way inside. He darted to the living-room window and crouched down, listening – silence. The TV was off … what was she doing?

A sudden high-pitched alarm sounded from his trouser pocket and he scrambled to pull out his mobile phone, his heart thumping. *Fuck!* He pressed the phone to his ear and listened.

Trouble at the docks. John was demanding his presence. So the boy was back. In a crouched run he returned to the Audi, surprised at his disappointment at not completing the job tonight.

Anna Clarke would have to wait.

22

Anna opted not to light the stove, having returned from the gym so late. Despite the heating on timer, she felt cold in the house. She changed into pyjamas and pulled on a hooded sweater, before popping a frozen lasagne into the oven.

Her conversation with Jason, when they had stopped for a break, had been disappointing. But not altogether surprising. It was news to him that Helen Clarke had been born in the Soviet Union – she could tell from the way his mouth had dropped open.

"Your father never said, but then, why would he? We were good friends, but never discussed life *before*, if you know what I mean."

She had sipped from her water bottle and nodded. She knew if she spoke her voice would betray her disappointment. She had hoped Jason might have some answers, but all he had were questions.

"Do you think it had anything to do with their disappearance?" he asked.

At that she had nodded. "How could it not? Alex doesn't necessarily agree, but why would they hide that from us? I mean, they obviously wanted her to *stay* hidden."

"Did your mum have any relatives you could reach out to?"

"I'm working on it."

That was the truth. Her search for answers was progressing slowly. She'd had so little time alone since Vivian had reminded her of the powers of the internet and the desire to start searching was growing. She just needed some space to get her thoughts in order ... she hoped tonight would offer enough time to find more pieces of the puzzle.

The house felt empty and deathly still – the tick of the kitchen clock and hum of the fridge were amplified in the crushing silence. She thought of Myles and wondered where he was. He had said he was going abroad for work but had offered no further information. Anna didn't want to press him for details – not yet anyway. Putting Bach's Cello Suite No. 1 in G Major on her father's record player, she closed her eyes, letting the familiar sound fill the living room. Her mother's favourite music had always calmed her down – now it presented unanswered questions. She pulled her mobile from her sweater pocket and texted Alex.

Just listening to Bach, again! Nothing yet from Myles re Robert Evans' business card. Am about to continue internet searches for any info. Did you find anything else in the attic?

His reply came instantly.

No time to look up to now – was snowed under at work and Sam's working late so was with Chloe all evening. Will keep you posted.

Anna felt uncomfortable as she read – Samantha was working late *again!* She could imagine how Alex's mind would jump to the worst conclusion and how miserable he must be feeling right now.

The beeping of the oven drew her attention. In the adjoining kitchen she arranged her lasagne and a glass of water on the small table, adding a mug of coffee to the meal, before pulling her laptop towards her. Her internet searches from the previous evening were still open – the newspaper articles covering the disappearance of the cellist Yelena Vasilieva from London yielding so much information: that Anna's mother, the woman she knew as Helen Clarke, was born in the town of Omsk, that she was the daughter of a successful businessman and was a talented cellist who played with the Moscow Orchestral Reserve.

The newspaper articles she found had gone into great detail about Yelena's talent and her disappearance from the orchestra's hotel when she visited London in 1978. It was a scandal that drew speculation of defection and veiled threats from Soviet politicians.

But the story that had seemed so explosive fizzled quickly to nothing, moving from a front-page headline to a small column within a matter of days. From what Anna could uncover, Yelena was never heard from again, and press coverage dwindled quickly. There were no statements from the police in London or any British politicians. Her theory that her mother might have been a Soviet spy appeared to be merely a cliched assumption.

There was little information on Yelena's mother – the articles focused more on her father, Maxim Vasiliev. He was a businessman, although the newspaper articles didn't go into detail. Rather they focused more on his fledgling membership of the communist party – he was never referred to as a politician and, reading between the lines, Anna understood that to mean he was a low-level member, not in a powerful position. Certainly not powerful enough to have anything done about his missing daughter. He died in a boating accident in 1990, twelve years after she disappeared. Anna felt sorry for the man she was beginning to think of as her grandfather – he had died never knowing what had happened to Yelena.

An article from newspaper archives covering his death was available online – she read with curiosity, paying close attention to the black-and-white image of two women turned away from the camera, standing outside a building, heads wrapped in furs to protect them from the cold.

"Yelena and Annika Vasilieva pictured following the service for former businessman Maxim Vasiliev."

Her fingers hovered over the laptop keys, her mind joining dots and linking names. Her grandmother was also called Yelena … fingers flying, she searched for any mention of the woman in all the newspaper articles available to her. There was nothing. It was as though she didn't exist. Any article about a woman named Yelena Vasilieva was in relation to the young woman who disappeared on a warm September night in London.

Swallowing the last of her lasagne, Anna turned her attention to her aunt, Annika Vasilieva. She was mentioned in many articles as merely the "sister of the missing cellist". There were no personal articles attributed to her, no quotes from her in relation to her sister's disappearance.

Annika Vasilieva. The name had stayed in her thoughts throughout her busy day, aching to be typed into search engines as soon as she had time. Alex's visit had rendered her too tired to concentrate the night before ... but now, even though the clock was edging closer to midnight, she couldn't rest. She felt this woman, if she were still alive, could answer so many questions.

She wondered if her mother had named her after her own sister. Annika and Anna were versions of the same name. Each time she thought about that her eyes filled with tears. Her mother may have chosen to leave her old life behind, but surely in naming her daughter she had displayed her love for her sister. Anna's own family had been split in half ten years ago – she knew the pain of losing people she loved. Why had her mother chosen to disappear?

Finally, the name Annika Vasilieva yielded results – in a newspaper article from San Antonia in Texas, in the United States. In 1985, the engagement of Annika Vasilieva and Daniel Garcia was announced in the *San Antonia Journal* in their "Births, Death and Marriages" section. Annika would marry Daniel in the fall and live on the family ranch.

Anna rested heavily into the back of her chair. She gulped down her coffee, wincing as the cold liquid turned sour in her mouth. Her aunt, if she was still alive, had married an American man and was possibly still living in Texas. There might be cousins and, more importantly, answers to be discovered. Pushing away a weary tiredness that threatened to derail her plans, she began to search again. For Annika Garcia this time, on Google, Linked-In, Facebook, Twitter ... whatever and for however long it took.

23

"We're leaving. *Get up!*"

The woman opened one bleary eye and closed it again quickly. The curtains were open, the morning sun blinding. She pulled the duvet over her head. The sounds of rustling and grunting were easily decipherable. He was packing. Quickly.

"*I said get up!*"

He pulled the duvet roughly to the floor and she had no choice but to sit up against the pillows, frowning at him. She felt the protest building inside her, although she already knew that what she wanted would make no difference.

"Shouldn't we stay here? I have champagne to sleep off – a whole bottle!"

"*Up!* We have a new plan."

He turned away from her and returned to the open suitcases he had placed on the desk and the chair near the hotel-room window. She could see their clothes neatly folded in piles inside, his mask in its soft pouch on top. Her wigs were still stacked on a shelf in the wardrobe – he wouldn't touch those, he thought they were filthy. "Other people's hair!" he had said with a shiver when she showed him. It intrigued her that he couldn't touch them but had no trouble wearing a rubber mask of his dead father's face. The thought made her giddy.

"Where are we going?"

"To a new hotel. Still in the city but we need to change location."

"OK then." She hopped out of bed and headed to the shower.

He wanted to rage at her to get dressed – he was done with this hotel and the flecks of blood he imagined were still in the bathroom from the scouring of his body yesterday – but he wanted her to clean herself too, so he said nothing. She stank of booze and sweat, and he felt nauseated just hearing her breathe.

She had insisted they celebrate and unwind, explore the city she had never visited before. Last night, she had drunk herself stupid while he watched her, feeling what he always did around her – fascination mingled with disgust. She brought out the worst in him, but allowed him his fantasies ...

He had decided they needed a car. Hiring one would not be an option obviously, so he would steal one. That had never been a problem for him and it would be easy now. They would get a taxi to the suburbs, steal a car, and drive back into the city. He imagined CCTV images of them would be circulating now, so they would have to be careful. One more taxi journey, and then they would bounce between stolen cars, leaving no traces behind.

Sound came from the bathroom: the hiss of the shower, and something else. Was she singing? He paused outside the door to listen. Shaking his head, he wondered what would happen if he walked out of this hotel and left her behind. Or if he opened the door to the bathroom and silenced her, finally. But he thought of the money and the task at hand – there were to be two more kills before the end. He needed her until then. After that?

After that he could be rid of her once and for all.

24

In Victus, Anna spotted Vivian at their customary table at the back, head bowed low over her laptop. Anna ordered a latte and Danish pastry and carried them to the table.

Sitting down, she blew on the foamy milk on top of her coffee. After only five hours' sleep – her internet searches continuing long into the early hours – she had expected to feel exhausted. But she felt invigorated. The realisation that she had found her mother's sister, after a whole life thinking she had no extended family, was an exciting prospect. And it had been far easier than she had hoped. She hadn't wanted to ask any more of Myles just yet, not unless she truly had to. He was working on finding Robert Evans, if that were possible. And she had to admit, a part of her had enjoyed reading the newspaper articles about her mother and weaving digital threads through her mother's family. It had felt like following the clues in a treasure hunt.

Lost in her thoughts, she waited for Vivian to notice she had arrived.

"Anna! Jeez, you gave me a fright!"

She grinned. "What are you so engrossed in? I hope it's not about the 'serial killers' you imagine are running around!"

It was intended as a joke and she cringed slightly as Vivian's eyes narrowed.

Vivian stirred her coffee before speaking, her voice low. "Oh that! Well, they *are* serial killers, Anna. Are you OK? I thought you were a bit quiet yesterday after the press conference. I know I was a bit … forceful, but you know that's the nature of the job, right? A journalist has to push buttons to get to the truth, especially when certain detectives are holding back."

Anna paused, thinking. Her comment had been intended to be flippant but it seemed Vivian had been waiting for her to bring up the subject. Normally, she avoided confrontation, especially with someone she cared about – but Vivian had surprised her yesterday.

"I'm fine, Vivian. It's just … yesterday felt like an ambush. DS Ryan has given the media everything he can, and it seemed like you were trying to goad him into saying more, that's all." She decided it was best to move on and held up her hands in a 'truce' signal.

Vivian pursed her lips. She seemed to be considering what to say.

"Maybe you're right. I have an interview for a new job anyway. And I think I've a good chance of getting it."

Anna raised her eyebrows and smiled around a mouthful of pastry. This was good news.

"It's with Banba Productions! As a presenter and investigative reporter for their new TV slot. I'd *love* the role!"

"Oh, wow, Vivian, that sounds amazing! *Um* … who are Banba Productions?"

Vivian leaned closer, her eyes gleaming with excitement.

"They're this amazing new Irish production company, run primarily *by* women, *for* women. And named after Banba, you know, the patron goddess of Ireland?"

Anna stared at her blankly, never having heard of the goddess in question.

"Anyway, they will have several slots a week on TV and radio, and I'm interviewing for the investigative reporter role, as I said. It's well paid, Anna, and would be such a step up for me. No more pressuring detectives for something juicy enough to make the front page." She smiled, somewhat apologetically. "I have to come up with an idea for a crime-related documentary and present it to them next week. If I get the job, I'd start work on it almost immediately! On television! I'm thinking about covering a cold case, you know, an unsolved mystery. It could be the start of something big for me!"

Anna beamed. "Good luck – you'd be great at that! What an opportunity! Are your parents delighted?"

Vivian's face darkened. "They're a bit preoccupied with Gareth actually. He's been in his room for days, refusing to speak to anyone. Who knows what's bothering him this time? I feel bad for him but there's no way he'll talk to me. I wish I could do something to help."

The air around them was suddenly heavy. Vivian's worry about her brother was palpable, deflating her earlier excitement. She met Anna's eyes and smiled, making a physical effort to shake off the gloom. "How did your internet searches go?"

Anna couldn't keep the grin of excitement from lighting up her face as she filled her friend in on the success of her online sleuthing. "I think she could be my aunt. She has a Facebook profile – it's set at private but in her profile picture she really looks like my mum! I've sent her a message asking her to call me."

"Did you? What did she say?"

"Well, she hasn't seen it yet. They're six hours behind us. I'll be checking my phone all day for a response – I doubt I'll get any work done!"

"Well, call me the minute you hear back. Will you tell Alex?"

Anna nodded. "He called over and we patched things up. I'll tell him, but not until I know for sure it's her. Her name's Annika ... just like my name. Mum must really have missed her sister ... all those years apart ..." Her eyes shone with tears and she blinked them away rapidly, unable to meet her friend's sympathetic gaze.

Vivian drained her coffee and leaned closer across the table. "Your parents' disappearance is a pretty big mystery. But not a crime, as far as we know." She pulled at her bottom lip, deep in thought.

Anna narrowed her eyes and shook her head. "You're unbelievable! It's a good job you're my best friend or else I'd be highly insulted. Forget it, Lois Lane! My parents will not be the focus of your Banba Productions cold-case documentary!"

Vivian smiled and squeezed her hand. "Sorry! But it was worth a try. It's a very intriguing story. But, seriously, as I've offered many times, if you ever want me to take a look at the whole thing from a journalist's perspective, you only have to say. Who knows what information might be thrown up if we bring the case back into the public eye?"

Frank Doherty almost knocked Anna out of his way as he stomped through the open-plan room. His strained shirt buttons had finally given in – two had popped open in the middle of his large stomach. His face was a red, thunderous jumble of features as he punched open the stairwell door and disappeared. His presence in the room had sucked any happiness out of it. As the door closed behind him there was a collective sigh of relief among the clerical staff.

"What's wrong with him?" Anna asked, handing Lauren a cappuccino.

"What's *right* with him?" She gratefully took the cardboard cup and opened the lid, blowing on the coffee before taking her first sip. Her eyes closed in momentary pleasure. She pushed her glasses up with her little finger, bracelets jingling. "More drama here this morning before you arrived!"

She leaned conspiratorially closer to Anna, who had switched on her computer and was waiting for the files to load. Lauren could always be relied upon for the office gossip.

"There's a guy due in from the FSI later – about whatever the mess with Dean Harris is about. Also, another body turned up!"

Anna quickly turned her chair fully to her colleague.

"It's a teenager, a drug addict according to his record. He's known to gardaí. It's thought he started dealing recently. Anyway, he turned up dead in the middle of Patrick Street. It's awful!"

A shiver shook its way through Anna. She wondered if this body was connected to the others that had been discovered. As if reading her mind, Lauren leaned closer.

"Detective Molloy is handling this one."

"Not William Ryan?"

Lauren shook her head. "Evidence says it's not related to the cases he's working on."

"Well, that's good news, at least." She thought of Vivian and her eagerness to write the macabre serial-killer story, feeling immense relief this particular crime wouldn't be added to her list.

She turned back to the tower of files awaiting attention on her desk yet couldn't propel her hand to reach for one. For the first time in her three and a half years in the office she felt no interest whatsoever in collating the data or compiling reports. Her eyes strayed to her mobile. She knew it would beep loudly if there was an incoming message, yet she couldn't help but check it anyway.

She looked at the stairwell door Frank Doherty had almost taken off its hinges. She didn't envy the Forensic Science team member who was meeting him to explain whatever the problem was with the DNA in the Dean Harris prosecution.

After his Chief Superintendent was murdered he had assumed the role. It offered him renewed vigour, one which had evidently been long ago lost. With this promotion he could redeem himself after the handling of the Gallagher shooting and dispel any doubt about his effectiveness. He had a demon to exorcise now.

A short time later, Anna watched as a visitor was led upstairs by a uniformed garda. He looked professional, in light grey trousers and jacket, with a briefcase in his hand.

"Nice suit," Lauren muttered, watching him pass their desks, "but it's a suit of armour the man needs to face Doherty. Oh, by the way, have you seen this?"

She threw the morning newspaper to Anna – it landed on her desk with a thump. The headline **SERIAL KILLERS TERRORISE CORK** jumped from the front page.

Vivian's smiling face in the top corner caused Anna to groan and bury her face in her hands.

Later, she had difficulty recalling what files she had worked on that morning. Her attention was almost equally divided between checking her phone for a reply from Annika Garcia and watching the stairwell door for any sign of the FSI representative leaving the building. A steady hum of noise pulsed around the office floor. Normally the beep of fax machines, ringing telephones and the low din of her colleagues' conversation combined into a soothing blend of sound. Today each ping and beep was a harsh wail of distraction.

As each hour passed, she was aware it was another hour closer to Annika Garcia waking and reading the message on her phone. She had struggled over the wording … **Hello, I think I'm your niece** … had seemed too brutal an opening, and she had abandoned it. But sitting in her cold kitchen long into the night had yielded little inspiration, and in the end she had just typed from the heart. She knew that if this woman halfway around the world *was* her aunt, she would learn two things from the message: that her sister had lived long after her disappearance in London, and that she was now missing again, presumed dead. A knot in the pit of her stomach told Anna what she already knew – it would be a horrendous message to wake up to. And perhaps something the woman might chose to ignore. Perhaps like Alex, she would like to forget the whole thing. It was a stark reality to realise this lead might amount to nothing.

Just before lunch, William Ryan escorted the FSI representative from the building. With every cell of her body tingling on alert, Anna watched them go. Both men looked unsettled – William's hair was an untidy mess, as though he had run his hands through it many times. The other man's red tie was pulled too far to the left, as if he had been struggling through the conversation so much he had sought to loosen it for air.

This didn't bode well.

As William returned to the office he paused at Anna's desk. His blue eyes were kind.

"Let me take you to lunch."

She nodded and, as she gathered up her things, she heard Lauren mutter, "Oh, God it must be very bad!"

With a heavy heart, Anna followed the detective out of the station.

25

John Gallagher flexed his shoulders, folded his shirt, and dropped it onto a chair. He lay face down on the table, positioning his head in the circular face cradle that allowed him to breathe through the process. He inhaled, the heady smell of bleach mixed with metal filling his nostrils. Anticipation and a feeling of peace settled over him. It would hurt, just as he wanted it to.

"How did it feel after our last session?"

He didn't know her name and it didn't matter. If she had noticed his fading bruises, she never mentioned it – she didn't ask questions, and he didn't invite conversation. The tattoo gun hummed in her hand, and he felt her gloved fingers prod his back, admiring her artwork.

To get what he wanted would be a long process, one he was willing to tolerate. It was symbolic. This pain was his by choice, not inflicted by men that overpowered him. He was reclaiming what it felt like to suffer, under *his* terms. Every second of this pushed the torture he had endured by the Meiers even further from his memory.

"The whole back is a large job, and the design you chose – a phoenix on fire – it'll take a few more visits yet."

He sighed, impatient. They'd been through all this. Her fingers continued prodding the design on his back, moving the skin over and back.

"Well, it looks great. I'm going to start adding some colour today, so get comfortable."

The needle pierced his skin – John sucked in a deep breath and clamped his teeth together. The design was something he had found online and it was an instant decision. The phoenix, rising in flames, a symbol of strength and rebirth … its meaning was so powerful for him. For the first time in weeks, he felt truly alive. That night at the docks, standing in the damp mist, heat had seared through his veins at being back in the thick of it again. He wanted that feeling to continue, and when the first rush of ink pierced him, the feeling intensified.

He *was* back – the business would be his within a few years, and he realised how quickly things would unravel if he didn't show everyone that the attack by the Meiers was inconsequential, easily forgotten. He saw himself now as the phoenix – he had survived the flames, and his rise from the ashes would be truly spectacular.

26

"It brings me no pleasure to have this conversation with you, so the least I can do is soften the blow over lunch."

Anna watched the detective she had grown to admire so much over the last few months. William Ryan wasn't yet a full year in the Lee Street station, but they had grown close. Trauma was a bonding force, she thought. She had turned to him when she had pieced together the puzzle that identified the link between the assaults Dean Harris had committed. He had also been there for her the night she was attacked and almost killed over the memory key Kate had given her. In the weeks after he had kept in touch with her while she recovered at home, updating her on the case details, filling in the blanks. They shared a mutual respect.

"Thanks for all your hard work, by the way, on the shooting case, and the killing at the weekend. I appreciate you prioritising the reports."

"No problem. It looks like there's very little to go on."

He gave a defeated smile, and she wished he would get on with the reason he wanted to talk.

The Italian restaurant off the main shopping thoroughfare was busy this lunchtime. Muted operatic music, with candles to punctuate the low light, combined with the rustic décor gave an authentic feel to the small space. Anna's memories pulled her to a family holiday in Rome, her brother's constant request to drink wine at the pizzeria near their hotel laughingly brushed off by their mother.

She attempted to smile across the table, but it was just a jerky twitch of the corners of her mouth. There had been little conversation as they walked and even less since they arrived at the restaurant. She traced the blue check on the tablecloth as she waited for the detective to tell her the anticipated bad news. Looking at him made her nervous – his flushed face and tightly set jaw cast an angry aura around him, one she wasn't accustomed to.

"As you know, we had a rep in this morning from Forensic Science Ireland. Just to clear up what we were told last week by an email and a telephone call. This necessitated a personal visit!" He exhaled heavily, causing the candle on the table to flicker between them. He seemed worn out from the subject.

Their food had arrived, but neither touched the steaming plates.

William kept his voice low as he continued. "Let me say this is very much a *human* error, and an isolated one. FSI have always done exemplary work, and they are as disappointed as we are." He pushed his hands roughly through his hair again. "There's no easy way to say this, but the use of the DNA collected after Harris's arrest was compromised. The prosecutor is concerned it may be inadmissible in court."

She had expected some version of this truth but, still,

hearing it out loud, she couldn't help her mouth falling open. Her heart pounded loudly. Gulping at the water in front of her, she swallowed hard.

"How did this happen?" Her voice was cracked and brittle.

William picked up his spoon and began to move carbonara sauce around his plate.

"One of the personnel assigned to the case, a woman whose name is being kept out of it for data protection reasons, was investigated in recent weeks." Disgust dripped through his words. "She made a number of mistakes, mislabelling, that sort of thing. Her attendance was sporadic and recently she was seen staggering and slurring her speech. She suffered a bad fall in the lab and injured herself … to make a long story very short, she's an alcoholic and she was drinking at work." He shook his head. "She was a senior forensic analyst, and everything she worked on had to be independently verified."

"So, someone else can verify the DNA sample? Or take it again? And connect his DNA to the crime scenes?"

William avoided her eyes. Finally tasting his food, he spoke around a mouthful. "It's not that simple. Everything this person touched lately is deemed tainted, and Harris's solicitor is pushing for him to be released on bail pending resolution. He's requested the charges be dropped given the circumstances, but the DPP is pressing ahead. It's a legal mess right now."

Anna rubbed at the space between her eyes, the tightness of a migraine threatening. She did her best to ignore it. "Where does this leave things?"

"As I said, Harris is still in custody but his solicitor will put a petition before the courts to have him released while this is being sorted. I expect he will be out before the end of next week."

Anna shovelled a forkful of pasta into her mouth, just to stop her teeth from chattering in fear and frustration. Dean Harris was a monster who deserved to be locked away. She hoped all was not lost, for the victims especially.

"His defence is just pathetic – he claims you and he were in a relationship, and that the break-in was part of a role-playing fantasy. Absolute rubbish!"

She gagged on her food and he silently passed her a napkin. After a few seconds she could breathe easy again.

"Why did you bring me out to lunch, detective? I mean, I appreciate it, but you could have told me at work. The idea of him back on the streets makes me nervous but I'm a big girl, I can handle it."

Wiping his mouth with his own napkin, he studied her carefully. The intensity in his blue eyes chilled her and she reached for her glass of water, to occupy her shaking hands as much as anything.

"I guess I'm a bit concerned about you. I know you had a tough time last year and I can see it still affects you. Don't get me wrong – you're a strong person and obviously able to defend yourself. But it's OK to be vulnerable, Anna."

His gentle concern made her eyes fill and she dug her fingernails into the flesh of her palm.

"Tell me, do you have good support around you?"

She lowered her eyes to the blue chequered tablecloth, wondering why she felt so uncomfortable.

"Of course … there's my brother, and my friend Vivian. I'm close to Lauren at work, and Myles ..." Finally she met his eyes and smiled, hoping she looked and sounded confident. "I'm OK."

"I hope so. Remember, there are supports at work you can access, and don't be afraid to use them." He inhaled, looking tense again. "I'm afraid there's more – we believe you're a direct target once Harris is released. He spoke to his cellmate about you, and not in flattering terms."

The restaurant suddenly felt claustrophobic, the walls closer than they had been before. She gripped the table edge as though it could stop her from sinking into the abyss of Dean Harris's world.

"Go on."

"It seems he holds you responsible for getting him caught and, I quote, 'ruining his life'. Illogical, I know, but the man isn't exactly a shiny example of male evolution. He told his cellmate you were a liar and a violent lunatic who deserved what was coming, that being, revenge as soon as he got out of jail."

A snort of shocked laughter burst from Anna. "You can't be serious!"

"I'm afraid I am. His cellmate was inside on physical assault charges and talked to a garda on his release. Initially I didn't give it any thought – there was enough evidence to put Harris away for years. Hopefully that evidence still holds!"

Anna swallowed hard, the pasta she had eaten earlier a solid lump in her chest. She wiped sweat from her upper lip and rubbed at her temple. The migraine was pulsing now, drilling into her thoughts. She'd have to get pain relief if she were to continue working today.

"So, what happens now?"

"Now you get a proper security system and a panic alarm installed." William answered with such conviction she realised he had already thought this through. "An intruder alarm and a panic button on each floor of your house will make you safer and make me feel better. I will personally guarantee that if a panic alarm is activated from your address, it will be responded to immediately. We'll also tail Harris once he's released, as long as the budget allows. I want him to know he's being monitored."

The look on his face told Anna that whether the budget allowed or not, he would be on Harris's back. She sank heavily against the back of the wooden chair, toying with her food, turning the pasta into the sauce over and over with the fork. Alex had brought up the need to instal a security alarm, and she had agreed. But in the weeks since Myles had told her about her mother, she had been consumed by that, and all thoughts of a security alarm had been cast to the back of her mind. She resolved to get it done as soon as possible, but the idea of panic buttons in her house seemed extreme.

"You don't look convinced. I assure you – we can keep you safe!"

"I'm sure you'll do all you can. It's just … isn't a panic button a bit over the top?"

"Panic alarms are very common, both for people who feel under threat and for medical emergencies. Is it the disruption to the house? I've been promised the process is very neat and discreet, you'll hardly know the fitters have been inside the house, and the buttons are only visible if you know where to look."

"You've researched this already?"

He nodded and resumed eating – his appetite seemed to have returned now that the worst of the conversation was over. "I have a company lined up, just give me the green light. Dean Harris is a predator and I believe he has targeted you. It may have been bravado and empty threats, but I don't want to take any chances. I don't know exactly when he'll be out but I want you to be ready when he is."

Back in the office, Lauren greeted Anna with a hug as soon as she returned. A chocolate muffin rested near her keyboard.

"I thought you might need it. I actually ate my own while I was waiting. The stress of this place! If I don't fit into my wedding dress, I'll sue the department!"

Anna laughed, despite the growing nausea she felt. Reaching for some painkillers in her desk drawer she downed two and checked her phone – still no message from Annika Garcia.

"Well?" Lauren prompted.

Anna scooted her wheeled chair across to her friend's desk and filled her in.

Later, as she tried to concentrate on her tasks for the day, she found her mind wandering. Crime statistics could not compete with the worry about Dean Harris getting out of prison and back on the streets. She trusted William Ryan when he said they would keep an eye on him and would want the man to *know* he was being watched. And she trusted too that if he *did* come calling to her door again, she could again use the self-defence skills her dad had taught her up until ten years ago, up until he disappeared from her life. She was counting on it.

27

London, 1978

The summer of 1978 was cooler than expected in London. Mr Lewis had insisted Michael take a short, black leather jacket from the excess stock, and he was glad of it as he made his way to the pub after work. He was a little later than the others, having stayed behind to finish up his filing. With his father's flat cap in place and his new leather jacket to buffer the surprisingly low temperatures, he hopped off the bus and hurried along the narrow street.

Bob had insisted they go out for drinks to celebrate Michael gaining his black belt, even though he said he had no idea what that meant. He had eagerly agreed to the night out. They left it up to him to select the venue, and so he chose his local, not far from Warburg Street. He hoped to get to know Boxer and Roy properly over a few beers – he was still too immersed in the accounts to do much else, and he looked forward to being on friendlier terms with them. Boxer was a sociable sort, always returning the morning greeting and offering a jibe about Bruce Lee. Roy seemed quieter and indifferent, surly where the others were friendly.

Sometimes Michael met the man's eyes, and found him hostile, even suspicious, which he found confusing. What had he done wrong? Time hadn't improved things – he hoped spending time together out of the office and sharing a few drinks might.

He was in a buoyant mood, thrilled to have been awarded his black belt. He could barely remember why or how he had got involved in martial arts – he just knew that it made him feel alive in a way other sport didn't. He felt more satisfied with the job he was doing at work too. The pile of papers had been reduced to less than a foot high.

He had explained what he needed the staff to do.

Bob had been the most sceptical.

"Write down everything?" He met eyes with the boss, who had an amused look on his face.

"Yes. Clearly. I can then enter it properly into the ledger. It's the only way to run things without incurring any fines or problems."

Mr Lewis hadn't said much, as usual. But he had smiled and nodded his agreement. Later, Michael had walked into the office after lunch to find him peering into the new filing cabinet. He had jumped as if a loud noise had startled him, quickly stepping back.

"Just checking out the new filing system!"

"Of course, Mr Lewis. They're your files after all!" He kept his voice light and jovial, but he was curious as to why the man didn't just ask for a run-through of the system he had created.

"Well done – it all looks very professional. I appreciate you taking over the wage and utilities payments as well. Gives me a bit more time to drum up new business." He slammed the metal drawer closed and the sound clanged around the office. Pausing on the way back to his desk, he turned to Michael. "Keep up the good work!"

Lewis wasn't invited to the night out – Bob had decided it was better to leave the boss out of their fun. When Michael arrived his three co-workers were already there, seated around a circular table, their pint glasses almost empty in front of them. He called for another round and joined them. Boxer and Bob were smoking, lighting each new cigarette from the stub of the last. A ring of smoke hung low over their table. A red bump on the bridge of Boxer's nose told of his latest fight. He smiled warmly as Michael sat down, the injury appearing not to bother him.

Bob's eyes rested on Michael as he shrugged off his coat.

"Here he is now! London's answer to Bruce Lee!"

Michael smiled patiently – the joke was wearing a bit thin but they seemed to enjoy it.

"I could have used you in my corner last night!" Boxer said with a laugh.

"Our very own bookkeeper and security man, all rolled into one." Roy spoke quietly and eyed Michael as he spoke. "Congratulations."

Michael nodded his head in thanks, though he detected a hint of sarcasm in the man's voice.

The barmaid brought their drinks and passed them around. Roy eyed her appreciatively, leaning back in the seat with a loud wolf-whistle, a smile playing on his lips. Michael knew the girl – she had grown up a few doors down from him. He thought she was far too young to be leered at by a man double her age.

"Thanks, Beth." He nodded to her and she moved away quickly, her cheeks flushed.

"Don't scare off the talent next time," Roy muttered

sourly. He leaned across the table and helped himself to a cigarette from Boxer's pack.

Bob laughed easily. "Lay off, Roy, she's just a kid anyway." He raised his glass. "To Bruce Lee, also-known-as Michael Clarke, our very own ninja!"

Boxer laughed and raised his glass, clinking it so loudly the head off his fresh pint of beer sloshed over the side.

Michael duly clinked glasses, and couldn't help noticing Roy did the same slowly, with exaggerated reluctance.

"Prefer a bit of boxing myself," he muttered. "A proper British sport!"

"I'm sure I read boxing originated in Egypt." Michael smiled over the rim of his pint glass. He swallowed, wincing at the bitterness of the beer. He knew he should leave it – he didn't know Roy well, and the man appeared to be in a sullen mood, much like every day since they had met. Like a man spoiling for an argument. Best not to antagonise him. He was taller than Boxer and rangy, with long limbs. His legs were spread territorially under their table and Michael had to sit on the side of his chair as there was no room for his own legs.

Suddenly setting down his pint, his face twisted, Roy muttered under his breath, "Let's see what you've got then!" He probably thought he had the element of surprise on his side when he swung a fist directly at Michael's face, but it was a clumsy manoeuvre, hampered by too much alcohol. Michael blocked it easily before twisting his wrist around to grab Roy's fist in his own hand. He pulled him close, their faces only inches apart.

"Don't make a fool of yourself."

He spoke quietly, so the others wouldn't hear, then quickly released Roy's fist and sat back. Blood flooded the man's neck and face and he picked up his glass with a shaking hand. For a moment Michael worried he might use it as a weapon.

After a few tense seconds had passed, Roy drained the glass and pushed it across the table.

"That's me done. Early start. You too, Boxer – come on!"

"What? We only just got here!"

But he complied, grumbling, grabbing his coat.

When they were gone Michael noticed Bob exhale deeply before his grin returned.

"I thought they'd stay longer. Roy's in foul humour – no change there! Ah well, their loss – let's get hammered!"

Nana Clarke rescued them at the front door, hours later, when Michael had trouble getting his key in the lock. Manoeuvring the two staggering men to the kitchen table, she made them sit down and appraised them while they grinned at her. Tutting, she turned to the grill. Her white hair was bundled into rollers and she tucked a few loose strands under her nightcap.

Michael gazed at her adoringly.

"I love you, Nana Clarke!" he slurred, and she slapped his hand but was smiling broadly.

"You boys need food. And lots of tea."

"Isn't she something, Bob? Nan, this is my friend Bob Evans."

"Charmed. If anyone needs to be sick, please aim for the sink."

Michael raised his eyebrows to Bob, who was watching Nana move around the kitchen with a grin on his face.

"Then, lads, we are going to play cards! Forty-five, and I won't cheat much, I promise! Now turn out your coins and we'll have some fun!"

That was the first night, and it became a ritual. As July slipped by into August and the summer nights were cool and long, Bob was a Friday-night regular. He and Michael rode the bus to the local on the corner after work for two pints, then it was back to Nana Clarke's for a grill and cards, often playing until the sun came up. Bob slipped into their little family, and to Michael it seemed that two easily became three. There was louder laughter in their terraced house every Friday night than there had ever been, the neighbours banging a shoe on the wall when the raucous laughter grew too loud and the night too late. Nana Clarke was happy – she enjoyed looking after "the two boys". Bob laughingly accused her of cheating every Friday night, and she smirked as she scooped her winnings into her skirt pockets. He called her Nana Clarke too, and Michael thought he felt a real affection for her – she was hard not to love, in his opinion. She greeted Bob with a hug every Friday night, the sofa made up for him, his favourite crackling bacon grilling. He always complimented her hospitality and thanked her profusely each Saturday morning when he left.

"He's a nice boy, your friend" was a thing she said often. That, and "Mr Lewis is a very generous man!"

She was right. Michael's wages were above that of most young men in London, and he was kept well-dressed. But, as time passed, he had a growing feeling that something wasn't right.

Weeks ago, he had discovered some anomalies in the accounts, but he had hoped that as time went on and his knowledge of the company grew things would become clearer. So he had delved deeper into the ledgers, and his confusion had turned to concern. Some things just didn't add up. While the customs documents seemed perfect – he could account for delivery dockets at the port, prepared by Lewis and scribbled on by Bob – some paperwork was non-existent. At first he thought he had misfiled the dockets, then he concluded that perhaps documentation for those particular transactions had never been created. Worse again, he still could not account for how the Turkish supplier was paid. He should advise the boss – but first he wanted to run things past Bob.

"Look, mate, did you ever hear the saying 'Don't sweat the small stuff'?" was his friend's response.

Michael couldn't keep the exasperation from his voice. "This isn't small stuff though! This reflects badly on me as a bookkeeper, Bob!"

Bob patted his shoulder. "Some things are looked after by Lewis exclusively. He has a good relationship with those suppliers – they go way back. And it's only a couple of orders a year. Don't worry about it."

Michael frowned. "I'll have to ask Mr Lewis to document it though to complete the –"

"Leave it to me!" His voice was firmer than Michael expected. "*Seriously*, I'll take care of this. Don't bring it up, OK?"

The force in his answer only fuelled the certainty in Michael that something wasn't right. And this was the second time Bob had fobbed off his probing questions, the other time being about the girl, Yelena. Nana Clarke had said many times he had a curious mind and had warned him about asking too many questions. So once again he swallowed his concerns and told himself that the longer he stayed in the business, the clearer things would become.

28

Cork, 2019

"Dean and Anna sitting in a tree,
Anna's gonna pay for what she did to me.
Pretty blonde hair and big brown eyes,
Filthy little mouth tells dirty little lies.
When we meet there'll be such a mess,
Where I'll bury you is anyone's guess!"

Dean liked to make up songs and poems while he stared at the bare walls in his concrete prison. It helped him to pass the time. Because, these days, he had a lot of time stretched out in front of him, with little else to do but think.

Sure, some parts of the prison were roomier than others, and some of the inmates were friendly. He was pleasantly surprised at the quality of the food – there was even a TV room. It was the waiting that bothered him the most... hour after hour, wondering what further injustices he must suffer. The greatest injustice of all was being in this hell-pit. His freedom denied, his comforts removed, all because of *her*.

Each morning, for the first few moments after opening his eyes, he actually forgot he was in jail. It was a cruel trick his mind was playing. He always woke early, earlier than his cellmate. After a few seconds of glorious peaceful nothingness, he became aware of sounds: clanging and banging, metal against metal. And shouting – men calling to each other or authoritarian voices shouting commands. The sounds were distant yet close enough to spike a dreaded familiarity that clenched his stomach. Then the noises made by his cellmate began, the man rousing from his own sleep – fingernails scratching skin, grunting and snorting phlegm. It sickened Dean to have to breathe the same air as him. Each new day brought fresh torture – he had been caught, he was locked up in here, and he was desperately scrambling for any excuse to get out.

Anna Clarke was lying! They were lovers, and it was all a game, and she had changed her mind, that's all!

The laundry room was his favourite place in here. The smells were more pleasant than anywhere else in the prison. Detergent and fabric softener, lavender scented if he wasn't mistaken, were far easier on the senses than other men's bodily odours. This room was sweet-smelling, like a woman. Like any of the women he had visited over the last few years, before he made the mistake of visiting *her.*

Every day the pain of her attack assaulted him again. He had taken to opening and closing his mouth continuously, a tiny up-and-down movement that had become an obsessive tic. A clicking sound rang loud in his ears each time, and he silently raged in anger. *She* had done this. The doctor said it was just a hairline fracture and he would be fine, but he wasn't. Toffee would forever be off-limits, meat was almost impossible to chew, and apples had to be cut into small pieces, as though for a child. If he heard the words "just give it time" once more he would kill someone.

The little bitch had a lot to answer for.

He wasn't to know she could do karate or kickboxing, or whatever she had done. She was the perfect target, until suddenly she wasn't. Living alone, in a house with a dodgy back-door lock, she was just his type. Everything had seemed ideal but quickly blew up into a catastrophic mess. He was aware of a tremor in his hands every time he thought of her, and he had discovered singing songs about her to be a great remedy. Best to stay positive.

"Harris!" A prison officer stood in the doorway, watching him.

Dean raised his eyes and stared impassively. His jaw was still slightly swollen, and he could get away with not speaking to these people, for now.

"Visitor for you."

He was surprised to see his solicitor waiting for him in the interview room, his folded hands resting on the table. He didn't stand as Dean entered nor offer more than a nod of greeting. Such rudeness grated on him. He noted the man's watch, almost too big for his skinny wrist, and the expensive cut of his suit as he sat back down, unbuttoning his jacket. His poor mother was paying for the best legal help they could get – he'd better be worth it.

"Mr Harris, I'll get straight to the point."

"What, no pleasantries?" he drawled. "No 'How are you Dean? They treating you alright? How are you sleeping?' No concern for my welfare?" The mechanics of speaking caused his jaw to ache, and he cursed Anna Clarke again.

The solicitor drew in a deep breath and Dean saw his eyes twitch slightly, as though the man were trying to stop them from rolling to the ceiling.

"I'm here to inform you there's been a technical

difficulty with the DNA evidence collected after your arrest. The use of that sample has been compromised. The prosecutor will do all he can to tie this up quickly but I think we can move to have you released on bail in the meantime. Let me explain the –"

But no explanation could be heard. Dean began to laugh, a truly satisfied sound from deep inside him, born of sheer relief. His jaw throbbed in pain but he couldn't stop. He was growing hysterical, his laughter louder and louder in the small interview room. The man sitting opposite him looked slightly alarmed, his eyes darting to the door, then his watch. He carried on speaking, delivering his message, but Dean could only hear fragments over the sounds of his own happiness.

"… terms of your release … stay away from the alleged victim Miss Clarke … do nothing to jeopardise …"

After a few minutes of having his words drowned out by unstoppable laughter he leaned across the table, impatient, and said: "*Mr Harris*, do you understand what I have told you here today?"

Later in his cell, while the man in the bed opposite tossed and turned seeking comfort, and shouts echoed and bounced in the halls, Dean rested his head in his cradled hands on the pillow, unable to keep a smile from his face. His eyes roamed the ceiling overhead, the scratches and cracks in the plaster, the initials drawn on there. He would add his own **DH** before his release, he decided. With a little smiley face too. He would be out of this concrete cage in a matter of days, and he didn't mind leaving his mark here before he left for good.

The shouts of other men reverberated around the cell

and in his mind, as they did every other night, but he began to sing his favourite song again, drowning them all out.

"Dean and Anna sitting in a tree,
Anna's gonna pay for what she did to me.
Pretty blonde hair and big brown eyes,
Filthy little mouth tells dirty little lies.
When we meet there'll be such a mess,
Where I'll bury you is anyone's guess!
Poor little Anna, whatcha gonna do?
Dean's getting out and he's coming for you!"

29

The River Lee was rough, the tide high and racing in angry ripples. Tom stared into its murky waters, a shade between brown and green that looked wholly unpleasant. From his vantage point on the third-floor office block, the city looked serene: traffic mutely inching forward, his fellow Corkonians walking hurriedly, heads bowed against the stinging January wind. Only the river betrayed the vast turmoil of its city's people: the anger, the swirling underbelly that, for the most part, lay hidden.

"You need to get your affairs in order." His solicitor's voice penetrated his thoughts. "Once the gardaí come calling with a warrant, there's absolutely nothing we can do, legally, but provide what they're looking for."

Tom turned from the window to face the man – he was sitting behind a desk so large he wondered if it were a metaphorical shield against the clients that would sit opposite. Various plaques and honours were hung on the walls of the room, reminding him of Victor White's qualifications, should he feel he wasn't being offered sound advice. He sat down again in the leather chair opposite, adjusting the button on his suit jacket, the leather creaking under his weight.

"I understand. You've spoken to the accountant? Everything is as it should be?"

The solicitor nodded and rested his elbows on the table, his fingers steepled under his chin.

Tom was irritated by the look on his face, like a priest about to council a sinner.

"I'm not an accountant, but yes, all looks to be in order. As you're well aware, Tom, the full extent of your business dealings are your own. I've never sought to be appraised of –"

"Yes, yes, plausible deniability and all that!" Tom snarled.

"The thing is – the Lee Street station have sought to question you so many times, and I fear now they have good reason." He sat back and ran his hands along his perfectly straight tie. "I've done all I can legally to stall and delay, claiming harassment and so on, but when the time comes you must cooperate. Unfortunately, David – God rest his soul – brought too much attention to the family in recent months. The assaults on his partner drew too much notice and the recent dealings he had with that that foreign criminal gang ... there is enough evidence to *know* David was involved in conspiracy to sell stolen classified data pertinent to national security. I'm afraid, were David alive, he would be in such trouble with the law that I could not help this time, no matter what favours I could call in. All of this has brought considerable attention to your business portfolio."

Tom smiled at the man coolly, his anger contained. The rage he felt at his son's behaviour and lack of care for the family business had long ago abated. David's mistakes were borne of his impetuous nature, but Tom felt compassion for his son – he knew he had only done what he did last year to impress his father, to show him he could handle taking over the business. The problem was that where David was concerned, things usually went awry.

Tom had always intended it would be John to take over. John was so ruthless it unnerved the men around him; such a reputation was effective. No other man dared to invade their streets. Business dealings with other bars and club owners remained cordial – competition was a good thing for a vibrant city – but drugs were Gallagher territory, protected by John and Ely Murray, a brutal tag-team of violence. Handling stolen goods was a lucrative side-line – everything had run smoothly for so long it was impossible to imagine any plausible threat. John remained eager for business to continue as normal, but Ely … he could feel the man's growing frustration.

He turned to the solicitor who had been on his team from the very start, a man he had made rich beyond his wildest imagination when he was a young graduate starting out.

"Have you pressed the gardaí further on the search for Kate Crowley?"

Victor White stared at Tom for a moment before he answered, his expression unreadable. "Well, yes, of course. At this stage, they are certain she remains abroad. The French authorities have been notified that the gardaí believe she's in France. It's the only logical explanation, knowing that her sister flew there the day David was shot. However, there's been no progress on locating her."

"And the enquiries we have put out? To the contact you have in Paris … any update?"

He shook his head. "Nothing so far. But I have people across France and Spain, and they have their own men even further afield. We'll find her."

"I'm working on something else. I've found a friend of hers who might have information. Here in Cork."

The solicitor's eyes widened and he leaned forward. "I must urge caution there, Tom! Your position with the gardaí is already precarious!"

Tom opened his mouth to speak but the other man held up his hands. "I really don't want to know."

30

All afternoon Anna checked her phone for a reply from Annika Garcia, but in vain. The little ticks beside the message she had sent didn't even turn blue to indicate she had read it. Minutes rolled into hours as the afternoon stretched before her. She knew her work level would be classed as 'unproductive' today, but for once, she didn't care.

Lauren had been horrified at the prospect of Dean Harris's release and the threats he had made.

"I think you should move into your brother's house!"

"Don't be daft!"

Anna knew her friend had a point, but she found her brother's over-protectiveness stifling. Still, she resisted the urge to reread the reports of the assaults Dean Harris had committed. She knew it was him, flawed DNA or not. She wondered about the threat he had made against her – was it credible? William Ryan seemed to think so. He was afraid for her, enough to want her to install alarms in her house. Fear was one thing, but panic was another – her father and Jason had long ago taught her how to control her fear, to steady her breathing, and to defend herself calmly. Those skills had worked that night in her house. She had to trust it would save her again if she needed it to.

The day stretched into evening and dusk replaced the light. She said goodbye to Lauren as a message from Alex came through on her mobile.

How are you today?

Fine, she lied, **You?**

Good. Any progress with the online searches?

Some. Anna didn't feel like going into it by text. **Will I come by after work to fill you in?**

Yes! I'd love to see you! Sam is working late. Chloe is heading to bed soon, so it'll be just us. Any chance you'd pick up dinner? I'd love a beef korma from that place near your office.

Anna quickly texted her agreement – they had shared this takeaway many times before. The food would have to be heated up by the time she had driven to Kinsale, but the idea of sharing dinner with her brother was a welcome one. It certainly beat eating alone with only thoughts of Dean Harris for company.

Before she shut down her computer she sent a message to Sam, pushing away the restless thoughts about her late nights at the office.

Hey, I'm still in the office & I hear you are too! I'm picking up dinner for Alex – want me to order anything for you? Would be lovely to catch up later!

In a way, Anna was hesitant, her thumb hovering before pressing send – this was a probing text message, and she knew it. The intricacies of her brother's marriage were none of her business. She had always been careful not to intrude too much into his private life – he had given her so much already. But her gut instinct told her this was the right thing to do. It was no big deal – offering to pick up dinner for her sister-in-law didn't imply she was spying on her, right?

As she collected her food thirty minutes later, there was still no reply. The restaurant also sold drinks to take away and Anna added a couple of soft drinks to her order, smiling at the image of Father Christmas embossed on the glass bottles, clearly stock left over from Christmastime. Chloe could enjoy one of those tomorrow. She tried not to think about Samantha and resolved not to mention the unanswered text to her brother later.

Outside, the bracing cold stung her face and her breath formed a halo in front of her as she walked through the streets. It was still freezing – she thought of Lauren's wedding in a few weeks' time and hoped it would be warmer by then. They had toyed with the idea of heading to the sun for a long weekend, to escape the cold for a while. In the end, Lauren had been too busy with last-minute wedding preparations and the idea had passed.

As she reached the station car park, a vibrating sensation and loud trumpet sound from her pocket announced an incoming call. Samantha!

"Sam! Did you get my –"

"Anna! *Please!*"

It was a whispered, urgent plea, her voice an ice-cold grip on Anna's heart.

"*Please! Help me! My boss ... I think he –*"

Abruptly the call ended. Turning on her heel, the takeaway carrier bag swinging in her hand, Anna broke into a run.

* * *

The building Samantha worked in was attended by a short man in uniform. He looked old enough to be long retired. He was probably doing the evening shifts no-one else wanted to top-up his pension, Anna thought as she passed his counter quickly. The randomness of the thought surprised her but it was better than worrying about what had happened to Samantha in the four minutes it had taken her to run there.

Steadying her breathing as best she could, she raised the bag of food, called out "Delivery, fourth floor!" and gave a friendly smile. The security guard waved her on. As she rode the lift to Samantha's floor, she thought that it really had been *too* easy to access the building late at night and grimaced at her own thoughts – she was spending too long typing up crime reports, seeing suspicion in everything and everyone.

Anna had been here before to visit Samantha and knew her desk was situated in the middle of the large open-plan room. At the back of the room was a row of small offices with glass windows that faced both onto the street and back into the main office space. She assumed the bosses were stationed there, the better to keep an eye on the staff.

She moved to Samantha's cubicle and saw her bag and coat, and her computer switched on. But where was she? Anna deposited the takeaway bag of food and the glass bottles of soft drinks on the table and looked around her. The place seemed to be empty. On the other occasions she had been here it had been full of people and the noise their hustle and bustle generated – now that it was deserted, it was eerily quiet.

Or was it? She held her breath, hearing a sudden muffled cry from one of the offices that caused her heart to pound in her ears and her adrenaline to surge. Picking up one of the glass bottles, but hoping she wouldn't need to use it, she moved quickly towards the office, her footsteps muffled on the deep carpet.

The cry rose in volume. The office door was wide open, desk chairs pushed to the wall. Samantha was bent backwards over the desk, pinned there, struggling with the weight of a man on top of her. His face was buried in her neck. She had her eyes closed and her face was shining with sweat as she frantically pushed against his chest.

She cried out again, *"I said get off me!"* but it made no difference. The man was too big, his weight a leverage on top of her that she couldn't escape.

Anger surged in Anna; quickly she quelled it, long ago taught by her father that it served no valuable purpose. She assessed the situation, her Taekwon-Do training replacing any other thoughts. The man was at least six inches taller than her and looked about sixty pounds heavier. His arms had a powerful look that could only be explained by pumping weights. He was strong. The office space was small, and he had all his weight on Samantha. Anna needed him to move, and for that she would need the element of surprise.

Gripping the neck of the glass bottle she smashed it hard against the door frame. Its bubbly liquid spilled onto the carpet as the sound of the breaking glass shattered the silence and broke the man's momentum. He jumped up as though he'd heard a gunshot. Red-faced, dishevelled, momentarily he looked startled, then furious.

Samantha quickly darted from the desk.

"*Who the fuck are you?*" the man blurted, and stepped towards Anna, his face twisted in anger.

She immediately dropped the bottle and adopted the martial-art ready stance, her feet shoulder-width apart, her arms held in front, fists closed. She was calm and she was ready.

Instinct stilled the man's movements – he stepped back and raised his hands in surrender.

"*What the hell do you think you're doing?*" she said, glaring at him.

He stepped back further, his thighs connecting with his own desk. He kept his hands high and feigned a laugh.

"There's no harm done, just a little misunderstanding. Isn't that right, Samantha?" He looked to his right at Samantha, but Anna didn't take her eyes off him. In her peripheral vision she could see that Samantha was steady on her feet, and she could hear her ragged breathing. She motioned with her left hand for her to stand behind her, and her sister-in-law moved quickly.

"*Call the gardaí!*" Anna instructed. "This man sexually assaulted you and I'm a witness. *Call them!*" Samantha didn't move.

Her hesitation seemed to give the man the confidence he needed. He pushed himself from his desk and shoved past Anna. Stopping in front of Samantha, he jabbed his finger in her face, anger colouring his skin. "You had better mind your manners if you want to keep your job. You've been teasing me for months, not to mention the money you owe me. You say one word and I'll see you fired. It's your word against mine. *I'm* the star around here, remember?"

He grabbed his coat from the back of a chair, glared at Anna once more, and stormed from the office. As he walked quickly away from them through the open-plan room, he buttoned his coat and smoothed his hair back into place, no doubt to present a calm exterior to the security guard on his way out.

Anna narrowed her eyes in disgust.

Samantha seemed to crumble in front of her. Her legs gave out and she sank to the floor, shaking and sobbing loudly. Anna knelt beside her, not saying anything, just rubbing her arm. Sobs echoed loudly around the empty office. After a few minutes she sagged against the open door, her tears and energy spent. Anna stepped over her and back into the open-plan office to retrieve her coat.

"Here," she held it out, "you're freezing!"

Samantha shrugged it on with trembling hands, leaning her head against the door, her eyes tightly closed. Tears leaked down her cheeks.

Anna waited quietly beside her, feeling at a loss as to how to comfort her. Eventually she said, "Are you going to tell me what's going on?"

"*Oh God!*" she moaned, lowering her forehead to press it against the palms of her hands. "I've made such a mess of things." She turned to look at Anna and groaned, "Alex is going to be furious."

"I think Alex will just be glad you're not having an affair," Anna said with a smile.

Samantha returned her smile sadly and wiped her wet face with her fingertips. She pushed herself up into a standing position and held out her hand for Anna. Together they moved to her desk in the open-plan section and sat down on two swivel chairs.

Samantha took a deep breath – she was pale and shaking still but making a conscious effort to steady herself.

Anna passed her a soft drink. "You could use some sugar."

She took a long drink, then with a shaking hand wiped her mouth and took a deep breath.

"I really shouldn't be telling you this!" She sighed, a weary, defeated sound. "A few months ago, things got a bit … tight, financially. As you know, a while back Alex invested in new software for his accountancy firm. That used up most of our savings to be honest but it made sense at the time. We had to replace my car … then, just a few weeks ago, we had the chimney fire – the insurance company *still* haven't paid out! We used what was left of our savings to fix the damage and were considering taking out a loan, but we really didn't want to do that. I had some shares that I could cash in if we needed them, and it seemed like a good idea at the time. But it wasn't enough – the shares were worth a lot less than I had expected. Alex hasn't been sleeping – he's seemed very agitated since what happened to you last year." She cast Anna an apologetic look.

Anna looked away – the attack last year had almost killed her. That, and the break-in to her home by Dean Harris, had caused her brother considerable stress. He thought of himself as her guardian, even though she was a grown woman. He had moved into the house for a short while after the attack – to think he was having sleepless nights because of it caused her heart to ache for him.

"I didn't want to worry him about money when he was already so stressed out!"

"I'm sorry you found yourself in that position. I really am. You were vulnerable and I suppose 'hot shot' here offered to help you out?"

"Yes." Samantha's lips trembled around her words, her voice low, barely above a murmur. "He's only in our office a few months, promoted from the States. He's brought in loads of clients and is about to be made partner. Anyway, he was really supportive at the beginning, and we worked really well on a project together last year, and I confided in him." She began to cry again softly. "A few weeks ago he offered me an advance on my pay if I agreed to work more overtime, and I jumped at it. The company has a strict policy on advances, but Blake said he'd square things with the owners, and not to worry about it. I told Alex the money came from the shares, we fixed the house up, and life went back to normal. I planned to pay back the advance when the insurance money came through, but that could be weeks, or months!"

"But then your boss, this 'Blake', started being difficult?"

Samantha nodded. "Blake Landers, yeah. He kept demanding I work weekends, and often it was just us. He said my performance was slipping and that my output wasn't enough. I knew that was a lie – I was doing the same amount of work I've always done, more if anything! He stopped being supportive and kept reminding me I owed him. I was terrified of him in the end." She looked at Anna. "How could I have been so stupid? He began making inappropriate comments, asking me out for drinks after work ... I should have put a stop to it, I should have just told Alex about the money. Tonight he suggested dinner and I said no and he just ... snapped. Said I'd been teasing him and he'd had enough. Oh Anna!"

Anna gripped her hand. "None of this is your fault, Sam! You trusted a colleague and he took advantage of that. I understand Alex wasn't in a good place last year. But I'm always here for you – I wish you had asked me for the money!"

Samantha shook her head. "Alex would never want me to burden you!"

Anna felt a rush of annoyance, biting back her anger. She wasn't the teenager Alex had to take care of anymore! Now, Sam had found herself in a terrible situation because neither of them was prepared to ask her for help. They both knew the trust-fund money Bob had provided was mostly untouched in her bank account, and she would have gladly given it to them. And, despite her suggesting it, Alex had never liquidated his share of their family home. She knew the house was worth a lot and had broached the subject many times – she wanted to buy out his share, to pay him what was his. He had always insisted they would sort it all out in time, that it would be an ordeal legally, and to let things be for now.

Anna was going to insist this time. She and Alex needed to finalise what had started ten years ago. They would have to declare their parents legally dead; then they could sort out their assets once and for all. She swallowed a lump in her throat at the thought of it, but she knew it had to be done.

"I'll probably be fired for taking the advance!" Samantha sniffed and buried her face in her hands.

"I wouldn't be so sure about that," Anna said confidently. "Landers just sexually assaulted you! *He* will be fired, I guarantee it! I've seen plenty of cases like this at work – the company will want to end this situation quickly and avoid any bad publicity or legal problems."

Samantha shook her head. "You don't understand. It'll be my word against his, and you heard him, he'll say I made the whole thing up. He'll say I came on to him."

"Probably. But you've a witness."

"I guess that's true." Although somewhat relieved, Samantha looked tired and very pale. "I still have to tell Alex."

"Come on," Anna said, hopping up. "You need to get home and talk to him."

Samantha allowed herself to be pulled to her feet. As Anna gathered her things into her handbag and switched off her computer, she noticed tears were still flooding her face. She made no effort to wipe them away.

"Anna," Samantha said softly, catching her arm, "tonight could have ended very differently. Thank God you answered my call!"

31

Ely Murray was cold and more than a little intrigued. Anna Clarke led a busy life. Following her was proving both interesting and frustrating, and the half-thought-out plan of bundling her into a car seemed out of the question. The most he hoped to achieve was breaking into her house and detaining her there while Tom Gallagher drove to meet them – let the man ask his questions of her in her *own* house, rather than try to bring her to them.

She was busy and rarely alone, it seemed. Today, she'd had lunch with a detective in the city, and then worked late into the evening. Although the Lee Street Garda station car park had been deserted when she left, he still wouldn't risk approaching her there. He had watched her from the shadows of a multi-story car park across the street and was heartened when she walked straight onto the footpath outside instead of towards her car. A quick trip to a takeaway restaurant and he was following her again, before she took a phone call and sprinted right up to the entrance of the office block she entered. An old man at security had asked him his business when he followed her inside, and Ely had quickly muttered he was at the wrong address, his eyes darting to the security cameras mounted in the corners of the entrance hall.

Now he had returned to the shadows again, his coat collar turned up against the wind. He wore a black woollen hat and scarf wound around as much of his face as possible. The scar, long ago earned, was prominent and remarkable – if Anna Clarke remembered their encounter in the ladies' bathroom in the Mad Hatter club, she would remember the scar. People always did.

He straightened up as a man stepped outside the office block. Early thirties, he wore a heavy dark coat over his suit. Ely watched him standing at the kerb, bringing a cigarette to his lips. He cupped his hand around the cigarette as he lit it, taking a deep drag, exhaling to the sky overhead. He stayed there for what felt like a long time, drawing deeply on the nicotine, the wind buffeting his coat.

Ely watched the man scowl as he turned his head towards sudden movement at the revolving glass doors. Two women had emerged: Anna Clarke and a companion. They linked arms, standing still, staring at the man who glared at them, spitting words that Ely couldn't hear in their direction. The man threw his cigarette at the ground in front of them and turned away, heading towards the main city streets. The women watched him go. Ely stepped further back into the shadows, keeping the women in sight.

It happened suddenly. As the man was standing on the footpath near a set of traffic lights, not far from Ely's hiding spot, a single car pulled away from the kerb where it had been parked. The road was otherwise deserted. The car pulled up alongside the man and the passenger window was lowered. Ely observed the scene curiously and noticed the women were watching too. The man bent forward, close to the car, as though to speak to the occupants. Suddenly a gunshot rang loud and red mist sprayed from the man's face into the wind. He fell to the ground. The women's screams mingled with the squeal of tyres as the car sped away.

Ely's heart leapt in horror. He exhaled heavily, a cloud of chilly air in front of his face betraying his position. Anna brought her mobile phone to her ear and looked directly at him. As the wail of sirens pierced the night, he turned and walked into the dark.

Later, Ely had trouble closing his eyes to sleep, eventually abandoning the idea. He returned to his living room, the red glow from his cigarette the only thing piercing the darkness. Images from the scene played on his mind. The man on the road was definitely dead – pieces of his flesh had littered the footpath.

The calm demeanour of Anna Clarke had slightly unnerved him. She had looked shocked – Ely could remember her large eyes, wide in terror, and her pale face. But unlike her friend she had stayed calm and called the gardaí. She was a woman he would be wise to respect.

One aspect of the incident, a detail he could not be sure was real or imagined, refused to leave his thoughts. The passenger of the car, a woman, had behaved in the most bizarre way. She had been holding something up to eye level, holding it steady with both hands. A red light on the device had cut through the darkness of the car – to Ely, it looked like she had been holding a camcorder. But it was her hysterically silent laughter that had unnerved Ely the most – the wide-mouthed shake of her head as the victim jerked backwards from the force of the gunshot.

32

It was close to midnight when they had finished giving their statements to the gardaí.

William Ryan had been especially interested in Anna's account that the passenger was a woman, and that she had been holding a camera.

"I only saw them for a fraction of a second but I'm sure! She was holding *something* and it had a small red light. It's *them!* The killers. And I could swear the driver turned his head to look at me!"

"Seriously?"

"Yes, I ... well, it was dark, but ... it seemed like he turned and looked right at me. There was a man also, almost hidden in the entrance of a building, standing quite near the victim. Can you check the on-street CCTV?"

"We'll do that. I hope to have it shortly. But think carefully about everything you think you saw tonight, Anna – you've been exposed to all the evidence in this case, and sometimes when we *want* to see something badly enough, we do."

She mulled over his words as she drove home. Samantha was quiet in the passenger seat, in no way capable of driving. She had barely been able to make her statement, shaking and crying throughout. Anna imagined it was the events from earlier in the night, and perhaps the fact that she knew Blake Landers personally, that had compounded her shock. She had vomited twice at the station – Anna just wanted to get her home to rest.

She felt fine. Obviously, it had been a terrible thing to witness, but she had calmly phoned the emergency services after taking what turned out to be a uselessly blurry photograph of the car registration number. She had assessed Blake Landers from where she was standing – he was clearly dead.

Her lack of panic and shock niggled at her though – shouldn't she have been more horrified, like Samantha was? Wouldn't anyone be? Perhaps it was her job, handling reports of the grimmest crimes in the city and county, that had acclimatised her to such scenes? She had no explanation for how calm she currently felt. And there was something she couldn't stop thinking about, edging out all other thoughts – the turn of the driver's head, the heat from his eyes as they met hers. William Ryan had seemed sceptical, but she was sure of it. The driver had looked right at her just after Blake Landers was shot. Almost as though he was checking to see if she had seen what happened, if she had witnessed the horror. So much of this just did not make sense – including, what did any of this have to do with her?

Alex was sitting in the living room, typing on his laptop, and looked up in surprise as they came in. "Finally! Sam! Are you OK?"

She sagged into the door frame, her face pale and tearstained. Anna helped her to the sofa, easing her into it.

Alex hurried to her side and embraced her.

"Anna, what's happened?"

Anna heaved a deep shuddering sigh and, sinking into an armchair facing them, recounted everything that had happened that evening.

"So is the guy dead?" Alex asked when she at last fell silent.

"Yeah," she nodded, "no-one could have survived that."

"Jesus! What a horrific experience!"

"Yes, I'm OK but Sam needs time to get over it all." She got up and brought in the takeaway food she had left in the hallway, resting it gently on the coffee table in the centre of the room. "I'll leave this here. It'll need to be heated up, obviously." She doubted anyone would be hungry.

Alex didn't say a word, unable to take his eyes off his wife.

Anna touched his elbow. "I think she'll need to rest before she can speak about it."

"Does she need a doctor?"

"No. She was checked over at the station. She just needs to rest."

She let herself out.

Her hands shook as she pushed the key into the lock, and she felt some relief that she was finally experiencing the shock of what she had witnessed. Stepping into her house she shivered. It was more than the cool temperature – it was the emptiness. Tears stung her eyes as she turned on the lights, dumping her keys in the bowl on the hall table and her bag on the sofa in her living room, before moving into the adjoining kitchen. She had intended to make herself a cup of tea – instead, she opened the fridge and pulled out a half-empty bottle of wine. It was one of the bottles she and Myles had shared last weekend.

Moving to the sofa she passed the bronze trophy her father had won, resting on the bookshelf. Touching it gently with one finger, she smiled at the memory of the self-defence games her dad had played in the back garden with her and Alex. The events of tonight in Samantha's office could have been so much worse – lately she was intensely grateful to her dad for all he had done to keep them safe.

She turned on the TV and flicked aimlessly through the channels – she needed noise to drown out the thoughts that swirled in her mind. As always, the house was too quiet. Exhaustion washed over her in nauseous waves – perhaps it was loneliness that had become a physical feeling? Pulling out her phone she dialled Myles' number, not caring it was the middle of the night.

He answered on the first ring, surprising her.

"Hello! I was just dreaming about you!"

"Did I wake you?"

"Not quite – I'm glad you called. I miss you."

"Me too. Where are you?"

After a brief pause, he answered, "I'm in Brussels."

She realised she hadn't expected him to answer.

"Are you OK, Anna?"

"Not really …" Her voice wavered.

For an hour, she filled him in on the events of her day: lunch with William Ryan, detailing the failures of the DNA analyst, the attack on Samantha and the killing of Blake Landers. Myles listened and asked questions, his soft words of comfort encasing her in the warm feeling that she wasn't alone. By the time they said goodnight, she felt lighter.

When she made her way to bed, she checked her messages again. Annika Garcia was still on her mind, despite everything else. But there was nothing from her. Selecting a playlist of Bach classics on her phone, she drifted off to sleep to the soothing sounds of her mother's favourite instrument.

33

The punchbag in the local gym bore the brunt of Anna's frustrations before sunrise the following morning. Jason wasn't there to spar with this morning, and the bag swung wildly. Still, it offered a release, and she felt better for it.

By nine she was in her brother's house, collecting Chloe for playgroup.

"Are you sure you don't mind?"

"Alex, it's fine, I told you. It's no big deal if I'm a little late for work. I'm owed some flexitime. In fact, I've taken tomorrow off – Vivian is getting the keys to her apartment today and I'm helping her move in. I can drop Chloe off again tomorrow morning if you and Sam need to go to any meetings?"

She meant with Sam's employer, assuming there would be a lot to sort out. He touched her arm, his face full of gratitude.

"Thanks, that'd be great. We're meeting Sam's boss. He's horrified at the whole thing and trying to decide what to do. I honestly think they care more about the fact that

Landers is dead than what he did to Sam." He looked away, angry, colour rising up his neck and flooding his face. Eventually he looked at the ceiling.

"Well, don't forget, I witnessed some of what he did to her and have given my statement to the gardaí. How is she?"

"Still asleep. She's normally an easy sleeper, but I gave her a sleeping pill anyway. Mine." He had been prescribed them ages ago.

Chloe skipped into the room, the novelty of her aunty bringing her to playgroup making her hop in delight.

"Come on, you!" Anna smiled fondly, helping her into her coat.

"Will you come and see my drawings on the art-wall?"

"Of course!"

"And can I show you the sandpit and the nature table?"

"Definitely!"

The little girl slipped her hand into Anna's. "Can I sit up front in the car with you?"

"Absolutely not."

Anna had a meeting with William Ryan at eleven to go back over her statement from the night before. His mouth was a thin, grim line, his lips almost invisible, as he greeted her at his desk. Dark circles under his eyes betrayed his tiredness, his jerky movements revealing too much coffee. She wondered if he'd had any sleep since they last spoke.

"You were right by the way." He moved files from a seat beside him and gestured for her to sit down. "The passenger of the car filmed the shooting. And we think it was a woman. Security cameras from office blocks on Albert Quay captured the best image of the occupants of the car. We have a pretty clear image of a person with long hair and a narrow build holding up an item matching the size and shape of a camcorder. The images are only as good as they *can* be, but given what we know already, I'm convinced."

"And the driver?"

"Male, most likely. Wearing a baseball hat. It's impossible to see anything of his face. They stole the car – the Technical Bureau are examining it now. What I find interesting is that the car was idling at the kerb, waiting. Shortly after you and your sister-in-law left the building, they pulled up alongside the victim and shot him. Do you know the man? Any connection other than the fact that your sister-in-law worked for him?"

Anna shook her head quickly. This was making her feel a little breathless.

William exhaled and rubbed at the sides of his face.

"Do you still think he looked at you, the driver?"

"*Right* at me!"

"Could it be possible he just looked in your direction?"

She shook her head.

"I've been awake half the night thinking about this. If they wanted to avoid CCTV and witnesses, then why would he look around him? He actually turned his head away from the victim to look at me! There was another man standing in the shadows in his direction, and he never looked at him, as far as I can remember. Just at me. Which is freaking me out, to be honest."

William's blue eyes softened and he sat up straighter.

"Alright, let's go through all this again. I don't think you should be worrying but you are, so let's run through what we already know. Maybe we can put your mind at ease, OK?"

Anna nodded, feeling a rush of affection for him. He

genuinely cared that she was scared from the encounter of the night before.

"We've established no link between the first two victims. Do *you* know them? Seán Doyle and Marian Selway? Any connection there?"

"No, nothing. I don't know those people at all." If she had, she would have informed him already, excused herself from working on the case, but she appreciated he was trying to reassure her by covering every possible detail.

"We've established that the car the killers were driving last night was parked at a kerb and approached the victim when he crossed the street. This *feels* different. You were with your sister-in-law, so there were two of you and up until now they seem to favour victims that are alone. But there were witnesses this time, and it didn't deter them. There are quieter streets in the city, but they chose one with three visible people on it. People that could call the gardaí and give statements ... it doesn't seem right. It's a massive coincidence that you're working on the case and were speaking to the latest victim before he was killed."

He rubbed his chin, watching her closely. She looked scared and as perplexed as he felt. He had hoped to reassure her there was no reason to be worried, but he realised he was failing badly at that. It seemed a coincidence too far to think she hadn't been involved somehow. He was sure there was *something* in this change in the killers' behaviour. They had been so careful to avoid witnesses before – last night, that hadn't deterred them. Why not?

"OK, you keep thinking things over and if you remember any connection to Blake Landers or the other victims, you know where I am. And you're off the case. I'll pass anything that needs doing to someone else, OK?

Somehow you're involved in this – we just need to figure out how."

She smiled, grateful he hadn't dismissed her, thankful that he believed she saw the driver look right at her. But terrified at what this might mean.

"Why are they filming the murders?"

"Now *that* is the million-dollar question."

The rest of the day dragged on for Anna. Lauren wasn't at work, having booked the day off for pre-wedding appointments. She missed her friendly banter and gossip, even the clanging sound her bracelets made as she typed out her reports. Vivian's mobile was going straight to voicemail. Anna was a little surprised Vivian hadn't sought a statement from her but was grateful she didn't have to decline a request from her best friend.

To Anna, it felt like she checked her phone every ten minutes for a message, but there was still no response from Annika Garcia. It was a gloomy thought that perhaps there never would be. She felt she had exhausted all the available articles online about her mother's disappearance in 1978 ... the idea that perhaps hiring a private investigator wasn't such a bad idea kept niggling at her throughout the day. She had the card somewhere for the investigator she had booked, and then decided not to use after all, before Christmas ... she decided that if she'd heard nothing back from Annika Garcia by the end of the week, she would call him.

She ordered a takeaway and spent the evening in solitude. Her night was lonely – Myles was unable to phone due to a late work meeting, texting his apologies. She thought about visiting the Pearsons, her neighbours. Their home had been burgled and Mr Pearson attacked not too long ago – in fact, it was when they decided to have a house alarm fitted in the days afterwards that Dean Harris had taken the opportunity to scope out Anna's house, seeing that she lived alone. She had promised them she would visit more often – they had been good to her and Alex after their parents' accident. But tonight, she couldn't seem to shake off the slump of a low mood and muster the energy to call over.

She thought about going up to her own attic, to see if there could be any clues about her mother's past hidden in the boxes there. Alex was searching his own, after all. The thought filled her with dread – she always felt claustrophobic in that small space. She knew it would be futile anyway – she had searched through the boxes of memories only weeks ago, finding nothing but clothes and photographs. And her mother's cello propped against one wall. Now that she knew more of the truth, she found she didn't want to see it again.

She stared at the TV screen without really watching anything, not bothering to check if anything more interesting was showing. Her thoughts strayed to Kate … they often did. Always wondering where she was, if she was safe, if she had found her sister and nieces and was making a new life away from the Gallaghers. She hoped so – even though Kate had run out on her, she could understand why. Kate had been terrified of the trouble she had unwittingly created. She hoped her old friend had found peace.

The shooting of Blake Landers refused to leave her mind, the images and sounds darting into her memory every few minutes. Was she going crazy to think the driver had looked right at her? She really thought he had … but what possible reason would he have to do that? To taunt a witness? That didn't fit with their previous methods … in fact, none of it did. It was too public, leaving two women behind that could give detailed descriptions, could alert the gardaí immediately … the killers had taken a bigger risk this time. But why?

The only bright point in her night was a text message from Vivian, showing a photograph of a set of keys, accompanied with a grinning emoji. Smiling, Anna texted her congratulations, before deciding to head to bed. She'd had enough of the quiet loneliness of her evening.

From her bedroom window, as she drew the curtains, she watched the quiet streets around her house. There were no cars parked on the kerbs this evening. The estate was quiet.

Before she turned out the lights, she pulled her hand back from the photograph of her parents that she kept in her locker drawer, chiding herself. This was becoming an obsession! Did she really think she could find them alive? She knew her brother was right – the most likely outcome from her sleuthing would be disappointment and heartache.

Ely Murray exited the city centre bar and turned the collar up on his coat. It was raining, a light mist that drifted around him and dampened his face, and he walked briskly. He had business to complete tonight, a personal project, and had turned off his mobile phone. Tom Gallagher was calling him and blustering about the girl every day, and it grated on his nerves. He intended to deal with the problem, to sort things out once and for all. But tonight, he had other things to attend to, and he didn't need the man griping in his ear.

Before the week was out, he would get the answers his boss was looking for. For now, he had his own future to think about.

34

On Thursday morning, when Anna returned home from dropping Chloe at playgroup, a white van was parked outside her house, with two men sitting inside. Behind that, a grey Audi pulled away and drove towards the exit of the estate. She frowned as she pulled a grocery bag and latte-to-go from the car – she kept seeing that car around. Perhaps one of her neighbours had changed vehicles. Before she could ponder on it further, the driver of the van climbed out and walked towards her.

"Miss Clarke?"

"Yes – can I help you?"

He stuck out his hand in greeting. "Richard Stokes. Stokes Security Solutions. I received a call this morning about an urgent job. You're having a security system installed, I believe?"

Anna stared at him, stunned. It was only days ago the idea had been raised – William Ryan certainly moved fast! Come to think of it, she didn't remember agreeing to have anything fitted at all. She felt a little perturbed but offered the man in front of her a smile.

"Come on in." She led the way into the house, noting that the passenger, a younger man, had exited the van and was unloading a toolbox from the back.

Richard wiped his feet on the mat and surveyed the hallway while she moved towards the kitchen, unpacking the groceries. When she turned around, the house felt smaller with the two men standing in her living room.

"We'll set up intruder alarms beside the front and back doors and one panic alarm here, beside the bookshelf. A second one will go in your bedroom. The gentleman I was speaking to was very keen to get this done today."

Anna felt her eyes pop involuntarily. "OK ... this is very quick ... and you want to install *two* panic alarms?"

He held his hands up in surrender. "Just following orders!"

She smiled quickly, "Sorry, it's just ... Detective Ryan is certainly very eager to secure the house!"

The younger man spoke for the first time as he riffled through the toolbox on the floor. "Oh, it wasn't him. We got our orders from a Detective Henderson." He looked at his boss for confirmation. "Myles Henderson, was it?"

"Something like that. Email came through first thing this morning – this takes priority, all the way from the top!"

Standing in the archway between the kitchen and living room, Anna smiled politely but her thoughts raced. From Brussels, her boyfriend had pulled some strings and arranged for her house to be protected as soon as possible. Pretty impressive for an intelligence analyst ... she felt flattered, sort of. She thought she knew *who* Myles Henderson was – exactly what he did in the Crime and Security Branch of the gardaí was a complete mystery to her.

Richard was talking again, drawing her out of her thoughts.

"I'll get started down here and then you can show us where to go upstairs. It won't take long and you'll never know we've been here, Scout's Honour!" He smiled. "Everything will be operational from today and I'll give you a complete run-through. Any questions?"

She shook her head.

"Then any chance of a brew to shake off the cold?"

"Of course!" She turned to the kitchen and filled the kettle, mulling over what she would say to Myles as soon as she had the chance to call him.

35

"So, it was the same killers?"

"I'm certain of it. The victim was shot in the head. And the front passenger filmed it – on-street CCTV and footage from security cameras on the surrounding businesses as good as confirms it. This man and woman are now responsible for three murders. Seán Doyle in Clonakilty, Marian Selway in the Rebel Event Centre and Blake Landers in the city centre last night."

Frank Doherty shook two white pills into his hand and began to crunch them quickly.

"Same gun?"

"Looks like it. A .22 calibre revolver. Landers suffered similar injuries to Seán Doyle – a close shot, where the bullet scrambled around inside his skull and stayed there. No exit wound and death was quick."

"At least that! Where are we with updates on the DNA at each scene?"

"Unfortunately, we've very little to go on. A partial tyre mark in Clonakilty, which is offering little so far. We did get reports of locals observing the same vehicle, a large beige type of jeep, driving around the roads on the three mornings before the shooting. The school-bus driver reported it as well as several others. So I'm sure the killer, one of them at least, drove around looking for a pattern in someone's routine, a driver travelling alone on a quiet road. Unfortunately for Mr Doyle, he fit the bill. That vehicle is still unaccounted for. But if the killers travelled into the city it could have been dumped anywhere."

"So they drove around looking for a victim ... anything else?"

"We're still waiting on a report from the hotel room they used there. In relation to the second victim, the CCTV footage from the Rebel Event Centre is as good as useless – the killers are heavily disguised. The car used in last night's shooting was stolen in Glanmire about an hour before the attack – it's been found in a city-centre car park. The technical team are going over it – I don't expect to find prints or anything useful. This couple are very careful. But it *is* the right car – blood spatter found on the passenger side door is expected to be a match to Blake Landers."

He expelled the air in his lungs heavily – after summarising all the available data on the three cases, the only thing that was certain was that the same couple were suspected of the murders. The *why* remained elusive.

"There's no common link between the victims?"

"Nothing. Seán Doyle and Marian Selway lived quiet lives and were very different people. Blake Landers lived a life that bears no similarities with the other victims." He looked down at the notebook resting on his lap. "Aged thirty-six, he's lived in Cork for four months now. His parents and two brothers live in Boston in the United States.

He was sent here from a stockbroker company in New York, is well regarded in his field and the Cork office requested his skills for a specific project. They wouldn't say more than that. An apartment was rented for him for six months. There's nothing of interest there aside from some old credit-card receipts that give us a clue as to his recent movements. He has frequented a strip club a couple of times in the city, but nothing else untoward. He was a regular gym user – he's a member of a city-centre gym and uses it on average three times a week. The manager there said he always trains alone and doesn't seem to chat much to the others there. Gyms can be like that though, solitary like. Our investigation shows he lived a quiet life while he was here, and that's about the only similarity he has to the other victims."

"What are your thoughts on why these people were targeted?"

"Honestly? It all seems opportunist. Wrong place at the wrong time. Except …"

"Well?" Frank rubbed impatiently at the back of his neck with an already damp handkerchief.

"I feel uneasy about this latest killing. I'm concerned about a change in pattern."

"Go on."

"Seán Doyle was killed on a quiet country road. A deserted road, first thing in the morning. Marian Selway had her time reserved by the killers for a private tour of her workplace. Both set-ups left little risk of witnesses. When Blake Landers was shot, the M.O. is completely different. There *were* witnesses, at least two of them. Anna Clarke and her sister-in-law, Samantha Clarke. And an unidentified male that was quite near the victim when he was shot. So, three potential witnesses. One of whom, Anna, is working on the case and believes the driver deliberately looked at her."

"So? What does this mean?"

"I don't know yet. Possibly nothing, just the killers getting lazy in choosing their victims – they drove around, spotted Blake Landers nicely positioned at the side of the street and went for it – disregarding the presence of witnesses. Or maybe there's more to it. It's a huge coincidence that Anna Clarke was in a confrontation with the victim just minutes beforehand."

Frank nodded, his lips pursed.

"Anna doesn't know any of the victims personally and can offer no explanation. I'm keeping an open mind on whether there is something more than a random selection of the victim here."

"I don't think there's enough there to warrant any concern," Frank said decisively. "Seems like another opportunist killing to me. But take her off the case – there's plenty of clerical staff to choose from. I don't need any mistakes because someone on the team is getting jumpy."

William nodded stiffly.

"It sounds to me like there's nothing to go on for the reason behind this – this – killing spree," said Frank.

"Well, maybe that profiler I've asked for could shed some light but, to be honest, there's isn't much to profile. A couple who seem to enjoy killing people in a variety of ways, and film it for ... fun? I don't know." His right leg bounced on the floor as he spoke.

"The press coverage doesn't help," Frank muttered sourly, his eyes finding the morning newspaper amid the jumble of papers on his desk.

William frowned as he read the latest headline.

SERIAL KILLERS STRIKE AGAIN

"At least they ran the image of the couple ... although, that's pretty useless. I don't like the headlines either but there's no harm in the public being extra-vigilant."

"But it makes us look incompetent! Pressure is mounting from Dublin. We need an arrest here!"

William leaned back in his seat. He didn't disagree. But with almost nothing to go on, he didn't hold out much hope. A profiler from Dublin was looking over his case notes, and his team were working every angle conceivable – it wasn't enough.

"We need a bloody miracle!"

Colin Forde pushed open the door and poked his head between the space.

"Didn't you ever learn to knock, Forde!" Frank growled.

"Sorry! But we've got something. Hairs found in a hotel room on the South Mall. One of the housekeeping staff got them caught in the vacuum cleaner this morning, and only remembered the photos in the paper as she was pulling them out. Long red hair."

William hopped up from his seat. Leaning across the desk he tapped his finger on the newspaper and grinned.

"This could be our miracle!"

He leaned over the shower/bath combo in the hotel bathroom. He couldn't see anything of interest, but he knew enough to know that what mattered was hidden to the naked eye. He cleared his throat.

"So? What do you think?"

"Let's see!" The Tech Bureau's analyst reached an arm to the light, the switch was flicked, and the small bathroom plunged into complete darkness.

The whole surface had been sprayed with luminol.

Immediately the hairs on William's arms stood to attention – he leaned closer to see. A blue pattern, devoid of any distinct shape, sprayed across the surface of the bath. Blood. Enough to suggest this was a crime scene. Whoever had showered here had attempted to wash away enough blood to leave behind the biggest miracle William could have hoped for.

"One of the forensics guys asked me to get you to leave."

Colin Forde stood at William's side – he was sitting at the small desk in the hotel room. Colin had his hands pushed into his pockets and hovered nervously, darting glances around the room. The place gave him the creeps, knowing *they* had been here. His supervisor looked to be deep in thought. He had been in the hotel room for hours now, his shoes and hands covered, a plastic hat over his hair. He was in the way but reluctant to leave.

"Did you get their alias from reception?"

Colin grimaced. "Yeah, they told the story again about being robbed and having no ID or credit cards. Paid in cash and checked in as Mr and Mrs Michael Myers."

"There could be any number of Michael Myers in the world but I'm guessing it's the character from the slasher films … no-one thought the name strange?"

Colin half-smiled. "I guess the receptionist isn't a horror-movie fan." He shifted his feet uncomfortably. "Michael Myers wore a mask in the films, by the way. Quite like the one visible on the CCTV in the Rebel Event Centre."

William shook his head and let out a low whistle. "These two are something else … curious that they are not seeking to carve out their *own* identity, but instead claiming the names of other, even fictional, killers." He pulled at his lips, deep in thought. Finally a groan of exasperation escaped him. "Wait until the press get hold of these details. I really need that profiler to get back to me!"

Sighing heavily, he pushed himself up from the seat, facing Colin now, light dancing in his blue eyes. He looked tired, but there was excitement there too.

"We're making progress! We know they stayed here, Colin! They slept in that bed and showered in that bathroom. One of them washed Marian Selway's blood off their own skin. The man, I bet. The woman was too far back, too busy filming. How did he travel back here covered in blood?"

Colin could only shake his head. His chest ached with the need to get out of here.

William spun around and surveyed the room, his eyes taking in every fibre and particle, all of it potential evidence.

"Very soon we'll have their fingerprints, or real hair fibres or some other type of DNA. No-one can live in a hotel room for a few days and leave no trace behind. And once we have that we'll have them!"

"But it won't tell us much more than who they are."

William put a hand on the younger man's shoulder.

"But *who* someone is, is all I need to know!" He buttoned up his overcoat.

"Interesting that they continue to film each murder. For their own gratification?"

"Or someone else's!"

William's eyes bored into Colin's with force as a slow smile broke across his face. "Bonnie and Clyde, Dr Jekyll, Michael Myers ... do you know what they all have in common? They all got caught, or stopped, in the end. One way or another, their madness ended. And so will this!"

36

"This place is gorgeous!"

Anna was sitting cross-legged on the wooden floor in the large open space that was Vivian's kitchen, dining and living room. An open pizza box on the floor held the crusted remains of dinner – two suitcases and four cardboard boxes were stacked against one wall.

"Isn't it sad?" Vivian drained a glass of water. "Twenty-seven years old and all I have to show for it is four cardboard boxes! All my worldly possessions in four measly boxes – and they're not even full!"

Anna laughed. She wiped her mouth with a paper napkin and rose to her feet, stretching her back to the left and right. They had scrubbed the apartment for over an hour before lugging Vivian's things up one concrete flight of stairs to her brown wooden front door.

"Are you staying here tonight?" The two bedrooms were empty of furniture – a delivery truck was due in the morning. "You can stay at mine, you know that."

Vivian held out her hand and Anna pulled her up.

"Thanks, but I want to stay here. Brenda is video-calling later and I want to show her around. I have a sleeping bag here somewhere," she gestured to the cardboard boxes, "and a quilt. I'll be fine."

"OK. Well, I'm teaching at six, so I'd better go." Anna hugged her friend and left.

As Vivian waved from her apartment door, she felt truly delighted for her to have forged such a close bond with her birth mother and moved into her very own apartment. She had also been confirmed as through to the final round in the Banba Productions interviews – it was an exciting time for her. Anna was glad there was some good news floating around.

The children ran past Anna into the Taekwon-Do Tykes class and she smiled warmly at them. They looked so adorable in their little white suits, their earnest chants of the tenets of Taekwon-Do ringing around the room. As she walked among them, she realised Chloe would be old enough to join soon – she would bring an application form to Alex's house later when she called in for dinner. She had said she wouldn't call to her brother's tonight after class – she could do so any night, and he and Samantha had a lot to discuss, probably preferring to be alone – but he had insisted. After class she made her way there, the early winter darkness settling around her. The roads were quiet as she drove the short distance. Samantha answered the front door, immediately pulling Anna towards her into a tight embrace.

"I owe you so much!" she whispered, her eyes shining in the dim hall light.

Anna followed her into the kitchen, relieved her sister-in-law's shock seemed to have abated.

After dinner, and after tucking Chloe into bed, she joined Alex and Samantha in the living room. They were sitting side by side on the sofa, their bodies pressed into each other. Looking at them, she felt a pang of longing for Myles. The house was chilly, even though the heating was on – the fireplace was still empty and half-built. The conversation of the night before, of their financial troubles, were forefront in Anna's mind.

Clearing her throat, she began the speech she had rehearsed while scrubbing Vivian's windows, but Alex beat her to it.

"Sam and I have spoken a lot today, about everything that happened with her job these past few months." He took his wife's hand in both of his own. "Obviously, I'd have preferred if Sam told me what was going on, but I *do* understand her reasons for not wanting to burden me. After everything that happened to you last year, and with Mum and Dad's ten-year anniversary as well, I've not been sleeping well." He looked at Anna, finally meeting her eyes. "Actually, scratch that – I've not been sleeping *at all*. Sam didn't want to add any pressure on my shoulders but I'm telling you, Anna, what I hold her – I am absolutely fine, and capable of handling pressure! I am here, for both of you, no matter what!"

Samantha wiped at her eyes, and Anna found she had to look away, into the empty hearth. The thought of her brother struggling to sleep, unable to calm his mind enough to rest, troubled her. He had been her rock for the last ten years – both her brother and her father. Guilt wound into her thoughts – she knew her dogged determination to find the truth about their mother was causing Alex even more stress.

"Anna, we owe you a huge debt of gratitude! What happened to Sam last night was horrendous, and there's no doubt in my mind it would have been a lot worse if you hadn't been there. Once more you've proved yourself more than capable in the face of danger. Calm, confident." He smiled sadly, "I remembered you always were more interested than me in the self-defence games Dad played. I'm just glad his love of martial arts passed on to you! He'd be very proud of you."

She had to swallow a few times before she could speak, and her voice faltered. "Well, I'm glad you're OK, Sam! Did you speak with your boss?"

She nodded. "We had to attend a meeting with the owner of the company this morning. The man was horrified as soon as he heard what happened. He believed me, which was a relief! The company money Blake Landers had loaned me was written off. I think they'd be happy if I never mention the whole thing again."

"I guess now that he's dead there's nothing to be pursued."

Alex shook his head in anger. "No doubt he'll be portrayed as an innocent victim, not the creep that he was!"

Samantha placed a calming hand on his knee. "To be fair, he suffered an awful death."

He sighed, and they were silent for a few moments, each lost in their own thoughts.

Anna wondered how the investigation was progressing at work – having been out all day, she had no idea if any developments had come to light. She felt sure Blake Landers had been killed by the couple responsible for the other murders. Vivian's colleague had covered the story but, while they cleaned her new apartment today, neither had wanted to discuss it. Both of them remained in the dark as to what a new day had brought.

She felt exhausted by the time she left. As she pulled into her housing estate she found the kerbs empty of parked cars. She attempted to search the driveways for unfamiliar grey Audis as she passed, but it was dark and she was tired – she concentrated instead on reaching home.

As she climbed into bed a text message from Myles brought a smile to her face.

Goodnight, Anna, I miss you! I'll be dreaming of you!

Well, sweet dreams then! she replied. **Oh, and thank you again for arranging to have the panic buttons installed, even though it's a bit overkill! You're a very efficient knight in shining armour!**

His reply made her grin: **M'lady.**

She settled under the blankets and switched off the light, hoping sleep would come quickly. But her brother's pale and drawn face was all she could focus on – that and the sleeping tablets he had mentioned recently. He still couldn't sleep … After all Alex had done for her, there was no way she could let him be so burdened by financial troubles, not when she lived in a house that was half his.

She sat upright again and switched on her bedside light. She felt wide awake now, a decision forming that felt so right, so timely, she couldn't shake off the feeling of certainty.

She was going to sell this house.

She had lived here all her life, and had thought she would continue to do so, but lately she felt lonely and isolated. It wasn't just the memory of Dean Harris's break-in, or that it felt empty without Myles or anyone else to scent the air and fill the pockets of silence. This house represented her past, hers and Alex's, and their parents. While she still lived here, she was trapped to it, and Alex was bound to the role he had fallen into when their parents disappeared – her protector, her pseudo-father. The house was full of ghosts – the memories of people that once occupied its space, the air heavy with silence after their laughter had disappeared. Every time she turned the key in the front door and stepped inside this house, she was pulled back into a jumble of memories that wound around her, holding her in place. Keeping her and Alex in this void where neither could move forward. The house felt like an ancient ruin of what was once a happy place.

Her heart pounding loudly in her chest, she knew she had reached a pivotal point in her life – she didn't want to just buy out her brother's share of the house. She wanted to sell it, to liquidate the last of her parents' assets, and give her brother what was his. And she wanted to start over. In a new house, a different one, where she could make fresh memories.

She knew there would be some legal things to take care of – but she wanted to move forward. A new house would mean a fresh start – separating this link to the past might help them to move on.

Switching off the light again, she settled into bed, confident sleep would come now. Her mind felt calmer, clearer than it had in days, and she felt that sleep might come easier tonight.

Her phone vibrated on the locker and she reached for it, smiling in anticipation of Myles' message.

But it wasn't a text from Myles.

Her heartbeat raced wildly in her chest as she opened it.

It was a message from Annika Garcia.

Anna. Forgive the delay in my reply. I almost didn't return your message. Or I almost replied to say "No, sorry, wrong lady!" But in your profile photograph I see my sister. You look so similar, only with brown eyes instead of blue. I guess perhaps your father's eyes. I won't pretend Yelena's disappearance has been easy, but I have built a new life. From your message, I understand you are suffering as I did all those years ago – she has disappeared from *your* life now. Everyone deserves answers, but I regret to tell you I have little to offer. If you like, we can speak by video message soon. I would so love to see you! Perhaps together we will put some ghosts to rest.

37

London, 1978

Once Michael convinced himself there was something suspicious going on in the business and silenced the part of his brain that loudly protested it couldn't be true, it was easy to find proof. Soon, any doubts that lingered were truly quashed, his worst fears and suspicions confirmed.

It was Saturday, a bright and crisp morning. The streets were quiet, most people only rousing from slumber this early in the morning. His breath fogged the air in front of him and his cheeks stung – a sure sign autumn was on the way, as Nana Clarke would say. He was dressed in his tracksuit as he walked from the bus stop to the working man's club, where his Taekwon-Do school ran their classes and provided a space to train, his gear bag slung casually over one shoulder. He could make out the lights in the windows in the club house, and lowered his head, walking steadily.

He became aware of a sound behind him, the low rumble of an engine. A glance over his shoulder brought confusion – a white Ford Granada, its distinctive red stripe and blue police light on the roof giving him pause. The car stopped too. He felt rooted to the footpath, his eyebrows drawn in uncertainty. A policeman stepped from the vehicle and moved towards him, his companion staying in the passenger seat.

"Michael Clarke?"

"Yes."

"What's in the bag?"

A pause, while the shock of the situation settled over him. "Training gear." He jerked his head in the direction of the working-men's club. "I train in Taekwon-Do there."

The policeman raised his eyebrows. "Taekwon-Do? That a martial art?"

Michael nodded and the policeman dipped his head towards the bag.

"Open it up!"

He crouched to the ground and unzipped it.

"Slowly!"

He'd had to do the very same thing for Mr Lewis only months ago, but his heart thumped a lot harder in his chest this time. Keeping his hands as steady as he could he did as he was told, removing his white top and pants, his black belt, a small blue towel, and bottle of water, making a messy pile on the footpath beside him. He held the bag wide and tilted it upwards to show it was empty.

The policeman nodded. "Right. Someone wants a word. Get in the back and don't make a scene."

Michael's heart hammered uncomfortably in his chest. Images of newspaper articles flashed in his mind, of men and women accused of bombings and acts of terrorism in London and throughout England, all with Irish-sounding names. He thought of the scenes he had watched on the small television in his nan's sitting room, showing men led away in handcuffs, protesting their innocence. Swallowing hard, he knew he had no choice but to go with them. To protest would mean he'd be arrested – that would be a difficult situation to get out of. He thought of Nana Clarke … she would tell him to cooperate.

So, he did.

In the police station he was shown to a small room and left to sit there for over forty minutes, alone. The room was stiflingly hot and sweat dripped between his eyebrows and pooled on his upper lip. He hadn't spoken since his arrival at the station, where he had confirmed his name, date of birth and address. He asked no questions, made no protestations, and if the policemen found his calm demeanour strange, they didn't say so. He concentrated on steadying his breathing, his hands folded on the table in front of him. The spike of his adrenaline in the car journey was a feeling he remembered before the recent black belt assessment. He used the memory of that experience to calm himself, to remember that learned response, and now he felt somewhat better. He knew he had done nothing wrong and tried to ignore the niggling fear that that might not make any difference.

The door opened and just one man entered, his shirtsleeves rolled up, his eyes not seeking contact. He folded his tall frame into the chair. His hair was thick and cut short, greying around the temples. He offered no smile or greeting, just placed a thin file of paperwork on the table between them.

"Patrick Michael Clarke, date of birth fourteenth of March 1956, correct?"

"Yes."

"Patrick, but you use the name Michael."

"I don't *use* the name – it *is* my name."

257

"I am Mr Smith, Counter-Terrorism Division."

Michael shook his head, his heart sinking, his shoulders slumped. He pulled his hands back from the table and rested them on his lap.

"Mr Smith? I don't suppose you can show me some ID?"

The man observed him coolly, his face not registering any emotion.

"You don't seem overly concerned as to why you were brought in, Mr Clarke."

Michael met the man's eyes as he spoke. "I know the score. I'm Irish. I've read the newspaper reports about bombings and terror threats. I live in London, for God's sake, I know what's going on. I know you don't need a reason to lift me and bring me in. Are you going to tell me what it is you think I've done?"

The man watched him quietly as he spoke, his own face still giving nothing away. After a pause he continued as if Michael had never spoken.

"You're second-generation Irish, right?"

Michael nodded.

"Raised by your grandmother in Warburg Terraces."

He thought of his nan, how this would break her heart. He prayed for the man to get on with it.

"And you work for James Lewis, the merchant. We know all about you, Michael. All about your dad's death at the docks, about your high marks in night school. How did you end up working for Lewis?"

Panic screamed silently inside his head. The niggling doubts at work ... the girl at the hotel ... this was about Lewis, and he worked for the man.

He licked his lips. "I ... I applied for a vacancy. What's this about?"

258

"Do you like working for him. Nice boss, is he?"

His fear was growing, his heartbeat loud in his ears. "He's alright. What's going on?"

"You've not worked there long. Not six full months. You're a bookkeeper. Expensive course that, in night school. How did you afford it?"

"What? I ... well ..." He stopped, afraid to speak, worried that anything he said would be twisted and turned.

"Let me guess – your grandmother paid for it. I'd say she's paid for a lot of things lately that are beyond her usual budget. Do you want to know how I know that?"

Michael remained silent this time. He felt fire in his face and the force of blood rushing in his ears. What did his grandmother have to do with this? Had she done something illegal and drawn trouble upon herself? The area they lived in was full of low-level criminals, but Nana Clarke had always steered clear, and made sure he did too.

Mr Smith, as he called himself, pushed a photograph across the table. Michael studied it, his eyes cast down. He didn't know the man in it, standing on the doorstep of their terraced house, in conversation with his grandmother.

"Paddy McManus. Great name ... he deals in stolen goods. He's serving time at Her Majesty's pleasure, and his small-time criminal escapades are falling apart. He loans money, did you know that?"

His heart sank.

"When a person can't repay fast enough, he draws them into his business – if you could call it that. Your grandmother got drawn in over a year ago because she couldn't repay a loan she took to put her grandson through night school. We have evidence she has been holding stolen goods, including cash and jewellery for McManus. Great set-up really; who'd suspect a little old lady? We have plenty of evidence – enough for a conviction."

He slid more photographs across the table and Michael picked them up one by one. It was her, taking possession of bags and envelopes at their front door. His grandmother looked scared and very old. He marvelled at how indiscreet it all was and wondered where in the house she had hidden the items. Tears blurred his vision and he roughly brushed them aside.

"Are you … are you pursuing this?"

"A crime was committed. Handling stolen goods. Assisting an offender. Take your pick."

"But she's an old lady!"

A shrug of indifference. "A crime is a crime."

Michael slid the photos back across the desk. "No judge would send her to prison. She was forced into it!"

"No, she wasn't, Michael! She borrowed money from a man she knew was a criminal. She brought this on herself." He sighed and shifted in his seat. "But maybe you're right. Maybe the judge will go easy on her. Or maybe he won't and she'll die in prison. Either way, I reckon the stress and the shame of it all will kill her." He shrugged and it was clear – it made no difference to him.

As though ice-cold water had been poured over him, Michael felt his skin begin to tingle.

"How is this your concern in Counter-Terrorism? What does this have to do with me?"

The man leaned across the table, his eyes bright. "You're a bright chap, Michael! I'm giving you an opportunity. I'm offering you the chance to walk away when this is over. You and your grandmother. Free from any and all convictions.

Because *you're* in trouble too!"

He licked his lower lip again, thoughts racing. *What the hell had she got them mixed up in?*

"We've had our suspicions about Lewis. Even went sniffing around a few times but there's not enough for a warrant. I've nothing confirmed. We can never find *anything*. The man presents as legitimate but we know he's rotten! We know there's something to find, except we have no proof, not even a hint of something enough for an official search. *It's so frustrating. Can you imagine how frustrating this is to me, Michael?*" He leaned across the table, his finger jabbing the surface to emphasise each word. He was a man possessed with acquiring something that lay just out of reach and he desperately wanted Michael to understand.

He inhaled a shaky breath. "Suspicions of what?"

"Lewis's sympathies lie across the water with his ancestors. Do you understand me? He presents himself as a Royalist in many ways, a true English gentleman – he's even gone fishing with the Prime Minister's aide, for God's sake! But we've been paying close attention – the man's crooked. Bent as a fisherman's hook. Playing the English gentleman while serving his cause."

He bunched his fists and spread them wide on the table. Colour rose in his face as he spoke, warming to the topic of catching Lewis red-handed.

"We know a little – but every time I get an inch closer I'm pulled a foot back. Do a little digging and you find the man is Irish by parentage and has managed to present an entirely different picture. All I have are suspicions and I need more. He has connections, but I can't touch him without proof. Or a *hint* of proof enough for a search warrant. I want *you* to help me find something. You've access to all his paperwork, and now you've a reason to dig deep. You're going to be my man on the inside."

Michael stayed still – his hands, clamped together on his lap, were damp with sweat. His mind was blank save for what the detective was telling him … Lewis was crooked. The girl had alluded to it, the Soviet from the hotel. And he had his own suspicions. With a growing weight of dread in his stomach, he realised he was in too deep to walk away now.

"There's nothing to report. Nothing I've noticed anyway." He hoped the lie might buy him time, but even as he spoke he knew it was useless.

Smith nodded slowly, considering. "That's plausible. You're a trainee, fresh out of school. It's why he hired you. I've no doubt that was deliberate. And you're Irish too, a perfect fit."

He stared intently at Michael and his eyes lit up in excitement.

"You're sweating, Michael … look at you! You've found something, haven't you! You have your own suspicions … I can read a man, Michael Clarke. You suspect, but not enough to leave. And you're not even sure he'd *let* you walk away. No, you know too much!" The man was exuberant, squirming in his seat, his face flushed with the hint of victory.

Michael scratched the side of his neck, finding it slick with sweat – he had absolutely no idea what to do.

The detective leaned back in his chair and spoke softly, as though to invite him into his confidence. "You're an Irishman. I get it. But one thing I've learned in this job is that most Irishmen want to live in peace. I think you're one of those, am I right? Do you know how we will win the war on terrorism, Michael? How we can stop the loss of innocent lives?" He paused, for effect. "With people like you."

"People willing to grass, you mean?"

"People who want peace. People with the understanding that if they don't cooperate they will find their loved ones dying in prison." His threat echoed around the small room.

"And if there's nothing to find?"

The exuberance and excitement were gone – Smith's face was unreadable again.

"There's *always* something to find. This is how it will go – you find what I need and alert me, then you keep your head down and get on with your life. I won't call on you to give evidence – you and your nan will stay out of it from there. I'll say it was an anonymous tip-off. Happy?"

At Michael's silence he sat back and smiled, but it didn't reach his eyes.

"I'm offering you two choices. You either make an enemy of him, or you make an enemy of *me*."

When he got home, she was sleeping on the sofa, the TV still on, the fire dying away to embers. He watched her from the doorway, drawing deep breaths to calm down. She had raised him, given him everything. And she had made a mistake, one he had the power to put right. But at what cost?

Bob noticed his changed mood on Monday. He observed him silently for a while before coming to perch on the edge of the desk.

"Alright, mate?"

"Yeah ... why?"

"You look rough. Nana Clarke OK?"

Michael smiled. "She's fine. She said to remind you that you owe her a packet of ciggies and can bring them Friday night."

Bob laughed as he made his way back to the desk. "I have to work late. Stock being moved and the lads need me to fill in dockets – remind me to hire men that can actually read and write next time! If you two are willing to wait up, I'll be there by eleven."

Michael smiled at his friend but knew it wasn't the easy grin Bob was used to.

"You sure you're OK?"

He jumped up, grabbing his coat. "Need some new ledgers. Be back in a while."

Outside he walked a few hundred yards before stumbling against a wall, leaning against the hard concrete, hands on his knees. He drew deep breaths through his nose and tried to steady the heaving sobs that forced their way up his throat. The realisation that his friend would be implicated too had hit him and he felt winded. After a few minutes he straightened up and smoothed his jacket, hoping the security guard in the little hut near the entrance hadn't seen him.

Smith was right – things didn't add up in the business. And Michael believed Smith when he promised he would spend the rest of his life in jail if he didn't cooperate – him *and* Nana Clarke. He remembered a lecture his nan had given him once, about men having to make choices, and about right and wrong. He was faced with a choice now – as much as it left a sour taste in his mouth, his loyalty lay with his grandmother. If he went to prison, or if she herself was locked up, he knew it would kill her.

38

Cork, 2019

Music reverberated around the Mad Hatter nightclub at such volume John Gallagher could feel it pulse inside his veins. The large space was hot, condensation dripping down bare brick walls, mingling with the sweat of the dancers crowding the floor. He watched from the shadows, or what sufficed as the nearest thing – a small alcove between two concrete pillars. The whiskey in his hand was a cheap imitation of the real thing his father supplied in his own club, the weak sting of its aftertaste an insult to his palette. He knew why he had come here – their own club, the Oracle, would be too busy with people wanting something from him, to talk to him, to touch him. People wondering if he was still in the game ...

But he wondered why he had gone out at all.

He swallowed the last of the cheap whiskey and began to push his way through the crowd with his elbows – the semi-naked women writhing to the music were coated in a repulsive sticky sweat he had no desire to touch. One of them stepped in front of him, her eyes glassy and ringed in smudged mascara, her lips pulled back around swollen gums. He knew what she was looking for – she was a junkie, and a repeat customer – but he shoved her aside, disgusted.

On nights like this he could understand why his brother had sought out the big time. Selling classified security information to foreign mobsters was ambitious, something he never thought David would even contemplate. The reward on offer must have been huge. Perhaps it had seemed better than wading through the stench and filth of the rest of their business dealings. Better than standing in the cold and rain at the docks, wondering who was stealing from them. Drinking cheap liquor in clubs where the junkies sought you out … yes, John could understand why David had wanted more. He just regretted that his brother had never confided in him – together they could have made it work.

David's deception had changed the way people viewed the Gallaghers these days. Once there had been respectful nods, now heads dipped and hands cupped around mouths that whispered rumour and ridicule. His night at the docks had renewed his spark though – he had seen the fear and respect in his men, and he wanted more. He resolved to get back into the heart of things again – he'd given his parents enough grieving time. If he could only convince his father to do the same … Tom was losing everything, blind to the slow seep of his respect and control. His only focus was on finding some girl he thought had answers to the whereabouts of Kate Crowley – everything he had worked for was bleeding to death so slowly he didn't even realise it. John knew it was up to him to pull his father out of this slump.

He climbed into the back of a taxi and muttered his

address, turning his attention to his mobile phone. He had no desire to engage in mundane conversation with the driver. His jeans were wet and he touched his hair, surprised to find that wet too. It was raining heavily and he hadn't even noticed. The light of his mobile phone lit up the back seat of the car. He had received a message while he'd been in the club – reading it John felt his pulse race. Business was progressing – he was growing richer by the second. His side-line was dissolving the veil he had hidden behind these past weeks, like acid melting flesh. He leaned into the seat and closed his eyes, feeling more content than he thought was possible.

"Dad?"

He was surprised to see his father sitting in the dark at the kitchen table when he got home, but not as surprised as Tom, who jumped from his seat, spilling a glass of milk over the surface.

"*Shit!*" he grabbed a towel and began to mop up.

John moved towards him. "Here, let me help you." Pulling some paper towels from the rack, he laid them on the puddle of milk and scooped it up. He became aware of his father's eyes on what remained of his finger and turned to the bin.

Silence was loud in the otherwise quiet room – it was a long time since they had spoken more than a few words.

Sitting down at the table, he kept his hands in his lap.

"Are you alright, son? Been out with some friends?"

John grimaced at the hope in his father's voice.

"Yeah. We went to a club." He knew the lie that he had been socialising with people would please his father, and maybe put a stop to his irritating worry. "I was thinking about the shipment. Have you heard anything?"

Tom shook his head.

"The cigarettes have vanished without trace. I have absolutely no idea who would dare to pull a stunt like this. Ely spoke about a new supplier for the street dealers as well, but things have been quiet there the last few days."

"Since the kid's body was found?"

"The message was received. I'm guessing whoever targeted the shipment to the docks is someone else."

John rubbed at his jaw, feeling the prickle of stubble. "Or maybe not – could be someone changing tack. This has never happened before. Why now?"

"Timing is everything. David's death has left us vulnerable. And of course, a man down. Plus, I've kept you out of things these past weeks ... that might have been a mistake."

John resisted the urge to say *I told you so*, keeping the conversation focused on the business.

"What about Alan Ainsley? Could he be behind this?"

Tom straightened in his chair, visibly relaxing as he shared the burden of his business with his son again. "I don't think so. There's no sign of the man besides that flight to London. To be honest, I'd almost forgotten about him."

John narrowed his eyes – it was as though his father was a different person.

"The man owes you, Dad, owes *us*! We forget nothing! He will pay his debts. We need to appear strong and united, and the message has to get out that it's business as usual."

"And is it?"

"It is now, yes. I'm feeling ... more like myself. I'm ready to be fully involved now, all you have to do is give me the green light."

Tom clamped his hand on his son's shoulder, grinning broadly.

"You're right!" His voice quivered and he paused to compose himself. "You should know there's some fall out from what David was involved in. Murray's Garda contact told him a file is being prepared for the DPP regarding the business." He exhaled forcefully. "Whatever that means! I suppose we should expect the gardaí to come knocking with a warrant any day now."

"Are you serious! You're just sitting here!"

Tom's eyes darted to the ceiling – Mae was asleep, in bed early for once. He motioned with his hands for John to be quiet.

"Calm down, everything's in order. The solicitor is on top of things and the accountant has worked his magic." He paused and looked his son in the eyes. "I need you back in the game. It's half a business without you. Murray is busy running things and trying to find that girl. I could use your input. The man is dragging his heels on it – I've no idea why!"

"You're still determined to find Kate Crowley?"

The sigh that escaped Tom was loud and deep, and his shoulders rounded. To John he suddenly looked very old.

"I promised your mother. She needs this … we both do!"

He slid the CCTV image of Anna Clarke across the table.

John hadn't noticed the photos there – he realised now his father had been sitting in the dark, in the middle of the night, obsessing over this girl. His eyes studied the image, though the darkness of the kitchen made it difficult to make out little more than their shapes in the alleyway.

"Well, why isn't she here then, helping you resolve this?"

Tom shrugged. "That's a question for Ely Murray. I gave him the job of bringing her here days ago – the man has one excuse after another."

"Such as?"

"Well, for a start, she's Garda staff. Murray doesn't seem keen on this and thinks we shouldn't touch her. And according to him she's rarely alone. She *lives* alone for God's sake! Plus, she's some sort of kickboxer or something, he thinks she'll be trouble. He's been parked outside her house for days, but for various reasons he's not had the balls to nab her. Pure incompetence! The man is getting … I don't think he agrees with this so he's dragging his heels. Now he's suggesting I go to her – he thinks it'd be more straight-forward."

"To break into her house some night and ask your questions?"

The kick of excitement in his son's voice washed over Tom, the light in his eyes shining in the dark kitchen.

"I've been asking you to let me take care of her, Dad! I'll ask your questions. I'll get your answers." He patted his father's hand. "Let me look after this for you. And you can concentrate on taking care of Mum."

Tom placed his other hand on top of his son's with a smile, a wave of relief washing through him. He should have trusted John days ago when he said he could deal with this – he could see now his son didn't need shielding, didn't need more time to heal from his injuries. He was more than capable. Fixing this family was all that mattered – that meant avenging David's death, and if John would take over where Ely Murray was failing, Tom was satisfied the matter would soon end. His eyes settled on the girl in the CCTV photograph, Anna Clarke, and he smiled.

"To have you take care of this would mean the world to me, son!"

39

The sound of churning coffee beans inside Victus drowned out Anna's laughter as she watched Vivian roll her neck from side to side and grimace.

"I knew you should have stayed at mine last night! I guess the floor wasn't very comfortable then?"

"Ugh, you guess right! Luckily, my furniture arrives today. Do you have any of your migraine tablets?"

Anna fished two from her bag and slid them across the table. Vivian popped them into her mouth, washing them down with her cappuccino.

"But a girl still has to work – now how about a statement for the paper? You were a witness to the shooting the other night. Oh, come on, don't look at me like that! I've been assigned to follow-up on it and you're a star witness! You must have known I'd ask eventually, once all my other sources had dried up. Now that you're off the case you can give your best friend an inside scoop!"

Anna shook her head. "Sorry, no can do! It's in my contract at work. And besides, the whole thing has already been reported in all its gory detail. Haven't you got everything by now?"

Vivian sighed in resignation. "Yeah, but an eye-witness account would get me back on the front page." She popped the last of her bagel into her mouth. "Never mind."

Anna gripped her friend's hand across the table. "She messaged me! My aunt! Late last night. And she wants to have a video call soon!"

Vivian's eyes bulged in excitement and she squealed, before suddenly looking serious.

"What's wrong?"

"It's just … you've wanted answers for so long, and what if you don't like what you hear? And you don't know this woman – can you trust her?"

Anna sipped her coffee slowly … it was a fair question. Annika Garcia was a total stranger. But she felt irritated. "*Ugh*, you sound just like my brother!"

"Well, maybe he has a point!"

"Maybe he does." Suddenly her earlier excitement deflated. "But I should speak to her – if she *is* my aunt, I'd be mad not to explore that!"

"Of course! But … just be careful."

"She's on the other side of the world! She can't hurt me, Viv!"

"You know that's not what I mean."

Vivian's warning echoed in her mind for the rest of the morning. The woman, possibly her aunt, was a complete stranger, and this was a longshot. But she had to try. And after all she had been through lately, she felt sure she could handle whatever Annika Garcia might have to tell her.

Filling in the blanks about her mother's life would be a

bonus that might help to explain what had happened after her parents' car accident. And maybe she would be able to tell her more about her father, Michael Clarke, too. Despite the warnings from Alex and now Vivian, she couldn't help but feel that finally she was close to the truth.

40

"Right," he said as he scanned the assembled team, "talk to me!"

Frank Doherty folded his hands together on the desk in front of him and waited. His usual brusque manner was compounded with something else ... something William found to be eagerness.

"It's a week since Seán Doyle's murder in Clonality and our killers have been busy. You said they are filming all the killings. Let's hear what you've got."

William stood up – he preferred to pace as he outlined the details.

Detective Gardaí Colin Forde and Grace Thompson were sitting beside each other, both with notebooks open and pens poised. They already knew all the information William was about to discuss with the Chief Superintendent but were ready to record any new thoughts and observations.

An array of enlarged photographs was pinned to the noticeboard and William pointed to one showing the triangular markings in the grass. "These markings match a standard model

274

tripod and we are certain one like that was used to film the shooting in Clonakilty. We know Marian Selway's death was recorded and we believe Blake Landers's was too."

"For what purpose?" Doherty asked, bunching his fingers under his chin, his elbows on the arms of the chair.

"I'll get to that." Taking a deep breath, he carried on. "The couple we are looking for are mobile and organised – they stayed in Clonakilty for four nights prior to the shooting before moving into the city. The hotel rooms they stayed in are a minefield of DNA – I'm sure you can all appreciate just how many fingerprints and DNA samples are left behind in each hotel room. The woman wore gloves on check-in and check-out in Clonakilty, so nothing traceable on dockets at reception but we continue to work on the bedroom."

"Gloves?"

"Yes, black. Weather-appropriate."

"A clever move." Doherty popped gum into his mouth and began to chew.

"I don't think it was calculated. More likely just due to the cold. She left fingerprint evidence at the hotel here in the city on the check-in docket, so I don't think it had occurred to her that we would be able to track her down. The couple *are* organised though. We know at least one of them drove around the roads in Clonakilty to choose an appropriate victim. There's a marketing leaflet in the city-centre hotel room for the Rebel Event Centre advertising private tours, so we believe that's how Marian Selway was selected. Street cameras show the car they stole in Glanmire was parked kerbside on Albert Quay, as if waiting for Blake Landers to leave the building. They ignored the fact there were witnesses that time. We don't know why. But we are getting closer. We have a positive fingerprint match for the woman, as I said."

"So, who is she?"

William nodded to Grace, indicating she should take over, and sat down. Grace didn't feel the need to stand. She cleared her throat and began, looking between the three faces as evenly as she could.

"Erin Beale. We have positive confirmation of a match on both her left thumb print and right index finger."

"So, she has previous?" Doherty hadn't heard this particular update. He leaned forward, his excitement at a positive identification of one of the suspects palpable.

William took the lead again but stayed in his seat, passing around sheets with a woman's photograph and brief details typed underneath.

"Erin Beale, age twenty-four, born in Wicklow. This photograph is about seven years old, and so pretty useless. Her history is a sad one, in many ways."

"Aren't they all?" Doherty muttered sarcastically. "Go on then, what's her sob-story?"

William met his eyes. "It's quite significant, to be honest. For one thing, it led her down this path. Erin Beale came to the attention of –" He stopped as his mobile phone began to ring. "Ah! Saved by the bell. I have managed to track down a specialist who examined Miss Beale, well, one of them, and if you'll bear with me ..." he fiddled with the buttons on his phone, wincing at one point as he thought he had cut off the call, until finally placing it in the middle of the table between them all.

"Ms. McNamara? This is Detective Sergeant William Ryan. Thank you for returning my call. I am in conference in the Lee Street Garda station here with a number of other detectives, and I've put our call on loudspeaker if that's OK with you?"

A pause followed, until finally a woman cleared her

throat. "Yes, that's fine, detective."

William exhaled and smiled. "Good. I'll introduce you to my colleagues first. This is Doctor Alice McNamara, clinical psychologist specializing in cognitive behavioural psychotherapy. I hope I've got that right?"

He called out the rank and names of the others present, and each mumbled a greeting, keen for the call to progress.

"I read your profile after our earlier conversation – there are many strings to your bow, but behavioural psychotherapy is essentially your specialist field?" His tone was brusque but polite and it was clear he felt huge urgency to learn all he could.

"That's right, yes."

"Great!" Sitting back a little, he spoke clearly. "In our earlier call I appraised you of the situation we are dealing with, and what we know of Erin Beale so far. We appreciate your discretion, and your willingness to talk to us. Please tell us all you can about your dealings with Miss Beale. And before you mention client confidentiality, we do of course appreciate the need for this, but as I understand it, records can only be released if they're subpoenaed from the courts. We are dealing with a triple murder here and we simply don't have time for solicitors to go through the red tape. I assure you the ball is rolling where that's concerned and the preliminary request has already begun at our end."

He looked at Colin Forde, raised his eyebrows, the meaning clear: was it sent? Colin nodded and he pressed on.

"I must stress to you – we are investigating a series of quite gruesome murders and believe Miss Beale to be a danger to others. Everything you can tell us is vitally important. Can you help?"

There was a moment of silence, then the sound of

rustling papers. When the doctor spoke again William felt his shoulders relax.

"Of course, I understand. But there's only so much I can tell you, in any case – I haven't seen Erin Beale for over seven years now, and even then I never officially diagnosed her. What determinations I was able to make were … well, not as conclusive as I'd have liked. Nevertheless, I did make notes at the time, and if it can help I'll certainly assist your investigation."

"Thank you … we'll appreciate all you can tell us."

The gathered detectives stared at the phone with bated breath.

"I was contacted by Erin's GP when she was sixteen, at the request of her aunt. I should explain – Erin had a difficult childhood, the extent of which we don't fully know. Sometime around her eighth birthday her schoolteacher contacted social services with suspicions of neglect. Erin lived with her father – I honestly don't know the whereabouts of her mother. Once the social worker visited the family home Erin and her father disappeared. She didn't turn up for school and the family home was empty when gardaí checked the property. Nothing more could be done at that time, despite efforts to locate them."

William looked at Grace, mouthing "Follow this up" and she nodded, writing in the notebook.

"They resurfaced four years later, living rough in Dublin."

"They were homeless? Not even in sheltered accommodation? A man and a child!" Doherty was angry at the idea of it.

"Yes – it has become too common in recent years. Remarkably, Erin was found to be in good health and good spirits – she told gardaí and social workers she and her father had been homeless for a few years. She was placed in the care of her aunt. Her father eventually disappeared again, presumably to the streets, or perhaps died."

"So, she lived with her aunt from the age of twelve?"

"Yes. And she appeared well cared for and was making progress, of sorts. But according to her aunt she never slotted in well to the family dynamic and had many different expressions of anxiety and depression. A certain amount of that would be expected, of course, given her earlier years. But into her teen years she progressively displayed behaviour that alarmed her aunt and she sought help with the family doctor. She was disruptive in school and at home, and there were some manic episodes. It was an escalating situation, albeit over a period of years. I was asked to give an opinion – her GP is an acquaintance, personally and professionally."

"And what was your opinion?"

A loud sigh crackled through the phone before the doctor continued. "I would have liked more time with Erin. She didn't cooperate well, and she disappeared again shortly after our sessions. I understand she was arrested a few years later for public disorder offences and drug use in public … at the time I examined her, she was almost seventeen. If I were pushed to give a diagnosis, I would say she suffered from an attachment disorder, or more specifically Reactive Attachment Disorder. It is often a consequence of some form of mistreatment or abandonment from the parent or primary caregiver. It *could* lead to a person having maladaptive mindsets regarding relationships and often they are drawn to dysfunctional ones. Erin certainly showed evidence of that. Going unchecked, untreated by either therapy or medical intervention, it's quite plausible this could spiral into a diagnosis of Dissociative Personality Disorder. Given what you've told me, it *could* be this, although it's very rare. It sounds like Erin is 'breaking away' from the reality of life and showing signs of unpredictable behaviour. She could be susceptible to more manic episodes like the ones her aunt reported, possibly depression, anxiety and so on."

Silence followed her words, as each person in the room attempted to digest what she had said. Grace was writing furiously in her notebook, her eyebrows drawn together.

"Would assuming different identities tie in with this?" Grace asked, attracting a nod from her superior.

"Absolutely, yes."

William thanked the doctor for her time and, after establishing she had nothing else to add, he ended the call.

The room was quiet, each one considering the doctor's opinion of Erin Beale.

Grace was the first to voice her thoughts.

"A person like this ... suffering from this mental illness ... we know she's taken on an American persona at the hotel in Clonakilty, English in the Rebel Event Centre, Russian, I think," she looked at her notes, "in the city-centre hotel breakfast restaurant. She uses wigs and make-up to disguise herself. We know nothing about the man except that he wears a mask and prefers to let her do the talking. They use fake names and have barely left any traces behind ... realistically speaking, we are searching for people who keep changing. People who want to be invisible."

"But she doesn't use these wigs and clothes, the personas, to blend in!" Colin said. "Instead, they make her stand out! It may seem like they are trying to stay anonymous, but she does everything in her power to be noticed – the wigs and make-up, the clothes, the accents ... they mark her out as different. He wants to go unseen – she wants to *be* seen. They only thing they seem to agree on is the kill."

William grimaced. "Well, that's a chilling idea, but you're probably right. And her theatrics may be their downfall. We are *this close* to finding them. They are slipping up." He gestured to Colin. "Remind us of what the Technical Bureau found in the South Mall hotel."

Colin lowered his head to read. "Fingerprints on marketing paraphernalia, that match Erin Beale. One strand of human hair but treated with chemicals in such a way forensics can confirm it's a wig, that match the colour and length in the CCTV at the Rebel Event Centre, and blood in the bath in the hotel bathroom."

"Blood?" Doherty swallowed hard.

"Two types. One a positive match to Marian Selway. The other is likely the male in this couple. The killer, as the CCTV showed in the Rebel Event Centre."

Doherty rubbed both hands over his face. He looked tired, but there was hope in his voice. "You've done well. The DNA evidence is catching up with them. And we know who *she* is. What I'm even more curious about, to be honest, is *why* they are doing this. And why film it all? Personal kicks?"

A knock at the door drew their attention. Lauren, from the clerical staff downstairs, stepped inside, smiling brightly. "DS Ryan? There's a woman downstairs to see you from Phoenix Park."

William hopped out of his seat. "Show her up, please!" he said with a smile.

Turning to the Chief Superintendent he grinned broadly.

"I believe we are about to come closer to finding out!"

41

"Thank you for taking the time to come here. In person. Although a telephone call would have sufficed. Nevertheless, we appreciate it."

They shook hands and William made the introductions. Jennifer Morrison shook each hand in turn, nodding in greeting. She looked like a businesswoman in a pin-stripe trouser suit and briefcase, but she was a member of the force. The journey from Phoenix Park, the Garda headquarters in Dublin, would have taken most of her morning, yet she had deemed it necessary to speak to them in person. Frank Doherty was impressed, and slightly unnerved. In his professional experience, personal visits from Dublin were never a good thing.

"Your role is as a profiler for serious crime, is that right?"

"Yes, that's correct, among other things."

"And you've been on the road most of the morning?"

"It's not a problem, the road is much improved now. I'm visiting my mother in West Cork this weekend so it suited to make a detour into the city."

He looked at his wristwatch. "Well, it's almost lunchtime. We'll work through if nobody objects." Small nods of agreement were enough to convey their assent. "Grace, run across to Victus and get some takeaway coffees and a selection of sandwiches like a good –" He caught himself just in time, and smiled at her tightly.

Grace looked between the other faces, Colin and William, her meaning settling uneasily. "Sorry, but are you taking the piss?"

"I'll go!" Colin jumped to his feet. "I could do with some fresh air. How do you take your coffee, eh, Miss Morrison?"

She smiled warmly at him from where she was standing, pinning enlarged photographs of her own onto the noticeboard. Tucking a strand of brown hair behind her ear, she said, "Americano, please, with a small drop of milk."

As he weaved between the traffic to the other side of the street where the coffee shop was located, Colin breathed in deeply. The air was heavy with exhaust fumes, not the *fresh* air he had hoped for, but it was good to get out of the conference room and away from the images on the board. Ever since he'd set foot in the hotel room where the killers had stayed, he'd felt a heaviness crawl over him. This was the first murder case since his allocation to detective, and the most macabre thing he had ever experienced. It just kept getting worse. People that killed, seemingly for fun, and filmed it? It made him shiver every time he thought about it. The blue luminal stains on the bath had freaked him out – it was blood, the victim's blood. In the Rebel Event Centre, he had stayed near the large glass walls and looked out over the city, rather than at the puddle of blood and little pieces of flesh he imagined were still visible on the carpet. He'd had trouble getting to sleep that night. The morgue images of Seán Doyle and Blake Landers had been just as disturbing – he imagined they were stamped onto his brain, waiting for him when he closed his eyes. He wondered if he was really cut out for detective work. He had a sneaking suspicion he might be in over his head.

As he waited in line for his order to be ready he almost laughed out loud, remembering Grace Thompson's face when Doherty had told her – the only woman on their team – to go and fetch the coffees. *She* had the stomach for the work, he thought. And the guts to stand up to Doherty too. He admired her, just as he did William Ryan. And he had to admit, the work was interesting. No two days were the same. Maybe he'd give it a few more weeks …

Soon he made his way back to the conference room, two large paper bags in his arms, hoping the woman from Phoenix Park had finished her business and he wouldn't have to sit through any more graphic images. Very quickly he realised this wasn't to be his lucky day.

She was still in full flow.

"I work mostly on very serious crime – murder, human-trafficking, exploitation, and so on."

"Sounds bleak."

"It is, but we get results. In my department we try to gain as many insights as we can into the mind of the criminal, to better try to understand their motivations and compulsions. Psychological clues are vital. We work across a broad range of specialisations – co-operation with other divisions, nationally and internationally, is key."

Doherty nodded, slurping his coffee quickly. "Right, tell us what you know. It must be important – you drove all the way down."

She smiled at him, unperturbed by his gruff manner. "As I said earlier, my mother lives in West Cork and I'll stay overnight with her. That was arranged anyway but, to be honest, what we are working on ties in with what's happening here in Cork, and I wanted to pay a personal visit. It might be easier to explain it all, and I need to examine all your data from the three murders, starting with Seán Doyle last Thursday."

William pursed his lips, thinking. It was becoming clearer to him that the three murders over the past week were part of some bigger picture. He rolled up his sleeves, eager to know what Jennifer Morrison had thought was so important. When he had requested help from a profiler, he hadn't expected a personal visit to the station. He felt impatient to know everything she knew.

"Of course – we'll do all we can to piece this together. Getting these people locked up is our main objective. Let's get to work!"

The sandwiches were finished, the last of the coffee growing cold in the cardboard mugs – Colin quickly cleared the debris into the paper carrier bags before Doherty could motion for Grace to do it. He left the bags on a table to the side and sat down slowly. Jennifer had finished attaching evidence photos to the noticeboard and she moved to stand beside them. Crime scenes, corpse photos, zoomed-in images of wounds and discarded weapons – it was worse than Colin could have imagined. CCTV images of the suspects offered little identification but the similarities to the murders in their own city were startlingly similar in two obvious ways.

In the other crimes displayed on the board, there were *two* killers, two suspects in each case.

And one of the two was filming the crime.

"These CCTV images and crime-scene photographs were taken across Europe – the data has been shared with us through our colleagues in Europol. This cluster of killings here ..." she turned and pointed at three photographs showing an array of dead bodies and weapons, "occurred in Spain. We were consulted only because most of the countries within the EU had a similar set of cases – murder, committed randomly, by two suspects, where there is clear evidence that one filmed the event."

She paused, and the silence in the room was oppressive, broken only by Doherty, crunching something between his teeth. As he seemed to do constantly lately, he pulled a handkerchief from his pocket and mopped the back of his neck, damp patches visible when he lifted his arm.

"So, let me get this straight – this is happening across Europe?" he said.

"Yes. We monitor crimes nationwide in HQ, of course, but initially it wasn't realised the first killing, the shooting of Seán Doyle, was filmed. Once that was established, it was already known the murder of Marian Selway had been filmed, and we became concerned we are dealing with the same thing."

"Which is what exactly?" The confusion in Grace's voice matched how everyone else in the conference room was feeling.

Jennifer drew in a deep breath before she continued.

"Experts in cybercrime across Europe have been working on this. You've all heard of the Dark Web, I assume? The European Cybercrime Centre is tasked with dismantling criminal sites online, but it's a painstaking task. This case has fallen into their remit. We believe the murders are filmed and uploaded as part of a criminal enterprise, for voyeurs and so on. This man ..." she pointed to a photograph of a middle-aged man, balding and thin, sitting on a plastic chair with his arms folded, "Francois Moreau, was apprehended in the French city of Angers on Wednesday. His partner in crime, literally, was killed when a homemade bomb exploded too soon. He's slowly beginning to cooperate with the authorities – he has disclosed some of the details and, as you might expect, he's quite a disturbed individual. He's only drip-feeding information one piece at a time – he seems to enjoy keeping the investigators guessing. He spoke about a "Film Critic" that he sends the videos to – this person seems to control things, but he would give no details on that person's identity. I believe he's afraid of that individual, which would tie in with how these things work."

She paused and drank some water, before looking again at the assembled faces. She had their complete attention.

"Moreau's computer yielded some interesting facts. Not everything yet, but enough to know what we're dealing with. The 'Critic' as he or she is called, is in charge of everything in each location. Those that commit the murder can choose their own victims or the "Critic" can direct everything, from location, weapon, even who to kill. The couples that carry out the murders are not all as concerned about concealing their identities as the man and woman here in Cork. Europol have a lot to go on in identifying suspects in Germany and Italy, for example, and the investigation is at a critical stage."

"Jesus Christ." It was barely audible – Doherty was stunned. In his whole career he had never come across anything like it.

William leaned back in the chair, clasping the cool metal legs of it as he spoke.

287

"So, all this is part of a type of murder club operating across Europe?"

"I can say with one-hundred-percent certainty that that is the case. Unfortunately, Cork has been swept up in it."

"But why?"

"All it takes is someone with the inclination to explore the Dark Web to stumble across an appealing website and express their interest. There's a large amount of money at stake and the killers are competing for the top prize. We've established that much. There will be a finale on Sunday, the winners announced then."

"A finale?" Colin swallowed hard.

"It seems the competition, as it's viewed, will conclude on Sunday."

"So the clock is ticking."

"Yes. From our information you can expect at least one more murder before then. The more spectacular the better, according to Moreau. Either we end all this by catching the perpetrators or the cyber forensics team dismantle the website and apprehend those running it."

"Or *they* end it," Colin said quietly, "by filming their last kill for the finale."

Doherty exhaled loudly as William leaned forward, looking at his detectives solemnly, resting his chin on his cupped hands.

"The people running the thing, on the Dark Web," he turned to Jennifer, "do they know Francois Moreau was arrested and his partner killed?"

She shook her head. "One thing he *did* say was he isn't expected to upload another video to his film Critic until Sunday morning. Lack of contact from him shouldn't raise any alarm bells."

"Well, that's something." Doherty sighed.

Grace raised her head from her notebook. "Their Critic, as you called it, could be based anywhere. So we should concentrate our efforts on finding the killers."

"Agreed," William said. "These people are smart. They need somewhere to stay and they need Wi-Fi if they are to upload their next film. These two factors offer us an opportunity. We target hotels, guest houses, internet chatrooms and public libraries. We don't search for names or nationalities – we search for couples that checked in without ID. No-one is to try to detain the couple – they are violent and dangerous. Our only chance is to track and locate them. We'll start co-ordinating this now – I want teams out there within the hour."

He rose quickly, pushing in his chair. The meeting was over.

He addressed the group once more before their tasks began.

"Someone contact the press. I want a message sent out – the public are already warned to look out for the couple – now we issue a warning to the people of Cork to stay out of their way and not to approach them."

"Understood," Colin said.

Grace and Colin left together, their heads bowed in conversation.

Doherty cleared his throat and shook Jennifer Morrison's hand again. He didn't manage to look at her as he muttered his thanks – he had calls to make to his colleagues in the other stations, cooperation to request and absolutely no idea how to explain this to them while keeping his incredulity from his voice.

"Do you need anything while you're here?" It was just William and Jennifer left in the room and he began to help her remove the last of the images from the noticeboard.

"I could do with a desk for a couple of hours if you can manage it? And I need access to everything from your investigation."

"Sure, we can sort something out."

William's eyes found the clock on the wall. The sound of the seconds counting down was loud inside his head … there would be one more kill by Sunday …

One more, at least.

He had opportunities now to catch the couple, to end the murders and save lives. But if the opportunities didn't come to fruition *they* would succeed, and possibly disappear.

He would do everything in his power to avoid that – he just hoped that was enough.

42

Lost in the details of her report, Anna snatched up her ringing desk phone quickly. As the caller spoke a smile spread across her face.

"You sound busy!"

"*Myles!*"

"How are you? I didn't want to call your mobile in case Frank Doherty is around – I've heard the man is grumpier than ever these days!"

She laughed. "He has his moments. Are you still abroad?"

"Yes, until the end of next week. Listen – the reason I called you is I found information on Robert Evans. I'm sorry it took so long – I was waiting on a colleague in the UK to get back to me."

Her breath caught in her throat.

"The phone number on the business card is long disconnected. The post-office box is legit, or was – it hasn't been used in years. Both were registered to a business named RE Consultancy with an office address in London. It was a low-profile business, a bit ambiguous in the way a lot of consultancy enterprises are … the company wound up about five years ago. It wasn't registered to Robert Evans but a different name – nevertheless I think he is the man you're looking for. He was questioned by police actually, back in the late seventies, but there wasn't enough evidence to convict him of any charges."

Anna nodded mutely, stunned. She hadn't expected so much information from the jumble of numbers on the card. The man had been questioned by police? And he was her dad's friend …

"There's not a lot of information available about Robert Evans other than a few facts: he never married, never bought any property, and there are no children registered to him. The last known and documented evidence of him existing in the UK is in 1978."

Alarm bells rang loud in Anna's mind as the thought formed – that was the same year her mother disappeared.

"But he has resurfaced. I had to dig *very* deep and pull in a favour but … I found him. He's currently in bad health and living in a care home near London. Do you want me to give you the address?"

It was some time later that Anna regained her senses. She was aware of the buzz of the office around her, of Lauren moving over and back to the photocopier, telephones ringing, the smell of fresh coffee as mugs were brought from the canteen. Yet she felt detached from it all. She stared at the image on her screen, elbows on her desk, fingers knotted under her chin. The care home Myles had told her about was a one-storied red-brick structure with small windows, set in front of lush green gardens, in colourful bloom when the photo was taken. The Royal

Haven Care Home provided end of life care and respite care for seriously ill patients. And one of its current residents was a man who had claimed to be her father's friend, had facilitated the transfer of half a million euro from a trust fund, and who just might hold the key to unlocking some of the mystery surrounding exactly who Helen and Michael Clarke were.

Having spent ten years in the dark, with only unanswered questions about *where* her parents were, in the space of two days Anna had found her mother's sister and her father's friend, and the question that screamed inside her now was *who* they were. She finally had a chance to find that out.

Wiping her sweating palms on her jeans before she picked up the phone, she drew air deep into her lungs. It was time to call her brother and see if they might find answers to both of those questions.

43

Moscow, 1978

As August drew to a close the days were long and warm, with barely a puff of wind to stir the air. Their apartment was too small and hot in the midday heat, even with all the windows open. Yelena hugged her mother goodbye, grabbed her favourite red coat and carried her small suitcase with her as she and her sister took the train into the city and made their way to Red Square. She would be collected from there by car, to journey with the orchestra to the airport, beginning her tour of England. The first concert was scheduled for London, in the Royal Albert Hall. Thinking about her trip brought a shallowness to her breathing that worried her, a tightness to her chest that she didn't understand. So she did her best to push all thoughts of the orchestra, the London hotel, and the scheduled meeting with the Englishman out of her mind. It helped that her father had been at work when she left the apartment – she already knew what she needed to do in London – he had made his instructions clear.

That afternoon the crowds in Red Square were sparser than usual, perhaps because of the heat. Yelena walked slowly beside her sister, intent on drawing out their time together, the sights of the surrounding buildings so familiar now she barely saw them. Her arms felt heavy and hot with her coat slung over it, and her blouse was sticking to her skin with sweat as she gestured to a wall in the shade. They moved to lean against it, and she rested her coat on top of her suitcase, feeling happier in this reprieve from the heat.

Annika was quiet – she had been all morning. The sisters didn't speak much when their father was in the apartment, but even after he had left for the factory she had appeared sullen and upset. Yelena had attempted conversation on the train ride but was unable to penetrate her sister's mood, which remained dark and brooding, her face turned away. Even as they strolled slowly around the square she was silent, lost in her thoughts. They had bought lunch from a cart on the street, and Annika's remained untouched in her hand, wrapped in its white paper napkin.

Now she turned to Yelena, finally breaking the silence.

"I have been thinking through everything, every possible option. I think it is time for us to say goodbye."

Yelena laughed in surprise and popped more cheburek into her mouth. The pastry was greasier than their mother made it, and she licked her fingertips. She winced slightly as the grease stung a fresh cut, the result of too much practice at her father's insistence. She hoped it would heal before the concert next week in London.

"Goodbye, sister!" She swallowed and laughed again, hoping to raise a smile. "Until I see you in three weeks!"

Annika smiled sadly and looked away.

Yelena watched as her sister plucked small bits of her snack apart and tossed them on the ground, a reflexive move she wasn't conscious of making. She stared into the distance, unaware of her sister's eyes watching her. Yelena placed a hand on her sister's arm, her unease mounting.

"Annika?"

She turned to face Yelena again, tears spilling onto her cheeks.

"Yesterday I heard him speaking. Father, I mean. Some men from the political party called to his office. I was at the front desk and he didn't know I could hear." She swiped her hand through the air, to dismiss the finer details – they didn't matter. What mattered, and all she had been able to think about, was what she had overheard. "I heard Father make the agreement. When you return from London you will be married to Comrade Kuznetsov."

Yelena burst into laughter again, her hand shooting up to her mouth. She smiled incredulously at her sister. Was this why she had been so quiet? Worrying over something so unbelievable … she must have misheard!

"Don't be crazy! He's older than Father! The idea is just –"

"Not the old man, his *son!* The younger Kuznetsov." Her voice faded sadly into a whisper.

Yelena felt the dart of dread and horror in her stomach. A familiar feeling, one she had experienced since her teens, anxiety at the things her father expected her to do. To practice her cello until her fingers bled and grew calloused, to smile and acquiesce to men that stood too close, breathing their sweat and desire all over her. And recently, the trips to London, to help him do business with a man she was growing increasingly afraid of. Now this …

"But his wife …"

"Yes. Beaten to death and six months pregnant," Annika continued in a whisper, her eyes darting left and right, fearful of listening ears, though there was no-one nearby.

"The family blame an intruder, say it was a random attack, but it was *him!* Even the dogs on the street know the truth. Leonid Kuznetsov beat his pregnant wife to death, and his father's powerful friends brushed it away like she didn't exist. Like she didn't matter! Now his father says he needs a new wife. He needs to appear respectable."

"But Father would never ..."

"Wake up, Yelena!" Her voice rose in despair – she needed to make her sister understand. "Father is desperate to rise in the Communist Party. Comrade Kuznetsov can open the doors he needs. And for that he is willing to pawn you to his murdering son."

She sobbed, a strangled sound from deep inside her. Yelena stared at her sister's face and knew that she spoke the truth. She believed her – Annika had not imagined the conversation. She knew she could not appeal to their mother for help – she had accepted her place within her marriage a long time ago. And the implicit expectation for her daughters was clear.

Annika turned suddenly and gripped her upper arms. Alarm sparked in Yelena – she had never seen her sister look so serious. It scared her. More than her father scared her, or the Englishman.

"Pay close attention to me, please!" Annika sucked in air, shaking her head as though to push aside any doubts about what she had to say. "We must say goodbye now. There can be no other way for us. Father's plans for you are ... are ... diabolical! You are so much more than what he thinks you are!" Annika paused and appeared to sway a little. Yelena worried that her sister was about to faint but her grip on her arms tightened. "Sister, I love you. More than I have ever loved anyone. When you are away from here, in London, an opportunity may present itself to you, a chance to leave your future here and start a fresh one. If it does, promise me – you *must* take it and leave us, for your own sake."

"No!"

"Think about it, Yelena. What is waiting for you in London? And worse, what is waiting for you when you return? This is not a life we can survive! You have no choice!"

Yelena lowered her eyes to the ground, unable to speak. Birds pecked at the flakes of pastry and bits of meat at their feet, heads bobbing, beaks darting over and over. For a fleeting moment she envied them – their greatest concern seemed to be scooping up the next morsel of food. And they were free to do as they pleased, to come and go as they chose, while she was prisoner ...

When she looked at her sister again, she resembled a stranger. Annika looked older somehow, with dark shadows circling her eyes and her lips were cracked and stretched into a tight line. Yelena knew she was right – she must escape, somehow.

"You really think I should ... disappear?"

"There is no other way. Take any chance you get to flee from the guards at the hotel. Perhaps there is someone who could help you?"

Yelena thought of the young man, the bookkeeper with the warm brown eyes and easy smile. She wondered if she would see him on this trip to London – perhaps she could turn to him. With an angry shake of her head, she pushed him out of her mind – it was merely a fantasy. He worked for Mr Lewis, after all. Why would he help her?

"But, Mother ..."

Annika gripped her hand. "Mother made her choices a long time ago and she stands by them."

"What about you?"

She smiled, but it was weak, wobbling, and faded quickly. "I will miss you, sister, but I'll leave here too, as soon as I can. We will both be free of him. We deserve better than this!"

Tears sprang from Yelena's eyes suddenly, her violent sobs taking them both by surprise.

"Annika! I'll never see you again! The world is too big, and I can't ... I can't ..."

She could no longer speak and she sagged against the wall – her legs giving way, she sank to the floor. The birds scattered before her with frightened squawks, some taking flight, others fleeing to a safe distance before circling around again, the crumbs still in sight. Annika crouched beside her and rubbed her shoulder as she cried.

Her voice in Yelena's ear was firm and clear.

"If an opportunity presents itself, you *must* take it, Yelena. You must leave and never come back. It is the only way you'll survive."

44

London, 1978

Michael replayed the detective's words over and over, day and night.

"There's always something to find."

In truth, he knew he had already found it – the inconsistencies that had bothered him before. Bob had fobbed him off and nothing had changed.

He pondered over it all for many nights, lying awake, turning over and back in his single bed. This had to be the key to unlocking what Smith was looking for.

And the girl ... Yelena. She had said her father was a business associate of Lewis's, but he could find no evidence of that. He still wondered what was in the suitcase she had received from Lewis. He remembered her question, "Are you as bad as the others?" and found the idea that she thought he was Lewis's money man flooded him with shame.

An opportunity arose to speak to his boss a week after his encounter with the man calling himself Smith.

Lewis was in the office for the afternoon, taking calls at his desk, his voice booming around the small space. It was just the two of them. After what felt like hours, he wrapped up the calls and pulled on his overcoat.

"How is your karate training going, Michael?" he asked conversationally.

He was surprised by his interest – the man was usually indifferent to everyone else's personal life. Today he appeared to be in a great mood and Michael seized his chance.

"Great, thanks, Mr Lewis – although it's Taekwon-Do – but never mind. Actually, I wanted to speak to you about something in the accounts, is that OK?"

"Of course! I'm at your disposal!"

He was beaming – still Michael felt some apprehension.

"Thank you. I can't find any documentation to account for payment for the shipments from Turkey. Are there more papers I need to work on, perhaps kept somewhere else?"

Lewis was pulling on leather gloves and stopped. He flexed his fingers inside the leather, forming a fist with one hand. "Anything else you want to know?"

Immediately Michael knew he had made a mistake. He had stepped over a line, the air in the room suddenly infused with tension. Lewis's body language offered a warning – his smile disappeared, his mouth now twisted and sour. His eyes, like small stones set deep in his face, stared hard at Michael, full of suspicion.

"*Er*, no. That's it," he lied. "Just wondering if perhaps I've overlooked something."

Lewis stepped forward, closing the space between them.

"I'm trusting you, Michael, to keep my accounts in order. Do you understand? If there is something you need to make appear, or disappear, I expect you to do your job. Trust is very important to me. Am I making myself clear?"

He nodded, hoping his eyes didn't betray his understanding and disgust.

"Of course, Mr Lewis."

"Good. I'll be back in an hour." He was gone, letting the office door slam behind him.

Michael moved to the glass window and watched him walk through the warehouse, pausing briefly to chat to Roy as he did.

He turned away and sat down heavily at his desk, resting his chin on his fists. That brief exchange with Lewis had sparked a rush of dread. He knew that if he hadn't had the conversation with the Counter Terrorism man, he might have missed the subtle threat in his boss's voice. Despite Bob's warning, he might have kept querying, innocently trying to understand. He *did* understand now. Smith was right. His boss was crooked, and it was clear that if evidence of that could be found in the accounts, he expected Michael to cover it up. But Smith expected an update soon ...

The question was, which enemy was he prepared to make?

45

Cork/London, 2019

They ordered wine on the flight, although Alex left his mostly untouched. Anna had hoped it might help with her mounting claustrophobia but wasn't surprised when it didn't. As soon as they were air borne the thought screamed inside her head – *I can't get out!* Immediately she felt it, a crushing weight on her chest, black spots dancing in front of her eyes. The last time she had felt this was when she hid in the storage closet the night Myles was shot. She gripped the armrests as she tasted vomit, cursing inside her head. Clamping her lips closed, she drew air in through her nostrils and began to count, releasing the air again slowly. The fog clouding her brain began to clear as she mentally recited the tenets of Taekwon-Do slowly, over and over. After a while she opened her eyes.

"You OK?"

"I will be."

For the next hour neither could sit still. At one point Anna realised she had forgotten to set her new house alarm – in the rush to make the flight she had done nothing more than throw some essentials into a bag. She didn't think Dean Harris had been released in the last twenty-four hours – DS Ryan would have told her, so she pushed the worry about it firmly out of her head.

She had brought a book but quickly gave up on it, the swirling letters on the page refusing to form a coherent pattern. Alex attempted a newspaper crossword, but the noise as he tapped his pen on the page grew so loud she eventually covered his hand with her own.

"Try to relax!"

"*You* try to relax! You haven't been able to sit still since we took off!"

He was sitting between Anna and an elderly man who occupied the aisle seat and he was beginning to look particularly uncomfortable. A single bead of sweat ran down his cheek and disappeared into the creases around his frown. She nudged him.

"Do you want to swap seats? You seem a bit … squashed. You look really uncomfortable."

Alex removed his elbows from the arm rests and cupped his hands on his lap.

"Nope, I'm fine."

"You don't seem fine, you seem … OK, I'll shut up!"

His glare made Anna laugh.

"Oh, come on!" she said quietly, conscious of possible listeners around them. "I know it's tense, waiting, but in twenty-four hours we'll know more truth about our parents than we have for our whole lives! Aren't you excited about that? Robert Evans agreed to speak to us tomorrow morning, and our phone call with Annika Garcia is at ten tonight. We'll have answers soon, maybe not *all* of them, but more than we ever dared to hope for. I bet we'll get really useful information to tell the Missing Person's Bureau, and maybe it'll be enough to reopen the investigation! Try to stay positive!"

Alex had been the one to suggest they fly straight to London and see Robert Evans as soon as possible. Surprised by his response and keen not to lose any momentum, Anna had quickly agreed and had taken some annual leave to finish work early. Samantha and Chloe were in Dublin for the weekend, visiting her parents, the zoo and catching up with friends. He wouldn't be needed at home and was caught up on work – it was perfect timing. Now, he seemed like a man having second thoughts.

He was intrigued by the fact that Roberts Evans had agreed to meet them without hesitation or surprise – the man had ignored his calls and messages ten years ago. Now that they had found him, he agreed to meet in person, and Alex was suspicious. He didn't voice his concern to his sister – excitement illuminated her face and she beamed at him now. She expected she was about to find answers to all her questions – what troubled him was that he didn't think she had given any consideration to what those answers might be.

Anna watched her brother carefully – she knew when he was stressed out. He had said, only last night, that she could lean on him for support, and Myles had advised her to tell him the situation about Dean Harris. He knew Alex would want to know. Looking at him now, she couldn't do it. Knowing her brother wasn't sleeping well and watching him squirm under the weight of his anxiety, she decided to continue to keep that information to herself.

Their hotel was central and spacious, with free WIFI and a stocked minibar. All that had been available at such short notice was a twin room, and after she had unpacked her small case Anna busied herself with entering the WIFI code into her laptop, keen to be set up before their Skype call with Annika Garcia. Alex unpacked slowly and called Samantha, chatting to Chloe too, smiling for the first time in hours. She watched him, glad to see his mood improve. After the call ended he flicked through the book she had left on her bedside locker, brooding.

"Isn't it amazing I was able to find Annika Garcia online? I would have paid a private investigator to find her, but Vivian was right – the internet is a fountain of information! Everything is accessible if you know how to search properly."

"*Mmm.*"

"Do you want to go get some food?" She was keen to pass the time – it was dragging here in the hotel room.

He nodded, although he didn't think he could eat. Still, it would be better than sitting in the small room, waiting for the seconds to tick by until ten o'clock.

The nearest restaurant was a burger chain popular with tourists. They walked the short distance quickly, and Alex felt somewhat revived. The air was cold and fresh, and he tucked his chin into his scarf as they walked, passing throngs of people emerging from the nearby tube station. Anna was quiet beside him, her hands deep inside her coat pockets, her head down against the wind.

Once their food arrived they both realised they were ravenous and eating distracted from the silence between them. As they moved on to coffee, Alex finally spoke, sounding more like himself.

"I know you can't really discuss cases from work, but I meant to ask you if there was any progress on the murder of Sam's boss?"

Anna shook her head. "Nothing that I'm aware of. It might be connected to the other killings that happened, but the investigation is on-going."

Alex whistled through his teeth. "That could have been you or Sam. It's crazy what's been going on!

I wonder what she's like. Are you sure she's Mum's sister?"

"Well ... yes. As far as I can tell, she is Annika Vasilieva and her sister was Yelena. It has to be her!"

The restaurant was busy, the sounds of diners a cosy backdrop to their conversation. Alex drained his coffee too quickly and felt his heart racing in his chest. After his earlier slump, now he felt agitated and restless.

"I still can't believe what Myles uncovered about Mum ...Yelena." Suddenly he was keen to talk. "Now we know she has a living sister ... we had no idea. She always said she had no family. Why did she lie?"

Anna could only shrug – she felt annoyance creep over her. "Why are you going over this now? We'll know in less than two hours!"

He looked away, affronted. She was the one who had refused to let the mystery drop, now she was irritated that he wanted to discuss it.

"Myles certainly is handy to have around –all the information he keeps finding for us." There was an edge to his tone and Anna wasn't sure if her brother meant what he said.

"You think he's meddling?"

"I'm not sure I'm comfortable that he accessed Mum and Dad's file and found out what he did. Yet he couldn't find any more? Or anything about Dad? It would have been better if he gave us the whole story instead of half the truth.

But what's done is done, and here we are."

"Yes exactly!" Anna was defensive, her voice rising. "Closer to the truth that we've ever been, and it's all thanks to Myles. Would you rather be in the dark for the rest of your life?"

"To be honest," he fixed his eyes on hers, "that depends on what we find out."

46

Cork, 2019

Ely Murray had scaled the smooth, high wall surrounding Anna's back garden easily. It was a feat he doubted she could do, being a lot shorter than he was. A heavy metal gate, locked with a steel padlock, secured the side of her house and back garden, the wall an added safety feature. He had approached the house from the garden of the neighbour behind, and noted no dogs, no sensor lights turned on to disturb him. Now he was standing in her small garden, the back of her house illuminated only by the moon. There was no security light on timer, but there did appear to be an alarm system – the white box with its pulsing light slowed his progress. He shrugged – he would have to tread more carefully.

He knew she wasn't home – his Garda contact had called earlier to say Anna had left work early, speaking to a colleague about flying to London. Ely had driven to Cork Airport, breaking every speed limit possible, but congested traffic at the Kinsale Road roundabout slowed his progress, and there was no sign of her at the airport. Presumably, her flight had departed before he arrived. He had called his contact back and made him check the system – she hadn't booked Monday off work. So, she was due back to Cork on or before the last flight in from London on Sunday night. Again, he would have to watch and wait.

On his last visit here he can been disturbed before he could check out the back of her house. Now he peered inside the patio doors that led to her kitchen. The house was in darkness and his view obscured by a thin white curtain that didn't quite cover the glass doors. There was a frosted bathroom window to the side, offering nothing useful. He checked the metal gate – it was secured with a steel padlock too big and heavy to break without some tools. She was safety-conscious, to a point. Remembering how she had pummelled the punchbag, he doubted she was careless. He would bring reinforcements on Sunday night, he decided – once she was secured, he would call Tom Gallagher to come to the house to question her. It was the safest option. And one he found himself increasingly looking forward to. As much as she intrigued him, he was tired of this task and looked forward to returning to other things.

He mounted the wall in a running jump and hoisted himself over, dropping back down into the grass of the house behind. There was little need for caution – he was dressed all in black, and every house was in darkness. Still, as he made his way to the front of the house he paused, crouched low beside the hedging that separated her house from the neighbours, and watched the street in front of him. Nothing. All houses were dark, all curtains were drawn and still. The street was empty.

Straightening up, he stepped quickly to the living-room windows. The curtains were open – she had left in a hurry.

Light from the streetlamp and the moon offered enough illumination to allow an outline of her living room – a small area, with sofa and armchair facing the TV, a low coffee table in the middle. He saw a set of shelves against the wall, crammed with books, and what looked like a trophy glinting in the darkness. An archway separated the living room from a room at the back of the house – the kitchen he had peered into earlier. He moved to the front door – he had already decided this would not be a viable option. There were still elements of the plan to be worked out …

He darted back to his car, parked at the kerb beside the house, and lowered himself into the driver's seat.

"Murray."

His heart constricted inside his chest as a man sitting in the passenger seat spoke.

John Gallagher.

Ely inhaled sharply and fought to steady his nerve and his hammering pulse.

"John. I'm surprised to see you here." He glanced over his shoulder and out the sides of the front windows – there was no waiting car that he could see. John must have instructed whoever drove him here to leave.

Ely pushed the key into the ignition and started the Audi.

"You'll be wanting a lift back into town?"

"Let's sit here a while first."

John's voice was soft, a purr that unsettled Ely. John was dangerous and unpredictable – Ely knew that better than anyone. His father had tried to keep him on a leash recently, but that seemed to have come to an end. He was wearing dark leather gloves, and the sight of them chilled Ely's blood.

"What is it, John?"

311

"It's as if you don't want to bring her in. How long is it now since you were told? She's just a girl, short and skinny. There's no point checking out her house. She's not here."

"Yes, I know that." But how the hell did John know that?

"She'll be back Saturday night. She has an evening flight booked. The thing is, Murray, I am ten steps ahead of you. You're like a dead duck these days."

Ely stayed quiet, waiting. If anyone else spoke to him like that he would lose his teeth. John, or any of the Gallaghers, had never disrespected him before.

"Drug dealers afraid to talk to you, missing stock, now a girl that keeps giving you the slip ..." John tutted theatrically and looked out the windscreen at the night sky. "You're lame while the rest of us are running, do you know what I mean?"

Ely inhaled again, filling his chest. What the hell was John playing at? They had been brothers-in-arms for years – he had given thirty years to the Gallagher business and watched John grow up. Thirty years protecting that boy, teaching him, guiding him away from fistfights that would become manslaughter, from deals that would go sour if he didn't shut his mouth. Ely had killed to deliver John safely from the clutches of the Meiers, mere weeks ago! And now, such disrespect ...

"You'd better watch your mouth, John!"

"Or what?" John laughed softly, grinning broadly. "You going to set your little girlfriend on me?" he nodded towards Anna's house. "I hear she's good at knocking men out – hardmen too. *Men. Just. Like. You.*"

The words hung between them and John's grin remained in place, enjoying how his words settled on Ely's face. A car pulled up behind them, its lights off.

"I've enjoyed our little chat," John said brightly, opening the car door a fraction. "The way I see it, I stepped back for a few weeks and the business is falling apart." His voice was serious again. "You're not up to it anymore. You're out, Murray. Done. Do you understand me? Disappear – I owe you that much. I'll take care of the girl."

He climbed lightly from the car and disappeared into the darkness.

As the car behind drove slowly from the estate Ely sat still, in shocked silence, staring after it. Quickly, anger punctured his disbelief. Thirty years … bodies burned and turned to ash, and he had just been told to disappear, that he was out.

With a sharp laugh he flexed his foot on the accelerator, the roar from the exhaust fracturing the stillness of the night. He didn't care if he woke the neighbours.

Let them come.

There was fire in him yet, and he had nothing to lose.

47

London, 2019

Suddenly, there she was. Silver hair falling softly around her face, blue eyes shining amid a fan of wrinkles, a slight smile as she gazed uncertainly from the screen.

"Oh, my goodness! You really are Yelena's children!"

Her voice was husky, her accent almost fully American but with the soft rhythm of something else. She was sitting at what appeared to be her kitchen table, the background showing a homely and bright room full of photographs and potted plants. She began to cry. Wiping at tears that flowed down her face, she gulped, trying to compose herself, her shoulders shaking.

They stayed quiet, waiting for Annika Garcia to be able to speak.

Anna felt numb, as though she was alive yet unable to do anything other than sit and stare. As soon as the video call had opened on her laptop she knew it was her aunt. Her mother's sister. An older version of the woman she had not seen for over ten years. There could be no doubt – the tilt of her head as she spoke, the slant of her cheekbones, the oval shape of her eyes ... she was an aged version of their mother. And here she was, in the flesh, or the closest form of that she could be from the other side of the world.

"It's so amazing to see you! A son and a daughter ... forgive my tears ... I never expected this!"

Alex reached for Anna's hand and squeezed it, both sitting on her bed, the laptop resting on the small locker beside them. He hadn't said a word, not even a greeting, when the video call began. It was Anna who had thanked the woman for agreeing to speak with them and had made the introductions. Tension coated his fingers in sweat as they squeezed hers.

"Breathe," she murmured from the corner of her mouth, never taking her eyes from the screen.

He flexed his shoulders and did as instructed, his breath shuddering into the space in front of them.

"Again, thank you so much for speaking to us, we really appreciate this. It's such a shock for us to see you too – we didn't know we had an aunt."

Anna winced, hoping the fact that her sister had never spoken about her wouldn't come as a blow to Annika. The woman smiled, seemingly unconcerned.

"I expected as much. When Yelena left for London all those years ago, I told her to take any opportunity to leave and never look back. I'm glad she followed my advice!"

"What? You told her to leave her family? To disappear?"

Annika laughed softly, dabbing her cheeks with a tissue. "Yelena didn't like to be told to do things, but on this occasion she actually followed my suggestion." She paused, studying their stunned expressions. "How much do you know about your mother's life?"

Alex cleared his throat and spoke for the first time, his

315

voice barely audible. "Very little really. She never told us she was from the Soviet Union, or a cellist. She never mentioned any living relatives."

Annika nodded to herself and wiped at her eyes again. "Yes, that makes sense. It's what I told her to do."

Anna gripped her brother's hand tighter. She couldn't believe what she was hearing.

"Please tell us everything you can! She has been missing now, with our father, for ten years! Anything you can tell us about her that could help ... we ..." She stopped as a lump formed in her throat, so big she felt she couldn't breathe. Alex's hand left hers and rested firmly on her back. "We'd really appreciate all you can remember. I ... *we* ... need answers."

Annika smiled at them, her sympathy radiating through the screen. She appeared more composed now, tucking the tissue into the sleeve of her jumper.

"You poor children, what has she left behind?" she muttered sadly to herself, shaking her head. With a trembling hand she reached out and touched the screen, as though to touch their faces, her eyes shining.

"If only my mother could see you! She would have been so happy to see Yelena's children! She died last winter."

"We're sorry to hear that." A grandmother, that had been alive up until recently, never knowing they existed ...

Annika swiped her hand through the air in front of them, a mannerism that was so like their mother's. "It was a blessing she went in the end." She pulled back her shoulders, steadying herself. "Yelena was five years younger than me ... she was gifted and beautiful, even as a small child! She was a difficult younger sister to live up to!" She laughed quietly. "You know, it is only as adults we realise our parents are human beings, you understand? That our parents are flawed just as we are, that they are not perfect, and sometimes they act only in their own best interests. Our father was a very … imperfect man. He was a businessman and he wanted to be a politician. He was never very high up in his political party, but he liked to pretend otherwise. He imagined he was many things … but really he was weak. Having a child as beautiful and talented as Yelena made him strong. This was a time in what is now called Russia when it was difficult to get ahead. In fact, that is still true in many places. But if you were gifted …"

She swallowed some amber liquid from a glass they hadn't noticed before on the table in front of her.

"My father was killed some years ago. My mother telephoned me then to come home – I had not spoken to him in a long time. I returned to comfort my mother, to make sure she is taken care of. My parents didn't attend my wedding here in Texas. They did not meet my husband. I prefer to keep my old life and my present life separate."

She looked away from them to the side of her kitchen and became lost for a moment in her memories. The shadow of loss was cast on her face – these were memories she would rather forget.

"Our father was the manager in a textile business then, but he never was satisfied. We had some level of wealth though – even in those days of communism not everyone was equal! Yelena and I had music and ballet lessons, and it didn't take long for father to realise he had a daughter that was very talented, a prodigy you might say! As I said, gifted as children like Yelena brought great advantages to their families, and they still do. She could do amazing things with the cello and she was very beautiful, and suddenly my father grew more successful. He was confident then – he had a new life. He was invited to meet other businesspeople and politicians – he expanded the range of textiles he used and traded. He was obsessed with having ... *more*. He found some allies in powerful people who loved to admire his young daughter ... Yelena became his most prized possession."

Anna met her brother's eyes in alarm, remembering his words that they might not like the truth they so craved. There was bitterness in their aunt's voice, and regret.

She looked at them sadly. "Yelena grew up understanding she was the key to our family's success, to my father's power, and she always had to perform. Our mother had no voice – to our father she was nothing, and for many reasons she accepted that." Her mouth twisted and soured at this. "Yelena became all that mattered and she hated it. She was a loving sister, and we were close. But our father would permit nothing except practice and performance. Practice and performance! As a young girl, it was the cello she had to showcase. As she grew older and more beautiful, my father realised the powerful men he so needed to be around wanted to admire her, and more ... she was nothing but a pawn. Her whole existence was held hostage to his ambition. He treated her terribly ..." She lowered her head and wiped at her eyes again, stifling fresh tears. "I escaped – I was overlooked, insignificant to him. I was pretty but she was beautiful, I was intelligent but she was wonderfully gifted. I was given an office job in the business – that was quite progressive of him, really – and I took it gladly, to learn and gain skills to escape him. Yelena won a place in an orchestra and our father was overjoyed – she cried in my arms that night. She wanted to escape this life he was carving out for her, but there was no way out. Worst of all were her trips to London with the orchestra. There she met an Englishman, and everything changed for the worse."

Anna felt Alex stiffen beside her. She dared not breathe and break this spell yet longed to cover her ears. How could things have become even worse for their mother in London?

"She visited London on two occasions with the orchestra before the time she disappeared. Our father arranged for her to visit this man, to please him and to transport things back from him."

"What things?" Anna's voice rose in alarm.

Annika's shoulders hitched to her ears. "I never knew. She would never speak of it. All I know is she was terrified of this Englishman and the things she had to do." She wiped at her eyes slowly. "She telephoned me once – the orchestra had several KGB officers accompanying them to prevent anyone defecting, especially the main stars, but she wasn't one of them, despite her talent. She was free to move around her hotel and she managed to telephone my office. The Englishman had grown obsessed with her. She was terrified of him. During her third trip to play with the orchestra in London she telephoned me, and I reminded her to run as soon as she got a chance, and to never look back!"

Annika paused – her eyes were bright with tears and memories, her face wet and blotchy. Anna and Alex stayed still, each caught up in the story and the terror that at any moment the woman would stop talking.

"She hugged me the day before she left for that trip. It was August 1978. I remember it so clearly. It was the last time I ever saw my sister!" She sniffed. "I told her to take whatever opportunity she could to disappear. She was miserable and scared." Suddenly she smiled broadly, a new memory bringing her happiness. "I remember father's anger when he heard she had gone! He blamed me of course, and I still have the scars from his anger." She shifted in her seat. "But Yelena was gone! She had done it! I was terrified for her – for months I prayed for news, but it was difficult to get foreign newspapers, and our father wouldn't speak of her again – he was in disgrace. Father was in a lot of trouble with his political friends and he slipped from grace in the community – he had stepped outside his station. It was a difficult time!"

Her eyes focused on them again – her voice was soft when she spoke, almost a whisper.

"Yelena telephoned me once more at the office, just to say she was safe. But life at home became unbearable – mother urged me to go. A chance came to travel to America and I took it. Mother worked hard to get me away from him … I could not leave a forwarding number at the office in case she telephoned me again, and so I never heard from her. Until I received your message, Anna … my goodness, how you look like her! And you say she was married? To a nice man?"

Anna nodded mutely. Yes, she wanted to say, to a very nice man. A kind man, one who loved his wife and made her happy. One who played self-defence games with his children and taught them Taekwon-Do while his wife laughed and encouraged them. One who was a businessman, and an Englishman … but she found she couldn't speak at all.

48

London, 1978

In several industries across London there was growing discontent – trade union calls for strike action grew louder each day. Michael read about it every morning in the newspapers, yet he could scarcely recall any details. His own job, and the situation he found himself in, were all he could think about. *Almost* all he could think about ...

Despite his best efforts he couldn't get the Soviet girl out of his mind. He had heard the phrase that a person's eyes were like windows to the soul, and having met Yelena Vasilieva, he believed it. Her pale-blue eyes had shown him she was both afraid of her visit to Lewis's house and resigned to her fear. Her relationship with Lewis bewildered and unsettled him – she was young enough to be his daughter, why had he summoned her to his house? And what was in the bag he had given her? The more he thought about it the more he wondered if she had anything to do with why Smith was interested in Lewis. He told himself to forget about her – he had barely spent any time with her – but he couldn't. And when he read in the newspaper that the orchestra was returning to London for a concert at the Royal Albert Hall, he made up his mind.

Tickets to the concert were too far out of his financial reach. But treating his grandmother to afternoon tea in the hotel where Yelena had stayed before was not. So he made the reservation and wore the smartest suit Lewis had given him, determined that if she were in London he would find her.

The look of awe etched across Nana Clarke's face as she stood in the entrance of the Banks hotel made him laugh. She wore her best dress and coat, her hair neatly pinned – Michael felt a rush of protectiveness swoop over him as he watched her. She looked smaller and more tired than he remembered. His conversation with Smith had unlocked many thoughts Michael had long ago abandoned as too painful – she was vulnerable, and he was all she had. He was the only person who could protect her, who could take care of her. As she had taken care of him.

"Lord above!" she whispered as her eyes moved from the chandeliers to the long mirrored reception area, to the well-dressed clientele that moved slowly around them. "We really have come up in the world, Michael!"

He tugged her arm gently. "Come on, we've a reservation to keep. I'm sure the tearoom is just as nice." She let him guide her to the left, where double glass doors off the main entrance led to the tearooms. He had asked where they should go when he made the reservation, and he was glad: walk with authority, command respect, present the image of a man in control. Even if he felt entirely unsure of what the hell he was going to do ...

Nana Clarke gasped audibly as the doors to the tearooms opened and they were led inside. Their table was laid out in a crisp white tablecloth with a delicate lace overlay, decorated with a selection of shiny silver spoons and tiny forks. In the centre of the table a large silver teapot rested beside fragile-looking china cups and saucers.

"Do you think it's Tetley's?" Nana whispered, eying the teapot, and Michael laughed out loud.

Almost immediately a waiter arrived and placed a square of white linen on their laps with a flourish, his gloved hands swishing through the air. Nana Clarke met Michael's eyes and giggled, and he swelled with pride at being able to treat her this way. A three-tiered serving tray materialised in the centre of the table, filled with delicate sandwiches and scones, clotted cream and jams in tiny pots. The top tier boasted a selection of bite-sized cakes and pastries.

As the waiter poured their tea Nana reached across the table and squeezed Michael's hand.

"Well, this is the most special treat I've ever had!" She beamed at him. "It must be costing you a small fortune, and for once, I couldn't give a tuppeny damn!"

Michael laughed heartily again – she was flushed with excitement and he was glad she was enjoying herself. He looked around him – as excited and happy as he was, Yelena was on his mind and he wondered again if she was staying in the hotel. The tearoom wasn't busy – there were only three other tables occupied, two with couples and one with a gentleman, head bent low reading his newspaper in between bites of his scone. He had scanned the hotel entrance while Nana Clarke had been enthralled by their surroundings, but there had been no sign of Yelena. He made up his mind to excuse himself when the time was right and make enquiries at the reception desk.

They passed an hour enjoying easy conversation, Nana

asking Michael to tell her more about his job. He tried to steer the topic away from work, feeling somewhat disloyal. Stirring his tea slowly with one of the tiny spoons, the reality of his situation flashed like a bright light. Because of Lewis and the generous wage he was paying, Michael was sitting here, in this expensive hotel, treating his grandmother, and dressed in a fine suit and coat. Yes, life had changed since he started working for Lewis – he finally had money in his pocket, for one thing. But the knowledge that Lewis had drawn the attention of the Counter-Terrorism detectives weighed heavily on him, as did his curiosity about the Soviet girl. If he could speak to Yelena again, maybe she could help him understand.

While Nana Clarke accepted another silver pot of tea from the waiter he excused himself to go to the bathroom. Her fingers wiggled as they hovered over the pastries and she nodded, lost in the happy moment.

He grinned as he walked to the reception desk – one of the men standing there was free and he squared his shoulders as he approached.

"Excuse me. I wonder if you could help me. Is Yelena Vasilieva staying here? She's playing with the orchestra from the Soviet Union and stayed here previously."

The receptionist quickly shook his head.

"I'm sorry, sir – we don't have any guests of that name. I'd remember that. No musicians in the hotel, I'm afraid."

Michael nodded, unable to muster a smile around his disappointment. He thanked him and stepped away, almost colliding with a tall man standing behind him.

"Excuse me ..." he muttered before he stopped. He recognised the grim expression, the thick hair greying at the temples. His eyes bulged slightly as he realised this was the man who had been sitting a few tables away for the last hour, reading his newspaper – this was the man who had hauled him into the police station and threatened to lock up his grandmother unless he found incriminating evidence against Lewis. *Smith*. Michael was surprised at how easily the man had blended into the background and gone unnoticed.

"Lovely thing to do, treat an old lady to afternoon tea." He had his newspaper folded under one arm, his hat held loosely in his hand. "She's looking frail, mind – would hate to see her lose her home comforts and end up in a prison cell."

It was a moment before Michael could speak again, his words strangled by shock and anger.

"*Are you following me?*" He spat the words in an angry hiss.

"The clock ticks and you are awfully quiet … I haven't heard from you."

"I have nothing to say!" Michael's eyes roamed the hotel reception area as he spoke, looking for anyone he knew, anyone from work, praying this very public conversation with the detective would go unseen.

"I have a man in customs." Smith leaned against the shiny reception counter with a casual grace. "Tells me an interesting shipment is coming in tonight. Our friend has paid him to make sure it gets through without any extra checks. Now why would he do that?"

"Sounds like you already have an informant. You don't need me."

He shook his head. "It's not enough. It won't get me a warrant when Lewis has his hands in the pockets of men in high places. I need more."

Michael looked at the ground, heat flooding his face – the

sounds around him, greeting calls and friendly chat, were suddenly so loud he couldn't think clearly. He rubbed at sweat that felt slick on his upper lip. He had seen the paperwork about a shipment arriving from Turkey that was to be repackaged overnight for Scotland. It didn't make sense to him that it had to be done urgently, and that the only paper evidence he could locate were the prepared customs documentation – there was no order, no trail of documents. He had found that suspicious, but not enough to phone Smith. Or perhaps he was just reluctant …

"I think I'll have a chat with Nana Clarke, see what she makes of it all." Smith's voice was soft, his tone relaxed, and it make the threat of his words all the more sinister.

Michael stepped closer, closing the gap between them, and fought to keep his voice steady.

"I'll find your evidence. If there *is* anything to find! And you can leave us the hell alone!"

"You'd best get back to your nan." Smith rested his hat onto the top of his head and turned to go. "Hate to see her get a stomach-ache from too many pastries. You wouldn't want her to suffer, not a good grandson like you."

Later that night, feeling more wretched than he had in his whole life, Michael made his way to the warehouse. It felt too traitorous to wear any of the coats Lewis had given him – instead, he wore his dark zip-up jacket, his father's flat cap in place too. He had mulled over the problem of bypassing the security hut – in the end, he decided there was no other choice but to have a chat with the regular guard and lie to him. There was no way to circumvent the small portacabin, and he doubted he could hide in the shadows – the port was well lit and secure. He adopted the walk he used when he wanted to appear confident, like a man with nothing to hide.

"Evening sir, can I help you?"

"Hi, Mr Jenkins, it's Michael Clarke, from Mr Lewis's warehouse. How are you?"

"Ah, Michael! Busy spot this, this evening."

Michael smiled – his hands jammed in his pockets, he rocked casually on his heels but his thoughts raced. Who else was there? Were Boxer and Roy already in the warehouse? Were the crates already being packed up?

But he managed to appear calm. "Oh yes?"

The night shift was lonely – evidently the security guard was eager to talk.

"Aye. The two men that help Mr Lewis out were here earlier – gone about half an hour now though." Michael exhaled in relief. "Mr Lewis too – his car left not ten minutes ago. You just missed them."

"Oh, that's a shame. I've left my gear bag and I need my training kit. Won't be long."

Jenkins passed a clipboard to him and he signed his name, familiar with the out-of-hours procedure. The idea of the gear bag had come to him earlier that day – the guard was familiar with the sight of the bag slung over his shoulder and he was confident the story wouldn't raise the alarm. "Getting cold tonight," he remarked as he scrawled on the signature line. Nana Clarke had often used that trick whenever a man called to the door collecting rent or some other money due – keep him talking, keep things friendly.

"Certainly is."

"You have a pleasant night. I won't be long, cheers!" He waved as he walked away and stuffed his hand back in his pocket. He didn't think he could successfully look casual if both arms hung stiffly by his side, his shoulders tense.

His sense of unease grew with each step. The warehouse was not completely dark – several lights were left on overnight for added security. If his hunch were right, the warehouse would be swarming with detectives soon. He would be out of a job, but hopefully, the nightmare that had been the last few weeks would be over.

Using his set of keys he let himself in and pulled the door shut behind him. The soft lighting inside the warehouse cast long shadows among the wooden crates and stacks of boxes. He stayed still, waiting and listening, barely breathing. When he was certain he was alone he moved quickly towards the back of the wide space, knowing the five pallets received and bound for Scotland would be located there. There was enough light overhead to read the paperwork typed on the front – Mr Lewis had done that himself this morning.

Michael hoped he was right, otherwise he would have trouble explaining his actions – he kicked at the two metal latches on one of the wooden boxes until they gave way. The noise was loud and echoed around the warehouse but he had come too far now to be worried about that. He pushed open the lid and peered inside, angling his head so his shadow didn't obscure his view.

Leather. Sheets of it, in brown and black.

"*Shit!*" he muttered, pulling it out.

Smith was wrong – there was nothing but leather. It was wrapped in plastic, rolls of it, bound in thick layers. He noticed dust on his fingers and moved some more of the leather bundles aside at the bottom of the crate, noticing they were packed in four layers among thick carpets of wood shavings. He rooted through the crate, side to side, top to bottom, and when his fingers hit metal he stopped. There was a metal object right at the bottom of the crate, in the centre. Taking a deep breath, he pulled out all the leather until it was in a heaped pile on the floor beside him, and stared open-mouthed at the fifth, the bottom, layer of the crate.

Guns. Nestling among the wood shavings was a row of guns – twelve in total.

He collapsed into a sitting position on the floor. Rubbing his hands over his face he was surprised they came away drenched in sweat. His shallow breathing was the only sound he could hear, but somewhere deep inside he was screaming. He could not believe it – Smith was right after all. He remembered the man's words… *"Lewis's sympathies lie across the water with his ancestors."*

How the hell had he got mixed up in this? A sob burst from him when he thought of his friend – Bob was in the centre of this mess, probably as guilty as Lewis.

His eyes moved to the other four crates. He had no intention of searching them too – he didn't care. Jumping quickly to his feet he began to load the leather back into the crate, haphazardly, attempting to conceal the situation enough only to disguise his snooping for a little while. Smith would have to be called straightaway – the crates could be moved by morning, and then the nightmare would continue – the threats from the detective, and the knowledge that the man he was working for was illegally importing weapons.

Hauling up the wooden lid he pushed it back in place. The locks were broken, but that could not be helped. Pulling the scrap of paper from his wallet with Smith's number on it, he made his way to the metal staircase and jogged up, his breathing laboured now. The office door was locked, and as he fumbled with the set of keys, he froze. Noise. From the meeting room across the hall. He ducked quickly to the ground, crouching out of sight, straining to hear more.

The sound he could hear was weeping – a woman, crying quietly. He rose and crept to the door, trying the handle. It was locked, but he had a key. When he pushed open the door his breath caught in his throat. It was *her*, the young woman from the hotel: Yelena. She sat hunched on the floor in the corner farthest from the door, her knees drawn up to her chest, her eyes wide in terror as he entered the room.

"Please! No!" She had been crying and her breath came in gasps.

"Are you OK?" Michael cursed himself for asking such a stupid question. He stepped towards her.

"No!" she screamed, terrified. "Stay back!"

He held up both hands and inched closer. "I won't hurt you. It's Michael – we met before, at the hotel. Do you remember me?"

She sniffed and ducked her chin so that only half her face was visible. "Yes, I remember."

"I read about you in the newspaper. You're with the orchestra that are visiting and playing at the Royal Albert Hall. What are you doing *here*?"

"Are you to take me to him again? I won't go!"

His panic at this situation and his surprise at finding her here were fading, and now he could take in what was obvious before him. Her pale-blonde hair was messed, as though pulled roughly from the chignon she had tied it in. Her stockings were ripped on both legs – they had been torn apart. Her cheek was a bright, raw red, where a hand had slapped her. Anger surged inside him – Lewis was a monster, and he was going to deliver him to justice. He stepped towards her.

"Yelena, please trust me." He held out one hand towards her. "I won't hurt you. I am actually just about to call the police. I've found ... well, weapons in one of the crates, and I think Lewis is planning to send them to Scotland. I think you should talk to the police too ... tell them what he did to you ..." His voice shook as he looked at her.

How he would love to have Lewis standing before him now!

She rose to her feet, slowly, holding on to the side of the office desk for support. Her hands went to her skirt and then her hair, attempting to smooth them both. Her sobs had subsided and she was breathing easier. When she met his eyes, curiosity burned inside the pale blue.

"You are telling the police about him? About the weapons?"

He nodded. She bent down and reached for something beside the desk, then slid a small black suitcase across the floor. He hadn't noticed it before now – it was identical to one she had pulled from the taxi all those weeks ago. "Then you can show them this. This will be evidence too, I think."

She sniffed and wiped at her face as he knelt down and clicked open the clasps. His mouth hung open and he sank onto the dirty linoleum. The suitcase was full to brimming over with neatly stacked bundles of cash. Bank notes of each denomination, all stacked on top of each other. Suddenly, the cogs turned and settled into place, and he looked at her.

"*You're* how he makes the payments. You travel with the orchestra and you bring the money ... *home?* To your father, to Lewis's business associate! Importing from Turkey is just a ruse ... the guns are coming from the Soviet Union!"

She nodded and a faint smile played on her lips, as

though she was relieved he had figured out the truth. "There is another man too, a Turkish man. I know his name – I will tell you everything! But you cannot involve my father, please! My mother and sister will be destitute if he goes to jail, they will die on the streets if he brings shame to the family … *please!*" She was crying again, suddenly, harder than before.

He crossed the office and took her in his arms – she felt tiny, shuddering against his chest. His hand went to her hair, stroking it, and she didn't resist. After a few minutes she pulled away and looked up at him, her eyes straying to the telephone on the desk.

"I telephoned my sister – I won't go back this time. You can take the suitcase and give it to the detective. I don't care. But please – keep my family out of things when you talk to the police!"

He nodded. He could do that. He didn't want to cause her any more pain.

A sudden thought struck him. "Lewis locked you in here – but he must know you'll be missed at the hotel. Which means he's coming back! Come on – we have to get out of here!"

Her eyes filled with tears again but she reached for her red coat on the desk, gathering her handbag up too, and took his outstretched arm. Picking up the suitcase, he took her hand and they left the office. Once he had her safely in his house, he could call the detective from the phone box at the top of the street.

They walked past the security hut with heads bowed, and if Jenkins saw them he made no comment. The bus journey felt longer than it should have. She took the window seat and watched the city lights blur past – he noticed tears fall, silently, and stayed quiet beside her. He wanted to pat her hand or put his arm around her shoulder, but he sensed she wouldn't welcome it. The suitcase was wedged between his knees and its weight drilled into him – evidence of Lewis's crimes, and more behind them at the warehouse. He was glad of the silence, it allowed him to process what he had learned tonight. At their stop he tapped her arm gently and she wiped her face, standing and following him to the door. During the short walk to his terraced house, they stayed a slight distance apart, no words passing between them, her heels loud on the cobbles.

Later, she rested on the sofa while he and Nana Clarke counted the money in the suitcase at the kitchen table. Ten thousand pounds. Exactly. His grandmother flopped into the kitchen chair with a thud, pale and breathless.

"You should have told me what was going on."

"Why? Would you have advised me to do anything differently?" he asked gently, and she glared at him harshly.

Her anger quickly turned to tears.

"I'm so sorry, Michael. I never expected it would end this way!"

The sight of her crying alarmed him – all his life, his grandmother had never been anything but strong and stoic. His heartbeat raced at the sight of her losing control.

He rubbed her arm as he fervently promised, "I can fix this, Nana!"

"*I don't see how you can!*" She was shouting now, gulping air as she spoke, "If the detective is right, and your boss is supplying weapons, you are in *serious* trouble!" Her head nodded towards the sitting room. "Not to mention this girl's father." She rocked back and forth as she cried, her arms wrapped around herself, her words now a whisper. "Mr Lewis is obviously some sort of … well, I don't know, but a very dangerous man! You're in over your head, Michael! Just let me go to jail if it'll keep you out of trouble. Go back to your boss and carry on as if this never happened. I'll be fine!"

He sat down opposite her, his head in his hands. "It's too late for that! And there's no way you will go to prison. But I think if I don't deliver something to Smith, *I* might!"

"So you tell Smith and then what? The people Lewis is supplying … *maybe it's the IRA, Michael!*" She was whispering now, scared of the words she was speaking and what it meant. "It's too dangerous!"

He gripped his hands together on the table. "We don't know that! But … oh God … how do I get out of this?" His eyes pleaded with her – all his life she had had the answers.

Crying softly, a defeated sound that broke his heart, she rested her hands on his arm. "Love, I don't know!"

From the kitchen doorway, a soft cough alerted them. Yelena rested against the open door with her arms folded, her eyes puffy from sleep and tears.

"You need to telephone the detective and tell him what is in the warehouse so that Lewis will go to prison." Her voice was strong and clear. "I have changed my mind – I will talk to your detective. I will tell him everything I know, in exchange for papers … new identity … I know it can be done."

"What about your sister? And your mother?"

"My father needs to be stopped. Perhaps things will be OK for them. My sister … my sister …" she took a deep breath, "she told me an opportunity would present itself and that I must take it. So that is what I will do." She wiped at her eyes and squared her shoulders. Her mind was made up.

"Then we disappear. Lewis is a – a bad man with bad connections, like my father – if he goes to prison he can still cause you trouble. So, we take the money. The police do not know we have it. We disappear for a while." Her eyes rested on the old woman crying softly at the kitchen table. "Three of us. We go away until the heat has settled."

"Dust," Nana Clarke said with a hiccup, "until the dust has settled." She turned to Michael. "How long would that take, do you think?"

He couldn't believe the hope in her voice – she was considering this?

"Are you sure you don't want to go home, Yelena? Think this over carefully! I'm sure the police could help you."

Her face was still pale, with shadows under her eyes, her cheekbones sharp and hollow. She had been through so much – but she was resolute.

"Without the suitcase of money, I cannot go back. I will go with or without you both."

He turned his back to them, moving to the window, staring out at the moon-filled sky. He had to protect his grandmother from anyone that might want revenge for what he was about to do. And he couldn't let her go to prison. He felt drawn to Yelena. He believed that she had no intention of returning home with the orchestra, to whatever life she wished to leave behind. Maybe he could make this work. What choice did he have?

He turned to face them.

"Only Lewis knows about the money?"

"And my father. And the other man, the one in Turkey."

"Well, they're hardly in a position to complain. What do you think, Nana?"

Sighing deeply, she moved towards him. "I truly think we have no choice. It's too late to turn back the clock. Phone the detective."

He left them in the house to pack and prepare to leave. The night was cold, the sky clear, and he walked quickly. The telephone box was located at the top of his street – stepping inside, he was assailed by the smell of urine and vomit. Swearing, he plucked up the receiver, fed in the coins and began to dial. Despite the late hour the phone was answered on the second ring.

"Michael! Why are you calling so late?"

"Bob, I can't stay long. I just wanted to tell you I'm sorry – there was nothing I could do. And I … listen, don't go to the warehouse tonight or tomorrow, OK? In fact, lay low for a while. Do you understand what I'm saying?"

Silence on the other end of the line told him his friend understood exactly what was happening.

"Jesus, Michael, what have you done?" It was difficult to hear him, he spoke so low. *"They'll kill you!"*

He ended the call, pressing the cold metal of the receiver against his forehead.

What, indeed, had he done?

Pulling the detective's phone number from his pocket for the second time that night, he fed more coins into the payphone, and sealed his fate.

49

London, 2019

The glare of the morning sun pierced the darkness of the hotel room, through curtains too thin to preserve sleep. Anna heard the hiss of the shower as she lay still, her eyes adjusting to the dark. They stung with the grit of dry tears, and she pressed her knuckles into them to ease the pressure.

When Alex stepped from the bathroom he was already dressed. Rubbing his hair dry with a towel he moved to the curtains and opened them.

"Not a bad day," he said softly. "Dry at least."

He met Anna's eyes as she stretched and sat up.

"You look terrible."

"Thanks," she muttered, swinging her legs onto the carpet. "Did you manage to get any sleep?"

He shook his head. "No, but that's nothing new. Come on, get ready. I've ordered room service and it will be here at quarter past."

She moved into the bathroom and turned the shower on – the hot water pummelled her shoulders and she surrendered to its weight, letting it unknot the tension she felt.

The night had been long. After they ended the call with Annika, promising to speak to her again soon, both had sat in stunned silence for so long that Anna had felt the chill of the night press around her. Then they had dissected every single thing she told them, repeating it all to commit it to memory. Knowing their grandfather was abusive and had ill-treated their mother was a stomach-churning blow – sadness had hung heavy over them. But "the Englishman", the man obsessed with her mother, the man she was afraid of … could it be their father?

"Absolutely not, no way!"

"So, who was he then? Annika said he was an English businessman. Dad was English, and a businessman, and you lived in England before I was born …"

"It doesn't make sense. It's someone else!"

"Then who? And how did she escape him?"

Questions rose and fell, unanswered, until exhaustion rendered Anna unable to continue. Her last memory before succumbing to her silent tears, and then sleep, was of her brother, sitting on the edge of his bed, his head in his hands.

The Royal Haven Care Home was over thirty minutes by taxi from their hotel. They travelled in silence, each watching the blur of the passing city as it merged into countryside, neither able to voice their thoughts. Anna felt like the taxi was propelling them forward while her whole being wanted to go back, as though she was on a rollercoaster and couldn't get off. She knew this was all her fault, this feeling of dread that bounced between them. She had pushed for this, exploring all available information to see if it led to answers. Now she wished she could turn back time. Alex sat beside her, his hands knotted tightly in his lap, his eyes closed. She wondered if he had finally fallen asleep.

In her mind, Annika Garcia's face was clear, the fine lines and features so familiar. She looked so like her sister – it was like looking at the older woman their mother could have been... *should* have been.

Helen, Yelena, had been happy. Her life in England and Cork had been peaceful and full of love, Anna was certain of that. She had spent the last few weeks wondering who her mother was, blindsided by the news of her true identity. That, and the fact she had disappeared from her home and family, had offered a clear path to solving the mystery – find out the truth about their mother and they would find answers. Yet now they were more confused than ever, and the focus of the mystery had shifted to their father. Michael Clarke. The English businessman. As the taxi hurtled them towards the only contact they had from his time living in England, she felt a ripple of fear roll over her. Finally, she shared her brother's trepidation – what if they didn't like what they would hear?

The entrance to the Royal Haven Care Home was flanked by imposing redbrick pillars that obscured much of the driveway. Large gardens to the left of the building were dotted with lawn chairs and some wheelchairs, their occupants sitting quietly, wrapped in coats, with blankets on their knees. Several turned their heads and watched with interest as the taxi pulled up and they made their way inside.

Alex seemed to have come alive. For a man who hadn't slept all night his eyes were clear and determined, his step quick. As the taxi pulled away he strode purposefully to the reception desk and rapped on the bell.

"Good morning. We have an appointment to speak to one of your residents. Robert Evans."

339

"And you are?" The receptionist was brisk, clearly busy, but she smiled to soften her words.

He handed over his passport and made small talk about their trip over from Ireland as he signed the visitor's register, pocketing his passport again once the woman behind the desk was satisfied.

"You're going to get a bit chillier, I'm afraid. Mr Evans is sitting outside by the water feature." Her eyes met Anna's and she smiled sadly. "He doesn't have long, poor man. Are you family?"

"He was a friend of our father's," Alex answered tightly.

Anna felt her tongue was attached to the roof of her mouth, which was completely dry. She couldn't speak. Despite the cold she found she was sweating – with a gloved hand she wiped at her brow. A tight feeling around her temples warned of an impending migraine and she gritted her teeth.

As they walked back out the front door and turned to the garden Alex stopped and grabbed her elbow.

"Anna … I don't think we are going to like what Robert Evans has to say."

She opened her mouth but he tugged on her arm harder.

"Please, try to prepare yourself! I don't have a good feeling about this. The man's sudden appearance ten years ago, the trust fund … I bet he's only talking now because he's dying. Dying men want to confess their sins… whatever happens, whatever he says, promise me you will remember we sought this out. We *want* to know the truth. OK?"

His eyes were wide and fearful and she found it unnerving.

"You and I can handle this, Anna. Mum and Dad have been gone for ten years. Nothing is going to bring them back. We've got through it. Let's not let whatever we learn here this morning set us back. Promise me!"

She blinked quickly and nodded, still mute. Everything felt frozen and stuck – words were forming but refusing to leave her mouth. On shaky legs she followed her brother across the lawn to a circular stone fountain, and the thin figure sitting in a wheelchair beside it.

Robert Evans was enveloped in layers – his coat was thick and padded, a blanket-sized scarf was wound around his neck and shoulders, a rug across his knees. He wore a dark blue woollen hat pulled low almost to his glasses. He pushed it up a fraction as they approached, his pale-green eyes watering in the cold air. Gloved fingers twitched on his lap – Anna wondered if he was nervous. His lips were thin and cracked, cheeks ruddy from the cold but devoid of the zig-zag veins and liver spots that normally accompanied old-age. He appeared frail, uncertain, and entirely unremarkable.

Two folding chairs had been placed in front of him for their visit, and they sat down quietly. His eyes appraised them, resting for longer on Anna.

"I wondered when I might see you two again. You look like him, you know… oh, and you're *her* daughter alright. The Soviet. The musician. I can't remember her name. I only met her a few times but looking at you … it's like going back in time. God, he was obsessed with her!" He looked into the distance, remembering.

Alex cleared his throat and the man in front of them snapped back to the present.

"Mr Evans, thank you for agreeing to see us. We want to ask you some questions."

Robert Evans smiled and he nodded as he spoke. "You

can call me Bob. Yes, I remember you. Michael Clarke's son ... God, this is taking me back! And what was your mother's name?"

"Helen. Or ...Yelena. We've only just found that out."

The old man laughed, the strength of it surprising them both.

"*Ha!* I bet you think she was a spy!"

Anna met her brother's eyes briefly and looked away.

"*Aha!* You do! The old cliché! She was no spy, just a girl in over her head."

Anna began to tremble – she felt frozen sitting by the stone water feature in temperatures that hovered around zero. And the man in front of her was beginning to scare her. She wanted this to end.

"What did you say her name was? Your mother?"

"Helen. Yelena."

He shrugged. "Means nothing to me. I didn't know her. Well, I met her a few times, before, but then they left." He swatted the air, as though swiping at flies. He was animated now but repeating himself. "Left us in such a mess! There was so much trouble, you could hardly imagine it! After all the boss had done for him!" Spittle flew in front of his face and he coughed, pulling a handkerchief from his sleeve, pressing it to his mouth. They waited silently as he composed himself.

"How did you know Dad? Can you tell us anything about him that might help us understand?"

Anna's voice surprised them all, including herself. It shook around the words but she leaned forward, staring at him, compelling him.

"You have no idea, do you? My goodness, you have his eyes. Brown and serious – I bet you're good at sums too, the both of you. He was a whizz, your father. The best bookkeeper I ever met. Too clever for his own good! Too curious, wanting to know everything about everything."

Alex exhaled quickly, impatient now. "We've come a long way to see you, Bob. You gave us the trust fund after the disappearance of our parents ... you must know something about what happened to them! Please!"

"Yes, of course ... I ..." He began to tremble violently – it was disturbing to watch. Tears leaked from his eyes and his hand shook as he sought to wipe them away – he looked utterly tormented. He started to cough again, his whole body jerking. "Oh God! Oh God!" He twisted in the wheelchair as coughs racked his body. "He was my ... my best friend. We used to call him Bruce Lee!" More coughing, and this time there was bright-red blood on the tissue when he dabbed his mouth.

They looked at each other in alarm, each wondering should one of them run inside the care home for help. Bob was crying uncontrollably now, spit mingled with blood on his chin.

"Oh God! My best friend. And I ... I ... *I killed him.* Oh God!" He wheezed and retched, doubling over.

The ground began to tilt as Anna watched him, as his words echoed in her head. She tasted vomit in her mouth and gave in to it – suddenly she was on her hands and knees on the frosty grass, gasping for air. Wiping her mouth, she looked at her brother in alarm, as he leaned over the wheelchair, his hand clamped around the gasping man's wrist.

"Don't you dare die, you old bastard! Not today! Before your time comes you're going to tell us everything!"

50

"We were supposed to bring him into the business. I say *business* but, well, you know. Michael was Irish, young, and a good bookkeeper, easygoing … he fit the bill. Lewis liked him, though you wouldn't have known that, but that was just his way." He swallowed some of the water the nurse had brought and coughed again, but softer this time. His eyes shone with tears and maybe regret. Or perhaps it was just the wind.

Anna leaned forward to speak but Alex raised his hand, his meaning clear: let him tell his story while he still can.

"I heard the police got to him first. They threatened his grandmother or something … lovely lady, Nana Clarke." His smile was wistful. "I never knew what happened to her in the end." He gulped more water and winced, as if swallowing caused him pain. "What Michael found in the warehouse was the tip of the iceberg and gave the coppers everything they needed to open the whole thing up. Lewis went down for years. I don't remember the actual sentence he was given, but he died in prison eleven years in. That's a long time for a man to be inside, and to end his days there

... his life destroyed ... of course, I know it was deserved."
He smiled sadly to himself. "We ruined many lives, it's
hard to argue against that. We supplied weapons, in the
beginning, but like in all things we followed the money. Yes
... Michael thought he had it figured out but he saw so very
little really. The detective found the lot within a few days."

"You managed to escape jail?"

His eyes focused on them again, moving between their
faces.

"Michael called me and told me to lay low ... he was a
good friend. I tried to call Lewis but it was too late and the
damage was done. The guns were found on his property,
and the detective got himself a warrant and searched
everything Lewis had ever touched. There were three men
sent to prison from the warehouse operation: Lewis, Boxer
and Roy. They were caught in the act, you see! Because I
wasn't actually in the warehouse that night, and because
Lewis convinced the police me and the few others knew
nothing about his operation, we escaped jail time. The
coppers were disappointed but there wasn't enough
evidence to convict us. Lewis was clever that way – made
sure we could continue things on the outside. He wanted to
provide for his family, after. His wife got five years," a
sudden burst of laughter, "can you believe that? A posh
lady like that was a crook all along!"

The laughter reignited a coughing fit and they waited.
Anna felt her brother placing one hand over hers – she
squeezed it and found it trembling slightly.

"The night they died?" he prompted quietly.

Bob lowered his eyes to the ground and fresh tears
leaked from them, rolling to his chin, dripping onto his
scarf. He drew in a shuddering breath.

"I had forgotten about Michael, about my friend. Mostly. Sometimes I wondered where he was but I tried to put him out of my head. Life carried on well enough for me after the others went to prison. He had warned me to stay hidden and so I did. About six months after the court cases ended and Lewis got sent down, I carried on where we had left off – on a smaller scale, but I kept the business going. I had his contacts and a lot of his resources and with his blessing I became the caretaker, you could say. I supported his daughters and looked after his wife when she got out. I set up a consultancy business using an alias and I carried on as before. Made sure to keep good accounts – Michael taught me that! – and my head down – I was the most invisible businessman in London!" He smiled at this description, and they sensed he was proud of his accomplishments. "Had to wind it up about ten years ago – coppers are a lot smarter these days. And my lungs aren't what they used to be."

Anna was surprised that her father had been close to this man – Bob had just described them as good friends. He was a criminal – he spoke of supplying weapons and said that was the "tip of the iceberg". She felt some comfort in his words that her father hadn't been part of the business.

"Lewis died in prison as I said. Boxer is still inside – he got into a fight and a man ended up dead." He shrugged. "Boxer was never very good at knowing when to leave things alone. Roy … he got out after ten years and worked with me. It took him a long time to trust me, seeing as I was one of the few that didn't do any time. But he came around." He eyed them tentatively. "He hated your father. Blamed him, said Michael Clarke had cost him everything."

Anna shifted in her seat. Her face felt wet and she

346

touched her cheeks – she was crying softly – the part about her parents' death could not be far away.

"While he was inside, Roy's wife left him – took his three kids and scarpered up north. He looked for them for years – his kids meant everything to him. Searched everywhere, he did. But she had disappeared. In his mind, *that* was Michael's fault too ..." He wiped at his eyes and gulped in air. There was weariness in his voice now – it was so soft they feared he would surely have to stop talking. "I listened to him prattle on about Michael Clarke for over ten years. I told him to shut up, to move on, but he never could. Even when he found a new woman and was doing well for himself again, he couldn't let it go. It was real, proper hatred." He lowered his eyes, no longer able to look at them. "He found Michael by accident. Had himself a new girlfriend and she convinced him to visit her daughter with her in a place in Ireland called Kinsale. I can still remember the phone call. Roy spotted Michael in a bar, having a pint with a friend."

"That must have been years later!"

"Yes, it was a long time after."

"What did he do?" Anna was surprised by the strength in her brother's voice while she felt barely able to stay upright in the chair.

"He phoned me. He wouldn't take on Michael alone – said he looked fit, like he was still doing his Bruce Lee thing. Maybe he was. In any case, I flew over to Cork. I wanted to see my friend again ... if it even *was* him. And I wanted to calm Roy down. He's a very volatile man, capable of ..." His voice cracked and stopped. Speaking was causing him to shrink in the wheelchair, to sink lower and slump slightly forward – he looked exhausted. Grunting, he tried to sit up straighter, seeming determined to push through the pain and tiredness and finish his story. His confession.

"Roy had a car hired and, when I met up with him, he had bought all sorts of things, rope, shovel … everything. He wouldn't be told! He said he'd never go back to prison – he'd rather die first. But Michael owed him, he said … he hated him! It was obvious what he planned to do."

"You should have told the guards!" Anna tried to shout, but her voice died in the cold morning air.

"We handle our own business. I argued with him, of course I did! I told him it was madness … but he wouldn't listen. We called to the house … Roy had followed your father home. I honestly don't think Roy knew what he was going to do – not really. He was hyper, manic, you know? I thought maybe we could all have a chat, but I guess I knew that wouldn't happen." He wiped his eyes, still streaming with water, either tears or the sting of the wind. He was rambling, talking in circles – Anna wished he would end this misery.

"As we arrived Michael pulled out of the house in his car. He didn't see us but I got a good look at him – it was definitely him! Older, but the same, if that makes sense. She was inside the car too, your mother. I recognised her as the Soviet girl … her father used her to transport money back. He had a supplier to send us guns and she …" His hands were shaking. "Anyway, they drove from Kinsale up to the city, then out onto the Dublin road ... we followed them for a long time. I don't know how long. It was dark and wintery – it was November I think. The weather was very bad, I remember that. Maybe it put people off heading out that night, because the road was quiet …"

Around them the garden grew colder – Anna hunched into her coat.

"After a while it was just us and them on the road. Roy sped up – God, he was so crazy. At one point I reached across and flashed the lights. I don't know … maybe to warn Michael? It was a stupid thing to do. I think he knew it was us or maybe that he had been found, or … who knows? He accelerated – all of a sudden he was ahead of us by quite a bit. And I guess he lost control of the car …"

They waited – his shaking hands dropped the bloodstained tissue onto the grass. This time when he coughed, he wiped his mouth with his hand, leaving his fingers bloody. After a few minutes he cleared his throat and continued, his voice barely audible.

"There was no-one else around – like I said, the roads were quiet that night. After they crashed I thought Roy would leave it, but he wouldn't! He ran over there … she had died in the crash. Michael was almost dead … almost. There was this window of time where the road was empty, and I helped Roy put the two of them into his car. We took all their things – we weren't thinking it through, we just … we knew we hadn't long before someone came upon the accident. We had to get out of there."

Anna remembered that a passing motorist had reported the car crash to the gardaí. If only the driver had got there a few minutes earlier, things could have been so different.

"We drove them away, drove around for a while, off the main road. Michael, he … he looked at me at the end, into my eyes … right when Roy …" A loud sob burst from him, spraying spit and blood into the air. "Eventually, we buried them together, buried everything, in a field. Roy was paranoid about DNA and going back to prison. He couldn't bear it. We cleaned down the car before he returned it to the rental place, and he flew back to London. I … I stayed around a while longer." He dared to raise his eyes to look at them. "You know, the funny thing is, if Michael hadn't phoned me to stay away from the warehouse, we'd never have known he had anything to do with it!"

He laughed a little, actually laughed, and Anna tasted vomit in her mouth again.

"I knew nothing about you two, not then. I went back to the house in Kinsale and I saw you." He nodded towards Alex. "You looked just like him when he was young, when we worked together. I felt so bad, I had to speak to you."

Alex shook his head roughly, and his voice was hard with anger.

"You shook my hand then! You said you were sorry for my loss. And you *knew* what you had done. Or what you had been a part of! You could have stopped Roy ... it needn't have happened!"

Bob stared at the grass, a whimpering sound escaping now and again.

"Is he still alive?" Alex's voice dripped with intent.

"Eh?"

"Roy!"

Bob nodded quickly. "He lives in Alicante now, with the same girlfriend. She's his wife now, I think."

"Do you remember the location of where you buried my parents? Or the general area?"

Bob's shuddering crying had resumed. Anna wiped her eyes and rose unsteadily – she had to escape, couldn't listen to anymore. She walked away, across the grass towards the large house. To be near him any longer was excruciating. Alex stayed, asking his questions, but she couldn't bear to hear the answers.

Pulling out her phone she selected Myles' number.

350

She needed to ask for his help one more time.

Two hours later they were ready to leave. Bob was speaking to two detectives, having moved inside to the warmth of the recreational room inside the care home. They had been given sweet tea, and though they protested at first, both found the hot liquid comforting.

A detective approached them and handed each of them his card.

"There's a lot to do now, obviously. But we will continue to work with Mr Evans to get all the information from him. I have both your contact details – I'll keep you informed of everything and will be liaising with the Irish Gardaí. I'm sorry for your loss."

Anna walked across the room, standing before Bob again.

"The trust fund. Dad never set that up, did he?" He could not meet her eye. "That was *your* money. Guilt money."

A nod, more of a twitch of his head. Every cell in her body ached to hit him, to hurt him.

"I returned to the house in Kinsale ... after. That's when I saw you. You were a teenager, just a kid. You and your brother arrived back to the house with pizza boxes ... I felt so bad! I wanted to take care of you both, the way Michael took care of me. I wanted to try to make up for ..." He covered his face with his hands.

"And the business card. Why did you give that to Alex?"

His feeble shrug was almost invisible. "Sometimes I wondered about that. Maybe I hoped you both would find me, or that I'd get caught. As it happened, I could never answer the phone. I hope you will forgive me." His voice cracked again.

She stared at his face for what felt like a long time.

"You're pathetic."

She had never heard her voice sound that way before, and it frightened her. Somehow she managed to walk away.

In the airport lounge they took a table, silently nursing drinks neither really wanted. Her phone beeped and vibrated on the table in front of them – a message from Myles.

"An arrest warrant has been issued for Roy Eastly. Myles will keep me posted."

"What does he do again?"

She didn't want to shrug or admit she really wasn't sure. Instead, she managed a small smile. "He's some type of tech-nerd for the gardaí."

Alex took a long drink from his pint of Guinness. His face was grey, the lines around his eyes and mouth exaggerated by stress and exhaustion.

"Bob seemed like a man relieved to tell his story."

"It doesn't sound like he did much to help Dad. After he kept him out of prison, you'd think he'd have tried harder to stop … he was right when he said he'd killed him. He may as well have!" She bit her lip and looked away, across the crowded bar. It was just a blur of faces, and the music overhead was loud but she couldn't make out the tune.

Alex's shoulders slumped so far forward his face was almost pressed to the pint glass as he swirled the liquid around inside it.

"You know, Anna … I've been thinking something – it's a thought that won't quit." He paused as her mobile phone rang again.

She snatched it up but quickly sent the call to voicemail. "Vivian. I'll ring her back."

Flexing his neck, Alex continued. "I've been thinking

that I knew they were dead all along. And I think I knew it was something ... bad, that led to that. Now we know *how* and sort of why, even by who ... I feel a strong sense of relief. Is that weird?"

She shook her head. "I understand how you feel."

"And now we can do something about it! We can get justice for them. We can give them a proper burial." He swallowed hard. "We can't change any of it but we might find closure. Or even... peace."

He squeezed her hands across the table. Somehow there was optimism in his voice – she hoped when her devastation had abated she might feel it too.

He straightened up and pulled his phone from his pocket, drawing in a deep breath as he looked at the screen. "Sam ... I'd better take this. I haven't told her anything yet."

He moved away from the table, standing at the entrance to the bar. She watched him, fearful to let him out of her sight.

Part of her couldn't take in what Bob had told them. He could have changed the outcome of what had happened that night but he chose instead to be a bystander – she would never forgive him. Thinking about her parents, about the fear her father must have felt, was too much. She consciously unclenched her fists on the table, watching the indents her nails had made on her palms fade away.

She wondered about her father's love of Taekwon-Do and everything related to self-defence, and the games he had played with them as children. Was it a natural interest he hoped to pass on to them? Or something more – fear that one day Lewis would find them, and he wanted them all to be prepared? Realising she would never know the answer brought fresh tears and she brushed them away – she was tired of crying. Alex's words had ignited a spark of hope – now she had a plan to get justice, something to focus on.

He moved through the tables and chairs, making his way back to her, his eyes shining, his face flushed.

"How did it go?"

"I didn't tell her. Not yet."

As tears slid down his cheeks he smiled. "Sam's pregnant. I'm going to be a dad again!"

51

Cork, 2019

On the plane journey home, he explained the fertility problems they had been having for a number of years.

"We hoped for a brother or sister for Chloe long before now but nothing happened. We talked about going to see someone about it, and to be honest it's really expensive. I guess now we don't have to."

Anna remembered the conversation with Samantha about their reluctance to take out a loan earlier this year, and her upset at having to use their savings … she understood more now about why she had accepted money from her boss.

"Chloe will be so excited!"

"God, this is the weirdest day of my life!"

Squeezing his hand Anna smiled softly at him, marvelling that she *could* smile after all they had learned in London. She closed her eyes before take-off, steadied her breathing and started counting – her plan to get ahead of her claustrophobic panic worked and she felt normal as the airplane taxied down the runway. If this feeling could be called normal.

"Alex?"

"Mmm?" He was hoping for sleep.

"What do we do now?"

He looked at her seriously and his voice was firm. "We grieve, I suppose – and then we try to move forward. We get the men responsible behind bars. And we give Mum and Dad the burial they deserve."

As they left London behind, she turned to the window, watching the lights twinkle below them, and let her tears fall.

Neither had more than hand luggage, so they left the Arrivals gate in Cork airport quickly. Anna felt relief at being home. The journey had been short but had changed so much. All she wanted was to crawl under the bedcovers and sleep, to let this day end. It was dark in Cork, the cloudless sky dotted with stars. While it had been cold in London and they were dressed for winter weather, the chill of the air outside Cork Airport took their breath away. They hugged goodbye quickly, both exhausted, and went to their separate cars.

Plugging her phone in to charge as the engine kicked into life, she noticed a voicemail, and listened as she manoeuvred the roundabouts out of the airport. It was from Vivian.

"Anna, I haven't heard from you. I hope everything's OK? Are you back from London? What did you find out? Sorry! Enough questions. I just hope you're OK. Oh, and I got the job! I start as an investigative reporter with Banba Productions next week! Call me soon!"

She grinned, listening to her friend. She had sounded so excited at the end of her message – Anna was delighted for her, knowing how much she wanted this job. She thought of Vivian's apartment, about her growing relationship with her birth mother, and now this career move, and felt genuine longing to meet her in person and hear all about it. And to talk over the whole weekend with her over a bottle of wine – she knew that would help to shift the sorrow she felt into hope for the future, into determination to put the wrong her parents had suffered to right. She could easily stay over in Vivian's, she had her overnight things, and she knew her friend would be delighted to see her.

At the final airport roundabout onto the main road, she had a choice to make, and she stopped, undecided. To turn left would take her into the city and out to Blackrock, to Vivian's apartment. If she turned right she would be home in twenty minutes, under her duvet in five more, and hopefully asleep straight after that. She chewed her lower lip – she needed sleep but talking to her friend might help her more. A car beeped behind her, and she turned right.

Home.

As Anna turned into her housing estate, she realised she had no memory of driving the last twenty minutes. She had been on autopilot and she shook her head, chastising herself. That was dangerous. She knew she was tired and had far too much running though her head to pay attention to anything but her thoughts. She pushed open her front door, stooping to pick up a flier advertising a new pizza restaurant in Kinsale, and walked through the hall, only realising as she reached the living room that she still held her keys and bag, having walked straight past the hall table. She moved through the dark living room to the archway that joined the kitchen and had to use her elbow to turn on the light switch.

The area illuminated and the whole room twisted in a terrifying jolt.

Sitting on a chair at the small kitchen table was a woman. She wore a brown-and-cream fur coat – it was a coat Anna had seen before. On CCTV footage. Her hair was an obvious voluminous blonde wig, and in her hand she held a camcorder. With her free hand she motioned for Anna to step closer.

"Hi darlin', welcome home. Don't be afraid." Her accent was American, an exaggerated southern drawl. "He won't hurt you. Much."

Her eyes moved to the living room and Anna followed them. There, a man had stepped from behind the open door. The hood of his dark jacket was pulled up and he was rigidly still. First she saw the long blade of the knife in his hand. Then she saw his face. But it wasn't a face – standing under the light she saw it for what it was. A mask. A grotesque, disfigured mask, with the eyes and mouth sewn closed.

Her bag dropped to the ground at her feet with a thud, her ragged breathing loud in her ears. And the woman began to laugh, so loud it became all Anna could hear.

52

It was as if she had fallen into a frozen lake. Her lungs struggled to take in oxygen and a sensation of pressure squeezed around her chest. She could not move. Very slowly her brain regained some semblance of understanding.

It was them.

They were in her house.

Standing beside her bookcase, near the archway, somewhere in the deepest sphere of her brain she realised she was standing in between them. She was the third point in a human triangle. While she stayed here she was safe, for a few minutes at least. She looked again at the man and at his knife. She could see no other weapon ... no gun. The realisation was a firework of hope inside her. She remembered the CCTV footage, the crime scene notes she had typed, horrifying photographs taped onto the noticeboard in the conference room. The pale faces of William Ryan and the others when they returned from the Rebel Event Centre. This couple ... they were a couple, a team. They worked together. The woman was the weaker one, the one who filmed the murder but didn't touch the victim ... didn't actually kill.

He was the one to fear.

Her eyes strayed to the TV, to the small space between that and the bookshelf, where the panic alarm was installed. Could she stretch out her arms and press it without either of them realising? She remembered William Ryan's words over lunch only days ago, *"I will personally guarantee that if a panic alarm is activated from your address, it will be responded to immediately."*

But it was out of reach.

If she could just step to the left and reach out ...

The man moved a stride towards her, as though sensing she was ready to move. Cursing under her breath, she stopped, willing her breath to steady, and abandoned the idea. For now. Squeezing the house keys in her hand, she felt more alive as the metal edges dug into her skin.

"You should see your face!" The woman laughed, wiping smudged mascara from her eyes. "Doesn't she look funny?"

The man ignored her. He hadn't moved any further.

"Drop the keys onto the floor, there's a good girl." The woman had composed herself now and raised the camera higher.

Anna did as she was told.

"Now move toward the sofa. We have a few questions for you, honey." The American accent was now more exaggerated.

Anna looked at the woman quizzically – what questions could they possibly have to ask her?

Instantly the woman's face twisted in anger. *"Do it!"*

Her heart pounding in her chest, Anna turned her eyes from left to right, from him to her.

"Now! Move!" The woman's anger intensified and she rose from the kitchen chair but didn't move any closer.

Anna sensed panic in her voice and stared at her face – and the woman recoiled. She put one hand to the other elbow, to steady the hand holding the camcorder. Anna saw it shake a little – things weren't going to plan. They had expected her to do what she was told, straight away. The element of surprise they had used on their other victims was gone – the moment had passed. This was new for them. She wasn't playing out her role as they had expected.

"I said move!"

"Go to hell."

Anna's voice was stronger that she had expected. Yet, at first, she wasn't sure they had heard her. She swallowed, trying to lubricate her throat which felt desert-dry.

The woman looked to the man, their mistake registering on her face. They should have jumped on her as soon as she entered the house, should have tied her up or killed her quickly. Now it was too late, and she wasn't acting like a victim – she was acting like she was playing for time. And time stood still – they didn't move, they didn't know what to do next.

"You see this space?" Her father's voice punctured Anna's receding shock, like a bright light piercing darkness. *"It's tight here, right? What can you do? Tell me, Anna, and remember … we use every available weapon, every available manoeuvre. Remember!"*

She had thought of little but her parents over the last few hours and suddenly her father's voice sparked inside her. She smiled at the memory of him, and their self-defence games in the garden.

Colour exploded in the woman's face. *"What are you*

smiling at!" Screaming now, spit flew from her lips. "Are you *seeing* this?" Her eyes found the man again, appealing to him.

Still, he didn't move.

Anna scanned the area around her and her heart leapt: her father's trophy. Grabbing it at the base, her hand clamped around the fighter's leg as he balanced to kick, she threw it at the woman as hard as she could. It didn't need to travel far to hit her. At the last second she attempted to dodge it but was too late – it thudded into the centre of her face and she fell backwards onto the floor with a shocked cry. The camcorder fell from her hands and lay on its side. Groaning, she cupped her hands around her nose, blood spilling between her fingers.

Anna heard the man growl in shock and anger as he moved forward and she readied herself. She saw his hand clench around the handle of the knife, his knuckles white. In less than two strides he would be upon her. She inhaled, finally able to fill her lungs and focus ... she was ready ...

She didn't hesitate – she was under threat. When he was within reach she unleased a physical assault on him that took him so much by surprise he lost all the momentum his size and strength should have given. His wrist was her first point of attack – once he dropped the knife she continued. Kneecap, groin, ribs, and finally, his head. Precise movements that shocked and inflicted pain, delivered so quickly he could do nothing but grunt and stumble backwards.

All the hurt and upset of the past twenty-four hours left her body as she drove him back towards the living-room door. He had no face, he wasn't real – he became Robert Evans and he became the punchbag Jason held steady five mornings a week, and only when she thought of Jason, and how far outside her discipline she might step, did she stop.

There was silence. The woman, finally, was silent. Her companion slumped against the wall and slid to the ground. With a shaking hand Anna reached out and pulled off his mask – it was wet with sweat and came away easily. He was ordinary, with normal features, not the terrifying figure he had wanted to be. With some relief she saw he was breathing. His eyes focused on her and he pushed himself up, slowly, staggering to his feet again.

A noise in the hall startled her. Anna's heart leapt – help had arrived!

But she was wrong.

A man stepped inside the living-room door and frowned at the sight in front of him. Raising his hand, he brought a shiny black object down hard onto the back of the other man's head – he crumpled to the floor again and the woman began to sob from the corner of the room, blood still seeping from her face onto the carpet. Anna watched in horror as the newcomer stepped towards her – the black object in his hand was a gun, and it was pointed at her chest.

He was taller than his brother had been, thinner too. His blue eyes pierced the way David's had in life. The hollow of his cheeks and his pale skin reminded her of the crime-scene photos of David in death.

"*John Gallagher,*" she whispered.

Narrowing his eyes, he smirked. "Clever girl. Let's see what else you know."

He waved his gun towards the sofa, motioning for her to sit there. More images from crime scene photos, like stills on a film reel, darted into her mind – files she had typed up, cataloguing the accompanying photographs, detailing vicious beatings where John Gallagher was the prime suspect. The word that had been mentioned in the station many times where he was concerned … *"sadistic"*.

On shaking legs, she stepped towards the sofa and lowered herself down into the seat. Her eyes found the panic button, agonisingly out of reach. Waving the gun, he gestured for her to sit back, as far into the cushions as she could. Then he perched on the edge of the coffee table in front of her, looking intently into her eyes. He was smiling. The gun was steady in his hand, a long shiny, metal object attached … a silencer. No-one would hear if he shot her – no-one would come. Her breath came in ragged gasps, the tight crushing feeling returned – she was terrified.

Her fear excited him. He rested one gloved hand on her knee.

"There's a devil on my shoulder, Anna, and he wants a word."

53

"You see, this is what you get when you send a fool to do a man's job."

He kept the gun pointed at her but he looked around the room, at the man on the floor, unconscious, and the woman whimpering against the wall. He shook his head in mock-disgust, tutting, his grin wide. He was enjoying himself.

"I told them to wait for me – I know you're a tricky one! Not laughing now, are you, sweetheart?" He leered at the woman before turning back to Anna. "You see, the plan here was to ask you some very specific questions before letting these two loose to do their worst. A simple solution to all my problems! My old man gets his answers and can stop obsessing about finding Kate Crowley, and I can wrap up my side-line, cash in, and life goes on."

He spoke with an easy, conversational tone, as if they were old friends.

"But I got delayed, you see – unavoidable when you're in business – and these two are *far* too fucking impatient, and just had to go in first." He grinned broadly at the woman as she squirmed on the floor. "You should have listened to me, sweetheart!"

Turning back to Anna, his smile was warm and bright. He pointed the tip of the gun at her temple, his eyes lighting up in excitement. "No matter, here we are! And I have it all worked out! I'll get my answers ... then *she* kills her lover and you, into the bargain, before turning the gun on herself! A breath-taking finale!"

"*M-me?*" the woman spoke from the ground, her words gurgling around the blood in her mouth.

"Yes, you!" he beamed at her. "You'll be the star of the show! All the way to the top! And this way, I get to enjoy it all. It's genius!"

The woman began to laugh, loud and frenzied, her eyes terrified and filled with tears, blood still dripping from her nose and mouth. The sound swelled around the living room. Anna longed to block her ears, shut her eyes, and erase the reality of them all. She was aware of an uncomfortable coating of sweat on her face and neck, her back, everywhere, like a second skin. Pain throbbed behind her eyes and she pressed her fingertips to the space between them.

The woman's laughter angered him. Pointing the gun at her he screamed, "*Shut up!*" To Anna, he leaned in a little, as though to confide in her, and muttered "What the hell is wrong with her?"

Her mounting fear caused her breath to come in lurching gasps. He had something to do with the killings ... what did he mean when he said, "wrap up my side-line?" And he had mentioned Kate ... she knew she was in serious trouble.

The sound of laughter subsided to sobs. With a satisfied nod he focused his attention on Anna, sitting on the sofa, him still on the coffee table, within touching distance. He tapped her knee with the tip of the gun.

"You've been fun to track! Kinsale to the city each day, boxing with your friend, coaching some little twerps in Kung-fu ... you're a busy girl! Did you like my little surprise the other night? Your friend getting shot – literally – in the face!" He laughed, his eyes dancing. "I got these two freaks here to follow you and scare you. Genius move to kill off someone you know right in front of you! Let you see just what they're capable of before it's *your* turn. Makes for better footage when the victim is truly terrified."

Anna thought of Blake Landers, of her certainty the driver of the car had looked directly at her ...

"And to think, Murray was watching in the shadows, thinking he was one step ahead!" He wiped his eyes, tears of laughter lingering there. "Oh yes, I know all about you. You think you're a tough nut ... but, you know, every nut cracks eventually."

He stared at her, his blue eyes hungry and appraising, and her stomach lurched. With the tip of the gun he traced circles on her thigh.

"You know, we could have tied this whole thing up days ago if you hadn't gone to London." He looked at her intently. "Luckily, we have until Sunday to submit the film. These two here have been hanging around getting bored in their hotel room, haven't you?" The woman whimpered, looking terrified. He turned back to Anna. "Why were you there, by the way, in London?"

She opened her mouth to speak but found herself unable to make a sound. It amused him and he waved the gun erratically in front of her face.

"Never mind that. Where was I? Ah yes, my plan! They

kill you and then each other, sort of, and I submit the film and collect the money. Easy. You can make a *fortune* on the internet these days! In the meantime, I might as well ask you a few questions. So, let's crack on."

He turned again to the woman and barked at her to pick up the camera, waving his gun at her to hurry up. She crawled along the floor, crying softly, and picked it up, struggling to hold it steady. He sighed in exasperation as she composed herself.

"Are you finally ready?" Rolling his eyes, he turned again to Anna. "Right – the rules! Every time you lie, I shoot you. We'll start with your left knee. Got it?" With his sing-song voice he sounded like a TV quizmaster, outlining the rules of the game to one of the contestants, and he pressed the gun against her kneecap.

Anna jerked her head down and back up, hoping it passed as a nod. She longed to lunge at him, to use her legs, anything … if he only moved the gun, if she could quell her fear and compose herself, all she needed was one split-second.

"Where's Kate Crowley?"

She swallowed. This was about Kate? It was easy to remember the details of the file at work – she still thought about her friend and wondered where she was.

"In France. Somewhere near Paris." It took effort to make her voice audible.

His eyes narrowed at her answer and he pursed his lips. "Everyone keeps saying that. Perhaps it's true. Why are you so sure?"

She wondered how he didn't know the finer detail – surely his father had pressed the gardaí for as much information as possible? It was the last known location of

David Gallagher's children, of Tom's grandchildren. She assumed he would know everything about the woman that had killed his brother.

"Natalie flew to Paris the day … the day David was killed. She had her children with her. Kate had no documentation when she left Ireland, none the gardaí know of anyway. But the … it's believed she managed to join her sister."

He looked away, out the living-room window, and tapped a steady beat with the gun on her knee.

"But you don't know for sure?"

She shook her head, rushing to add detail. "I've had no contact with her. You can check my emails and my phone. I don't know her exact location."

"Why did you help her? The night the two of you jumped out the bathroom window at the Mad Hatter club."

"I … I saw the details at work. I saw her name connected to David's shooting. I used to know her … I wanted to help." She shrugged weakly.

He raised the gun, shaking it in her face as he would a wagging finger.

"You know your problem? You don't know when to leave things alone. If you had minded your own business I wouldn't be here, I wouldn't have to –"

He stopped, his head swivelling to the kitchen. The woman dropped the camera and crawled backwards to crouch beside her companion. She too was looking towards the kitchen and had started to laugh again.

Anna felt the cold kiss of the night air crawl over her skin and realisation hit her – her sliding patio door was open.

John was on his feet, his gun raised. Before Anna could react, he bellowed, "*You!*"

Whatever he may have said next was lost. He fell backwards and landed between the coffee table and the sofa, an awkward angle that wedged Anna to her seat. A silencer had muffled the gunshot, and the woman's hysterical screaming drowned out any other noise.

Anna watched in muted horror as a dark stain spread across the front of John Gallagher's chest, turning the grey fabric of his jacket a deep red. A crushing weight on her chest and a dull ache behind her eyes warned her this claustrophobic panic could drown her. With a firm shake of her head she pulled her feet up and threw her body across the coffee table, slamming her hand onto the panic alarm. She felt no relief at finally pressing it, only fear. Reaching over the coffee table she pulled the gun from John Gallagher's gloved hand – then she stood up, face to face with a hooded figure in her kitchen archway. Standing in front of him, her chest rising and falling quickly, she pointed the gun and waited. Her hand shook – the gun felt heavier than she imagined it would, she wasn't even sure she could use it properly – and she added her left hand to steady her right.

Ely Murray stood still, his dark eyes on Anna's. Wearing a black jacket, the hood pulled up, he had a grey scarf wound around most of his face. He knew she wouldn't recognise him. She wouldn't remember him from the Mad Hatter. Oh, but he remembered her … after days of watching her and waiting for his chance, now here she was. She was breathing heavily, gasping, and her hands shook as she pointed the gun at him. She was scared. Yet he knew better than to think that mattered. He had seen what she was capable of … behind his scarf he smiled a little. He had a decision to make – shoot her and end this, or toy with her a little …

As he stepped towards her the first peal of sirens broke the stillness. Another time, he thought. He turned and quickly ran through the kitchen, out the back door. The white curtain billowed behind him as he was swallowed in the darkness.

Anna dared to breathe again and dropped the gun onto the carpet. The sirens were loud and shrill, and her body sagged in relief. She became aware now of another sound, wailing, so high-pitched it pierced her skull. The woman was screaming hysterically, her eyes on the growing red stain on the carpet where John Gallagher lay.

Anna looked at him – his chest rose and fell in spasms and she knew he would be dead soon.

No!

There had been so much death already … darting to the kitchen she grabbed a towel and made her way to his side, kneeling, pressing it against the wound. The sound of screaming mingled with the sirens and she felt utterly exhausted.

54

The doctor had insisted she stay overnight, despite her protests.

"But I'm not hurt. I'm completely uninjured!"

"That's not strictly true. For one thing, your blood pressure is too high. You're staying overnight for observation."

"Listen to the doctor, Anna, please!"

She had glared at her brother but quickly given up arguing with them. She was tired after their time in London – all they had learned had drained her. And the ordeal in her house had been terrifying. She realised she felt spooked at the idea of going home – so she didn't argue further, just accepted she was safer here for the night, and tried to sleep.

Surprisingly, Alex took little encouragement to go home. After the attack last year, he had insisted on staying by her side, for days afterwards. Now, once he had satisfied himself she was safe and not hurt, he agreed to go. His wife was waiting, his *pregnant* wife, and they had a lot to talk about.

William Ryan called in to her room for the second time about an hour after Alex had left. He was clean-shaven and suited, as usual, his long wool coat over his arm. It was Saturday night – Anna wondered if the man ever dressed casually and took some time off work. He had already taken her statement, and she knew tomorrow would bring more questions. For now, she felt happy to see a familiar face.

"What is it about you and trouble?" he asked softly, settling into the visitor's chair. She shrugged and smiled, hoping he had an update and was here to fill her in. She knew he would if he could.

"John Gallagher will live. He's not too far away – one floor up actually, recovering from surgery. I'm afraid your living-room floor is in a bit of a state. The technical team will be there for days yet – can you stay with your brother when you get discharged?"

She nodded – Vivian had already offered her the spare room in her apartment, but she and Alex had a lot to talk through and plan for over the next few months. She had already decided to spend a few nights with him while they figured out what to do next. She had no desire to go back to the house.

"What about the couple? Are they the people wanted for the murders?"

"Yes! The man arrested in your house is called Simon Gleeson. He's clammed up, refusing to say a word. He has a cracked rib and some bruising." He looked at her, somewhat quizzically, she thought. He knew what had happened in her house, but it seemed he had trouble believing her role in the man's injuries. "The woman's name is Erin Beale. She's fine apart from a bust nose and lip. She seems to be enjoying herself, answering as many questions as we can ask her, refusing a solicitor. She just wants to talk. Whether it's all true is another thing." He yawned and rubbed his hands over his face. "They *are* our killers though. Gleeson and her. She's already told us to refer to them as Bonnie and Clyde, and says John Gallagher is their 'Film Critic'."

"Their what?"

"It's connected to the Dark Web – we have some information on that already and it's pretty horrific stuff. We'll see what checks out. What we know is there's been a number of similar crimes across Europe and it appears to originate on an online platform, where people log in and pay to view the killings, ranking them for a cash prize. As I said, horrific. Each set of killers needed a link into the website, someone who controlled the money and uploaded the footage. John Gallagher was their link. The woman has told us enough to get a warrant to search Gallagher's computer and phone, and we have the camcorder recordings of tonight, and the other murders now too. She's keen to tell us everything, which makes a nice change."

Anna's eyes were wide as she listened. This was more disturbing than she could have imagined.

"Your link to the whole thing was John Gallagher wanting information on Kate Crowley. The family are still searching for her – it's understandable, I suppose. Although how they connected *you* to her is a mystery."

She wondered about Tom Gallagher, head of the family – was he involved? Or had another son left him out of a new money-making venture? She knew the gardaí had opened an investigation and would take any opportunity to search all the premises listed to the business. The Gallagher days of running criminal rings around the city seemed to be coming to an end – the sooner the better, she thought.

"Anything else spring to mind about the man that shot

Gallagher? Only his feet were captured on the camcorder earlier."

She shook her head, disappointed not to be able to help further. "No, sorry. Just dark eyes, tall, broad shoulders. The clothes were all black except for a grey scarf. I wish I could be more helpful."

He rose to go, resting one hand on her shoulder. "Not to worry. There'll be street cameras, CCTV in Kinsale from the businesses on the main street. We'll work with time frames and see what can be uncovered." He smiled. "Told you that panic alarm was a good idea."

With a wink, he was gone. Resting her head on the pillow, she hoped sleep would come quickly.

The rattle of the food trolley woke her before the sun was fully up. As she accepted the tea and cereal she became aware of a figure curled up in the visitor's chair, sleeping under a blanket. Her heart skipped a beat. *Myles.* She watched him sleep for a few minutes, wondering at the happiness just seeing him brought her. Leaning against the pillows she sipped the tea, smiling as he stirred and turned to her.

"Hello, you."

He rubbed his eyes and pulled on his glasses from under the blanket.

"Hello you too!"

"When did you get here?"

"Last night." He sat up and stretched his arms to the ceiling. "They're very strict here! I had to show them my badge to get in!" His eyes roamed over her critically, and she realised he was looking for injuries.

"I'm alright. I'm only still here because my blood pressure was a little high."

He looked sceptical but sat back and smiled.

"If you say so. You had a lucky escape from those people last night, Anna. You know, I've never been so happy someone accepted me butting into their business. Thank you for agreeing to the panic alarms. I know you didn't want to, and I'm glad you let me bully you into it!"

She laughed – she didn't mind admitting he had been right. She remembered their phone call the day the two men turned up at her house to install the alarms, and her annoyance at him taking the decision out of her hands. But Myles had convinced her – "Just humour me, Anna!" She was glad now. Without the added security, she didn't want to think about how the night could have ended.

"I thought you would be abroad for another few weeks."

"That's the plan. I flew in last night and I must fly out again this morning."

Her heart sank – seeing him made her feel alive, made her happy. And it was only to be for a few hours.

"Will you make Lauren's wedding? You're my plus-one, remember?"

He grimaced. "I don't know. I'll try. What I *do* know is I have a week off soon and I'd love you to come to Dublin with me."

She blinked in surprise. "Really?"

"My mother wants to meet you. And my brothers. They don't believe you're real. I'm the techie geek in the family and they think I've made you from spare computer parts."

She laughed so loud a nurse put her head inside the hospital room to check all was OK. Wiping tears from her eyes Anna settled again against the pillows. Myles moved to sit on the edge of the bed and took her hand, speaking softly.

"Things are progressing quickly regarding Robert Evans – his statement was taken again late last night. He's cooperating fully – it's like he's unburdening himself."

She nodded, sitting up again, fully alert now to his every word – she had nothing to say and didn't trust herself to speak anyway. Just hearing him say justice was about to be served was enough.

"He's cooperating with the police in London and the gardaí. As soon as he can give a reasonable idea of the location of the … *um*, bodies, the search will begin. Roy Eastly has been brought in for questioning." She gasped and he gripped her hand tighter. "I won't be directly involved but I'll make sure you're updated every step of the way! I know I'm away a lot but I'm *here* for you, Anna, I hope you know that."

His hug was warm and comforting and she clung to his shoulders, all the grief and fear that she had felt over the last two days making her whole body shake. He was the anchor, her grounding force. He was prepared to take two flights in twelve hours to be here for her and he would do everything he could to make the next few months as bearable as possible.

Despite all that had happened in London, and in her house, her heart felt lighter.

55

He watched the scene unfold with eager eyes, feeling calmer than he knew he should: no shaking hands, no sweat on his forehead. The Audi was parked across the street and fifty metres to the left of Gallagher's house. Ely was sitting in the dark, with enough of a view to see the gardaí pull into the driveway. The security gates had been opened shortly after the first squad-car pulled up and had stayed open. Gallagher's house was currently being overturned by men and women that had waited years for this moment.

He couldn't see the front door but could imagine what was happening. Several Garda cars and even more unmarked cars were parked in the driveway, blue lights flashing for all to see. Curtains twitched in windows of the neighbouring houses – he assumed the press weren't far away. One of the city's businessmen was in trouble – those that had long suspected he was a criminal would be gloating now. And men that had underworld dealings with Tom Gallagher would be panicking, wondering if the man had recorded anything incriminating or was willing to talk and cut a deal. Ely smiled in satisfaction.

As Saturday nights went, this had been busier than most. He had just finished emptying Gallagher's safe in The Oracle when his phone rang: John was seen following a car from Cork Airport, in the direction of Kinsale. The decision to follow was quickly made. He had no idea who the man and woman were in Anna Clarke's living room. The man had been semi-conscious, but both women had been alert, their eyes searing him. He had concealed his face and the scar that made him memorable – and even if they could identify him, it wouldn't matter. He had no plans to stick around Cork. He assumed what she had pressed on the wall was a panic button – clever. With a Garda station in Kinsale, it had taken only minutes for them to respond and he had made a quick exit. He wondered what might have been between him and Anna, how their encounter might have gone. But he had bigger things to worry about.

He picked up his phone and dialled. It was answered on the first ring.

"Is everything ready?"

"All set to go. The vans are loaded and on stand-by."

"Well, consider this your go-ahead."

They would meet in Limerick – four vans bearing different business logos were packed full of Gallagher's counterfeit cigarettes, stolen liquor, and drugs. His warehouse was empty – Ely considered they were doing him a favour really, removing the incriminating evidence. There was more gear, of course, and more money too, in the house and wherever else Gallagher had stashed it. Ely was happy to take what he could and get out.

He started the engine and it hummed smoothly. He had no desire to draw attention from any of the detectives and gardaí. In the boot of his car was a black gear bag containing over four-hundred grand in cash and a gun, still fitted with a silencer. Enough evidence to secure a lengthy prison sentence, probably in the same place as John Gallagher, if he survived.

For the first time in thirty years Tom Gallagher was weak. Both sons, heirs to the business, were out of the way. David had brought his death upon himself, never listening to Ely's warnings to stay calm, stay out of trouble and off the radar. And John … Ely knew his feral nature would land him in trouble one day, trouble so big his father couldn't get him out of it. Now, with the gardaí sniffing around, Gallagher's associates were jumpy and suspicious, his competitors circling and hungry. Ely had seized an opportunity ripe for the taking. He knew Gallagher had admired his cunning and talent for solving problems over the years… but he had made a mistake in never questioning his loyalty.

Ely and a handful of Gallagher's men had taken as much of his cash and stock as possible and planned to go to ground until the ripple this night had caused was calm and still. Then, if Gallagher had any fight left in him, Ely would be ready for war.

56

Detective Garda Colin Forde was standing outside the interrogation room, watching her through the glass. She couldn't see him, but he thought she knew he was there. Every few minutes she turned her head and smiled at the mirror, despite the sutures and bandages to her injured nose and lip – smiled to him, he wondered, or to herself? He remembered the doctor speaking about her possible psychological illness and thought to himself that it was probable this woman would be spared jail in favour of time in a secure psychiatric facility. Where maybe she could get the help she needed.

Stripped of her wigs and vulgar make-up she was pretty. Her hair was cut into what Colin knew was called a "pixie" style – his sister had the same – with a short blunt fringe, in a shade of dark brown. Her eyes were huge and bright blue. Without all the effort to hide, to mask herself, she was striking. Maybe that was the point, he thought. With his hands in his pockets, he watched her, thinking about all the horror she had been part of … what she had witnessed, and laughed through. He shivered.

The door banged open and William Ryan stepped into the room, two coffee-to-go cups in his hands and a croissant hanging from his mouth. As Colin relieved him of a cup he pulled another croissant, wrapped in a napkin, from his pocket and handed it over.

"Cheers, thanks."

"It's Sunday – the least I can get you is breakfast." He nodded towards the room and Erin Beale. "Is she still smiling at the mirror?"

"Non-stop. Is Grace getting in on this?"

"No. She's gone back to the hospital to take Anna Clarke's statement again and then she's heading to the house in Kinsale. The Technical Bureau are still there."

Colin nodded, suddenly feeling as though he'd drawn the short straw. He was to accompany his supervisor in interviewing the suspects then. He hoped they would start with the woman, before moving on to the man. She persistently refused a solicitor. A doctor was due to arrive shortly, and William hoped Alice McNamara, the psychotherapist that had been so helpful, would return his call and consider a trip to Cork today. Simon Gleeson insisted on his solicitor being present, and they were currently waiting on the man. He had expressed dissatisfaction at the early hour on a Sunday morning but was expected at the station soon.

"Do you think they did all this just for the money?"

William stepped closer to the glass and watched the woman.

"Who knows? Greater minds than ours will figure that out."

"The man … Simon Gleeson. He must be a psychopath. The woman said the mask he used was made to look like his father's face."

William turned away from the glass and bit into the croissant, licking crumbs from his lips.

"The longer I'm in this job the less I believe in psychopaths. Some people appear to be perfectly sane until they do terrible things."

He watched the younger detective closely.

"You know, Colin, I am aware this case has been difficult for you. For us all. But for someone so new to all this, I think you've done really well. Not every Detective Garda would have to deal with such gruesome crimes so early on. It's been a tough case."

Colin felt heat in his cheeks and looked at his shoes.

"I want you to know I value you on this team. You have a sharp mind, and that more than makes up for a weak stomach."

Colin met his eyes and they shared a smile.

"It's been that obvious?"

"As obvious as the vomit on the roadside in Clonakilty."

A uniformed garda stepped inside the door.

"DS Ryan? We've Simon Gleeson's solicitor downstairs."

William nodded and muttered his thanks. He turned again to Colin.

"I want you to open on this one – you up to that?"

Colin swallowed a burning mouthful of coffee as he nodded. "Sure. Absolutely!"

He would have to look the killer in the eye. He would have to slide images from his crimes across the table and ask the man to explain himself. He would put the mask, the death mask the woman had called it, on the table between them, wrapped in its plastic forensic pouch, and ask the man to explain why he felt the need to hide behind a rubber impression of a dead man's face ... there were many questions, and he felt ready to ask them all.

57

Two Weeks Later

The day was colder than she knew Lauren hoped for, but it was dry and bright with very little wind. Anna smiled from the bedroom window as she inspected the weather outside and was surprised to feel tears sting her eyes. They were happy tears in anticipation of her friend's big day, she told herself. And she almost believed it.

The bedroom in Vivian's apartment was actually bigger than her old one at the house in Kinsale. She wouldn't be going back there – her mind was made up. Too much had happened since last November, and how she felt about her childhood home had changed forever. She wished now that she had left the house sooner – then, the memories of happier times could be preserved before things had changed. Alex had advised her to remember that the good times within the house in Kinsale far outweighed the bad, and she knew he was right. Still, she hoped the 'For Sale' sign could go up before too long. Until she sold that house and found somewhere new, somewhere fresh, she was staying here with Vivian.

The day she had returned, to pack up the house, her hands shook so much she couldn't push the key into the front door lock, so Vivian had taken over. Thinking about it now, Anna realised Vivian had taken over almost the whole process of moving out and readying the house for sale. She arranged for the carpets to be ripped up and replaced, and the walls repainted. She had helped Anna to pack her whole life into boxes.

"Are you keeping the record player?"

"Yes, that was my dad's."

"What about the books?"

"Of course!"

"*All* of them?"

Alex took care of the attic, emptying the contents and filling the remaining space in his own. Their mother's cello, her red winter coat, boxes of their parent's clothes and family photo albums ... they had agreed what to do with most of it. The clothes, except the coat, should be donated to a charity shop and the photo albums shared between them. Copies of some of the photographs would be mailed to Annika Garcia. The cello ... who knew? For now, her house was empty, the possessions in boxes that lined the walls of this bedroom, a room she had quickly grown accustomed to.

After her shower she did her hair and make-up carefully, deciding not to dress until after she had eaten breakfast.

Vivian was at the island counter, sipping coffee and reading from a blue folder of papers. Working, on a Saturday. She turned with a bright smile as Anna said good morning.

"Happy birthday!"

Anna was briefly stunned – she had completely forgotten. That had never happened to her before. She laughed as Vivian wrapped her in a hug.

"I forgot about that!"

"Well, you *are* getting old! Here!" She thrust a small package into Anna's hands. "They're only small, but they'll go with your dress."

She blinked away tears as she pulled twinkling emerald studs from the box. "Thank you!" she murmured, putting them on.

She noticed a pile of cards and presents on the countertop and inspected them in disbelief. Alex, and one from Chloe herself, Lauren, and some of the others from work … there was even one from William Ryan.

"I've heard of people opening and closing their mouth like a goldfish when they get a surprise, but I've never actually seen it before!" Vivian laughed. "Sit down and read your cards, I'll make some fresh coffee."

The church was packed full of bodies in stylish coats and headpieces, lulled by a quartet of violinists as they waited for the bride. Anna's seat was saved by an usher, a young boy she knew was Lauren's nephew. She squeezed in beside some of her co-workers and their partners, smiling her greeting. Looking around her she mentally checked that the flowers looked as they should and everything was in its proper place. She knew all the details of the wedding, having listened to it all at work for so long, and was surprised to feel as apprehensive as if she had organised it herself. Once he was near enough she motioned for the young usher to come over to her seat. He looked a bit worried but made his way to her side.

"You're Adam, right?" she said softly.

"Yeah." He pulled at his collar, uncomfortable in the formal clothes.

"You guys have forgotten to hand out the Mass booklets."

His eyes widened, alarmed.

"Don't panic! They're stacked inside the confessional box on the left-hand side – just calmly hand them out now and no-one will ever know."

She winked at him as he walked quickly to the back of the church. She smiled broadly a few minutes later when he handed her the ivory booklet, muttering "Thanks!" as he passed.

She smoothed out her pale-green dress and touched her earrings. Vivian had been her rock over the last few weeks. There was nothing she couldn't put a positive spin on. When Anna had cried about the fate of her parents, Vivian had urged her to focus on the love they had shared, the happy times they had enjoyed together. When she had despaired at the evil nature of the people that had crossed her path in the last few months, Vivian had forced her to list out all the *good* people she knew who brought love and support to her life. As first she had resisted, shaking her head angrily. But slowly, as her friend urged her to think, those people had come clearly into focus.

Her brother, who suffered just as she did, who kept his love and his support firmly wrapped around her. Vivian, who was always listening and making her laugh, and Lauren, who kept up a steady supply of Victus coffees and treats on her return to work. William Ryan, his earnest blue eyes alight with determination to protect her. Even Frank Doherty, who almost refused to let her go back to work, insisting she stay home and rest, before finally conceding she might be better off busy. Jason, her trainer, and her dad's friend, who let her take centre stage in their Taekwon-Do Tykes classes, knowing how much it meant to her. And Myles ...

After his visit at the hospital, he had disappeared abroad again, and his return home had been delayed. She had opted not to bring another plus one to the wedding and planned to head back to Vivian's apartment as soon as she could. She missed him. His twice-daily telephone calls sustained her, barely.

She was pulled from her reverie by the crowd around her rising to their feet and the music changing – the bride had arrived. Anna's breath caught in her throat as Lauren began to walk up the aisle with her father, their arms linked, tears rolling down his face. She couldn't stop her own tears, wiping quickly to save her mascara.

"You look so beautiful!" she mouthed as her friend walked slowly passed.

"I know!" Lauren mouthed back, and Anna beamed.

Before long she was called to the altar to do her reading. On the rare occasion she had had to speak in public, it hadn't bothered her too much – today she felt a little jittery, her breathing a little shallow as she made her way to the front of the church. She stepped to the microphone, clearing her throat softly, her eyes seeking Lauren's.

She stopped, frozen.

He was standing at the back of the church, just inside the closed door, and she wondered how long he had been there. He looked good in a suit, with his hair tamed and smoothed into a bun, and his brown eyes crinkled above his warm smile.

Myles.

He was here, and her heart soared.

Epilogue

He stood at the corner of the road where it curved around to an open green area, and swung his arms wide, making a windmill. It felt good. He had escaped the concrete cage, all because some drunk had messed up the DNA samples. Freedom had taken longer to materialise than he had hoped, but he was out. Figuratively speaking, it felt like he had won the lotto.

He had already filled his lungs, burning them with the cold air, and he savoured the space around him. He would never get tired of this. An occasional drop of rain landed on his upturned face – he marvelled at the sensation, like liquid ice bouncing on his skin. He had missed this! A laugh burst from him as he realised he must be insane – no Irish person could ever miss the *rain!* Yet here he was, standing on the path, enjoying the chilly touch of spring.

With question marks hanging over the DNA evidence, the only thing that could convict him now was *her.* If she disappeared, maybe the accusation would too. It was her word against his. And if she were silenced ... this was reckless, he knew that of course, this spur of the moment visit could get his bail revoked and land him back inside. But he wanted her to know he was nearby, and that he could find out all about her life if he wanted to.

A tinkling bell interrupted his daydream. It was faint, almost lost to the breeze, but it was there, and growing closer. Soon she rounded the corner. She was taller than he imagined and bundled up in layers that he guessed added bulk to her small frame. She pushed hard on the pedals, ribbons on the handlebars of her bike blowing in the wind. Two pigtails popped out from under her helmet. Before long she drew up alongside him. He stepped to the side and blocked her path – she hadn't been cycling fast and she stopped easily.

"Hi!" His smile was large and friendly, or so he hoped. It made his jaw ache and he fought a scowl of annoyance.

The evening sun was setting behind him, the glare in her eyes. She couldn't see him clearly and raised a hand to shield her eyes.

"Hi." Her voice was soft and faltering.

What was she, five? He could see the uncertainty on her face – she had been trained to be polite yet warned not to talk to strangers. She didn't know what to do.

"Are you going for a bike ride?"

"*Uh-huh.*"

"I see little princesses on your bike – are those your favourites?"

She turned her head over her shoulder, looking behind her, possibly to friends or a parent that she knew was nearby.

Time to go.

"Don't worry, you don't need to be afraid. I just have a message for you. Can you deliver a message for me?"

"*Um* ... OK."

"I'm a friend of your Aunty Anna. Can you tell her I said hi?"

"OK ... what's your name?"

He smiled broadly. "Tell your Aunty Anna her friend Dean said hello."

THE END

Also by Poolbeg Crimson

Blinding Lies

Amy Cronin

Ten years ago, Anna Clarke's parents disappeared.
The mystery haunts her, and she hopes her job in a busy city Garda
Station will one day help her find answers.

The case of a man shot dead crosses her desk – and Anna is shocked to
discover that the main suspect is her childhood friend Kate Crowley.
Certain that Kate is innocent, Anna is determined to help her clear her
name. But first she has to find her ...

Tom Gallagher's son David is dead, and Tom believes Kate is responsible.
Now his older son John is missing – unable
to grieve for one son until he finds the other,
desperation can cause a man to do terrible things ...
Then the German Meier brothers descend on the city, intent on finding
an item David had offered to sell them. Even Tom doesn't know where it
is, but he suspects Kate Crowley must have taken it.

Kate is on the run. She is trapped in the dead man's
city – can her old friend help her find a way out?

In a week where a political summit is taking place and the city is on high
alert, Kate must struggle to stay hidden and stay alive.
And Anna is drawn into the twisted race against time,
falling deeper into danger.

ISBN 978-178199-723-9

Available on Poolbeg.com